continued . . .

"This second Shadows Inquiries novel can stand alone as a strong, well-written tale with an evolving heroine who's tough without being a sex goddess. Sylvie is a complex, flawed character, and that makes her interesting. The real-world setting keeps things believable." —*RT Book Reviews*

Sins & Shadows

"Dark and fascinating."
—Kat Richardson, national bestselling author of *Downpour*

"Sylvie is harder and darker than the usual paranormal PI, and this story is the better for it." —*CA Reviews*

"Ferocious, no-holds-barred Sylvie is abrasive but forthright—a heroine that any reader would champion. Rounded out by a series of well-developed characters and pulse-pounding action, this story looks to be the start of an excellent series."
—*RT Book Reviews*

"Lyn Benedict delivers one hell of a powerful story, expertly weaving Greek, Egyptian, and Christian lore and traditions together before tossing them into a modern setting . . . Sylvie herself is a tough cookie, one willing to boss around gods and monsters alike to get the job done." —*The Green Man Review*

"With fantastic characters, engrossing magic, and creative mayhem, Benedict gives us a new twist on the supernatural noir front. A fast-paced ride all the way!"
—Chris Marie Green, author of *Deep in the Woods*

"Pulls out all the stops. Sylvie does battle for no less than the fate of the world."
—Carrie Vaughn, *New York Times* bestselling author of *Kitty's Greatest Hits*

"A dark, gutsy urban fantasy filled with mythology . . . I'm looking forward to reading the next installment."
—*Fantasy Cafe*

Ace Books by Lyn Benedict

SINS & SHADOWS
GHOSTS & ECHOES
GODS & MONSTERS
LIES & OMENS

LIES & OMENS

A SHADOWS INQUIRIES NOVEL

Lyn Benedict

ACE BOOKS, NEW YORK

THE BERKLEY PUBLISHING GROUP
Published by the Penguin Group
Penguin Group (USA) Inc.
375 Hudson Street, New York, New York 10014, USA

Penguin Group (Canada), 90 Eglinton Avenue East, Suite 700, Toronto, Ontario M4P 2Y3, Canada
(a division of Pearson Penguin Canada Inc.) • Penguin Books Ltd., 80 Strand, London WC2R 0RL,
England • Penguin Group Ireland, 25 St. Stephen's Green, Dublin 2, Ireland (a division of Penguin
Books Ltd.) • Penguin Group (Australia), 250 Camberwell Road, Camberwell, Victoria 3124, Australia
(a division of Pearson Australia Group Pty. Ltd.) • Penguin Books India Pvt. Ltd., 11 Community
Centre, Panchsheel Park, New Delhi—110 017, India • Penguin Group (NZ), 67 Apollo Drive,
Rosedale, Auckland 0632, New Zealand (a division of Pearson New Zealand Ltd.) • Penguin Books
(South Africa) (Pty.) Ltd., 24 Sturdee Avenue, Rosebank, Johannesburg 2196, South Africa

Penguin Books Ltd., Registered Offices: 80 Strand, London WC2R 0RL, England

LIES & OMENS

An Ace Book / published by arrangement with the author

PUBLISHING HISTORY
Ace mass-market edition / May 2012

ISBN: 978-1-937007-50-8

ACE
Ace Books are published by The Berkley Publishing Group,
a division of Penguin Group (USA) Inc.,
375 Hudson Street, New York, New York 10014.
ACE and the "A" design are trademarks of Penguin Group (USA) Inc.

PRINTED IN THE UNITED STATES OF AMERICA

10 9 8 7 6 5 4 3 2 1

ALWAYS LEARNING   **PEARSON**

For my mother,
who is oddly fond of Sylvie's bad behavior

Acknowledgments

As always, there are many people who should be thanked for helping me bring this book to completion: the local Wednesday Night Writers, who had to hear more of my plot-wrangling than they ever wanted; Barb Webb, who kept a stick handy; and, of course, Caitlin Blasdell and Anne Sowards, who've both helped Sylvie run amok through the world.

PROLOGUE

Murder Unmemorable

"I DON'T KNOW ABOUT THIS," DETECTIVE RAUL GARZA SAID AGAIN. He tapped his fingers on the steering wheel. Afternoon sunlight spilled hot and heavy through the windshield and the open windows. The faux-leather seats had gone sticky and soft, as irritating as his incessant finger drumming. Garza scowled at the world from beneath his mirrored sunglasses.

He wasn't the only one. Sylvie Lightner had been sitting beside him in the unmarked car for the past three hours. In that period, he'd expressed his doubts about their purpose no fewer than ten times. A frustrated scream built in her chest.

Coming to Key West to help Garza hadn't been her idea, and it sure as hell wasn't something she'd do for fun. For work, on the other hand—as Miami's go-to girl for dealing with the supernatural nasties, this kind of moment was all too common, right down to the thinly veiled dislike Garza showed her. Made sense. Sylvie had so many strikes against her that it was hard to pick out which one bothered him the most. Unlicensed PI with a reputation for trouble? A vigilante who took care of problems the police didn't want to acknowledge? A woman with a liking for large-caliber weaponry, a smart mouth, and something dangerous in her blood? Or maybe Garza had caught wind of her change in reputation. It had been bad before. The *Magicus Mundi*— the supernatural world that mingled with the mortal one— had called her *L'enfant du meurtrier*, The Murderer's Child.

Now they knew her as the New Lilith. The dark heir to an immortal woman who had wanted to make war on her god. If Sylvie's reputation had been bad before, now it was abysmal. She was unpopular with everyone. Witches. Monsters. Law enforcement. And nosy and controlling government agencies like Internal Surveillance and Investigation, who would rather blame her for the magical problems than deal with them on their own. No one liked her; they all treated her with suspicion and fear.

Sylvie didn't understand it. It wasn't like being the new Lilith had done much to change her beyond increasing her innate resistance to inimical magic.

Beyond making us immortal, her little dark voice said. She ignored it. She often did. It was another genetic legacy, an all-too-active form of ancestral memory. It had its uses, not least its desire to survive, but it also was a little like having the world's most cynical and angry roommate living in her head. She hoped it was wrong about the immortality thing; on the off chance it wasn't, she'd started trying to play nice. Forever was a terribly long time to be friendless.

With that thought recurring to her more and more frequently, she had begun to treasure her few allies. So when Detective Adelio Suarez, her only friend in the Miami PD, asked for her help, the answer had to be yes. Suarez had told her that Garza had a major problem, *her* type of problem. Magical malfeasance with a rising body count.

"I must be out of my mind," Garza said, reaching for the ignition.

"Six dead men, three dead women in a nightclub two weeks ago," Sylvie reminded him. "Another eight down for the count last night, in hospital on IVs, still twitching. It's a classic dance-'til-death curse."

"I don't believe in curses," Garza said. He sat back, took his hand from the keys. Sighed. Spoke again. "I don't want to believe in curses."

"Hey," Sylvie said. "You believed in them enough to pick out the bad guy."

She opened the file folder in her lap again, though she'd memorized most of it. Marcel Braud. Twenty-seven years old. He looked bad on paper. Spoiled, rich, a history of smaller crimes: shoplifting, DUIs, and the habit of getting high and beating up his girlfriends. But he was sober now.

Sober enough to use black magic?

The first victim was his ex-girlfriend. The people who died were the ones who'd danced with her, or in her immediate orbit. Last night, the first one to fall under the curse was his current girlfriend, who Braud had accused of cheating. No matter which way Garza added it up, the culprit seemed the same. Braud.

Garza had told Sylvie that Braud, when brought in for questioning, hadn't done much to deny it, only smirked and asked what Garza thought he could do about it.

Which led to this. Sitting outside Braud's Key West condo waiting for their chance to go inside without witnesses. Garza's jaw kept jumping. She couldn't blame him. He was well out of his comfort zone.

She was in hers.

"Let's go," she said, as the neighbor pulled out and left the tiny parking lot quiet. The midday dead zone.

"Jesus Christ," he muttered, but followed her out of the car. "You sure about this?"

"He's killing people," Sylvie said.

"I meant . . . what's protecting us from him?"

"Me."

Garza watched her unholster her weapon, and visibly, carefully said nothing about a civilian drawing a gun like she meant to use it.

Sylvie tapped on Braud's door, and when he opened it, she stuck her gun in his face and let herself in.

Garza shut the door hastily behind them.

"What is this?" Braud said, looking past Sylvie and her weapon. "Garza? You again? I'll have your job."

"No," Sylvie said. "You won't."

· She'd come prepared to scare him senseless, to take away any magic he'd gathered. Until this very moment, she'd assumed he had possession of some malignant magical tool that could be removed from his custody. But there was a chain around his neck with a too-familiar bat-wing pendant. Part identification, part magical amplification.

He was *Maudit*.

His magic was inborn.

The energy in the room shivered, fluxed cold, pulling away from them like an icy wave washing out to sea. Beside her, Garza shouted, his voice scaling up in panic.

Sylvie's skin crawled; Braud smirked.

"Stop," she said. Normally, she wouldn't have bothered with that much warning, but she had a cop beside her. Her resistance to magic meant she could afford that momentary hesitation.

Garza, his face a rictus of pain, raised his gun and shot. Sylvie jerked aside; the air before Braud shimmered like an oil slick and let the flattened bullets slip down to ping hotly against the tile floor.

"Shadows!" Garza gasped. His face was blistering, tiny seeping pustules.

Braud jerked at hearing her identified, turned to look at her. Garza gasped in what sounded like relief as Braud's focus split between them.

Braud repeated, "Shadows."

Cold air rushed past her, sucking all the chill toward him. Heat sparked around her, stung her skin with points of fire. One of the *Maudit* top-ten favorites for removing an enemy: the immolation spell.

Sylvie stepped forward, ignored his increasingly desperate spell casting, ignored the heat that couldn't seep beneath her skin, couldn't boil her blood the way it was doing to Garza's. She sent a bullet toward Braud's skull.

A glimmer of that opalescent shield eddied between her bullet and his brains, then disappeared all at once, letting her shot hit home between his eyes.

He collapsed.

Garza had a quiet breakdown at the door; his hand jittered between his own weapon, his radio, his brow. Finally, he said, "He tried to kill me. He tried to kill—I was burning alive."

"And now you're not," Sylvie said. She eyed him carefully despite her flippant words. The welts on his face were fading fast, sinking back into his skin as the temperature around them dropped; the air conditioner whined, recovering from the sudden burst of heat.

Garza holstered his gun, kept patting at his face, his forearms. "My bullets didn't touch him."

"Magical body armor. It's a *Maudit* thing. They like to attach a few prepared spells to their amulets."

"Maudit?"

"Society of very bad men. Who have issues with women. I should have known when you told me he was killing off his girlfriends."

"You killed him. You carrying special rounds? Like silver?"

"No," Sylvie said. She didn't elaborate. Cops liked facts, and she didn't have any. What could she say? That her bullets somehow could be relied on to find a weakness in magical shields? She hadn't figured it out herself. "Call the hospital. Let's make sure the people he cursed are healed up, too."

"Then what?"

"Make him disappear?" She tried to sound like this was a first for her, that she was just as lost as he was. Garza eyed her sidelong, suspicious. Not surprising. She didn't do innocent very well.

She was going to catch hell for this one way or the other. She really hadn't been expecting to kill Braud, had expected a one-spell dilettante, the kind that could be scared straight. But the *Maudits* were a different type of sorcerer entirely: socially connected, rich, entitled, and far more talented than they deserved to be. Death was the only thing that stopped them.

Garza could have been killed. She'd endangered her client.

She should have come alone.

She was tired of going it alone.

". . . they're awake? Stopped seizing? No, no, no need to bother the doctor. That's wonderful. May I interview them in the morning? Perfect."

Sylvie eavesdropped shamelessly, felt a quick glow of satisfaction. That was that, then.

Garza disconnected. The unhappy tension in his face had changed out for a visible and grim contentment. Not the outcome he'd planned but one he could live with. "So, we make him disappear. How?"

"Your case. Your call." She'd love to push this off onto Garza if she could. Failing that, she certainly wasn't going to suggest a place to dump the body. There was foolhardy— shooting a sorcerer dead in front of a cop—and then there was just plain stupid—drawing a cop, no matter how friendly, a map to her occasional graveyard.

Garza grimaced. "God. Yeah. I can't believe I'm saying this."

"Didn't believe in curses either, at first."

"Fine. There's a drug spot. I'll leave him there. Braud has a past of drug-related offenses. A deal gone wrong in a drug alley will pass. Your gun on file?"

"No. What about the apartment?" There wasn't a lot of mess. Braud's magical shield hadn't saved him, but it had contained the blood spatter surprisingly well. And since the shield was keyed to the bat-wing amulet, it was keeping the blood spill close to the body.

"I know someone," Garza said.

"Figured as much." Sylvie shivered. Cops made the best murderers. Or accomplices.

• • •

WHEN SYLVIE HADN'T HEARD FROM GARZA IN A WEEK, WHEN THE finding of Braud's body passed almost without comment in the press—odd for a wealthy white man with a luxury lifestyle—she bit back her instincts that suggested no news was good news, and called him.

"Any fallout?" she asked, when he answered.

"Fallout?"

"With Braud."

"Who is this?"

Sylvie hung up, frowning. Garza's confusion sounded real. More, when she'd mentioned Braud, his attention had sharpened as if he'd been investigating Braud's death. Not covering it up.

Sylvie figured it was time for a trip back to Key West.

Hours later, she waved at Detective Raul Garza across a parking lot, and he raised a hand back in the halfhearted way one did when recognition was lacking. She let her hand drop. She wasn't as surprised as she should have been. Garza had been her fourth stop. Sylvie had visited some of the dance-'til-you-die-cursed clubbers, and none of them recalled anything more complex than someone *maybe spiking my drink*? One man, shifting uncomfortably from foot to foot, as if his feet felt bruised and tender, said he thought that maybe there'd been E going around.

When she pressed, tried to get them to admit they recalled more, remembered something magical, they'd locked up and stuttered like a skipped record, claimed headaches. She imagined, if she confronted Garza, he'd do the same.

Her jaw set; she tightened her grip on the steering wheel as she turned the truck for Miami and home.

The thing was, Sylvie had always known the world was blind to the *Magicus Mundi*, that people would ignore their own senses to come up with a more "real world" answer. It wasn't a werewolf that ate the family pet, it was an alligator. Fur? What fur?

People liked their world's being safe and sane and sensible. Sylvie had always assumed that the hard cases who denied magic even when it was happening big and bright and undeniable in front of them were *willfully* blind.

She'd never considered that they might have been blindfolded by someone or something else.

Maybe she needed to.

This wasn't the first time Sylvie had expected to have real-world fallout from a magical event: After the gods had battled in Chicago, scattering god-power and warping the city, she'd expected to hear endless speculation and theorizing. Instead, there'd been a news report about an inland storm and freak occurrences brought on by panic and strange atmospheric pressures. Strange atmospheric pressures that allowed children to bring nightmares to life, that set buildings to attacking each other, and lifted roadways off the ground like ribbons. Very strange pressures.

That was the most egregious example, but several hours of research later, Sylvie had compiled a list of should-have-been-noticed events. Chicago, obviously. The cursed bodies she'd found in the Everglades, more locally. And reading between the lines on newspaper accounts and her case files: another half dozen. It seemed like anytime the *Magicus Mundi* made itself felt with a significant death toll, something or someone swept it under the proverbial rug.

Sylvie, who believed in honesty, even if she didn't always practice it, found it insupportable. She couldn't stop people from pretending the *Magicus Mundi* didn't exist. But deliberately blinding them? The world was dangerous enough when you knew the predators existed, even subconsciously. If you weren't allowed to know? It was like being shoved into a room to take a test without even knowing what the subject was, and if you failed, you died.

She and her business partner, Alexandra Figueroa-Smith, would have to do some research. Find out who was behind it. Find out why they were doing it. And find out what it would take to stop them.

1

Fall Apart

SYLVIE HAD A WHOLE LIST OF THINGS SHE DISLIKED—MISOGYNIST sorcerers, incompetent drivers, government agents who raided her office illegally, trashed her security, and absconded with her files, lovers who were too busy to call, and cops who weren't—too many things to really enumerate or rank, but frantic phone calls from her clients were close to the top.

She liked frantic calls even less when things were theoretically under control. Her client, Lupe Fernandez, was supposed to be tucked up safe and sound at her parents' home.

Lupe's call had been brief, mostly unintelligible. It had been three minutes of sobbing, shouting, a vibration of mortal terror. When the call had disconnected, mid panicked babble, Sylvie knew something had gone wrong. Knew she hadn't done her job right.

That was the kind of thought that ruined her morning, sent her scrabbling out of her bed, grabbing at clothes, her gun, her keys, and heading for her truck at a dead run. Not the way she preferred to begin her days. Ideally, they'd start with waking before the alarm went off, having time for a leisurely cup of coffee, a morning jog, or swim if the day was too hot, then a late breakfast at her office, while Alex caught her up on potential clients.

If it were a really good day, when she woke, Demalion would be beside her, lashes dark on his face, the glint of blond stubble in slanting sunlight, sleeping as determinedly as a cat. If it were a good day, she'd get to lean over and nudge him awake, watch his pupils flare and fade as he blinked into morning light.

It hadn't been a good day for months.

Sylvie laid on the horn, cursed rush-hour traffic, and stomped on the gas, jerking her truck around a multitasking driver who had one hand full of coffee cup, the other full of cell phone, and was failing to steer with his knees.

Her throat was tight, worried about Lupe. The woman had been through so much already. Kidnapped by Azpiazu the soul devourer, used as a magical conduit, finally freed through Sylvie's actions. . . only to find she wasn't as free as everyone thought.

Azpiazu had slapped a shape-shifting spell on his victims as part of his attempt to control his own unmanageable shifting. When Sylvie had killed him and broken the spell that linked him to his victims, she'd thought it was over. Had seen the women home with the sense of a job well-done.

Then Lupe had called her the first full moon after, in total hysterics; the moon rose, and Lupe shifted into a werewolf in her screened-in patio. Reason enough for hysterics, but it had been far worse than that. Lupe hadn't been alone. Her girlfriend, Jenny, had been curled next to her on the patio swing. Jenny had needed 134 stitches in her face, chest, shoulder, and arm, lost three fingers on her right hand, and gained a cracked skull. She'd nearly bled out before Lupe woke the next morning and called 911.

Unsurprisingly, the two broke up. Jenny didn't really remember what had happened; the concussion and blood loss saw to that, but at the same time, Lupe said, Jenny was afraid of her.

Lupe was afraid of herself.

Sylvie had taken her out to Tatya and Marisol in the Everglades, two women, two *werewolves*, who she thought might be willing to help deal with the change. They had been. Again, Sylvie had thought, problem solved. Or at least shelved.

Sunlight lancing through her windshield from the car before her made her squint and wince, and realize she'd torn out of her apartment without grabbing her sunglasses. A small pain, though, compared to what Lupe was going through.

Finding out she was a werewolf was bad and freaky enough—curse-inflicted lycanthropy was insanely rare—but spending the full moon with Tatya and Marisol had proved that Lupe's problems were larger than that. With Tatya and Marisol at her side, Lupe had been braced to deal with the wolf-change, assured that no one would be hurt this time.

The problem was that Lupe *didn't* shift into a wolf. She changed under the moon, wasn't left a human between two monsters, but she didn't turn into a wolf either. For her second full moon, Lupe turned into a *jaguar*, all fury and rage at being caught between the two werewolves. No one came out of that unscathed.

Lupe didn't heal like Tatya and Marisol did, either; she was left with bloody bite marks that bled and scabbed for weeks. She bore the wounds without complaint, saying Jenny had had it worse.

Sylvie had started looking into witches, hoping to find someone who could break the curse. It was a slow, too-slow, process, trying to find a witch with the right ratio of power to trustworthiness, and they'd run out of time. It didn't help that three months ago, the ISI had helped themselves to Sylvie's files. The ISI was supposed to deal with the intersection of the *Magicus Mundi* and the real world, but they had chosen to use the information gleaned from Sylvie's files to run the few remaining local witches Sylvie could work with out of town. Business as usual with them. They would rather inconvenience Sylvie than do anything productive.

So for the third moon, last night's moon, Lupe had made her own arrangements. She'd gone to her parents' home while they were on a buying trip in New York City and locked herself in a zoo-quality cage that she'd set up in the home gym. Obviously, something had gone wrong. *Again.* Lupe couldn't seem to catch a break.

Sylvie changed lanes, got off the highway, and hoped Lupe hadn't killed someone. If that happened, she didn't know what she'd do.

Put a bullet in her brain, her little dark voice suggested. *You kill monsters.*

It was true. If she had been coming into the case from the outside, she would have shot Lupe already and fed her bones to the sea. But Lupe was hers. Sylvie had saved her from the sorcerer, and she was responsible for her well-being.

She was forced to a stop outside the gated community's security station and bit back her impatience. She'd forgotten Lupe's family had money and the paranoia to go with it. The guard leaned out of his station, eyed her beat-up truck, eyed her, said nothing. "Sylvie Lightner," she said. "I'm here to see the Fernandezes."

"Yeah, all right. They got back this morning."

He waved her on; the security mostly for show. He hadn't even asked to see her ID. But he'd answered at least part of her question. What had gone wrong? Well, for one thing, Lupe's parents had come home early.

Sylvie felt her lips thin, press tight. She hit the gas, let her urgency spill out with that last rush to get to the house.

She pulled into the long, curving, palm-shaded driveway, and cut the engine. The stucco facade, golden in the morning sunlight, seemed peaceful, at odds with the shrieking phone call.

The driveway was paved brick and stone, money spent on decoration because it could be, and led her to a double front door with a brass knocker kept well polished. It was cold in her hands despite the growing heat of the morning.

The door opened a bare person width to a middle-aged woman Sylvie didn't know and presumed was Mrs. Fernandez. Behind her, the house was dim and dark. Quiet.

"I'm Sylvie—"

"It's in back," she said as she opened the door. She didn't look at Sylvie.

"It?" Sylvie didn't wait for an answer. The woman's expression told her enough. Fear and distaste and horror all admixed.

Lupe. Her daughter. *It.*

Sylvie headed for the back of the house, for the exercise room Lupe had mentioned. *"I'll set up there. At least then, if I get loose, I won't shred the furniture."* Another woman stood in front of the gym door; this woman was younger, her face miserable with fear as she blocked the entrance.

Sylvie said, "I need to go in."

The woman—not sister, Lupe didn't have a sister, but maybe sister-in-law?—grabbed at Sylvie's arm. "She tried to kill him. We had to do it."

Sylvie shoved past, frightened now for Lupe, expecting to find her dead. It wasn't that bad. Close, but not that bad. Lupe huddled in the base of the cage, arms wrapped tight around herself, face hidden in her knees. Two men stood outside the cage, their backs to Sylvie but their stance unmistakable. Guns in their hands, aimed at the cage. Blood smell hung in the air, sharp and sweet and strong in the sterile confines of the home gym.

"Hey," Sylvie said. "Put 'em away. I got this."

"It tried to kill him," the younger one said. Lupe's brother. Sylvie tried to remember his name. Alex, thorough as always, had put together one of her overkill files on Lupe and her family. The brother's name was in it. Miguel?

"Manuel," Sylvie said. "Put it away. She's your sister."

"It's an abomination," Lupe's father—Alberto—said. "We should kill it." His words were brutal, his face cold, but his hands wavered.

"Put it away and get out," Sylvie said, losing patience. Lupe still hadn't looked up.

"You'll get rid of it?" Alberto demanded.

"I'll take care of her," Sylvie said.

He huffed, jerked his head at his son, and they ceded the ground. Sylvie waited for the adrenaline rushing her system to fade, but it, wiser than she, refused to go.

They could change their minds; they could come back

at any moment, worked up all over again, guns firing. Sylvie and Lupe weren't out yet. Relief was premature.

. . .

THE HEAVY PADLOCK ON THE CAGE WAS SNAPPED TIGHT, LOCKING Lupe behind bars, a beaten prisoner in her own family home. "Lupe. You have the key?" Sylvie tried to keep her voice steady, but blood smeared the pale tiles surrounding Lupe, a jumbled finger painting in shades of crimson and rust. The woman was injured, maybe seriously. Not dead. Sylvie could see the fine tremors running the angles of her bent elbows and knees, the shaky bellows of her rib cage.

"Lupe. Answer me!"

". . . they took it," Lupe breathed. "Put me back in and took it away."

Back in. She'd gotten out. Not good.

"Oh, fuck this," Sylvie said. She looked around, focused on the weight bench and free weights. That would do. She seized up a twenty-five-pound weight, swung it around, and brought it crashing against the padlock. The noise made Lupe scream, and it was echoed in the rest of the house. Sylvie dropped the weight on the broken lock, turned to greet Manuel with her gun raised. *"Out!"*

He held his hands up, gun pointing toward the ceiling, and backed out. "Your life," he said. "Your risk."

Sylvie followed him to the door, locked it behind him, dragged the weight bench in front of it, metal legs screeching over the tile.

"Lupe," she said. "Come on, what happened?"

"I changed," Lupe said. Her voice was a husk, ruined and wet. "Sylvie, I can't live like this."

"It's okay—"

"It's not!" Lupe jerked to her feet, faster than she should have been able to after trying to fold herself into origami. She was in Sylvie's face almost before Sylvie could blink. Sylvie stiff-armed her in the chest, knocked her back.

"Calm down."

"Why should I?" Lupe shouted.

Sylvie got her first good look at the woman since she'd entered the room and found herself in reluctant agreement. Why should Lupe calm down when things were so completely, visibly, wrong?

When Lupe had turned wolf that first time, she hadn't come back unscathed. Her teeth had stayed sharp-edged behind soft lips. When she'd become a jaguar, the shift back to human left her with a swath of spotted skin across her shoulders and back. Whatever she'd shifted into last night had left its own startling and far-too-noticeable mark: Lupe's irises looked like hammered brass, and her pupils were black slits. They should have looked like special-effects lenses, easy to explain. They didn't.

Lupe crossed her arms, long, tanned limbs crossing darkly over her white tank top, her white-linen pants. Blood spread scarlet near her rib cage. The shirt was smoked at the center of the bloodstain. A bullet crease. Close range.

Sylvie stepped closer, peeled the shirt up. Lupe winced. Superficial but bloody. Sylvie grabbed a towel from the weight bench, pressed it against the wound. It came away mostly dry. Lupe had bled hard, but she wasn't going to bleed out. She could wait for first aid. Sylvie threw the towel across the room, a drift of white in a mostly white room. Lupe's blood was the brightest thing in it.

"They shot you?"

"Wouldn't you?" Lupe said. "The cage didn't hold me. I almost killed him. Olivia came last night, waiting to welcome them all home. She brought my nephew, Sylvie. Two years old. She thought they were alone in the house, and I . . . I was loose."

"How'd you manage that, anyway?" Sylvie asked. The cage was first-rate. The bars were solid steel, none of them more than four inches from each other, closed at bottom and top, and, until Sylvie had smashed the lock, secure.

Lupe blinked dark gold eyes, and Sylvie understood what they reminded her of just as Lupe said, "I turned into a python. A big one. I almost crushed his rib cage. Two years old, and his aunt tried to make him a meal. I knew better, even as I closed my coils, but I couldn't stop."

Sylvie swore. It was all wrong. All unexpected. Were-wolf was bad, were-jaguar was worse—but Lupe had worn those shapes before while held by Azpiazu. She'd worn bear also. Sylvie had expected that to be the third shift, something big but containable. Not this. Not a reptile who shared nothing with humankind.

Lupe swayed closer; Sylvie smelled sweat, blood, and a musty underlay of old snakeskin. Her stomach turned uneasily.

Careful, her little dark voice warned. *She's dangerous.*

Dangerous enough to maul a woman, to take on two wolves, to try to smother and eat a child. A calculating brain with animal instinct.

"It's the curse, isn't it," Lupe said. "The curse that Azpiazu suffered. Now it's on me."

Sylvie thought of a slew of platitudes but chose not to lie. "Looks like."

Lupe's legs gave out; she dropped to the floor as fluidly as if she had gone serpentine again. "Why me?"

The question wasn't an accusation, but it felt like one. The other women who'd survived being Azpiazu's prisoners—Maria, Rita, Anamaria, Elena—had come out of it untouched except for nightmare memories and scarred foreheads where the binding sigils had been.

The binding sigil had held them prisoner to Azpiazu's will. Sylvie and her cohorts had disrupted the sigils on the other four, magically or physically. She remembered gouging at Rita in bear form, her marked forehead the only part of her still human. Sylvie had slashed the sigil with a sharp stone and her nails.

But Lupe, during the final battle, had been wounded and retreated beneath a bush. Her sigil had never been disrupted. It hadn't mattered. The spell had broken when Azpiazu died. It should have been a nonissue.

"We went back," Sylvie said, half in realization, half in explanation. "We dispersed the last traces of Azpiazu from the site to make sure he couldn't come back as a vengeful ghost. You still had the sigil whole on your skin. It acted like a beacon for those traces."

Lupe's skin was unmarked now. Her forehead where the sigil had been was as smooth as marble. The other women bore scars. Sylvie imagined the sigil groaning beneath the sudden weight of the curse and sinking through skin and bone, making itself at home somewhere in Lupe's body like a migrating bullet.

"So *you* did this to me?"

Excuses leaped to Sylvie's lips: She hadn't known. It shouldn't have happened. Azpiazu had started it. It was Tepeyollotl's curse. "Yes."

"What are you going to do to fix it?" Lupe said. "I've lost my girlfriend, I've fucked up my classes, and my parents want me dead. I mean, they haven't been happy with me since I hooked up with Jenny, but . . . they really want me dead, Sylvie."

"Yeah," Sylvie said. "I noticed."

Lupe's face crumpled as if she'd hoped Sylvie would protest, would tell her pretty lies about her parents just being scared, bullet crease aside. She scrubbed at her eyes, but the snake taint in them seemed to prevent tears from forming.

"We'll fix it," Sylvie said. "We'll find a witch who'll figure out a way—"

"That's what you tried last month," Lupe said. "I'm still fucked. And it's getting worse."

"Witches are a little scarce on the ground right now," Sylvie admitted. The witches with any real power had been leaving Miami in waves, fleeing Sylvie's gun, fleeing the ISI, fleeing the new god that was making Miami her home. The new god that Sylvie had helped create. Erinya had been a demigodling, a servant to the god of Justice—dangerous, but containable—until Sylvie had used Erinya to defeat the soul devourer's grab at godhood. Erinya got the shiny prize instead, becoming a full god, independent and unstoppable. Worst of all, instead of retreating from the real world in proper godly protocol, she insisted on sticking around.

Gods in the real world were always a disaster waiting to happen. They were pure power, and like a human shedding skin cells, shedding breath, gods shed scraps of power wherever they lingered. Witches could use that power, collect it for their own, but it was a risky habit. A god's power was more likely to burn out a witch's ability entirely than it was to recharge it.

Once Erinya had started making her presence felt, Sylvie's favorite go-to witch, Val Cassavetes, had disappeared somewhere in Italy, and taken Sylvie's witchy sister, Zoe, with her. She couldn't even rely on family.

The witches who were left? Scavengers who hoped to grow fat on the god's shed leavings. Untalented, untutored. Untrustworthy. Too small to be of interest to the ISI or too skilled at going to ground. The kind of witch who'd be just as glad to kill Lupe and use her bones for spell ingredients.

"Don't worry," Sylvie said. "We'll beat this. I'll broaden the search. I'll find a way to break this curse." The words felt empty in her mouth, fragments of faint hope. She wasn't a spell-breaker. Point her in the direction of the spellcaster, and she'd take him or her out of the picture, break the curse through brute force. But Azpiazu was three months dead, and the god who'd laid the original curse was a powerless shell who'd retreated to a realm Sylvie couldn't reach.

Lupe grimaced, all pointed teeth and animal distress, and said, "You'd better hurry. I'm running out of normal." As if to prove her point, she went from her crouch to a leap that took her to the top of the cage, then to the high window and through it. She left a bloody smear on the sill as her wound broke open again with the exertion.

Sylvie, thinking of the armed men outside the weight room, thought Lupe had the right idea, and clambered awkwardly, humanly, after her.

· · ·

WITH NO PLACE ELSE COMING TO MIND, SYLVIE DROVE LUPE AND herself to the Shadows Inquiries office, ushering Lupe in ahead of her. Lupe's bare feet were soundless on the dusty terrazzo floor, and Alex, wielding a broom with determination, grimaced as she splashed sawdust over Lupe's feet.

"Crap. Sorry, Lupe," Alex said.

Lupe raised her head; Alex sucked in a breath and retreated to the sanctuary of her desk. The lanky blonde looked uncharacteristically flustered, but Sylvie understood. There was something particularly horrifying about watching Lupe grow less human each month.

"There are some spare clothes upstairs," Sylvie said, disrupting the awkward moment.

Lupe headed for the stairs and came face-to-face with the workman coming out from beneath them. He dropped his toolbox, and Lupe turned back to Sylvie, fury and humiliation on every distorted line of her face. Her throat mottled darkly with passing spots. "Fix this, Shadows."

The carpenter, kneeling over his spilled tools, crossed himself as Lupe stomped upstairs. Sylvie said, "How's the safe room coming, Emmanuel? We're going to need it a little sooner than I thought."

"What's wrong with her?" he said. His dark eyes jittered over hers; then he looked up the stairs as if his gaze could drag Lupe back down and pin her in place until he understood the inexplicable.

"Nothing that's any of your business," Sylvie said. She kept her tone friendly but didn't bother with an excuse. She was tired of helping the world blind itself to the *Magicus Mundi*. Let him worry and wonder.

"Fair enough," he said. "I'm taking lunch. I'll have the room finished by this evening. Just need to finish up the ventilation system. Can't have you suffocating in there."

"Would defeat the purpose of a safe room," she agreed, and waved him off.

He stopped at Alex's desk, flashed a smile, and offered to buy her lunch. Alex turned him down but sent him away with a smile. Sylvie shook her head and tuned out the flirty conversation.

She peered into the narrow corridor that Emmanuel had excavated beneath the stairwell. She hated that they needed the room at all, but Alex had been agitating for one for months. After the ISI had tear-gas-bombed the office, Sylvie decided Alex was right.

Ideally, it would be a magical safe room as well, a place to store dangerous talismans or to hide from magical attackers, but that would require a trustworthy witch to build the proper shields.

A shift in the air, the scent of blood and antiseptic, and she turned to find Lupe at her side, peering over her shoulder. Her lips were pulled tight over her teeth, outlining the jut of her canines. "That for me?"

"If it comes to that."

"Guess it's a good thing I'm not claustrophobic." Lupe crossed her arms tight over Sylvie's borrowed sweatshirt. She shifted foot to foot. "You sure it'll hold me?"

"Long as you don't turn into a swarm of mosquitoes," Sylvie said.

Lupe grinned without amusement. "Right now, I'm not ruling it out."

Sylvie shot Alex a *help* glance. She was out of anything even remotely approaching comfort. Alex slid out from behind her desk, put a careful hand on Lupe's sleeve, and said, "You want to get in on our lunch order? I mean, I don't know much about shape-shifting, but it seems like hungry work."

Lupe followed Alex's lead docilely enough, even as she protested that she was too stressed to think about food. Sylvie took the opportunity to duck up to her office.

She left the door open, keeping an ear out for Lupe and Alex, and let her shoulders slump. She didn't like Lupe's changes. The curse was bad enough, but she really didn't like the level of violence that went with the changes. She needed a witch, and she needed one now.

Even if a witch couldn't break the curse, maybe one could ameliorate the worst effects.

Sylvie ran through her usual contacts in her mind, trying to figure out who was speaking to her this month, who was too busy to talk, and finally just admitted the truth to herself. There was only one person she was going to call.

She pushed back her rolling chair, propped her sneak-ered feet against the scarred wood desk, and dialed.

"Sylvie," Demalion said. Picked up on the first ring. And didn't that make her skin warm embarrassingly even though she knew the quickness was dictated more by prox-imity than desire. She'd caught him at a good time.

"Got a moment?"

"You've got trouble?"

"When don't I?" Despite the truth in that, she felt her voice relaxing. It had been three months since he'd taken his new body back to Chicago, three months that should have stretched the relationship between them to the breaking point. Instead, it had given them something they'd never known they had needed. Distance and the time to talk.

"Truth," he said. "I think you wouldn't know what to do with a vacation if you had one."

"You could come down early and find out," she said.

His voice roughed itself into a huff of not-quite-amusement. "Would if I could."

"Oh, damn," she said. "I know that tone. You're not coming next week." Disappointment sat sourly in her stom-ach. Time to talk was all well and good, but she missed being able to touch him. His resurrection from the dead and his departure had happened so close together that some nights she woke sweating, thinking he was only a voice on the other end of her line. A ghost she couldn't let go.

It had been difficult enough to let him go when he was determined to repay a dead man for giving Demalion back his life, when he had gone back to Chicago to fix what was broken in Wright's life. It hadn't taken too long for Wright's wife to smell a rat, to come to the correct but improbable answer that the man wandering around in her husband's body was no longer her husband. Once she figured it out, she took her son and the money Demalion offered and fled the city. Sylvie had hoped Demalion would return at that point. Instead, he'd rejoined the ISI under Adam Wright's name. That had been a harder pill to swallow. No debt owing there, just ambition and an ideology Sylvie didn't share.

Still, they were making it work.

She pushed away from the desk, spun to stare at her filing cabinets, assessing. Even without Lupe's case, she had too many small irons in the fire to go to him.

Before he could make apologies, she said, "Hey, you heard anything about memory modification?"

"Magical?"

"Would I ask otherwise?"

Demalion hesitated, thinking about it. "Individual or big picture? Are we talking Chicago?"

"That and others."

"No," Demalion said. "You know, it's weird, now that you mention it. I just sort of accepted it. People don't like to look beyond the ordinary."

"This is true," Sylvie said. "To my everlasting chagrin. You know how many of my clients wait until things are holy-fuck bad instead of coming in at first trouble?"

"You and the doctors. You really think there's something there? Something you want me to look into?"

"If you've got time."

"That's the problem," Demalion said. "Yvette is running us all kinds of ragged. Trying to get everything in place to impress whoever it is who funds us. Apparently, there was some type of . . . incident."

She could hear the air quotes through the phone, and said, "Let me guess. Someone served the big boss shrimp, and he's allergic?"

"Hell if I know," Demalion said. "Seriously, Syl. She's got things locked down tight. It's all need-to-know, and I'm a new hire as far as Yvette's concerned. Her inner circle is so busy that none of us low-levels have even laid eyes on them for days. But it's all trickling down."

"Things like that do," Sylvie said.

"I don't know when I'll be able to get a day off. God, I don't know when I'll even catch up on my sleep." If it hadn't been for his nearly tangible frustration, she might have shared hers.

"You have any idea what's going on?"

"Big picture, yeah," Demalion said on a sigh. "Political infighting. Yvette, Riordan, and Graves are all duking it out to be the new head of the ISI. They're all hell-bent on impressing the money man with their dedication and efficiency."

Sylvie grimaced. She knew Riordan. Wouldn't have liked him even if he hadn't been the one who had sent a SWAT team armed with tear gas into her office to collect her. He was too prone to attacking the little guys and leaving the big threats to sort themselves out.

"What happened to the old head?"

"Gods in Chicago," Demalion said. "They found a charred pelvis and skull in his office. Typed it for DNA. He's toast. It just took a while for the paperwork to go through."

"So Riordan's down here, posturing at me. Yvette's making your life difficult. What's Graves doing?"

"Nothing good, I bet. Man's a bastard. I worked for him for two months when I first came out here. Bad temper. Bad attitude. Distrustful."

"Sounds like typical ISI to me."

"Syl—"

"All right, all right. No job bashing."

"Graves hightailed it down to Texas after Yvette stole the Chicago office out from under him. He's pissed. Been making our lives hard by accusing this office of all sorts of things. Magical misconduct, mostly. He's heard rumors that Yvette is a witch."

"Is she?"

"Yeah," Demalion said. "Makes sense if you think about it. Who better to deal with the *Magicus Mundi* than someone who can step in and out of it."

"I do all right," Sylvie said.

"Yeah, don't try to pretend you're ordinary."

"So Graves doesn't like witches."

"Witches, psychics, half-breed monsters."

"Not a fan of yours, then," Sylvie said. It was more than just a comment; it was an invitation to confession. There were some things they'd talked about endlessly. Demalion's difficulty in adjusting to his new body. Demalion's relief when Wright's wife figured out that the man in her apartment might look like her husband but wasn't, and left him. Demalion's careful plan to rejoin the ISI without tipping them off that he had been with them before. He wanted to work for them, not be studied by them.

The one topic made conspicuous by its absence was Demalion's clairvoyance. He'd been born with it, a genetic gift from his inhuman mother, and he'd died with it. Sylvie wanted to know if he'd managed to reshape Wright's body to bring it with him, and he wasn't talking.

Lupe's voice rose sharply downstairs, but after a reactive jerk to her feet, Sylvie diagnosed the sound as brittle laughter, not a threat.

"Watch your back," Sylvie said. "Political infighting can get ugly and violent fast."

"I think Graves is more focused on Yvette than me. She's his target. Everything he hates in one tidy package. A high-ranking woman, a rival, and a witch."

"Graves sounds like a peach."

Demalion said, "Hey, Sylvie—"

"Yeah?" The tentative sound to his voice made her wary, made her tense up as his pitch went tighter, higher, noticeable only because she'd gotten to know this new form of his voice so well.

"I don't know that it matters, but Yvette and I—"

Sylvie went cold, flushed hot, read that little pause too clearly. "What, you hooked up with your *boss*? I guess she's convenient."

"No!" Demalion said. "Not currently. Then. Years ago. Before she was up in the ranks. Before you. Way before you. When I was a different man. I just thought it was something you should know."

Sylvie sighed. Just what she needed. An irrational reason to add to the rational reason she already had for disliking the woman: a government agent who was keeping her lover from visiting her. "Some things you should keep to yourself. Does she know? You said she's a witch. Will she recognize you?"

"She looks at me funny every now and then."

"Just great," Sylvie said. "Hope you had an amicable breakup, or you'll be on the damn dissection table before you know it."

"She wouldn't—"

"Wouldn't she? It would be a great way to get Graves off her back. To show him that she wasn't a crazy *Magicus Mundi* wannabe."

"You're ridiculously cynical—"

"You're ridiculously trusting for a government suit."

An argument hummed along the wires between them, ready to break out, and Sylvie wrenched them to a new topic. "I called because I need some info," she said.

"Anything."

And that right there was why he kept her on her toes. How he could go from defending the ISI to implicitly agreeing to give her information out of their files if she asked. . . Sylvie thought the inner workings of Demalion's mind might always be a mystery to her. Either he was the king of compartmentalization, or he judged and scaled every moment and every request.

Or, of course, he still had his psychic abilities, and knew what she was going to ask, knew it wouldn't tax his relationship with the ISI.

She waited, let the space stretch between them. But Demalion was too cagey to be caught out that easily. "Should I be worried that you're taking a long time to ask? Trying to think of the perfect way to phrase it?"

"You seen your mother recently?"

"Why do you ask?" The hesitation in his voice was enough to tell her that psychic or not, he hadn't foreseen that question.

"It's just a question. One with an easy answer, I thought." She spun her desk chair 'round. Now he had her doing it, overthinking every word.

Downstairs, the front door opened and closed, Alex heading out on a food run. Lupe's footsteps were soft on the terrazzo, but Sylvie, listening to Demalion's breath in her ear, could hear when Lupe's pacing faltered, when she sank onto the couch with creak of leather and the soft gasps of someone fighting tears.

"Sylvie—"

Sylvie lost interest in the game. "I was hoping she could find me a reliable witch. One with a healthy slug of power and a good attitude. One who will make house calls. I've got a client with one hell of a nasty curse."

"I'll give her a call, but don't count on anything. She's—"

"Still holding a grudge against me?" It was fair enough. Sylvie had gotten Demalion killed, bad enough for any mother. When that mother was the Sphinx and had spent a thousand years gestating the only child she'd have? Sylvie counted herself lucky Anna Demalion hadn't slaughtered her.

"And me," Demalion said. "I asked her to do something she didn't want to do. She's been ignoring my calls ever since. I don't think a human in trouble is going to get her to break her silence."

"Well, fuck," Sylvie said. "What about the ISI? You keep records, right? Of known witches in the country?"

"Mostly the ones who leave a trail of dead behind them," Demalion reminded her. "I could bring Yvette in on it if it's urgent. She's pretty damn skilled at what she does."

Sylvie choked back her gut reaction, a profane and profound negative. She thought about it, turned the idea around from different angles, and decided her gut instinct was absolutely right. "No. Absolutely not."

"She can probably help—"

"Michael, no. It's not a matter of ability," Sylvie said. "I think you'd see that. For one thing, my client can't afford ISI scrutiny right now. They'd lock her up and worry about the cure later."

"She's dangerous, then?" Demalion asked. "Sylvie. You take on some crap clients."

"Regardless," she said. "No on Yvette. Besides which, if you don't want her to associate your new life as Adam

Wright with Demalion? Don't point out that we're on good enough terms to help each other. Good way to blow your new and secret identity right out of the water."

"She might know—"

"And you want to confirm it? You trust her that much?" Sylvie heard the ugly edge in her voice and winced. It wasn't about jealousy. It was about the basics. Yvette Collier had two strikes against her. She was a government agent, and she was a witch. Both of those made her someone to distrust.

"Syl, the ISI is not your enemy."

"Did you forget they tear-gassed me and tried to make me vanish?"

Demalion said, "If they wanted you gone, they'd have done a better job."

"Not your best rebuttal ever, just so you know," she said. "They've been keeping a careful distance, I'll admit it, but it's not because they want to make nice. They're scared of me. Every time they get close to me, their agents end up dead or damaged. That caution won't hold forever. "

"You're paranoid."

"You're drinking the Kool-Aid. You want to believe they're the good guys, and I admit, their goals *sound* good. Study, research, integration of the *Magicus Mundi* with the human world . . . but what government group ever sticks that close to its charter?"

"At least they have one," Demalion said. "Your charter is all over the place. You've got the luxury of taking things on a case-by-case basis. We're the government. We don't."

"Fine," Sylvie said. Her cell phone creaked in her hand, plastic protesting her grip. "Just do me a favor. I bet they've got files on me—"

"You know we do. The new Lilith. Of course, we do. Not that they say much. We don't know what the new Lilith is. . . ."

"Don't look to me for answers," Sylvie said, irritated at his fishing. "But I bet the ISI recommendations aren't to wait until they figure me out. ISI's not much for live and let live. You want to believe in them, fine. Just realize that, sooner or later, you're going to have to pick a side. Them or me."

She disconnected with an angry stab of the END button, hit it so decisively that the phone not only truncated the call but shut itself down. Sylvie let out her breath in a shaky gust.

The new Lilith.

She'd been letting it slide, letting the words be nothing but another soubriquet people slapped on her. Loud-mouthed bitch. Shadows. *L'enfant de meurtrier.* The new Lilith.

Hiding from reality doesn't change it, her little dark voice purred.

All right then, she thought. One goal, two reasons. Find a witch who was either trustworthy or clued in enough to the currents of the *Mundi* to make the risk worthwhile. Use the witch to cure or calm Lupe's problem. Then use the witch to find out if being the new Lilith meant anything beyond the general resistance to magic and a potentially increased life span. Do all of it without letting the ISI spy on her business.

She grimaced and tossed her cell phone onto her desk, where it landed with a clatter. Finding a witch was going to take time.

We have time, the voice in her head suggested.

She might have time. More time than Sylvie could imagine if her fears were accurate.

Immortality loomed before her like a void, endless, pointless, terrifying. She closed her mind to it. She might have time.

Lupe didn't.

2

Unwelcome News

IT WAS PAST MIDNIGHT AND STARTING TO STORM BY THE TIME SYLVIE made it back to her apartment. The flash and crash of the night suited her mood well enough. Three days spent hunting witches for Lupe, and she'd managed to chase down a single reference to a *brujo* who specialized in shape-shifting curses and cures. It had been a long shot for a lot of reasons, most especially because he was supposed to live in Orlando. Sylvie knew it was unfair, but she couldn't take a Mouse-City witch seriously.

He'd been the real deal, though. He'd also been long gone when she got there, chased out of the city by the Green Swamp werewolf pack, who didn't like a witch encroaching near their territory. It had been a long drive for nothing. He hadn't left a forwarding address.

She shrugged off her jacket, removed her holster, looked at the empty shelves of her fridge, and called for Thai. If only all her problems could be solved that easily.

Sometimes, there were things that just couldn't be fixed. She wasn't ready to consign Lupe to that file, not when her curse was Sylvie's fault, but all the signs were there.

A god's curse on a mortal was a nightmare of pantheon

politics and power. Usually, the only way those curses were removed was by the god forgiving the mortal. Tepeyollotl, even if he wanted to, no longer had the ability to take back his curse; he'd lost that power to Azpiazu, then to Erinya.

Even if Erinya had his power, it wasn't her curse to remove. Gods didn't interfere with other gods' punishments, not unless they were willing to war over it. From what Sylvie understood, all the pantheons were carefully circling each other in a wary cease-fire.

Even so, maybe Erinya could help.

Sylvie shook her head. Asking Erinya for aid was a bit like asking the pyromaniac neighbor kid for help with a campfire. Something would burn, all right. The campfire, the trees, the houses. Erinya was a resource best left untapped.

Besides, Sylvie and Erinya were negotiating a wary truce of their own. Erinya wanted to hunt Demalion down. Sylvie had stopped her from doing so. She wasn't ready to rock that boat.

The doorbell buzzed, and Sylvie shook herself into movement, grabbing for her wallet.

She had just paid the delivery boy for three cartons of Thai when all the fine hairs on the back of her neck stretched toward the ceiling. She waved off her change and braced herself before turning around.

She should have expected it. Ordering late-night Thai was like sending up the Bat-Signal. Erinya tended to mooch whenever she could.

Erinya's habit of popping into Sylvie's tiny Miami apartment made Sylvie crazy, but she marked it up as part of the price to be paid. Erinya hadn't turned full god on her own. Sylvie had basically force-fed her the power. Now Erinya kept a close eye on her.

Sylvie regretted her actions at least once a day. But if she hadn't done it, a vengeful and broken Mesoamerican god would have turned Miami into a feeding ground, and there'd be no chance of delivery food after a long and hellish day, so maybe Sylvie had made the right choice after all.

The looming presence in her living room grew stronger, took on a crackle of lightning. "Yeah, yeah," Sylvie said. "Let me get you a fork—"

It wasn't Erinya making herself at home, propping her booted feet up on Sylvie's long-suffering couch, staining the pale fabric with indescribable bits of destroyed "sinners." Or flouncing around in her punk-goth wear—torn plaid skirts, fishnets, and spiky hair—demanding that Sylvie stop what she was doing and pay attention to her.

Instead, a man, midway between six feet and seven stood there, looking mildly disappointed. He had a kind face, but Sylvie's guts clenched hard; she dropped the cartons, fumbling for her weapon, though she knew there was nothing in hell she could do to stop him if he'd come gunning for her.

He might look human. Until you took a more careful look. Beneath his skin, an entire sky roiled, a landscape of lightning-struck clouds and looming thunderheads. She'd met him before. Worked for him once. Solved his case to his satisfaction.

She still counted him an enemy. Not least because he was her introduction to the messed-up world of godly politics: Kevin Dunne, onetime human, now the Greek god of Justice.

He frowned; her gun transferred itself from her hand to his. "I need to talk to you."

"Not interested," Sylvie said. She wanted to slip out into the night, but running was the wrong thing to do. The worst thing she could do.

The god of Justice was like any human cop on earth in that respect. Running equaled guilt.

Sylvie turned her back on him though it made her inner instincts protest, and picked up the dropped cartons. She found the one with the *mee grob*, grabbed the chopsticks, retreated to her couch, and did her best to pretend he was a particularly stubborn hallucination brought on by sleep deprivation and too much exposure to witchcraft in the past week.

She clicked on the TV, turned the volume to destroy-all-possibility-of-conversation, and he sighed. The tiny sign of displeasure shuddered down her spine, made her first mouthful of spicy-sweet goodness utterly mechanical. An act of will to chew her food and not give him the satisfaction of looking rattled.

He sighed again, and the TV muted itself.

She swallowed, and said, "Godly powers cover remote control of television? Who knew? Maybe your lot is handy after all."

"Shadows," he said, and took a seat opposite her on a chair that hadn't been there a moment ago. She tried not to like him for conjuring up a squashy, comfortable, obviously aged recliner. It'd be easier to keep up her hatred if he had magicked himself a throne.

"A throne?" he asked, reading her mind easily. "What have I ever done to make you have such a low opinion of me?"

"You blackmailed me into working for you. You let your Furies kill my lover when he was helping to save yours."

"Demalion came back," Dunne said.

Sylvie felt her heart stop, her breath lock up, as if she'd suffered a sudden blow to her chest. He wasn't supposed to know that.

"Did you think I *wouldn't* know?" he said, and yeah, it hurt to admit, but Sylvie had hoped that the god of Justice would have missed Demalion's less-than-triumphant return.

"Don't hurt him," Sylvie said. It wasn't pleading. It was a command, came out rough and certain and angry. It felt like a plea. What could she do to stop him?

"Erinya told me not to."

"Told *you* not to." And dammit, he'd drawn her into talking to him. Last she'd heard, Erinya took orders, didn't give them.

"That's why I'm here. Do you know what you've done?"

"I've done a lot of things, most of which you disapprove of," Sylvie said. "If I recall, you considered me . . . what was it? A trigger-happy vigilante? You would have let your Furies kill me except that you needed me."

"You gave Erinya god-power. You released her from my pantheon. She's running loose, killing people at will, changing the world, and she's only getting started."

"You think I don't know that?" Sylvie said. "Christ, Dunne, she comes here afterward to tell me about it. In detail. *Graphic* detail. She doesn't wash up first. It puts me off my food. And I've had to have the carpet professionally cleaned. Twice."

"So you understand it's a problem—"

"It's your problem. You know why you're pissed?" Sylvie was off the couch, in his face, her hands braced on either arm of his recliner, leaning over him in a way that had her common sense yelping in terror. "She's killing people at her will. Not yours. The only difference between Erinya now and Erinya three months ago? *She's* choosing the targets."

Dunne was gone from the chair, the chair vanished; Sylvie tumbled forward, caught herself, and found him behind her again. "Vigilante justice. I shouldn't be surprised you approve."

"I was out of options, Dunne. I had to protect my city, my world. There were only two choices left: me or Erinya. Would you rather I have kept the power for myself? Turned *myself* into a god?"

It took some effort to startle a god, since mind reading was as natural as breathing for them, but Sylvie had managed it. Dunne sat back again, this time on her couch, as if his concentration had been blown so thoroughly he couldn't even spare a thought for a familiar chair. He studied her, his brown-eyed, human gaze altering bit by bit until there was only a band of churning grey god-stuff instead of a human face.

No eyes, and yet Sylvie felt as *seen* as she had ever been.

"I hadn't been aware that was possible," he said slowly.

"Surprised the hell out of me," Sylvie said. "But so much for your godly omniscience." She was surprised to find that she felt disappointed. She had questions, and though she'd never wanted Dunne here, she'd been hoping to get some answers out of him now that he was. But he just looked blank.

Probably adding up how many people she might kill if she stuck around longer than a mortal's span of years.

That was the thing about god-power. It was heady stuff. Strong stuff. The kind of stuff that blew a mortal body into pieces. A human couldn't hold god-power unless they held immortality first. The only way Dunne had made the transition was by his lover, Eros, granting him immortality first. Even then, by Erinya's accounts, Dunne had nearly gone mad under the weight of godly power.

Sylvie had held the god-power for a horrifying minute, had even used it. She still woke from nightmares about those actions: using that kind of power, containing that kind of power—it had made her want to claw her insides out. Repulsive. Repellent. Wrong.

"The new Lilith," Dunne said thoughtfully. "You replaced her."

"Yeah, thanks, I've heard that."

Sylvie waited to see if he'd elaborate on the theme. If he'd let slip what being the new Lilith actually meant.

He merely said, "I see."

"So I've been told. You want to tell me what that means?"

"You don't know?"

"Would I *ask* if I knew?" Sylvie let all her irritation and frustration come to the surface. She made it a point of not asking things she could find out on her own.

"You'll figure it out eventually," he said.

"I'm impatient, sue me," Sylvie said. "Spit it out, Dunne."

He stood, rolled his shoulders; the light in the room shivered as if the storm core of him were passing overhead, dimming the real world. "You're her replacement. You kill things that shouldn't be killable."

Sylvie threw her carton of Thai food at him in sheer, sudden rage. He didn't dodge; the carton replaced itself on the table, not a single noodle spilled. "Look, asshole—" she said, and somehow that was the mistake. Maybe it was leftover cop, reacting to being disrespected, maybe it was his own burst of impatience—he loomed over her and pinned her to her couch with a look.

Thunder rumbled inside her apartment; the smell of cold rain was bright and strong and sharp, laced with the threat of lightning. When she looked up at him, there was nothing human in his shape, only churning cloud.

"You never thought about her at all, did you?" Dunne asked. "You killed her, and you didn't know her. Did you ever think it strange that she opposed her god so fiercely, acted against him as she could, and was never punished? She birthed monsters to destroy his peoples, and he did nothing. She walked with demons and erased the protective charms men put on their homes—she laughed when the demons crept inside and devoured his blessed children. And he did *nothing*."

She coughed, tore her eyes away from the angry, hypnotic surge of storm cloud, and said, "So he has a hands-off policy—"

"He *created* her. He had a purpose for her. You killed her. Now that purpose is yours. Lilith lived thousands of years and never was called to fulfill her purpose. *His* purpose. I don't know what it is, but I bet you won't like it. Whatever it is, it's important enough that he let her get away with murder."

"Stop," she said. Her heart raced in her chest, painful and panicky. She twisted, tried to escape his psychic grip. "Stop." She didn't know what the new Lilith was? Maybe because she'd never wanted to. Maybe it was safer not to know. More bearable.

"You'll be alive for a very long time, Shadows. Until he has need of you. Or until you're . . . replaced by another of her lineage, another shortsighted killer hungry for blood, filled with rage, refusing to bow to anyone."

"I don't want it," she said. Her throat crackled with dryness; her voice disappeared beneath the thunder of his presence.

"Oh, you know that lesson," he said. "We don't always

get what we want. I wanted a nice, orderly system for meting out justice. I got a Fury-turned-god wreaking havoc."

"What do you want me to do about it?" she asked. She felt horrifyingly close to tears. Blamed his presence for it, a sort of evil osmosis—the storm core of him drawing her salt tears to the surface. Her entire apartment smelled like a squall at sea.

"Stop her."

Sylvie laughed, a fierce crow of stunned disbelief. "What, you want me to do the job? She might be a god, but she's small potatoes compared to you. Deal with her yourself."

"She's not mine anymore," he said. "A pantheon of her own. Not a Fury. If I act against her, it's war across the heavens. You created her. Stop her. Kill her if you have to."

"She's my . . . friend," Sylvie said, and surprised herself by meaning it. That knowledge bolstered her, took her out of her own fears. So what if God had a purpose for her. She didn't have to do it. She didn't have to do what Dunne wanted, either.

"She's your responsibility."

"Fuck you," Sylvie said.

Dunne rocked back, going human-shaped again. His eyes narrowed; suddenly, he didn't look as gentle as he usually did in human form. "You want to use her against your enemies."

"No," Sylvie said. She crossed her arms over her chest, thought clearly how much she wanted him to go the hell away.

He ignored her, and said, "You already have. You sicced her on the ISI after you disposed of Azpiazu."

"I asked her to make us an exit," Sylvie said. "That's all."

Dunne flicked his gaze TV-ward. The channels shifted, blurred, landed on a local news station that wasn't local at all. The banner beneath said it was Channel 8, Dallas/Fort Worth. And it was *yesterday's* breaking news. The volume wound up; the newscaster shouted disaster into the room. An entire work force found dead, all asphyxiated at their desks. Forty people.

The news report suggested a gas leak.

"That's the Dallas ISI," Dunne said.

"I know that," Sylvie said. She kept track of their branches, knew the buildings they took over. The Dallas ISI was based out of a lakeside marina. The facade was distinctive, cement slabbed with a faded trio of white sails against blue waves. The boats slipped there looked normal but all belonged to the government. Expensive camouflage.

The TV flickered, shifted again. "How about this one? I know you recognize it. Or what's left of it."

She didn't at first. It was a picture as horrible and meaningless to her as a foreign disaster—all broken slabs of beige stone, glittering with dusty glass, crawling with reflected emergency lights and first responders. It was the cops' caps that tipped her off, sparked recognition out of anonymity: Chicago cops in late-afternoon sunlight. The video clips were choppy, cameras held by a series of unsteady hands before the professionals arrived. Flashes of gold light flared like special effects every so often, the dust catching and reflecting the lights.

The broken walls weren't beige; they were granite covered with sand. The skyscrapers to either side, though damaged, were familiar enough. The collapsed building was the Chicago ISI. Where she had killed Lilith. Where a resurrected Demalion worked.

The announcers were reading off death tolls like ghouls, adding new bodies on a ticker in the corner of the screen. Seventy-six dead. No, seventy-nine. No, eighty-three.

A pained, broken breath overrode the announcers. It took her a moment to realize it had been hers. Not possible. She'd talked to him just two days prior, and he'd been too run off his feet for anything more than just a *hi, miss you, wish you were here, sorry we fought*. Hadn't even been long enough to argue over anything.

"Do you see?" Dunne said.

She scrubbed hard at her blurring eyes, understood what he was implying and the sheer manipulative gall of it scoured away her fear and pain. "You're a bastard and a liar," she said, couldn't muster enough strength to make it more than a furious whisper. "*Erinya* didn't do this."

It wasn't the Fury's style. Erinya loved the visceral taste of battle. She wouldn't kill by alleged gas, wouldn't drop a building on her foes. She'd wade through their blood or consider it not worth doing.

"No," he admitted. "But she could have. You sent her after the ISI. She's cunning in her own way, could easily decide that your command not to hurt Demalion was overridden by your desire to hurt the ISI. While she might be a small god comparatively, the world's still going to bend to her will the longer she lingers in it."

"Is that even real?" Sylvie asked, gesturing at the TV. "Or is it a sick object lesson?" She pushed off from the couch, pushed past him—felt that nauseating vibration, that subsonic wrongness that indicated power—and leaned on her kitchen counter, stared at the dark mass of her backup gun in the half-open drawer. It gaped at her like an angry mouth. Metal shone within, a black tongue.

"It's real—" he started.

She turned, gun in hand, and fired until the clip was empty, making a violent thunder of her own.

Meaningless, of course.

The only thing she'd killed was her wall. Dunne was gone. The bullet holes in the thick plaster wall and the couch—changed from cream faux suede to a dark leather with brass nailheads at the arms and back—were the only signs that he'd been there at all. A reminder he had to have left deliberately. Gods changed things by their presence. Not all of the changes were as harmless as updating her furniture.

Sylvie set the gun down with a shaking hand and grabbed her cell phone.

Demalion's phone rang and rang on the other end. No matter how often she dialed, he didn't answer.

3

A Sea of Troubles

AN HOUR LATER, SYLVIE WAS POUNDING ON ALEX'S DUPLEX DOOR, feeling an entirely new worry jittering along her nerves. After she'd given up trying Demalion's phone, she'd started calling Alex.

Alex hadn't answered either. The phone hadn't gone directly to voice mail, her usual sign of "closed for business," and so Sylvie worried. She'd pushed herself into the Miami night, waved off her neighbor's tentative question about gunshots, and headed for Alex's place.

Sylvie knocked louder, called Alex's name. Guerro, her German shepherd, barked from inside, but Alex didn't appear. Sylvie felt anxiety spike. If the ISI were under attack, they'd be looking for someone to blame. They had to know Alex worked for Sylvie, had to know she kept the backup files, had to know Alex was the one who coded them. By grabbing Alex, they'd have an all-access pass to Sylvie's work history.

Just when her knuckles began to smart, when she considered breaking in to Alex's little house, footsteps stumbled in her direction, and Alex mumbled, "Yeah. Coming." The barking stopped.

She opened the door, leaned on the jamb, and stared at Sylvie with bleary eyes and smudged makeup that made her look like she'd decided to take up boxing. "Syl? It's really late—"

"It's urgent," Sylvie said. "You all right?" She slipped past Alex's slumped form, stepped into Alex's living room, and suddenly wanted a real answer to that question.

Alex was obsessively tidy. Always had been. But her home showed signs of disarray. Not a lot—a pile of dishes in the sink, rinsed but not washed, a few pieces of clothing flung over the couch, a tangle of dog fur not immediately vacuumed—just the usual detritus of a day or two left untended. Still, it wasn't like her.

"Just headachy," Alex complained. "Had a lot of them of late. I tried to sleep it off."

"Without taking off your makeup?"

"Syl, this isn't an interrogation. What do you want?"

"To find out if Dunne was fucking with me," she said, recalled to her purpose. "Demalion's in trouble."

"Fuck," Alex murmured. She rubbed her face, pushed away the sleepy languor, and said, "Shoot."

Sylvie filled her in, and Alex's expression grew miserable. "Demalion's tough, Syl. He's survived worse."

"Sort of," Sylvie said. "Just . . . just do your thing. Prove to me that Dunne was being a godly asshole, making me pay for not doing what he wanted."

"What did he want?"

Sylvie waved a hand, a not-talking-about-it-now gesture. "The facts, Alex? I really want to know whether Dunne's on the up and up."

Alex cast a last longing look toward her bedroom and dragged out her computer, blinked lashes gummed with mascara at the bright screen. "Give me a moment." She flipped the laptop open, held it over her forearm, typed with her free hand, as if she wanted to get it done as quickly as possible.

"I don't know if we can trust the news. He's a god—"

"Wasn't going for the news. Always go to the source," Alex said. She clicked through increasingly troubling screens, and said, "The ISI. Have a seat. It's going to take a bit."

"You think?" Sylvie said. "They started battening down the hatches months ago."

"Yeah," Alex said. "Paranoid, bad-tempered bastards. But I've got an in." Her lips curved into a tight smile. "Demalion's passwords."

His name fell into the space between them like a cold front. Alex's smile wiped itself away, traded for a squirming awkwardness, the taste of premature grief.

Sylvie roughed her voice into working order, said, "He's not dead yet, and he's going to kick your ass for snaking his passwords. He's stupidly loyal to that organization. Keep going."

It was unnecessary advice. Alex's fingers had never paused. "I'm hitting their memos to each other. Interoffice warnings. Red alerts, that kind of thing. Chatter's real. Talk about Dallas, about Chicago, about Memphis."

"Memphis? What happened in Memphis?"

"Something bad I'm guessing. They're sending around a list of precautions to be made SOP . . . Syl."

"What?"

"Another one just showed up. Savannah," Alex said.

"There isn't an ISI branch in Savannah." Sylvie kept pretty close track of them. They covered twenty-nine American cities.

"Well, not anymore."

Alex's jaw tightened, a white sliver in Sylvie's field of vision. Flickers of light against her skin, and she nodded. "Look at this." She turned the computer toward Sylvie. "Security video."

It wasn't what Sylvie had expected. The ISI tended toward government bland, but this lobby was stark beyond that. She squinted. Was that security glass around the intake desk? Something blurred the men behind it, made them look oddly distant.

When the woman wandered into view, captured the camera's eye, Sylvie was irritated, trying to piece together the nagging sense that she should know what this place was. Then the woman moved forward and shed her coat like a falling stage curtain. It fell fast and hard, as if it were weighted, but none of the security guards could look away from the woman.

She stretched long and lean and more *naked* than it seemed possible for someone to be. Her skin drew all attention, gleaming and alive with opalescence, as if milky feathers fluttered beneath her skin. She had bright eyes, supple limbs, a curling mouth as flushed as a fall apple. She held out her arms in invitation.

Sylvie's mouth dried. The men behind the desk, behind the security glass, jerked to their feet.

It wasn't a woman. Wasn't a man, either. But it encapsulated the most appealing of both.

A succubus.

The men opened the door—it *was* security glass hemming them in—stepped out. Other men and women came out of the depths of the building, clustered around the succubus's lithe form.

"Is that—"

"Yeah," Sylvie said. "Succubus. But what it's doing . . ."

Sylvie didn't understand it. Even if the succubus meant them harm, which it had to—no other reason for it to walk into the lion's den—it couldn't feed on all of them at the same time, and once it started to feed, it couldn't keep perfect control.

The man closest to the succubus reached out, brushed shaking fingers over the perfect, pristine cheekbone. The succubus's smile darkened. It bent smoothly, picked up its coat, revealed the weapon in it.

Sylvie sucked in a shocked breath.

This wasn't feeding. This wasn't hunger. This was slaughter.

The automatic weapon chattered in silence on Alex's small screen. The ISI agents, lust-struck, had no time for lust to change to fear. The security glass grew starred and spattered with blood.

On-screen, the succubus dropped the gun, drew a finger through a spray of blood that stippled its face like freckles, and sucked it clean. Then it turned and let itself out. A bar of light—the front door left open—draped over the bodies.

"Savannah," Alex said. "She killed all of them. Called them up and mowed them down." She shook her head, shook away the nerves. "There's no security footage in Dallas. Or Memphis."

"What about Chicago?"

Alex bit her lip. "You sure you want to see?"

"Play it."

Same thing. The lobby, familiar to Sylvie. There was the elevator where Demalion had cornered her, argued with her, before chasing her down the street and insinuating himself back into her life. She swallowed.

The beginning of the disaster was more subtle than Savannah's succubus. So slow, it took Sylvie time to notice. Dust crawled across the lobby floor, a slow ripple of shadow. Accreting.

Not dust.

Sand.

It swirled, trickled upward like a pulled thread, fitting itself into the seams of the building. The agent at the front desk stood, approached, hand on his gun. He reached out toward that tiny spinning thread of sand; it drilled through flesh, through bone—he jerked his hand back, a hole pierced right through, started shouting for help.

Too late.

As if his blood was the catalyst, the thread of spinning sand exploded into a tornado. It devoured the retreating guard, silica slicing him to ribbon. The building shook and blurred. The last glimpse Sylvie had was a pair of shining eyes at the heart of the whirlwind before the camera failed. Not a spell. A creature of some kind.

When Sylvie caught her breath, she could come to only one conclusion.

It's war, her little dark voice said. Coldness crawled her spine, edged her jaw and cheeks. To say she didn't like the ISI was like going on record saying that yeah, contracting Ebola was a bad way to spend the weekend. She distrusted them down to her very core. But she didn't like this. Especially didn't like the sense of organization behind the attacks.

One thing she'd always counted on was the *Magicus Mundi*'s disinterest in uniting against humankind.

So why now?

"It's a prison," Alex said. "Was a prison. Savannah. They just opened it. Skeleton staff."

"That might change things," Sylvie said.

"You think the *Mundi* finally woke up and said, enough? I can't imagine they'd like the idea of being put in cages."

"I don't know," Sylvie said. Never one of her favorite phrases. "If it were the human magic-users attacking, I might be more willing to think that it's a reaction to the jail. But the *Mundi* . . . if they were that easy to catch and cage, don't you think we'd have a zoo full? I'm not sure they care about us that much. About what we're doing."

"That look like disinterest to you?" Alex said.

On-screen, the succubus dropped the gun again, rolled its shoulders and neck with a visible satisfaction. A job well-done.

"It's too much and not enough," Sylvie said. "It's strange. Two different monsters, probably three if we assume Dallas's gas accident means asphyxiation—something neither of these monsters tried. They don't cooperate outside their own kind."

Alex drew her finger along the screen, tracing a pattern made in the shadows of filmed blood.

Sylvie continued thinking aloud. "If they've organized enough to make alliances, then why not strike all at once? Why strike day by day? Allowing the ISI to warn their other branches? It's pointless. And worse, it's ineffective. The *Mundi*'s a lot of things, but it's brutally efficient."

"Fear," Alex said, running her fingers over the keyboard, over the part of the world she could control. "Let them know what's coming and let them know they can't stop it. I mean, *can* they stop it?"

"I don't know," Sylvie said. Grimaced. Goddammit. She wanted answers. She wanted them now. "Maybe it's not a war. Maybe it's revolution. A series of uprisings, each spurred on by the previous one."

"Like an infection, spreading." Alex bent her head over the computer. "What can we do?"

Sylvie closed her teeth on another *I don't know*, and thought about it. "If it's an infection, there'll be a cause. If there's an uprising, there's a leader somewhere. Keep plugged in. Keep me informed. I got someplace to be."

"Chicago?"

Sylvie shook her head. "And do what? Pick through the rubble and hope I strike lucky? If they even let me get that far? No. If he can, Demalion will call us."

Alex raised her head for the first time in what seemed like ages. Her eyes seemed more shadowed now than when Sylvie had first woken her. "Let me guess. Four ISI agencies down. You're headed for ground zero. Trying to see if you can get yourself killed protecting people who hate you."

"Sounds bad when you put it that way," Sylvie said.

Alex's smile was perfunctory. "They gassed you, kidnapped you; you had to break out. If they weren't so scared of your pet Fury, you'd be back in their cells. But you're going to take the moral high ground and help them?"

"Miami might not even be next on the list," Sylvie said, "Seems to me, though, that there's a path being taken. From Savannah? There are two ISI offices in easy lines: DC and Miami. DC has its own building, but here, the ISI offices are in the hotel district. The ISI brought this on themselves but . . . there are too many innocent bystanders involved. Riordan does it deliberately, hedges his agents 'round with regular people. One floor of agency, fourteen floors of civilians. I don't have a choice."

Sylvie left Alex hunched over her laptop, one hand snarled into her short, wild hair, the other clicking through screens that opened and closed with such rapidity that it might as well be arcane magic that guided her. She hoped it was comforting.

Outside, out of Alex's sight, Sylvie's shoulders sagged. Her bravado faded. The nighttime air, hot and still, felt charged, electric with change. With chaos. The peace before disaster.

Her tongue felt dry and heavy in her mouth, choking her with the weight of all the anxious words she couldn't say. It tasted of cooling asphalt, unsweetened by the jasmine nearby.

Her phone was in her hand again, Demalion's number picked out. She closed the phone without pressing SEND.

Wondered, if he were dead, who would tell her? Not the ISI, who hadn't connected Adam Wright with Sylvie Lightner. Maybe Adam Wright's ex-wife would get the call. Maybe then she'd call Sylvie to pass the news on, that the man who'd taken over her husband's body had lost his own hold on it in the end.

Most likely, it would be Alex, hunting through the casualty roster, refusing to tell her over the phone. Sylvie would have to watch Alex picking the careful words, trying to be gentle, while her face telegraphed every detail. She scrubbed a quick hand across her eyes.

Cowardice, her little dark voice said. *To give up before the battle's even joined.*

Sylvie let its contempt steady her. It was right. It so often was. Older and wiser than she was. That genetic leftover from Lilith's blood. As if Sylvie's synapses occasionally fired in a different pattern, an older pattern, a memory trail that was laid in before she was born. A memory, given voice.

Demalion wasn't dead yet. And he'd survived worse. This, whatever it was, hadn't been aimed specifically at him. He'd survived when the Furies had torn his flesh apart and sent his soul fleeing to the first sanctuary it found: Adam Wright's body.

She had better things to do with her time than mourn him prematurely.

* * *

NEXT MORNING FOUND HER SITTING IN ALEX'S JEEP OUTSIDE THE hotel that housed the ISI while dawn pushed back the skyline, spreading reflected pinks and pale blues in the dark, slow, canal waters alongside the street. Her anxiety had dulled to a background simmer in her brain, an occasional skip to her breath when she thought of where Demalion might be, why he hadn't called. Boredom had always been a good cure for terror.

Sylvie yawned into her hand, thought about moving the Jeep again to keep ahead of the ticket-happy police who patrolled the hotel district. It was tricky, though. She wasn't the only watcher. She'd seen more than one agency SUV with suspicious shadows behind tinted glass. Keeping an eye on their perimeter.

She rolled down the window, sucked in a breath of Miami at morning when it was clean and green. The ISI surveillance made watching their HQ that much more difficult; she had to evade their eyes as well as the traffic cops while staying in close proximity. Really, she should have just slumped low, let the tickets accrete on the windshield, and let them assume the car was abandoned.

Alex would have bitched, though, and with the ISI on alert, odds were the Jeep would have been towed at first ticketing.

Sylvie squirmed; Alex's fabric seat covers wrinkled beneath her, creating uncomfortable ridges. She missed her truck and its leather seats and her stock of canned drinks and snacks. But Alex's Jeep wasn't bright red with a werewolf-clawed hood. Sylvie loved her truck, but it was the very opposite of subtle.

A gull wheeled out of the dark, white feathers reflecting the sun, heading for the docks and the fishermen chopping chum for a day on the water. Sylvie thought of those men, weathered by sun, stubble-faced, shirtless, wielding cleavers with one hand and slurping coffee with the other, and decided the ISI could fend for itself long enough for her to grab breakfast and a bathroom break.

• • •

SYLVIE WANTED REAL FOOD BUT COMPROMISED ON A STARBUCKS and took a seat outside, slanting her gaze down the street, where she could keep an eye on the art-deco front of the ISI hotel. The streets trickled to life; first, men and women heading to work, clogging the roads, bleary-eyed and cranky, their radios blaring NPR, Spanish talk radio, the shock jocks. When that rush passed, the early tourists began emerging from the hotels, equally bleary-eyed, but smiling or fussing and juggling maps and children.

Sylvie finished her first coffee, went back for a refill, and found the second seat at her outside table occupied when she returned. Erinya's boot scuffed at the sandy concrete; the other leg was tucked up beneath her. Her collarbone and cheekbones stood out like ridges under her skin, as if being a god was whittling her away.

She looked up as Sylvie approached, her eyes as black and starved as a starless night, and said, "I want coffee, too. And a croissant."

Sylvie turned on her heel and went back inside, resisting the urge to point out that Erinya could *create* any breakfast she wanted. It was better for everyone involved if she kept her godly powers unexplored. Gods shed enough as it was, warping the world by their very presence, unless they were very big on self-control.

Through the window, Sylvie watched Erinya testing her fingernails against the tabletop. Wood peeled back as easily as torn paper. Erinya used the slivers to pick at the mortar in the window seam, then dropped those stony chips into Sylvie's coffee, smirking.

Yeah.

Erinya was a lot of things. Self-controlled? Not so much.

Sylvie's mouth tightened. Little as she liked it, Dunne was right about that. Erinya couldn't keep coming around. The world, as it was, couldn't withstand her.

Sylvie collected Erinya's food and rejoined her. She waited until the erstwhile Fury had a mouthful of pastry to say, "You can't stay here, you know. You're damaging the world."

Erinya laughed. "The world's ruined already. I'm making it better. I killed a witch last night."

"You did," Sylvie said, flatly. She needed a witch and

couldn't find one to save Lupe's life, and Erinya was picking them off like low-hanging fruit.

Her attention veered back toward the ISI building as a crowd of people moved toward the entrance. Today, there was a doorman. An agent masquerading as a servant. She had to grin at the sight. Those bastards. Thought they were so clever, basing themselves out of a hotel, figuring no one would look for them there. Now they had to reap what they'd sown: They expected an attack and couldn't lock down without drawing exactly the kind of attention they didn't want.

Plus it did her heart good to watch the agent being harried by hotel guests, trying to hail cabs and cart luggage in and out, and getting stiffed for tips.

Erinya slurped her coffee, continued her tale, unprompted. "Her daughter was chained up in the pool house, had just given birth. The witch boiled the infant so it could be used for spellwork. Bones and fat, skin and tongue."

Sylvie's attention jerked back; her stomach soured.

Erinya leaned forward, hands flat on the table, nails digging in. Her expression was predatory, hungry. "I took her out of the world. She offered the infant's heart up for power, prayed for a god to attend her, offered her worship. She didn't specify which god. I was faster than the rest. *I* was already here. I did good. You should be *thanking* me. Not telling me to go away. You don't have the right." Arrogance rang in Erinya's voice, echoed across the water, rang against buildings like a trumpet's call.

People on the street shivered, staggered by the surge.

At Sylvie's feet, blood-colored flowers pushed through the pavement, spreading petals like opening mouths. Vines twined around them, curled up the table legs. Erinya growled; the jungle slunk back into the concrete.

"Did you let the daughter out of the pool house?"

Erinya blinked, sank back into her seat. Crossed her arms over her chest.

"Did you leave her there, chained in the dark, injured and afraid, grieving, calling for help?"

". . . I can go back."

"You can't stick around," Sylvie repeated. "I know your intentions are good, but you're a god now. You can't—"

Erinya's shoulders rounded; she caved inward. "I'm lonely. There's no one good in my god space. I don't like it there. I miss my sisters."

"I thought you were sick of them bossing you around."

Erinya's fangs, razor-edged, dented her lower lip. "I miss *fighting* with my sisters."

"Then make minions of your own," Sylvie said. "Make them mouthy. Make them tough enough to stand up to you."

"I could have you—"

"No," Sylvie said. "No."

Silence fell across the table; Erinya's sulking spread outward. The other patrons in the tiny courtyard let their drinks go, ignored their food.

A bird crashed into the glass storefront with an unpleasant *thunk* and bounced downward. The man closest to the bird jumped from his table, grabbed the corpse, and brought it to Erinya.

"For you," he said. His gaze was adoring. His hands, covered by the wings, trembled, giving the dead bird the illusion of imminent flight.

Erinya smiled, her human slipping. Her teeth gleamed like new razors; spotted feathers sprouted from her hair and nape.

"Thank you," she said. She leaned forward, kissed the man, claiming him for her own; he stepped away, dazed, his mouth bloody where her fangs had scored his skin.

Erinya licked her lips, plucked the bird's heart out with jagged claws, and ate it in a single bite, lapping at her fingers afterward. The smell of blood was sharp, as metallic as a bullet. Sylvie wondered suddenly if Erinya had killed the witch before or after she'd eaten the infant's offered heart.

Sylvie shuddered. "You can't stay."

"Do you smell that?" Erinya asked, her head coming up, eyes going unfocused.

Sylvie sniffed. She smelled a lot of things. Car exhaust,

coffee, the woman two seats over who had decided to go for broke when she slathered on the Giorgio. Erinya's bloody snack. The scent of salt air, a taste of canal rankness . . . and something else. Something slight, but pervasive, rippling along beneath everything else, lifting the other scents.

"What is that?"

"Something wet," Erinya said, shaking herself fastidiously. Catlike. When she'd been just a Fury—*just*—she'd seemed more doglike. Now that she'd incorporated Tepeyollotl's powers into her own, her animal aspect, more mythic than real, edged toward cat.

"How about a little more detail?" Sylvie shot a glance toward the ISI. All serene. Annoyingly so. She hated wasting her time.

"Smells old?"

"Old like a *Mundi* monster? Like the Sphinx?" Sylvie's heart skipped, equal parts anticipation and pain. Demalion was bright in her mind again, an absence that felt like a weight.

Erinya curled her lips into a satisfied smile. "Old like drowned bones. I know what they are. Mermaids."

Her gaze lasered into the canal. Sylvie almost protested. *Mermaids?*

The canal waters rose like a tsunami and slammed into the ISI building.

· · ·

THE SOUND OF IT WAS BREATHTAKING, A SOUND THAT HIT LIKE A body blow—the crash and thunder of pouring water, the gunshot cracking of glass, the screech of metal as cars were shoved aside. Beneath it all, another noise. Something wild and inhuman, like whale song fed through a broken autotuner.

Sylvie, on her feet, water rolling toward her, found herself with her head cocked just like Erinya, trying to focus on that sound. How many of them? Where were they?

All around her, people did the same, but without purpose. Just stood and listened to that alien song beneath the chaos. Ignoring the sheeting, foaming water rising, tugging at their feet, slapping up against legs like angry fish tails, spilling into shops.

No one reacted at all.

"Mermaids sing the sea," Erinya said. "Coax men into the water, drown them, lick the despairing froth from their lungs like a delicacy. But if the men don't jump. If they can't be coaxed . . ."

"The mermaids bring the sea to them," Sylvie said. For being surrounded by water, her mouth felt desert dry.

A little boy tugged curiously at his mother's hand, looked around, the beginnings of distress on his face. His hands flew, asking questions no one answered. No one noticed.

He squatted, slapped at the water reaching for his mother, crying. The water, darker than it should be, slapped back. The boy fell backward, limbs flailing, and went under.

The water was shallow on the ground, but the boy didn't rise.

"Eri—"

Erinya was already moving, surging through the waves; the waves jerked back, cleared a path. Erinya, shape-shifting as she moved, never set a paw to the water, dancing above it. She jerked the boy out of the froth with her teeth, flung him toward her back. The boy, showing more sense than Sylvie had expected, clung tight to Erinya's spiky feathers. Erinya vanished, and Sylvie was left, the only waking person in the mermaids' murderous nightmare.

Water cascaded down the ISI building, peeling stucco away in foaming, chalky ribbons. Sylvie put a hand on her gun, cast another glance at the dark canal waters. The mermaids were there, had to be. But they might as well have been on the moon for all she could get to them. If she was going to help the ISI, she'd have to do it one victim at a time.

Erinya would have been more helpful here, she thought. Never mind saving the child. But that was logic, that was reason, that was fear at being hopelessly outclassed. A gun did her no good if she couldn't get the bullets to her targets.

Really, she was grateful that Erinya was still child-focused, still protective. That Dunne-programmed core of her—*avenge crimes done to children*—had been untouched by her change in god status.

Sylvie swallowed, anxiety like the taste of dry metal in her mouth, and headed toward the ISI building. Ground zero.

It was hard to think, hard to hear with the roar of the water, but her little dark voice was an internal sound, something even deafness wouldn't allow her to escape.

Be grateful to Lilith, it growled. *Be grateful to me; without me, you'd be just another victim waiting for death to roll in with the tide.*

Water roared in her ears until they rang with the echoes of it, a waterfall that wrapped itself—rising and falling and rising again—around the ISI hotel, as tightly as a strangling vine.

One of the dark SUVs lifted off the asphalt, was swept swiftly into the canal waters, its glossy finish going dull as the water rose up to envelop it.

Something supple and quick rose out of the water, cracking the windshield with a single hard tail-lash, and vanished back into the darkness. It had been matte grey-beige, as rubber-plastic as a shark. Sylvie was left with the impression of rolling teeth and black eyes before the SUV sank, the men inside doing nothing at all as they were drowned.

Fuck, Sylvie thought. *Fuck it all.*

Water danced in the air before her, making breathing a chore, trying to filter out the rainbow shards of suspended droplets, flung into the air with such violence that they seemed like projectiles.

The main glass door was sheeted with water, crashing and foaming; dirty water roiled behind it—a blurry, ominous shadow.

Pressing up against the entry, Sylvie was soaked to the skin in a second as she forced the door open. The motion sensor had given up the battle at the first impact, seizing up. As she forded her way in, she cast a last glance back to see if Erinya might have returned, and caught a glimpse of another person moving among the bespelled. Dark-eyed, peak-faced, and frowning, he raised a hand toward her as if he might draw her back. His hair curled sleek and wet along his face, dripped like seaweed.

She shook her head. Witch or whatever—she was committed now. He was on his own.

The lobby was more peaceful than she'd expected, having had horror-movie images of bloated bodies suspended in seething waters stuck in her head. The lobby had been mostly empty when the waves struck, the clerks slumped over the desk, their legs bobbing in the water. The hotel security—*ISI agent*—seemed the only casualty, floating facedown in the water, jacket flaring wide, exposing his gun. A few guests, seated on lobby furniture, drifted, staring and uncaring through the room, bumping up against walls, unmoored from the earth.

Sylvie flipped the guard, but one glance was enough to tell her he was dead past reviving, skin already softening, bloating in the water.

She stripped him of his keycards, left him floating. Sylvie waded toward the stairs and the cascade of water coming down, a shattering amount of noise in the concrete confines of the stairwell. She gritted her teeth, wished for earplugs, thought she was never going to find the ripple of water soothing again, and headed upward. The mermaid song—penetrating concrete, steel, glass—followed, resonating in the walls as if the rebar that supported the building acted as enormous tuning forks.

Sylvie might be immune to the song's effects, but it set her nerves on edge.

The ISI had the fourth floor all to itself. Four flights wasn't much normally, but climbing through cataracts?

She was sweating hard with nerves and exertion by the time she made it to the fourth-floor door. Water flowed sluggishly out beneath the rim, and condensation beaded cold and foggy on the steel fire door. Sylvie ran the card through the scanner, hoping that the glowing red light meant it still worked.

The door beeped, shorted out, but the lock popped. Sylvie, braced for a flood, found herself staring into a magical aquarium. Water glimmered and lapped at the door but didn't do more than seep through at the edges. If she'd had any doubt that the mermaids had total control of their element, that wavering pool, a damp inch from her face, removed it.

The people below, the people dying on the streets, the people on the other floors—they were all incidental. The mermaids intended the ISI to drown. And the only thing she could think to do was remove the mermaids' targets and change their focus.

Here was her horror-movie moment. Through the water, made cloudy by loose papers drifting into the hall, by stirred carpet dust, she made out bodies. A man bumped up against the hallway ceiling, swaying in a killing tide, his tie drifting, his gun holster empty, the gun itself sunk into the waving anemone plush of the carpet.

She pushed her hands into the water. It gave slowly, cold and sucking. Sylvie shuddered, her certainty slipping. What was she doing? She couldn't save them if she couldn't even breathe. If there was anyone left to save.

If they hadn't died like Demalion.

She shook her head. No. For one thing, if they were all dead, the mermaids would have stopped singing. She could do this. She'd broken spells before. Accidentally, full of rage, or with luck and her little dark voice on her side. She could do it on her own. At will. On purpose. She put her hands back into the water, hunting the magics that held the wall of water in place.

Nausea churned in her gut as she crept up on it; her nerves fired in distaste as she felt out the spell's hold on the real world—a seaweed tangle of malignant intent netting the water.

The magics slipped through her fingers, defying her urge to pull.

Careful, her little dark voice said. *Careful.*

Preaching survival.

Risk your life for them? For your enemies? For the dead?

She faltered. It had a point. They were her enemies. How much of this determination to save them was her hoping to save Demalion by proxy? If they were all dead, all trapped below the water—it had been twenty minutes since the wave first broke. And the mermaids' song had never faltered. Twenty minutes of concentrated ill will.

A new sound impinged on her hearing. A rhythmic percussion traveling through the water, amplifying itself as it came.

Thumpthumpthump.

Thump. Thump. Thump.

Thumpthumpthump.

Sylvie didn't need to know Morse code to recognize that; the pattern was a part of pop culture.

SOS.

She'd never been able to turn away from someone pleading for help.

She delved back into the water, seeking to grab that intangible something. To break it apart. It slipped like a shoal of minnows through her hands, cold and slimy, her grasp slowed by the water.

No, you don't, she thought at it, and dug in harder, wet to her elbows, scratching her nails through the liquid, snagging that magic. It thrashed like an eel, stung her palms with a near-electrical protest that made her grimace and curse between tight-locked teeth. But she held on, and, millimeter by slick millimeter, she dragged it toward her, through the door, spurred on by the drumbeat SOS.

Just as her wrists breached the glittering surface of the water, her little dark voice spoke again. *Wait!*

Too late.

She broke the magic's hold, and the water *crashed* into the stairwell, sweeping her from her feet, slamming her—pinball style—wall to wall, then plunging her down the stairs.

Sylvie flailed, locked a hand on the guardrail, and hung on for dear life.

. . .

WHEN THE FLOOD SUBSIDED, WHEN SHE'D BEEN BATTERED BY CUR-
rent and cold and the dead agent slamming into her as his
corpse swept inexorably by, she uncrimped her hands and
staggered to her feet. She felt bruised all over, sodden,
cold, more in need of a rescue than a rescuer. But she had
to get moving; there was no guarantee that the waters
wouldn't rise to drowning levels again.

She labored up the half flight she'd fallen, headed into
the hallway, water swirling about her ankles. She scanned
the area swiftly, wondering where the SOS had come from.
The first two doors she opened sent more water crashing
down, turned corpses into driftwood. The water level, she
thought, was rising again. The hiss of water pressing in
through the broken windows.

Morgue, she thought. The ISI had a makeshift morgue.
She'd been in it. The room had been baffled, had sucked
the air into the room when the door closed. Close to sound-
proof. Maybe close to waterproof.

She tried to remember which door it was—in the refur-
bished maids' supply room—and found it, not by memory
but by the SOS starting up again, more desperate. She
tapped on the door, got voices responding.

"Is there anyone out there? Is it safe to come out?"

"No," Sylvie said, "Not safe. But safer. Open up."

"Is that you, Grace?"

"Just open the damned door," Sylvie snapped.

A furious set of whispers, then the door popped open,
revealing four soaked and shivering ISI agents. The room,
thankfully, was mostly dry. The water had only been up to
their shins, and it flooded out past her.

Sylvie stepped in, shook off like a dog, and looked
at them. "Let's move."

"Who—"

"That's Shadows," the agent in the back of the little
huddle answered. She recognized him: John Riordan, the
local ISI chief's son.

"Hey, Junior. Want out? We need to go now. I broke the spell but only briefly. If they put it back up while I'm inside the barrier? We're all dead."

"We're safe here," another agent said. "We can wait."

"For who?" Sylvie said. "Your security? They're dead. They're *all* dead."

John's teeth set; he shoved past the other agents. Sylvie braced herself for a fight, either physical or verbal. The look on his face was pure rage. But he only gained her side, and said, "Let's go, people."

Being the boss's son has its perks, Sylvie thought. The three remaining agents fell in line like good little ducklings.

Sylvie opened the door again. Looked out. A wet hallway shouldn't look that intimidating. But the water had risen noticeably in the few minutes they'd debated, moved faster, in purposeful ripples and rills as if snakes undulated beneath the surface. The hallway smelled like the sea, and it stretched out like a football field. The morgue had been nearly at the blind end of the hall, two hundred feet of enemy territory.

"Elevators?" John suggested.

"No," Sylvie said. "We'd have to pry them open first."

"First?" he said.

"You don't listen well, do you. You think water floods one floor of a hotel naturally?" Sylvie asked. "There's a *spell* calling the water. And there's a *spell* holding the water in place. The better to drown you with."

One of the agents said, "What's that sound?" His lean face was tight with longing; green eyes drifted closed, the better to focus on the thin threads of the song he heard.

"I don't hear anythi. . . wait. Yeah. What is that?" And there went agent number two. His heavyset body slowed, eased, relaxed.

The third agent, showing some sense, stuck his fingers in his ears, looking wild-eyed. It seemed to help, at least a little.

"Shit," Sylvie muttered. Fucking mermaids. She yanked the door closed, dragging it through the rising waters. "Junior. Earplugs?"

He shook off his own stillness more easily than she'd expected. The other men were close to catatonic. "Earplugs?"

"Cotton balls, paper towels, rags, *anything*?"

Sylvie glanced around, but the room was as empty as a broken eggshell. White and wet and useless.

He opened his mouth to ask, then shook himself, started ripping fabric from his shirtsleeve. Shoved the first scraps at the agent with his fingers in his ears. The others followed suit. Makeshift. Sylvie hoped it'd buy them enough time. If they all froze on her, they were dead.

Sylvie took a big breath, hoping that if the spell lock was restored—which she had to assume it was, given the rising water—that she could disarm it again and do so from the inside.

"Close the door behind us," Riordan said to the other agents. "If we can't get out, we can retreat."

They nodded, and Sylvie kept her mouth closed. She wasn't going to burst their bubble, but if the water filled the hallway again, that door might as well be glued shut. Water pressure would ensure it. The doorway opened out.

Riordan's jaw clenched, released; he cast a sidelong glance her way, and she raised a brow. He knew.

"Move," Sylvie said.

They waded into the hallway, the last agent forcing the door closed through the frigid water.

It hadn't been that cold before.

On her way in, the water had been chilly, water from below the sun's reach, but this. . . this was icy. Deep-sea icy. Abyssal-plain icy. It leached heat and energy, set her teeth to chattering. It swallowed light, turned the hallway to rolling shadows and splashes. Worst of all, the water reached above her knee.

"What's happening?" Riordan asked, as they headed into the hallway. Two hundred feet to go.

"You tell me. What'd you all do to piss off the *Mundi* so bad?"

"I don't know," he said. His teeth chattered. "I don't even know what's attacking us. The *Maudits*?"

"Mermaids," Sylvie said.

One hundred eighty feet. The water reached midthigh.

A new sound penetrated the hallway, a low moan, the complaint of masonry giving way. Doors burst behind them, before them, spilling icy torrents into the hall. Fingers-in-his-ears shouted, stopped cold, changed trajectory.

Riordan reached for him, but the man forded the water, waist high and rising, to catch the body cresting the surface. Long hair streaming out, as red as undersea corals, falsely alive. "Grace!" he shouted.

"Jack!" Riordan shouted. "Leave her."

The agent dropped her, but it cost him something; his pace slowed, his gaze dragging him backward. It slowed him, slowed them all.

Sylvie gritted her teeth, kept moving. They didn't have time to waste on argument.

One hundred forty feet.

"Mermaids," Riordan said. "Mermaids."

His lips were blue; Sylvie assumed hers must be likewise. She knew her steps were slowing, dragging through the water. Movement was an act of will, a heavy shift of hip and numb leg, left, then right. Leaning forward. Simply trying not to topple in. Keeping her hands raised above water, awkward strain on her shoulders.

"Fuck," Riordan said. "Why the hell can't the water flow *toward* the door?"

Sylvie forced her lips into a grimace. It was meant to be a smile. "Think there's enough bodysurfing going on in here, already," she said. His face darkened. Graveyard humor. Never an ISI trait.

"Shit." The curse slipped free. Behind Riordan, the count had changed.

They were down to three. Jack was gone, drifting back to join with his dead partner. Lost in the dark waters, lost silently, lost among the jetsam of floating bodies.

One hundred feet. Only halfway there.

Riordan turned. Sylvie grabbed his arm, dug her nails in, and yanked. "No. We stop. We die." As if her words were carried by water, as if her pointing out that there were still living agents was overheard, the mermaid song kicked up to a new, angry volume. The water jumped and bubbled with its force.

The two ISI agents stopped cold, faces slackening.

Sylvie shivered, loss biting as hard as the cold. She couldn't do it. She couldn't save them. The water was an icy hand at her heart. The distant door glimmered, water rising unnaturally to fill the gap.

Riordan, thank God, was still alert. "Grab one of them," Sylvie snapped. She wrapped her numb arm around the nearest agent and dragged him after her, saw that Riordan was doing the same to the other. Eighty feet left.

She'd save anyone she could. If she could get the door opened again—

The agent writhed in her grip like seaweed being torn from the seafloor, went slick and slippery in her arms. Her nails drew blood, a warmer, rosy drift in the gelid water. She couldn't hold him. The water was actively dragging him out of her arms, fighting her.

"I can't hold on. Help me," Riordan gasped. He went under as if he'd been yanked downward. A sinuous ripple of faster water suggested that was exactly what had happened. The mermaids were getting more and more precise in their song. A cold coil of water wrapped around her thigh, impossibly colder than the rest of the water, altered by magic. It tugged; she clawed at it with one hand, feeling the same spell that had been stretched over the doorway— the mermaids' song given physical shape and intent.

The agent in her arms slipped free of her one-handed grasp. The water rope rose out of the water, lashed around her waist, and dragged her under. She fought the riptide, felt the purpose behind it, and finally, clawing and kicking, got her head up and out of the water, sucking in great gasps of air.

She'd lost ground. A hundred feet to the door.

Warm skin brushed hers, and she yanked, came up with Riordan, sputtering, breathing. Alive.

His face was fierce, her grip on her hands brutal. "Don't let go."

"I won't," she said.

"God, won't they stop singing!" he said.

He was still aware, still fighting. It looked like it hurt him, though; his face contorted with effort.

"Watch our backs," she said. "We can't afford to get sucked under again. Even if we survive it, we can't lose the time."

Her feet were floating, rising above the carpet; she grabbed at the molding on the hallway wall, scraped her way forward, kicking off from doorjambs. Riordan was close to a deadweight on her back, all his energy going to fighting the song, to keeping an eye out for a single ripple of water in an entire hallway of moving waves.

Leave him, her little dark voice said.

No, she thought.

Forty feet.

He's a witch, her voice said. *Or he wouldn't be able to fight off the song.*

All the more reason to save his ass. She needed a witch who owed her one.

Twenty.

The door. Sylvie clung to the jamb, forced Riordan's weight between her and it, kept him floating, contained. Looked back.

No sign of the others.

She clawed for that magic netting; the thing she'd torn so easily before. As before, it tried to elude her grip. As before, she caged it in her hands anyway, guided not by physical sensation—her hands were utterly numb, useless meat—but by the revulsion that magic woke in her blood.

"Hurry," he whispered, his teeth chattering. If he was a witch, he wasn't a helpful one. His urgency raised hers to a painful level. She clawed faster.

This time, though, the netting refused to tear. She hung her entire weight on those magical bindings, kicked against the doorjamb, her face underwater, her breath bubbling out of her. It glowed under the water, with an icy bioluminescence, thick, anchored at a dozen points, fifty points, more . . .

That rope of water reached out again, wrapped her leg tight to Riordan's, geared up to pull them away from the door. Her chest heaved; her lungs burned. She didn't have time to fight it, too. Riordan slipped from between her and the door, his lips parting, whispering spells, whispering *let us go, let us go.* She could feel the shiver of intent, and it seemed to be working, at least minimally. The water trying to pull them down faded, gave her just that much more time to fight with the seal on the door.

As long as he could keep murmuring spells. There wasn't enough air to make her think he could do it for more than another minute, tops.

Sylvie grimaced, peeled the first of the anchors away. Despair got her nothing. Effort might pay off.

She doubted it.

Fear, bright, sharp, nearly overpowering, danced through her veins. She'd done this all wrong. Had been overconfident. Had been stupid.

She was going to pay for it. And she wasn't ever going to find out if Demalion had survived.

The mermaids' song—a vibration traveling her skin, the walls, the building—broke off on an awkward screech. Riordan jerked, flailed, sought air that didn't exist.

The spell on the door weakened.

Sylvie yanked and yanked and tore and scrabbled, using her hand, her feet, her teeth—the taste rank and vile, rotten oysters, scabrous and greasy in her mouth.

The netting tore.

She and Riordan tumbled headfirst into the stairwell; Sylvie gasped for air, lost the breath with impact against the far wall, whooped for air again.

She and Riordan skidded to the next landing and stopped, water streaming over them. Riordan groaned, got to his knees. "The others?"

"I don't know," Sylvie said. She forced herself to her feet.

"What happened?"

"Mermaids stopped—" Sylvie frowned. No, they wouldn't have stopped. Something or someone had stopped them.

Sylvie limped down the stairs, Riordan staggering and sliding after her, scratches livid on his neck where she'd clawed him in her attempts to keep him above the waterline. "Where are we going?"

"Out," she said.

The lobby's floodplain was draining out into the streets, draining back into the canal. People were waking all over. Sylvie could hear them screaming.

After the mermaids' song, it sounded like music.

The screaming took on a new and frantic pitch and Sylvie burst out into the sunshine, squinting, half-blind with exhaustion and sun dazzle.

"Holy mother of God," Riordan said from behind her. He fell back and sprawled on the concrete, crossing himself.

For once, Sylvie was in complete agreement. She'd seen a lot of things since she'd been made aware of the *Magicus Mundi*: witches and werewolves, gods and ghosts. But this was a spectacle even for her eyes.

Erinya, in full nonhuman form—a twice-tiger-sized mass of scales, feathers, and talons, and fangs that glistened scarlet in sunlight, her eyes great, empty, burning holes—was dragging a thrashing, writhing sharkish mass out of the canal: gills flaring, flashing red, thrashing tail slicing through the air with a sound like ripping paper, and a screaming maw of teeth under bulging, opalescent eyes.

Mermaids, Sylvie thought numbly, were nothing like in the storybooks.

Erinya dragged the screaming mermaid—God, it must be nearly seventeen feet long—right to Sylvie's feet and dropped it, then crouched atop it, looking for all the world like a nightmare cat bringing its owner a mouse.

The mermaid's tail slapped at Erinya, rough scale slicing at the Fury's hide; its front limbs pushed upward, trying to break the weight from its back. Sylvie found herself staring at its . . . fingers. Four of them, scaled, jointed like a crab, sharp enough that the concrete was chipping beneath its efforts. Erinya punched it on the back of its oddly flat head, stunning it, then dragged its head back so Sylvie could see its face. Nacreous eyes as large as eggs stared blindly at her, blinking in scarlet membranous tides.

"Want to ask it questions?" Erinya asked.

"Will it understand me?" Sylvie asked. Her hands were shaking. Her voice wasn't, but it took effort. Years dealing with the *Magicus Mundi*, and she suddenly realized she'd only just scratched the surface.

The mermaid thrashed, spat out curses in a dozen human languages, with a tongue as pale as a drowned man. "Do I understand? The water carries all words to our hearing. We know more about your world than you do."

Faced with that promise of understanding, Sylvie fumbled for words. She was under no illusions that the mermaid would talk, even if it could, but she had to try. Had to ask.

"Why attack the ISI?"

"They overreach," it said. It seemed to have no qualms with confessing. "They think to control what cannot be leashed."

"And in Chicago? That wasn't you in Chicago. Or in Savannah. You're working with the others?"

The mermaid twisted, left wide swaths of its dull scales on the cement; its breathing seemed labored. The water was mostly gone.

"We are ourselves. We don't mingle."

"So, not working with. Working for—" Sylvie said.

The mermaid gusted cold air over her feet—contempt.

"You killed my people!" Riordan said. "Why? Tell me, or I'll see you hung out to dry."

A for attitude, Sylvie thought. *D for common sense.* He was too close to that tail, and it slapped him off his feet, back on his ass.

Light flashed.

"We do what needs to be done," the mermaid said. "Do

not think that capturing this one makes a difference. We are the water. And water is everywhere."

"And you chose to attack now. At the same time as the other attacks. You want me to believe that's coincidence?"

"We do not mingle."

If it were possible for something without a human face to sneer, the mermaid was doing it. Sylvie said, "You came up with the idea all on your lonesome?"

"We do not mingle."

Erinya snarled; blood spouted out of the creature's flesh. The mermaid shrieked. Then its gills fluttered madly and stopped.

"I wasn't done," Sylvie said.

"I was bored. And it was arrogant," Erinya said. "It wouldn't have talked." Erinya turned the heart, a greenish mass the size of a man's skull, in her hands, eyed it warily. She licked it with a coiling serpentine tongue. Wrinkled her muzzle in reaction. "Fishy."

She licked it again, this time with a human tongue, a human face. Trying to decide if she liked it with a different set of taste buds.

More flashing lights.

Lightning? An early-morning storm blowing in on the heels of the mermaids' false tide?

Sylvie turned.

They had an audience. Not much of one—most of the bystanders were microfocused, trying to figure out what had happened to them. But some were gaping at Sylvie. At Erinya, sitting atop a dead mermaid, licking her talons clean of heart's blood.

"Is that . . . Is that a shark?" a man asked.

"Does it look like a shark?" Sylvie snapped.

He edged closer, drawn to the strange. "Oh my God. It's a monster." He looked up; Erinya smiled, bright and bloody, and he fell back, gaping.

"Riordan!" Sylvie snapped. "Your crowd, I think?"

Sylvie ducked another camera flash, the growing murmur of *oh, my God, a thing . . . in the canals, who caught it, monsters! Blown up by the storm, wasn't that a freak storm? No, the things made the storm. The other monster stopped it.*

Riordan rose shakily to his feet; his clothes were torn where the mermaid's tail had slapped him. But he was wearing a suit, and people were turning to him for an explanation.

Her problem was figuring out what the hell was going on, and she was no closer now than she had been.

Worse, actually.

Now she understood how little of the *Magicus Mundi* she really knew. If it hadn't been for Erinya, she'd be dead.

Sylvie looked back. Erinya had gotten tired of preening over her kill and vanished. Her presence lingered. The sidewalks bloomed with jungle flowers; her beastly footprints smoked in the wet asphalt. A child pointed them out to her mother, talking a mile a minute.

Sylvie wondered abruptly what Erinya had done with the child she saved from drowning.

Things were changing and changing fast. Sylvie, sore, soaked, cold to the bone, wasn't sure she could keep up.

She was going to need help. Erinya, unreliable, unpredictable, callously single-minded, might be the best she could get.

4

Making News

ALEX'S JEEP WAS MUDDY, SPLATTERED WITH CANAL REMNANTS, BUT it hadn't been one of the casualties of the mermaids' wave, hadn't been shoved into another car or dragged into the waters.

Even better, throughout the entire business, Sylvie had managed to hold on to the keys. She got in, squelching miserably, and blew out a breath. The drive back to Alex's went smoothly. All the major traffic—cop cars, news vans, gawkers—were headed in the other direction.

When she reached Alex's place, she was tempted to trade cars and head home, but she needed to check in. She needed to know if Alex had heard anything on the Chicago situation, and Sylvie's cell phone had died in the dunking.

She tapped on Alex's door, leaning tiredly on the jamb. Guerro barked once; Sylvie heard Alex hushing the dog, then Alex swung the door wide.

"Oh my God, Syl. It's all over the news. *You've* been all over the news."

Sylvie put a hand on Alex's shoulder, pushed her gently back inside. The woman was too excited to notice that she was blocking the door, and her neighbors were beginning to poke their heads out. Sylvie had had enough of gawkers. "My family call?" She'd be surprised if they had. Zoe was in Ischia, learning to be a good witch, and her parents had hit the other hemisphere, headed to Australia for an extended vacation.

"Wales called." Alex's duplex smelled of coffee and burned cinnamon toast. Sylvie thought toast sounded good. Warm and dry. Two words that otherwise didn't apply to her at the moment.

"How is Tex? Burning feet to help us?" She found the bread, a thick-sliced Cuban loaf, put a smear of butter on it, a lashing of sugar and cinnamon, and stuck it under the broiler.

Alex shook her head, a little smile touching her mouth at the mention of her necromancer boyfriend. "I wish. He's tangled up in that Alabama mess. Narrowed it down to kids playing at necromancy. Creating sort of their own zombie theme park." The twist of her mouth was wry. As if she knew it was bad but found it amusing anyway.

"What is up with that?" Sylvie asked. "I mean, I sure as hell wasn't a saint when I was a teen, and I know you were all juvie-girl, but c'mon, there's a difference between raising a little hell and raising *the dead*."

"Getting old there, Sylvie. Complaining about 'kids these days.'"

Sylvie pulled her toast out of the oven, juggling it from hand to hand, and stifled any ruder retort when Alex waved a cup of coffee at her.

Sylvie, feeling as obedient as Alex's German shepherd, sat down at the breakfast bar, shut up, and applied herself to breakfast. Killer mermaids were definitely a good thing for stimulating the appetite.

She wolfed down the slice, went back for more, and tossed the crusts to Guerro, sprawled on the couch. He snapped them down, beat his tail against the couch arm, and visibly hoped for more.

"So the ISI—"

"No," Sylvie said. "That's a postbreakfast conversation." She wanted a few minutes of peace.

Alex sat down on the breakfast bar itself, swung long

legs. "You can't save everybody. I mean, they had warning, and they couldn't save themselves. You can't beat yourself up for this."

"There's a difference," Sylvie gritted out, "between not being able to save everybody and not being able to save *anybody*. Including myself. If Erinya hadn't taken out the mermaids, I'd be a floater in a magical fish tank."

Alex's mouth turned down. Changed the focus of the subject. Too little, too late. Sylvie felt wired, edgy. "So, you know what you're going to say? I mean, the news is going to track you down sooner rather than later. Local woman and monster kill another monster."

"Guess the cat's well and truly out of the bag." Sylvie gnawed her lip, trying to figure out if it was good or bad. If whatever erased magical evidence would act on this event.

"Yeah, hard to squelch the news vans," Alex said.

Exposure had to happen eventually. The human world was expanding, searching, documenting; the *Magicus Mundi* would be revealed sooner or later. Sylvie had been hoping for that discovery for years. Secrecy allowed all sorts of nastiness to fester, be it government agencies or magical monsters. But this wasn't among the top ten ways she would have chosen. A monster attacking a major business district in broad daylight, killing US citizens? It was going to go over about as well as a terrorist attack.

Well, that was what it was, wasn't it, she thought.

People were going to freak.

The only thing average Americans liked more than their illusions was the chance to panic. To find an Other and fear it.

Sylvie wasn't fond of the *Magicus Mundi*—too often, when it and the human world intersected, humans got the worst of it—but she was sure that total terror was not the proper response.

Maybe, this time, if the reality censors kicked in, it wouldn't be such a terrible thing.

She couldn't believe it even as she thought it.

Alex, puttering around her kitchen, made an "Aha!" of triumph and waved the TV remote in Sylvie's direction.

"Take a look for yourself!" The TV turned on, savagely loud in the tiny apartment; Guerro's ears went flat, and Alex hastily muted it.

It wasn't like they needed sound. BREAKING NEWS scrolled across a bright red bar on the local channel. The scene was the one Sylvie had just left. Waterlogged people, destroyed properties—cars and businesses—palm trees with slimy, glistening trunks and spiky leaves that sparked with lingering beads of water.

Then the image backtracked, showed a tourist-filmed video that cut away from the palm trees to that sudden, rising wave. The video was image without sound, but Sylvie still heard the roar of that much water displacing itself vividly in her memories. She thought she'd be hearing it for days.

On-screen, the water slapped the building, slid down, and flooded outward, eating pavement in hungry gulps. The camera eye tilted—the mermaid's song, Sylvie thought, paralyzing the cameraman into a stupor.

Through his lens, the landscape surged and fell and foamed, a world of inrushing water.

The red bar scrolled on relentlessly, reading off disaster tolls. Four dead, multiple injuries—

Alex said, "That's not too bad."

"They haven't gotten inside the hotel yet," Sylvie said. "The death toll will go up."

"There you are."

It was true; horrible, but true. A new video, a *better* video shot by a professional hand, showed Sylvie and Riordan stumbling out of the hotel lobby, looking so much the worse for wear. Riordan's face going grey and gaping—

seeing Erinya and the mermaid

—the camera pivoted sharply, chasing whatever he was gaping at.

Sylvie winced, anticipating.

The images on TV. . . blinked. Gold light flickered and flared so quick it was only an impression that Sylvie took away rather than something she consciously saw. She leaned closer. "Did you see that?"

"See what? Oh, what the hell—" Alex said.

On-screen, Erinya, dressed in her gothy human form, ran up to Sylvie, grabbed her hand, and drew her down the street to where a thrashing tiger shark took up immense quantities of pavement.

"That didn't happen," Sylvie said.

"It was different before," Alex said.

"Turn up the volume."

". . . freak waterspout touching down in the city, today, washing up wildlife, and causing an unknown number of fatalities . . ."

"It was different," Alex said again. "I mean, it was you and Erinya, but Erinya was all—"

"I know," Sylvie said. "I was there, remember?"

Alex flipped stations, chasing news but finding only more of the same. "It's a cover-up," she said. "I can't believe it! I mean, how effective do they think that'll be? I TiVoed it the first time. I can't have been the only one."

"Alex," Sylvie said. "Show me the recording you made. Wait, no. Watch the screen. Do you see that?"

Alex squinted, focused, shook her head. "I don't know what you're wanting me to see."

"Image flickers," Sylvie said. "Goes gold for a second. A break in the image. Reality before it. Rewrite after it."

"Photoshop?"

"Too fast," Sylvie murmured. To splice in an image of Sylvie, an image of Erinya—human form—put them in motion, change out the mermaid for the shark, do it seamlessly enough that it didn't blur or warp the rest of their surroundings, the light and shadows? It wasn't possible in the time they'd had. At least, not by conventional methods.

She wanted to be surprised, but wasn't. The whole mess was confirmation of her theory that someone, somewhere was censoring reality.

Alex clicked over to the recording, and played it. "No, no way."

It was the same as the currently airing clip.

"How the hell—" Alex said. "Wait. That flicker you see,

that I don't. . . . This is that memory thing you've been researching. Alteration of public perception. How? *Magical* Photoshop?"

"Witchcraft, I think," Sylvie said. "Illusion's one of their favorite tools."

"What about a god hiding things?" Alex said. "Gods seem to want earth to keep chugging along in blissful ignorance."

"Yeah," Sylvie said. "But I can't see a god doing this. For one thing, we're too damn small. Too fragile in comparison. Plus, there's all the godly politics. This is affecting everyone. No matter who they worship."

Alex hmmed in response, already bent over her laptop, clicking away, her green-painted nails bright against the silver keys. "Yeah. I'm not the only one. Others saw the change. They're calling foul. Conspiracy sites are popping up fast. What do you think the memory wiper is going to do about them?"

"I don't know. Without knowing who or why, I can't predict their actions," Sylvie said. "Witchcraft covers anything from the *Maudits* to Val's research coven in Ischia, and they all have different motives."

She looked at the television clips again, playing disaster porn nonstop, and said, "More than one witch. A coven. That's an awful lot of reality to paint over. But I can't believe it's a local coven, not with all the hunting I've been doing for a single witch with a decent grip on power. A task like this? I don't know. It feels . . . big. Organized."

Alex opened her mouth, shut it again. It didn't matter. Sylvie had heard the thought clearly. It was the same one in her mind. *Wonder if Demalion had discovered anything. Before.*

"So. . . any word?" Sylvie went to the window, fiddled with the fraying edge of the batik curtain, wrapped her fingers in scarlet, green, and gold, and thought of macaws bursting into flight.

"Yes and no," Alex said. "Good news? He wasn't on the list of the dead, not as Wright, not as Demalion. Wasn't on the injury list either. Bad news? No one's heard from him."

"My cell phone's fucked," Sylvie said. "Waterlogged." The words were rote; she was concentrating on the peculiar sensation of relief trickling through her blood. She'd expected the worst.

"I've got a spare," Alex said. "There's a box." She waved vaguely toward her kitchen, toward a dusty box on top of the refrigerator.

Sylvie pulled the box toward her, peered in. "Alex?"

Alex waved a hand. "My father came by, gave them to me. You know, kind of like some families taking their kid out to dinner. Mine just hands out burner phones and reminds me that The Man is watching. Take one. You can at least call people on it instead of having to leg it all over Miami."

"What do you think I'm about to do?" Sylvie asked.

Alex looked up from the computer where she was bookmarking conspiracy sites like a fiend for later response, and tilted her head. "Hunting down the brainwashy witches? Calling to get the scoop from Val and Zoe? I mean, what good is it, having a witchy little sister, if she can't—"

"I'm going home," Sylvie said. "I haven't slept. And the witches aren't the problem. They're just covering up the problem." The sun streaming through the kitchen window seemed heavy and bright, but it also seemed distant. She felt cold and dark and empty. *Grief,* she thought. The relief that trickled through her wasn't enough to chase it away.

She closed her eyes, was suddenly back there in the cold waters, watching people watching the water without panic even as they drowned. She'd seen a lot of terrible things, but that was going to make it into her nightmares.

"Are you okay? You want me to drive you?"

She shook the memory off, and said, "No, stay here, stay online, see if you can get a better idea of how far the illusion goes. I mean, the video is step one. What happened to the newscasters who put the real one on? Did *they* forget? We can figure out a lot about the witches who did this by how they treat the people who saw the truth.

"Miami's pretty low on bad-cess witches at the moment. They're keeping a low profile if they're around at all.

They've got to know Erinya's hunting them. But that doesn't mean people aren't in danger from this. Charm, coerce, kill. Right now, someone's playing at charm, at illusion. We want to keep it on that level. Illusion spells are ugly, coercion spells are worse."

"Hey, Syl," Alex said. "You look wrecked. Go home. Get some sleep."

Sylvie scrubbed her face with her hands; her hair dripped down her neck and face, smelled like the churned bottom of a canal—fishy and rank. She grimaced. "Yeah. Okay. Just . . . call me, Alex. If you find out about Demalion. Call me at once. Good or bad. Limbo's killing me."

"I promise. Good or bad. I'll tap into the Miami ISI and see if he reports in."

Sylvie reached the door, turned back. "Wait. What? Alex, there's no one left. The mermaids killed most of them. Any survivors are going to be scrambling for order, not—"

"Mermaids?" Alex said. The perfect incomprehension in her voice froze Sylvie in her tracks.

"Mermaids," Sylvie said. She went back, directed Alex's attention to the TV, to the laptop sliding off her lap, forced her to look at the pages she'd bookmarked. "Conspiracy. Illusion. The ISI taken down a peg or two."

Alex shook her head. "Don't shout. My head hurts. I don't want to look at that." She turned her face away, closed her laptop, and slid it beneath the couch. Guerro whined, rested his heavy head in her lap. Alex's fingers tightened in his ruff as if she were falling, and the dog was her only anchor. When she opened her eyes again, her pupils were two separate sizes. A magical concussion.

Sylvie whispered, "Bastards. Bastards, all of them." This was why she hated witchcraft. It wasn't bad enough to force an illusion down people's throats, to make them doubt what they had seen. Somewhere, a group of witches was very busy making people forget they'd ever had doubt at all.

Alex's breathing was tight and hitched; her face pinched with agony. Sylvie got her off the couch, walked her into her bedroom, saw her put to bed with aspirin that couldn't really touch the source of the pain—having her brain altered by something unnatural.

Alex curled into her sheets, hid her face in the bright teal pillowcase, passed out. Sylvie shut out the lights and hesitated in the doorway. There was no reason to stay. Alex would wake up without remembering any of it, with only a lingering memory of a killer headache.

But she was young and healthy.

Morning news broadcasts, though, had more than their share of elderly viewers, people who rose from their beds with the sun. How many sudden strokes would there be, or inexplicable heart attacks brought on by magic forcing its way into their brains and rearranging things to suit some- one else's will?

On the TV, the breaking news listed thirty-seven dead and counting in a freak waterspout. NOAA scientists were being harassed for quotes on the "anomalous weather." Sylvie turned the TV off and headed home, chilled all the way through.

. . .

SYLVIE SQUELCHED UP THE CONCRETE RISERS TO HER APARTMENT and left a wet imprint on the doorjamb as she keyed the door open.

Her exhaustion weighed her down; her worries made her leaden, slow to realize she wasn't alone. She shut the door behind her, flipped the dead bolt, and started shed- ding clothes. Her Windbreaker slapped the floor, mostly dry, but soggy around the cuffs and hem. Her boots—she toed them off, sent them thudding across the room, where they left dark marks on the white walls.

"So, crappy days all around, huh?"

Sylvie jerked around; her gun stuck in her holster, the nylon deformed by the icy water and the rough and tumble of the morning, but she got it out, leveled it at her uninvited guest.

It didn't bother her guest at all.

Marah Stone, the ISI assassin, sat cross-legged on Sylvie's kitchen counter devouring cold soba noodles forked up with her fingers.

"Marah," Sylvie said. She licked her lip, nervous and unable to hide it. Sylvie had met Marah only twice, in brief meetings where the woman had been carelessly chatty and far too interested in Sylvie's life. She might have seemed harmless, only Sylvie knew two things about her. One, the strange, mottled birthmark on her arm and hand wasn't a birthmark, but a curse mark, which made her dangerous. Two, Marah had been the ISI's solution to an imprisoned witch. She'd ghosted inside, evading guards and convicts with equal ease, and killed the witch without taking any damage to herself.

Sylvie could live with that. She'd killed her own share of magical baddies after all, but Marah had mutilated the body afterward, in a way that just screamed psychopathy.

"Are you even listening to me? God, what a fucking long week this has been. I mean, I dig my way out of a very premature grave, face down a lurking sand wraith with nothing but nerve, haul ass halfway across the country, and you don't even have a clean fork. What the hell, Shadows. What kind of host are you? I had to load the dishwasher myself."

"Are those my clothes?" Sylvie asked.

Marah licked her lips clean of brown sauce, wiped her fingers—again—on a very familiar pair of jeans. "Mine smelled really bad. I didn't think you'd mind."

"I mind," Sylvie said. "I mind a lot."

"Ungracious," Marah said. "I even brought you the mother of all hostess gifts. Thought you'd be pleased. But no, I get bitched at for borrowing your clothes, eating some really, frankly, mediocre takeout, and a gun in my fucking face!"

Sylvie stepped back, holstered the gun, raised her hands, a my-bad, sorry gesture.

Simple rule to stay alive by: Don't piss off the assassin.

If Marah had wanted her dead, she'd be dead. Which meant this was exactly what she claimed it was. A visit.

Marah's marked hand slowly unclenched from where it

was white-knuckled around the bowl, visibly backing away from the urge to throw it at Sylvie.

"Fine," Sylvie said. "You've had a bad day. So have I. Let's not take it out on each other. I'm going to go take a nap. You can . . ."

Get out of my house.

". . . occupy yourself."

"I'd take a shower first, if I were you," Marah said. The last vestiges of temper in her face faded, shifted to a maddening smirk. "I left your hostess gift in there."

Sylvie belatedly realized that the noise she heard in the background was not the leftover aural trauma of the mermaids' watery attack, not even the homely sound of the dishwasher churning its slow way through its cycle, but the shower running.

The splash of the water was muted, not just crashing down on tile and curtain; something intercepted the spray.

Sylvie felt her nerves jangle, tighten. What an assassin considered a hostess gift might be something she really didn't want.

"Brought it all the way from Chicago," Marah said.

Sylvie's attention jerked.

"Chicago?" Her voice was hungry, vulnerable.

"I told you I had a crappy day, told you I had to dig my way out. Never said I was alone. I wanted to go straight to a nice hotel with a Jacuzzi and complimentary robes, but no, he insisted on coming here—"

Sylvie, heart in her mouth, headed for the bathroom, half-terrified, half-hopeful. Marah wouldn't have, couldn't have brought her a corpse. She might be dangerous, but she was mercenary enough to want something from Sylvie. And Sylvie would owe her one for this.

Even though the crash and sputter of water made Sylvie's gut churn, she couldn't stop herself. A hand on the doorknob, her pulse ricocheting in her throat, and she flung the door open.

"Hey, Stone, a little privacy? Near death and a road trip doesn't make us that close—"

Demalion stuck his head out from the curtain, blond hair damp and darkened, slicked to his skull, bruising on his cheek, his shoulder, but alive. . . . His lips parted, moved silently. *Sylvie*.

Sylvie crashed into the shower stall with him; his arms tightened around her even as she slid and slipped on the soapy tile, trying to get closer.

Alive.

She was laughing, wild, triumphant. Surprised.

Though she'd talked a good game with Alex, she'd been most of the way convinced to thinking him dead. She clutched him closer, the sleek, wet warmth of him making her think of selkie lovers, bit his shoulder, trying to hang on.

"Sylvie," he murmured, dragged her mouth up to his. Laughed low and hungry in his throat when she whined at having to release him from her teeth. "Too much time with werewolves?"

"Shut up," she said and smothered that laughter with her breath. She pressed closer, bare feet unsteady on slick tiles, hanging her weight from his shoulders. He caught her around the waist, snagging her belt loops, holding her tight, holding her up.

Sylvie, who normally relegated shower sex to something best left in the movies, felt his hands pressing into the small of her back, the dip of fingertips tracing heat beneath her waistband, and thought, *The hell with it.* She pulled away, grabbed the hem of her tee, and eeled out of it, all awkward elbows and jutting angles in the small space.

He caught her wrists while they were overhead, leaned in, pressed her back against the cool tiles. She arched into him, hissing, and he kissed her wrists, her palms, his breath as heated as the water splashing her skin.

"Clothes in the shower, Sylvie, really?" He ducked his head; the light in his eyes familiar even in Wright's paler shade, making it no surprise when the next kiss hovered at her mouth without connecting before descending to her throat, the rasp of his stubbled chin waking a thousand tiny nerve endings to singing pleasure.

"Tease," she said, tangling her hands in his hair— different, she cataloged. Demalion's hair used to feel like mink to her, back when he was original recipe. Now, it felt like raw silk, equal parts coarse and soft. Different, but wonderful.

He popped the button on her pants; she released his hair to help shimmy them off her hips. Both of them were breathless with effort and desire by the time the clinging fabric was peeled off, abandoned on the floor of the shower stall.

His hands closed on her hips, wordlessly urging her closer, tighter. She tried to climb him, cracked her knee against the tile, and swore, staggering backward, losing that brief press of connection. Missing it immediately. She whined in frustration—but that was shower sex for you, bumps and bruises and awkward clinches that broke just when they were getting really good, terrible footing, and someone's back always got slapped up against the chilly tiles.

Her tongue tangling with his, tasting heat and the bitterness of soapy foam, Sylvie thought, awkward or not, she wouldn't trade this moment for all the silk sheets and scented candles in the world.

At last braced, balanced, they rocked against each other, trading breathless frustration for laughter, and finally for a pleasure that had their voices cracking against the ceramic tiles, saw them sprawling in the morass of water and discarded clothes that soaked the floor. Her shampoo bottle had tipped, overlaying the scent of sex and the sea in the room with a lashing of citrus foam.

Sylvie kicked feebly at her pants, unblocked the drain, and put her head back to Demalion's shoulder and listened to the gurgle of water receding. In a moment, she was going to get up, shake this lassitude from her veins, drag Demalion with her to the bedroom, and never mind the assassin in the living room.

He stroked her wet hair, smoothing it from the wild kinks and curls it had worked its way into. "I should check in with the locals."

Sylvie stiffened, rolled away from him. "About that."

He propped himself up on his elbows. "What?"

"You haven't been watching the news."

He rolled up to sit cross-legged. He looked tired suddenly, and past the first flush of their reunion, she saw dark bruises on his arms, his hands, his shins. Marah's words came back to her—had to dig out of a premature grave—mixed with the memory of the collapsed ISI building in Chicago.

"The Miami ISI, too?" he asked.

"Yeah," Sylvie said. "Mermaids."

He shoved his hair out of his face, scrubbed a hand over a jaw rough with stubble. "Mermaids. Fuck. What the hell is going on?"

"Don't know," Sylvie said. She shrugged. "Beyond my pay grade. I got my ass kicked and for nothing. I'm sitting this one out. I've got a client who needs me more than the ISI does."

He stiffened all over, and said, "Are you shitting me? You're sitting this one out? My coworkers *died*, crushed or ripped apart by a sand wraith, and *you're sitting this one out*? What, just because we're government, we don't rate?"

Wow, she thought. Forty minutes, give or take, and they were at odds again.

Gunfire in the next room derailed their argument. Four shots, quickly fired, and a roar of something inhuman. They scrambled for the towel—the *last* towel; Sylvie grabbed Demalion's discarded shirt, draped over her sink, yanked it on, and bolted for the living room, Demalion crying out for her to *Be careful!*

· · ·

HER FIRST THOUGHT WAS THAT HER LIVING ROOM HAD GOTTEN A HELL of a lot smaller, filled with Erinya's inhuman shape. Her second thought, even less useful than the first, was to wonder if Erinya had grown. Her front feet, talons extended, crushed Marah face-first into the western wall of Sylvie's living room; Erinya's tail lashed against the eastern wall, knocking magazines and books from the shelves. She bulked twice as large as a tiger, scented the room with pissed-off animal musk and the cloying, damp weight of ancient jungles. Black porcupine spikes, tipped in scarlet and gold, rose from her back and nape, jutting upward in threat.

The carpet beneath her hind claws slowly transformed to loam, vines twining out of the listing bookshelf.

Lost in gaping, in yanking Demalion's shirt around her, it took her a moment to understand that there were words beneath the guttural rolling growl emanating from Erinya.

"Where is she? What have you done to Sylvie?"

"I'm here," Sylvie said. Her voice sounded thin against the vastness of Erinya's anger, but it was enough. Erinya's head turned; her nose wrinkled and flared, scenting her.

"You smell like old cat. Like him."

Marah squirmed, got her gun up, and shot Erinya beneath the chin, point-blank. The concussion of it filled the room and overflowed, much like Erinya herself. Demalion shouted in surprise, but Sylvie was just waiting for the aftermath.

She'd shot Erinya herself once upon a time, multiple bullets tearing into the demigod's immortal skin; the Fury had shaken the bullets off, healed the wound in minutes.

This time, amped up to full god status, the bullet only bloomed against her jaw, flattening out like a flower, and dropping to the carpet.

"Eri!" Sylvie shouted. "Stop it!"

The cops were going to be called. The last thing they needed was a clueless, trigger-panicky cop added to this bizarre domestic dispute.

Erinya's spiked hackles settled but hissed and rattled against her nape like a nest of angry snakes. "I came to see you, and she shot me. Can I kill her?"

Truthfully, Sylvie was stunned that Marah was still breathing. The assassin was tough; even now, she looked pissed instead of afraid, had her body braced in such a way that Erinya's strangling grip was uncomfortable, not breath-stealing.

"Sylvie!" Demalion said, clutching his towel in one hand, a gun in the other. "For God's sake, tell her not to!"

Sylvie jerked into speech. "Don't kill her, Erinya." At least, not now.

Erinya glared past Sylvie at Demalion, then calmed as if she'd read Sylvie's thoughts. She probably had.

She dropped Marah, shifted direction, leaped over the breakfast bar, and yanked open the fridge. "You never let me do anything."

Demalion slipped past Sylvie, helped Marah up from the floor. The woman rubbed her throat thoughtfully.

"What were you thinking?" Sylvie said to her.

"Hey, lay off," Demalion said. Marah coughed when she tried to contribute to her own defense.

Sylvie refused to feel bad. What kind of idiot took on a monster like Erinya with a gun?

We do, her little dark voice said.

That's different, she shot back. We're *different.*

"You okay?" Demalion asked. He tugged Marah as far from Erinya as possible in the small space.

"Not a problem," Marah said. Her gaze never left Erinya, shrunk back down to human size, human shape. "You often host gods in your apartment, Sylvie?"

"I host all sorts of unexpected guests," Sylvie said.

"I don't like her," Erinya said. She pulled a steak out of the fridge, a monster hunk of beef that Sylvie knew hadn't been in there. "Make me dinner?"

"Be a big girl. Put it in the oven yourself," Sylvie said. "How about Marah promises not to shoot you again, and you don't squish her like a bug. And, Eri? Can you get rid of the jungle?"

Her apartment was unrecognizable, and Sylvie, dreading the moment her neighbors called the cops, couldn't help but be distracted by the new plant life turning her apartment into a conservatory. She batted a flowering vine away from her face with unnecessary vigor. It left a dusting of rusty pollen all over her hand.

Marah and Demalion had their heads bent close together,

and it made Sylvie nervous. Demalion, on his own, she trusted to the ends of the earth. Demalion, with the ISI at his side? A little less.

"I wouldn't want anyone to kill my family either," Erinya said. "But if you had to, I'd forgive you. You'd forgive me, right?"

Sylvie said, "What are you talking about?"

Erinya shoved the steak into the oven—it flared scarlet with fire inside, and Sylvie closed her eyes. Erinya was a god, she reminded herself. Wouldn't burn the apartment down. Even if she'd turned the oven interior into a fiery pit of some kind. Erinya wasn't exactly up on electricity.

"Family. Her. You."

Marah coughed again. It sounded a little like a laugh. "Told you we should have had a chat. Months ago, I told you. Properly get to know each other. You know. Hey, I'm Marah Stone. I'm not just the ISI cleanup crew. I'm your cousin on your great-great-great-whatever side."

"Bullshit," Sylvie said.

Demalion's face reflected her own surprise, and Sylvie felt a flare of shameful relief that he didn't know Marah well enough to know that.

"Truth. But she wants to kill me," Erinya continued, hauling the steak out, barely warmed. She put it on a platter, looked at it without any hunger, and said, more quietly, "They *all* want to kill me."

"She's ISI," Sylvie said. "Kinda their raison d'être."

"It's a good reason," Marah said. "Her kind is dangerous. I mean, look at your apartment. Look *outside*."

Erinya's jungle hadn't lessened—Sylvie's apartment was one step away from growing moss in the damp, green heat. But a glance out the front window showed that Erinya's stress had translated on a much wider scale. The chlorine blue pool had gone green and dark; the vines that snaked around Sylvie's furniture also coiled around the sun deck, creeping into the laundry room. The carved, limestone alligator cracked like an egg and birthed a dozen small, squirming hatchlings.

"Erinya can control herself," Sylvie said, hoping it was true. It might not be. Gods leaked. That was a fact. Even Dunne, who'd been brutal in his self-control, had leaked. A new god, a god with a history of indulging her appetites? "And she will. Erinya, pull it back."

"Why should I?" Erinya said. "If I'm living on earth, why can't I redecorate?"

"You want to play house? Fine," Sylvie said. "Get a *house*, and leave the world alone. Pull it back."

"Not the boss of me," Erinya said, a familiar complaint. The flowering vines in the kitchen withered, crisped, and burst into dust. Sylvie would need to vacuum, but at least she wouldn't need a weed wacker.

"Good," Sylvie said. "Now, go do the outside. And make sure you get the little snappers out there. Kids swim in that pool."

Erinya scowled. "Don't eat my steak." Then she vanished.

Marah shook her head. "Yeah, she needs killing."

Demalion said, "Stone. Watch the attitude. Or you'll have Sylvie on your ass as well as Erinya."

"Not the boss of me," Marah sniped, imitating Erinya, gaining another growl, this one from Sylvie.

Demalion threw up his hands, disappeared into Sylvie's bedroom, slamming the door behind him. It had a distinct attitude of *women*!

Marah made a face as he left. "I thought he'd be in a better mood once he'd gotten laid. Of course, you two were pretty quick about it."

"What the hell are you even doing here?" Sylvie wanted to be in her bedroom with Demalion.

Marah drew a finger across Erinya's steak, licked the juice from her skin. "Lilith's side. So bad-tempered. No wonder you like that damned monster-god. Our side's a little more sensible."

"My side, your side. Whatever. You keep playing coy with that info. I don't think it really exists." She wasn't going to ask outright, no matter that she wanted, maybe even *needed* the answers. Marah was mercenary; Sylvie owed her one already for Demalion. She knew if she asked, Marah would add that to the tab.

"God, you're difficult." Marah leaned back against the counter, shifted her weight to one hip, crossed her ankles. "Go on, tell me who my daddy is. I'll give you a clue if you like. He brained his brother with a rock."

Sylvie hung her head. Oh yeah. Like Lilith's side of her genetic line wasn't enough to deal with. She tended to forget who helped father it. "Cain. You're Cain's line. I'm the progeny of Lilith and Cain, and you're the progeny of Cain and whoever."

"Got it in one," Marah said. "This?" She held up her red-stained hand, made jazz fingers at Sylvie. "This is the infamous mark of Cain."

Sylvie swallowed, thinking of Zoe marked in that way. Her witchy mentor—Val Cassavetes—had to have known. Had to have kept that secret from Sylvie.

"Your first kill, and it blooms if you've got the right blood in your veins," Marah said. "Comes with perks, too. Like a magic shield of sorts. God does seem to like us killers. I mean, you've got magical resistance, too, right? The new Lilith and all."

Sylvie didn't say anything, didn't trust anything Marah was saying either. No assassin was going to blithely show off their ace as simply as that. It was false sharing, designed only to make Sylvie feel obligated to respond in kind. She knew better than to fall for it.

Demalion, returning, dressed in clothing he'd scrounged from the oddments he'd left behind the last time he was in Miami, did fall for it. "So why doesn't Sylvie have the mark? She's half-Cain, and she's killed people."

He fiddled with the sleeves where they pulled a little tight across his arms. He'd added muscle to Wright's body since the last time he'd worn those clothes. Right now, Sylvie felt like he'd added some muscle to his head.

"Hey, *she's* in the room," Sylvie said. "And *she's* killed *monsters.*"

Demalion shrugged a bare apology. "It's not like you

know the answer, right? Aren't you curious?" Sylvie groaned. The worst of dating an agent. It wasn't enough for Demalion to know her; he wanted to know what had made her the person she was. Hell, he probably kept his own set of files on her, separate from the ISI's.

"Lilith's stronger," Sylvie said. "See, there's your answer."

"But Zoe's marked—"

"Hey," Sylvie snapped. Bad enough they were discussing her. Zoe was off-limits.

Marah's dark eyes were inquisitive, bright with calculation, but she was polite enough to back off the topic of Zoe. Not polite enough to drop the conversation.

Sylvie, heart beating oddly fast in her chest, wasn't sure whether she wanted the conversation to continue or not. Marah might have answers. Marah might be full of shit. Sylvie figured it was a fifty-fifty shot.

Don't trust her, her little dark voice whispered.

Not a problem, Sylvie thought.

Instead, Marah pushed herself off the counter, circled Sylvie, making her very aware that, of the three people in the apartment, she was the only one underdressed. "Lilith is stronger," Marah agreed. "But harder to wake. You had to have been exposed to her influence, somehow. An inoculation to wake the body to the virus's presence.

"You could have run into Lilith herself," Marah continued when Sylvie stayed stubbornly silent. "But from the files, you were already nipping at her metaphysical heels when you killed her. So not the progenitrix. Lilith's progeny? You play chew toy with a vampire? A succubus? A werewolf?"

"Does it matter?" Sylvie said. "I don't know how it happened. It just did."

"Details always matter," Marah said. "Especially when I'm trying to figure out which side you're on. You hang out with werewolves. And you're claiming friendship with a god who's violent and insane."

"Marah," Demalion objected.

"You can't tell me it doesn't bother you," Marah told

Demalion. "That she's close with one of the monsters who killed you? That's she made friends with the Fury?"

"It bothers me," Demalion snapped. "Is that what you want me to admit. Fine. It does."

"Yeah, Shadows," Marah said, jumping on the wagon she'd started. "You really should put that monster down. Whose side are you on, anyway?"

She looked at them both, Marah's expression calculating, Demalion's more honestly angry.

Sylvie felt her own rage surge back—judge her? Over Erinya? She said, "I'm on the only side I can trust. Mine."

"Well, then," Marah said. "Maybe we should find more congenial company. Check in with the locals."

"Most of them are dead," Sylvie said, bluntly. "Riordan's son survived."

"He's enough to start with," Marah said. "You coming, Demalion?"

"Yeah," Sylvie said. "You going with her, Demalion?"

"The agency needs us," he said.

"I can't," Sylvie said. "I've got a client in distress and some bastard fucking with people's memories. Making them forget what they've seen. On a citywide scale."

"*City*wide? I know you were looking into memory alterations, but I didn't realize the scale of it."

"Neither did I," Sylvie said, grimly. "And it's getting personal. It hurt Alex."

Demalion shook his head. "I know you're independent, but it's time to call Yvette in on this."

"She survived the sand wraith?"

"Taking meetings in DC," Marah said. "Bureaucracy saved her ass."

"Guess that proves she's near the top of the food chain," Sylvie said. "They're the only ones who benefit from bureaucracy."

"Yvette's surviving is a good thing," Demalion said. "Look, you said your plate is full. You've got your client. You've got us—"

"Didn't say I was helping the ISI—"

"You'll help me, right?"

"Yeah, but—"

"So, why not let Yvette take point on this memory thing?"

"Because I don't trust her," Sylvie snapped. "I can't be the only one who's noticed this memory gap. But I seem to be the only one who cares. So no, no passing this buck."

"Don't argue with her, Demalion," Marah said. "You'll never convince her. She's built to work alone. The new Lilith."

"I don't even know what that means," Demalion said.

"Yeah," Sylvie said. "Why don't you enlighten him, Marah. Since you know so much." She doubted Marah knew anything of substance. The ISI files, as Demalion had said, were empty speculation.

Marah grinned, a predatory shine of teeth. "How much is it worth to you? A favor? Maybe two?"

Then again, Marah was of Cain's line. Maybe she did know.

"One more," Sylvie said. "But I'm not killing anyone for you—*my* definition of anyone."

"Hey, I rescued myself," Demalion protested. "I'm not a favor."

"Deal," Marah said, waving him off. "One favor owing. It's simple, really. I told you. God likes his killers. Both sets of them. It's politics at its finest. You've talked to gods, you know the only thing they hold sacred."

"Noninterference with gods outside their pantheon. No more godly wars," Sylvie said.

"No more *overt* godly wars," Marah said. "But a free agent, who refuses to belong to anyone, who wreaks havoc—say a woman who disposes of the last Aztec god, strips his power, and gives it to a Fury. A woman who yanks said Fury out of her own pantheon and creates a new one—

"You're God's stalking horse," Marah said. "And for all your independence, you'll never know if you're working to his plan or not. The eternal killer who does his bidding even while you spit in his face and assert your disallegiance. You're his plausible deniability. Congratulations, Sylvie, you hit the jackpot. You're going to live forever. Or until someone else gets in a lucky shot and takes your place."

The little dark voice in Sylvie's blood was roaring in protest, drowning out her own voice, a tight rasp. "I don't believe you."

"Think it's coincidence that you're immune to most magics? That you can kill things way above your weight class? You're a stealth bomber in human form. He doesn't care who you kill, as long as you keep doing it, keep picking off his rivals. It's a long game. Maybe the longest game ever."

"Get out," Sylvie choked. "Out."

"Truth hurts," Marah said. She patted Sylvie's cheek; Sylvie slapped her hand away, and felt a weird numbing echo in her bones as her flesh hit Marah's. Like to like. Killers. God's killers. Spreaders of chaos and misfortune.

"Out," she whispered.

Demalion put his own hand out, a steadying touch at her shoulder. She shrugged him off.

"Fine," Marah said. "I could use some real food anyway. And I doubt your Fury wants to share." She headed out, jaunty and pleased with herself. Sylvie wanted to chuck something at her.

Demalion lingered, silent. When she met his eyes, he dropped his. Answer enough to a question she hadn't asked. Did he believe Marah? Did he think Sylvie's entire purpose in existence was to kill things? Yes. He really did.

Heat stung her eyes. She blinked furiously. "So how'd you hook up with her, anyway? Think you can unhook her? Maybe while dangling her over a cliff?"

"She saved my life. That's got to count for something."

"Yeah, it counts as another one I owe her."

"Hey, ouch," Demalion said.

Sylvie shook her head. "Sorry, sorry. You know I didn't mean it like that. Hell, that's one debt I'm thrilled to incur."

"You know, I did my share of the digging," Demalion said. "I could make a case for Marah and me being even.

Hell, we could probably even make a case for her owing me. I warned her the sand wraith was coming. Psychic perks."

Sylvie nodded. "Take it up with her."

Demalion, given his cue to leave, hesitated.

"What?" Sylvie snapped.

"Are you okay?"

"Dandy. I'm going to live forever, don't you know. Which is good because I'm busy. Got things to do. And hey, I'm waiting for Erinya to remember her steak. You want to be here when she is, when she remembers how much she dislikes you?" Her throat felt tight. She didn't mind being a killer, but she wanted to be more than just that.

Sylvie's new cell buzzed where she had dropped it, an angry hornet making itself known. She tore her gaze away. "I should—"

"Yeah," he said.

"You go and take Ms. Mercenary—"

"Yeah."

The phone rattled, and Sylvie said, quickly, "Be careful, Demalion. The ISI's in real trouble."

Demalion's tight, irritated expression cracked. "I know."

"This might be a good time to quit."

"Can't do that," Demalion said. "I believe in the mission."

"I know. Just had to put it out there."

She kissed him too briefly, let him go, and grabbed the phone, expecting Alex. No one else had the number.

Instead of her assistant, she got her sister in a temper.

5

Complications

SYLVIE MISSED ZOE'S FIRST RANT, CAUGHT UP IN WONDERING HOW in hell Zoe had gotten this number, distracted by Erinya's reappearing to claim her steak, by the sheer amount of noise in the background wherever Zoe was.

"I said, come get me!"

Sylvie pivoted, keeping Erinya in her view. She'd learned the hard way not to leave the Fury unsupervised. Erinya only studied her steak, then shrugged, dragged out a plate, and made a stab at being civilized.

"No," Sylvie said. "Where are you?" She knew the answer already, just from the loudspeaker in Zoe's vicinity spitting out distorted messages in English and a dozen other languages—an airport.

"LaGuardia. Heading home. You need to come get me when I land."

"I thought you were in Ischia. Safe with Val."

"Obviously, I'm not. Come get me, Syl. I don't wanna wait around. I've been traveling all night."

"Zoe, this is a terrible time for you to come back," Sylvie said. "Did Val send you? Does Val even know?"

Zoe huffed. "She's so damn patronizing. I'm not a child or an idiot. And I had to come back. School starts in three weeks. I've got back-to-school shopping to do."

"It's not a good time," Sylvie said, watching a god putter about in her kitchen, warping things as she went. Under Erinya's touch, Sylvie's coffeemaker turned upscale, spat out espresso; her tiled floor shifted to rough stone. "I've got house guests that aren't witch-friendly." Gods could burn out witches, leave them husked out and unable to do magic. Erinya, of course, liked to go one step further and kill them dead.

"What, your god-thing friend? Tell her to go away. I'm family. I come first."

"And you called Val patronizing," Sylvie said. "Fine. I'll be there. Give me your flight number." When she hung up, she found Erinya watching her as eagerly as a dog whose master had rattled the car keys.

"Are we going to the airport?" Erinya said. "I like the airport. Good hunting."

"You are not coming," Sylvie said. "I'm picking up my sister. She's a witch. Your presence will hurt her."

"Does she deserve it?" Erinya asked. "She's a witch."

"She's not sacrificing babies," Sylvie said.

"Not yet," Erinya said. She ate the last of her steak in one giant, mouth-distending bite. "Can't trust a witch."

"Go home," Sylvie said when she could speak again. "Redecorate your heaven and not my living room."

"It's my city," Erinya said. "I think that makes it my living room."

"It's *not* your city," Sylvie said. "Don't get possessive. Don't make me take Dunne's side."

Erinya vanished before Sylvie had finished talking, fading out on the first mention of Dunne's name. Sylvie filed that away, wondering if it would work more than once.

A draft touched her legs, the AC kicking on, making her shiver. Her hair dripped down her back; the thin poplin of Demalion's borrowed shirt felt clammy.

She sighed, tried to recover some of that all-too-brief happiness she'd had curled against Demalion in her wrecked bathroom.

Her phone rang again, a text coming in on the burner phone.

Alex.

I'm at the office. Meet me. Bring coffee.

• • •

LIGHT GLITTERED FROM INSIDE THE FRONT WINDOW OF SHADOWS Inquiries, hard to see in the sunlit streets of South Miami Beach, noticeable simply because Sylvie hadn't been expecting Alex to be awake and about anytime that day. Not after her magical concussion.

She really needed to stop underestimating Alex.

When she opened the front door, Alex greeted her and the Starbucks cup with determined cheer that went oddly with the bruising beneath her eyes. "Oh good, you're here. You need to see this."

"See what? I thought you were going to rest? Your head was hurting?" Sylvie came at it obliquely, unwilling to trigger another attack.

"'Swhat Tylenol 4's for. Took a nap, took a pill, feel loads better."

Sylvie said, "Yeah, that's why you look like someone socked you in the nose. You should be in bed."

"Let it go, Syl. You'll be glad you did. Look at this. Not me. I'll hit the foundation in a minute or two." She hauled her laptop across the desk, turned it to face Sylvie, the screen blurring with the vibration.

"I've been working on the Chicago site. Lots and lots of video being shot."

"Of the actual event?" Sylvie said. "The attack?"

"The sand wraith? No. I've been looking through the aftermath." Alex shook her head, answering two questions at once. Had the monster made the news? Had Alex lost memories of that attack, also? Answers: no and no.

"What exactly is a sand wraith?" Sylvie asked.

"Monster out of the Texas, New Mexico, Arizona area. I think it's a type of djinn that migrated eons ago. Anyway, that's not the important part. Focus, Syl. I've been searching through iReports on CNN. Look. Right there."

She cued the scene up: nighttime, the rubble illuminated by emergency lights, stone and wiring and metal making crazy, nonsensical shadows, not helped by the shaky-cam hand of the filmer. "What am I—"

Sylvie shut up. She knew what Alex had wanted her to see. Six hours ago, it would have filled her with relief. Now, she watched Demalion and Marah Stone pick their way out of the rubble, dwarfed by the slabs of concrete, limping, braced on each other, and felt her heart tighten up. Christ. One thing to know Demalion had had a close call, to see him bruised but whole in her shower, full of attitude, full of life; another thing to see him like this—his eyes dark holes in his skull, face a mask of concrete dust and blood.

"Syl? This is good. He's alive—"

"Yeah, yeah," Sylvie said. "Alive and in Miami. He made it here this morning. He's off hunting down the Riordans. Being a good little agent and reporting in—"

"You didn't call me? Fuck you, Sylvie. I spent hours scouring the Net and for nothing? When my head feels like it's about to rupture?"

"Thought you were fine," Sylvie said.

Alex burst into tears and flung the stapler at her; Sylvie dodged, listened to the metal crack against the front window, winced. Another thing for Emmanuel to fix.

"Hey, hey, I'm sorry, really sorry," Sylvie said. "I should have called you. I was going to. I thought you were sleeping."

"You should have left a message. A text. A fucking e-mail. I was so damn worried." Her words tangled, choked off, left her rubbing her eyes with the heels of her hands.

"About Demalion?" Sylvie felt like she was walking across an unexpected minefield. Alex was the calm one. Alex was the sensible one. Alex didn't throw office supplies, break windows, or curse her out. Alex didn't usually have her memory scrambled either.

"About *you*, stupid. You do dumb things when you're angry. And I'm tired. I can't keep up with you." Alex dragged her hands away from her eyes; she looked as tired as she claimed. More, she looked ground-down. Sylvie frowned. She couldn't be to blame for all of that. Some of that was Alex fighting the memory modification, courting the pain by poking around similar events.

"I'm sorry," Sylvie said again.

Alex jerked the laptop around, lips tight, not forgiving her that easily. "I compiled and skimmed about two hundred videos. My head's still spinning." She stabbed at the keys, brightly colored nails flashing like daggers. She turned the laptop back toward Sylvie, showing her window after window of stored video. A barrage of flickering information all set to a disaster backdrop. All of them with gold flares marking where the sand wraith had been erased from the world's memory. CNN, Sylvie noticed, was saying that two newspeople—a reporter and her cameraman—had died when the rubble shifted unexpectedly. Sylvie looked at the last images they recorded, caught another glimpse of Marah and Demalion, running fast from . . . something washed out in a flicker of light . . . The camera image jerked forward, following the reporter, who was, in turn, following a basic journalistic rule. If you see someone running, find out what they're running from.

Then the reporter disappeared into a cloud of dust and rubble.

"All of that. For nothing? Because you couldn't be bothered to call?" Her cheeks were flushed, feverish.

"Alex," Sylvie said. "I'm sorry. I can't go back and undo it. Can we move on? Hey—"

Sylvie reached out, jabbed at the keys, trying to get one particular video to stop, and only succeeded in losing that screen altogether. "Dammit. Can you find that again?"

"Is it important?" Alex asked.

"Might be," Sylvie said. "If I'm not seeing things. There was a bystander who looked familiar—"

Alex sighed. "And there goes my second surprise. You

know, sometimes it's just no damn fun working for you, Shadows. This the guy you meant?"

Sylvie came around to Alex's side of the desk, dragging the visitor's chair around with her. It couldn't be healthy to spin the laptop around and around like a top. Sylvie looked at the image—slightly blurry, but the one she'd spotted. A wiry, dark-haired man with a beaky nose, wearing the American uniform: worn blue jeans, white T-shirt, sneakers. He should have been totally nondescript. Except . . . Sylvie pushed play.

He was studying the wreckage, trying to be discreet about it. Not gawking like the rest of the onlookers. Scoping it out without drawing attention to himself. He walked out of one video into the next, his damp dark hair collecting a mottled coating of dust and sand, a clear sign of how close he'd managed to get.

"So he was in Chicago," Alex said. "Playing looky-loo. He was also in Memphis."

"Memphis," Sylvie said. "Did we ever find out what happened there?"

"Not a clue, but our guy was there. Maybe he knows," Alex said. She reached over Sylvie's shoulders, clicked another set of images onto the screen. Same man, same outfit, same damp, dark hair. Same careful prowling the border of chaos, betraying his interest by trying not to seem interested at all. Memphis. Chicago. Miami.

"So how'd you pick him out?" Alex said.

"Saw him here," Sylvie said. "Outside the ISI. Moving when no one else could. Immune to the mermaids' song."

Alex whimpered, and Sylvie swallowed back further comment, waited for Alex's eyelashes to stop flickering, her mind rewriting itself to someone else's commands. Finally, Alex sighed, said, "What were we talking about?"

"Him," Sylvie said, hoping she hadn't screwed things up, hoped she hadn't managed to link their mysterious bystander inextricably with the forbidden parts of Alex's memory.

Alex wrinkled her nose. "Oh yeah. I'm trying to find

him at the other scenes, but it's harder. Savannah and Dallas didn't rouse so much excitement, you know? The Savannah site was isolated. And the Dallas site was effectively cordoned off. Hard to be a face in the crowd if there's no crowd. Even harder to film a face in a noncrowd if there's no one to man a camera. And my head is killing me. The more I research, the worse I feel."

Alex let out a breath, drained her coffee like it was booze after a too-long day.

Fighting the conflicting memories. Whoever was doing the changing hadn't gotten into the ISI files to alter them. So Alex remembered those. But they were erasing the truth outside of the ISI, and Alex was dutifully trying to forget.

"Why don't you give it a break?" Sylvie said. "Lock the door, pull down the blinds. Take a nap."

Alex's eyes swept the couch; she leaned forward in her chair, as if she could simply fall into the couch by wanting it. "What are you going to do?"

"Check in on Lupe," Sylvie said. "I was supposed to do it this morning, but Demalion was at my apartment, and I got distracted."

"Distracted, huh?" A brief smile touched Alex's lips. "I guess I can forgive you for not calling me immediately."

"Distracted like he brought trouble with him. You remember the ISI assassin who killed Odalys?"

"Not like you ever introduced us," Alex said. "I know she exists."

Sylvie found the image of Marah and Demalion whirling to confront the sand wraith, Marah's hand upraised. She showed it to Alex. "That woman Demalion's leaning on? Marah Stone. ISI assassin. Big trouble."

"How big?" Alex asked.

"She's been in town for a few hours, and she's already tried to kill Erinya."

Alex clicked her jaw shut, then said, "I'm too tired to deal with that. Go away. I'm taking a nap. Check on Lupe. She left a message on the machine. She's found a witch she wants you to vet."

"She what?"

"She's impatient, I guess. Can't really blame her," Alex said, digging a camp pillow and blanket out of her deepest desk drawer.

"No one listens to me," Sylvie said. "I gave her the speech. I told her that you had to be careful, I told her—"

"Yeah, yeah, I was there. Go tell her again and let me nap." Alex dragged herself to the couch, sprawled over the cracked green leather, tugging the blanket over herself.

"See if you can find anything else on our mystery man. He had to have come from somewhere. For that matter, the monsters, too. Even if they were living among us, there should have been signs. Why attack now?"

"I don't know," Alex muttered.

"Crap," Sylvie said, glancing at her watch. "Alex, do me a favor? Pick up Zoe at the airport? I have a feeling Lupe's going to eat time."

Alex sighed hugely. "So unfair. Come in, tell me to rest up, then give me things to do. I will look into our mystery man. I will pick up your brat of a sister. But after a nap. Go away, before I throw something else at you."

Sylvie waved off the threat but headed out, right into the full heat of the day.

. . .

THE MOTEL LUPE WAS STAYING AT WASN'T IN THE BEST PART OF town; sirens were a familiar background melody, and the palm trees embedded in the sidewalk cutouts were hardly the type to gladden even an indie director's location scout, being stunted and soft.

But the motel was reasonably cheap, catering to long-term guests, and the neighborhood wasn't so bad that Lupe couldn't take her morning runs. There were even coffee shops and restaurants and a movie theater in the area—so why the hell couldn't Lupe just occupy herself in some safe way?

Sylvie found herself gritting her teeth as she parked her truck, made herself stop. She stepped out of her truck and found her teeth locking tight again as she heard muffled shouting. That was never a good sign. Even in a crap hotel.

Also not good? The fact that Sylvie could feel the tiny flare of unnatural forces rippling in the air, like a storm about to break. Guess Lupe hadn't waited for Sylvie to approve of the witch but dived in headfirst.

She booked up the stairs, felt the morning's bruises protest, and pounded on Lupe's locked door. "Lupe!"

"Help us!" a woman shouted. "Help!"

It wasn't Lupe. Lupe's voice had a thick rasp to it, an animal huskiness when she spoke. Sylvie hadn't asked if the rasp was original or if it, too, was a change forced upon her.

She tested her balance, her aches, then pivoted and kicked the door, with the expected result. She bounced off it. Even cheap motels tended not to skimp on the doors. Easy road to a lawsuit.

"Lupe," Sylvie said. "Let me in!"

The shouting on the inside broke off to a series of hushed whimpers and a low, feral growl. "Lupe," Sylvie said. She leaned on the door, slapped her palm against it repeatedly.

"I called the cops," a voice said. Sylvie jerked, found the day manager staring at her. Truculent, even in the face of her gun. Then again, he probably had one of his own.

"Great. You got a key?"

He stared at her, dark eyes under a crew cut, tattoos running the breadth of his thick neck. "Don't sue." He threw her the passkey and stomped back toward his office to wait for the cops.

Sylvie slapped the door again, said, "Lupe, I'm coming in."

Another whimper, another growl, a groan that was another voice altogether. What the hell was going on? She swiped the card through the reader, shoved the door open, and fell through the door.

Blood on the bed nearest the door. Bright and wet and freshly shed.

Dammit.

A crying woman in a long skirt huddled near the bathroom alcove. At Sylvie's entrance, she raised her head, eyes flaring wide with alarm. "Behind the door!"

Sylvie caught Lupe's wrist as the woman lunged—and it *was* Lupe-the-woman, which Sylvie was grateful for—and used Lupe's momentum against her, slung her onto the bed, crashing into the headboard. Crystal crunched beneath Sylvie's feet, cracked quartzite.

Lupe growled, a deep, inhuman rumble in her chest, and Sylvie snapped, "Stay there."

"She hurt me," Lupe said.

"It doesn't look like *your* blood," Sylvie said. Her client looked furious, close to insane, her hair a wild tangle, her eyes bloodshot, her hands clawing at the sheets, but she didn't look hurt.

"It shouldn't have hurt!" The woman—the witch—by the bathroom shrilled. She had reason to sound scared. It was her blood; the patterned skirt she wore was shredded. Her leg beneath the fabric was streaked and stippled with blood. Claw marks.

"Can you walk?" Sylvie said, cutting over her protests that she'd just been trying to help, that Lupe had gone berserk, that she'd tried to kill her—

"What?"

"Get out of here," Sylvie said.

"Not without Peter," the woman protested.

"Peter?" Sylvie echoed, and the low groan rose again. Keeping a careful eye on Lupe in case she freaked out again, Sylvie peered into the only space another person could be in: the gap between the beds.

The shadows separated themselves into a man in dark clothing crunched down into the gap.

"Fine," Sylvie said. "Get him up, go."

"But he's heavy—"

Sylvie lost patience. Sirens scaled through the air, getting closer. She leveled the gun at the witch, and said, "Should I motivate you?"

The woman scrambled to her feet, tripped over the edge of her skirt, gained her feet again, and started dragging her boyfriend out of the room. Sylvie waited until they had cleared the door to slam it closed.

"Get your stuff, Lupe."

"That bitch tried to *do something*—" Lupe said.

Sylvie did rapid math in her head. Another minute, maybe two for the cops to reach the motel, two minutes for them to get directions from the day manager, a minute to get their asses up the stairs.

"No time to talk," Sylvie said. "Move your ass, Lupe, or I'm leaving you here to deal with the police."

Lupe's jaw slammed shut; she snatched up her shoes. Sylvie grabbed her duffel bag, grabbed the woman's arm, and pulled her out the door, nearly tripping over the witch. No sense of self-preservation, Sylvie thought. The witch and her boyfriend should have been long gone; instead, the witch was trying to wake him, while they were still in the danger zone.

Lupe snarled; the woman yelped, and Sylvie jerked hard, her nails digging in to Lupe's skin. "Ignore her."

They descended the stairs in a slithering rush, half-falling, half-pulling, and Sylvie slammed Lupe up against the truck. "Get in."

Sylvie darted around the nose of her truck, got the engine started, and was backing out at speed before Lupe even had the passenger door shut. "You check in under your own name?" Sylvie's truck was distinctive, but not enough to randomly ID her. Not unless she was really unlucky, and it was a cop she knew.

Lupe's lips went tight and thin. Answer enough.

Sylvie slued the truck around and headed out of the lot as the cops were pulling in. She waited two heartbeats, three, checking her rearview to see if they were U-turning, then punched the accelerator.

They drove ten miles down the road before Sylvie pulled into a movie theater's crowded lot, parked her truck in a morass of other vehicles, and got out. She paced a tight circle, swearing, trying to figure the angles. So the cops had Lupe's name. They didn't have hers. Sylvie's truck was distinctive, but there were so many red Ford trucks in the city that the cops would get bored long before they ran down the one with the jagged scars in the hood.

Unless she was unlucky, and the cops were part of Suarez's brood. Then they'd know exactly who the truck belonged to. *Fuck.*

All right. If that was so, Suarez would come to her first. She could put him off. After all, no one was dead. No one was that badly injured. Sylvie hadn't committed the crime herself. She could come down hard on "I know nothing. Where's your warrant?" if she had to.

The witch . . . Lupe had torn up her leg, and pissing off witches was usually a one-way ticket to a nasty curse. Nastier than what Lupe was already suffering through? Not likely.

Sylvie let her breath out. Okay. She'd need to keep Lupe away from the cops, but that wasn't impossible. Not even particularly hard. Cash, another hotel, a tiny crime— hardly the kind of thing that would set them on a manhunt.

Annoying and time-consuming for Sylvie, and completely avoidable if Lupe had only listened.

She glared at Lupe through the truck window. Lupe glared right back, serpentine eyes gleaming in the shelter of the truck cab. Lupe didn't look like she'd learned her lesson. She looked pissed, even put-upon, as she crossed her hands over her chest and revealed that the nails of one hand were stained with blood.

What the hell happened?

When she put the question to Lupe, back in the close confines of the truck, her nerves prickling at the animal scent in the cab, Lupe stiffened in her seat, and said, "That witch fucked me up. Made things worse. She was just supposed to diagnose the curse. She brought it out. I changed, Sylvie. No moon, and I changed. Now it's right there, under my skin, ready to break free."

Sylvie tightened her jaw, said nothing. She couldn't think of anything to say immediately that wasn't an *I told you so* or *If you'd only done as I said*, and Lupe was nearly vibrating with tension, one breath from hysteria. "Tell me exactly what the witch did," Sylvie said, finally.

"What does it matter?" Lupe snapped.

Sylvie couldn't help but notice that Lupe's teeth were long and sharp, more than just the canines. Now, she had an entire mouthful of predator's teeth.

"Humor me," Sylvie said. "I just saved you from an awkward interview with the cops."

Lupe slipped out of the truck, letting her stress out by pacing just as Sylvie had done, kicking at the worn yellow lines on the pavement. "I don't know."

"Of course you know. You were there. Let's start. You were in the room, you called this witch who you didn't even know—"

Lupe growled.

"So you let her in. . . then what?"

"Her bodyguard sat on the other bed. Creeper. Just stared at us. Livvy—the witch—told me to lie down." Lupe's breath rasped in her throat. "I did. She put crystals on me, told me that they were going to find the seat of the curse . . . but they burned." She licked her lips, rubbed at her breastbone as if the heat remained. "I don't remember things clearly after that. She tried to get her bodyguard to hold me down. I think I bit him. And the heat just sort of . . . ripped me open, turning me inside out. Next thing I knew, she was screaming and throwing spells at me."

"Spells?" Sylvie said. She'd chalked the witch up as mostly show, a new age wannabe, who had managed to reach convinced-she-was status.

"Like wasps stinging. I don't know. She kinda got freaked when the spells didn't do much to me. Then you showed up."

"When did you get your licks in?" Sylvie asked. "Her leg was torn up."

"I don't know. Does it matter? She got what she deserved. Trying to trick me. Pretending she could help." Lupe's eyes flashed bright again, a glance Sylvie's way, her breath quickening. "Of course, that's all you're doing, isn't it? Stringing me along. Doing nothing? Studying me? Watching me get *worse*? Watching me become just like *him*?"

Her words grew thick, distorted; her face creaked strangely, as if the bones were shifting.

Sylvie had her gun up, leveled in Lupe's inhuman face by the time the woman lunged at her. Half animal. Human enough to recognize the weapon as a threat. Lupe dropped to a crouch, nails scratching at the concrete, the side of Sylvie's truck, the inhuman jut to her jaw shrinking.

"Back off. Back down. Chill the fuck out. Or we're going to have bigger problems than a pissed-off crystal witch and some overworked cops.

"I told you to let me handle it. But you couldn't trust me. You had to trust a stranger. You're lucky it ended the way it did. No one dead. Not them. Not you. You got a crap witch who exacerbated your curse. Boo hoo. You lucked out. You could have gotten the witch who said, 'Drink this! It'll help,' then vivisected you for spell components. Witches are tricky business. If I can't find someone local, I've got a backup plan—"

"Fuck plan A, I vote backup plan. And now," Lupe said. "Why are we waiting?"

"Because you're in no condition to face the TSA and an international flight. You lose control on a plane? Things can get worse, Lupe. Even if it doesn't seem like it."

Lupe nodded, calming down. Sylvie holstered her gun, noting that her fingers were trembling. She glared at them. They stopped.

"Why international?" Lupe said. "Another witch?"

"Yeah," Sylvie said. "One who's dealt with death curses before."

"Can the witch come here?"

"Working on that," Sylvie said. It was like the most frustrating game of missionaries and cannibals ever, all bounded around by difficult women: Erinya and Lupe and Val. Lupe couldn't fly to Ischia. Val wouldn't come back while Erinya was in Miami. And Erinya wasn't budging.

Sylvie had already struck one deal with the god—her

promise not to kill Demalion in exchange for god-power; Sylvie didn't have anything else to bribe Erinya with.

"Then what?" Lupe asked. "I just live like this? Turning into a bigger freak each day?"

"Better than the alternative," Sylvie said.

Lupe shut up, either shocked silent or furious.

The parking lot couldn't hold them for long. The movies had let out; people collected their cars, cast inquisitive glances in their direction—at the spectacle of two women arguing about witches, their voices carrying.

"Look," Sylvie said, dropping back to a whisper. "I'll think of something."

"Waiting sucks," Lupe said. "Where do I go now?"

"New hotel," Sylvie said. "We pay cash, keep a low profile."

"Yeah, 'cause a woman with snake eyes and fangs is so unmemorable," Lupe said. She flung up her hands before Sylvie could respond. "I know. I know. Better than the alternative."

"That's right," Sylvie said. She nodded toward the truck, and Lupe climbed into it, far more calmly this time.

Sylvie wished she thought the calm was more than skin deep. Lupe was breaking down, getting moodier, more aggressive with each day. The stunt with the witch hadn't helped.

But it had made one thing clear.

The witch really hadn't done anything wrong—she'd simply tried to run a diagnostic with the wrong tools. Sylvie had seen crystal witches work, using the clear stones to identify the type of curse—stones turning red, black, blue, all the shades of a malevolent rainbow. It was utterly passive, reactive magic.

Lupe shouldn't have had any reaction whatsoever.

If the stones had felt like they were burning her, that meant one thing only. The curse had dug its way in like a parasite, and fueled by a god's power, was actively protecting its new position.

Giving Lupe the happy ending she deserved was looking less likely by the moment.

6

Government Business

SYLVIE WAS EATING AN EARLY DINNER, HIDING OUT IN A PART OF town she didn't normally visit, waiting. Waiting for Suarez to see if her name had hit the system, if she could go home without getting dragged into the station by the police. Waiting for a call back from Alex to assure her that Zoe was home and bitchy and resting up from her jet lag.

Instead, she got Alex calling to say, "Sylvie. She's not here."

Sylvie flipped her watch—an hour past the time Zoe had said. "Delayed?"

"No," Alex said. "Her flight arrived on time. But I can't find her. I tried calling, but her cell's off."

Sylvie pushed her plate away, the sushi suddenly repulsive. Her heart beat unpleasantly. "Okay. This is what we're going to do. You're at the airport? Check to see if her luggage made it, and if it's still there."

"You think she had checked baggage?"

"It's Zoe. Of *course* she had checked baggage. Probably the maximum allowed." Sylvie closed her eyes, tried to remember. "I think it's dark green. Hard-sided. A matching set."

"Okay, what else?"

Sylvie sipped her tea, mostly lukewarm, set it back down. The cup chattered against the cherrywood tabletop. "You have your laptop?" She didn't wait for Alex's response, knew it would be a yes. "Dig up, oh. . . that smuggling case we had. Victor Arana. He owes us one. and he works at the airlines. Call him. See if Zoe ever got on the flight. If she's missing, we need to know which end it happened on."

Sylvie waved off the hovering waitress, trying to think of all the angles. NYC or Miami. Or god . . . Sylvie closed her eyes. The last time her family had been threatened, it had been Dunne doing the threatening. He wanted Erinya gone, and she hadn't agreed. He could have snatched Zoe from the plane anytime he wanted, midflight.

"All right," Alex said.

"Be careful. Keep me informed." A shadow crossed her table; she turned, and though it felt like turning away from her sister's plight, she disconnected. Suarez eased himself into the chair opposite her, rested scarred forearms on the table. The waitress brought him a menu, but he handed it back without looking at it, requesting coffee.

"So there's nothing on the line about you," Suarez said, his voice a deep, disapproving rumble. "Should there be? If I go through police logs, am I going to find something inexplicable with your name attached to it?"

"Not mine," Sylvie said. "My client's. She's got some anger-management issues at the moment. With reason."

"Yeah?"

Sylvie reached out, touched the scars on his arm, looked up at the scar winding over his face. "When you were in the hospital, I said you wouldn't turn into a monster after being attacked by a magical were-creature, told you shapeshifting via curse was rare."

"You did," he said.

"She wasn't as lucky as you. Azpiazu's curse shifted to her."

Suarez sat back, eyed her with a cop's ingrained suspicion. "You're volunteering information, Shadows. Why?"

"Because the way she's going, she might end up in your cells. You call me if that happens. It's not safe to keep her there. Not for your men. Or for her. Lupe Fernandez. You'll know her if you see her."

"Understood," he said.

Sylvie rose, and Suarez reached out with that quickness he had, so surprising in such a solid man. "Not so fast. Since you're in a sharing mood. I have two questions for you. There's some sort of monster killing people in Miami. You know what's doing it?"

"Depends," Sylvie said. "There are a lot of monsters in Miami."

He narrowed his gaze, losing patience. "Are you encouraging it?"

"Tell me about the people who've died."

"A woman, only this morning, fleeing down the street, swore that a monster tore her mother's head off and devoured her newborn baby. They sent her for a psychiatric evaluation. Last week, six men died, heads pulverized; witnesses claimed they saw something like an enormous cat. With feathers. Later, they recanted. Remembered nothing at all. What's happening? Tell me."

Sylvie debated pros and cons for a moment, then decided, hell with it. Suarez knew about the *Magicus Mundi*, and she didn't have time to play keep-away games. Truth, it was. The whole truth.

"We've got two separate problems, and neither is going to make you happy. The monster is the easy part. She's a Fury, and she's avenging dead or abused children."

"Enojada?" He sounded perplexed, and Sylvie remembered English was his second language. He was so fluent that she forgot. Not only that, but his curriculum would have been different. She wondered if they taught the Greek myths to children in Cuba, wondered belatedly why they taught Greek myths to American children anyway.

"One of the Eumenides," Sylvie said. "A Greek mythical monster, only less myth, more monster. A lonely creature, who's doing what we all do. Losing herself in work. Just, her work is full of dead people."

"Can I stop her from doing it? What do I need? SWAT team? Spell?"

"You can't stop her," Sylvie said. "The best you can do is take heart in the fact that she has very specific parameters for her kills. And that, so far, she has some sense of collateral-damage control."

Suarez growled. "A murderer who kills undesirables is still a murderer."

"Suarez, please," Sylvie said. "I don't have time to fight her now. I've got a client in bad shape, I've got the ISI bringing serious trouble to the city, and I've got a missing sister."

"Again?" Suarez said. "Leash that girl. She's trouble."

"She might be *in* trouble."

"Don't count on me to rescue her. We're short-staffed. Fifteen of our officers had to rush to the hospital today because their parents had had strokes or heart attacks while watching the morning news. When they did call in, they said the ERs were overwhelmed. I might not have your inside knowledge, but something seems wrong about that."

"I don't suppose mermaids mean anything to you?"

Suarez winced, pinched the high bridge of his nose, and Sylvie said, "That's what I thought. That, right there, is our second problem. Someone's playing cleanup with our brains. Well, your brains. Making you forget anything you were exposed to that was blatantly *mundi*. You didn't take any of those monster calls yourself, right?"

"That's right," he said. "People told me about them."

"I bet if you talk to the woman sent for the psych evaluation about her mother and the monster now, she'll remember something different. Will get a headache if you press. Might even stroke out, depending on her overall health. I bet your men won't be much different."

Suarez dropped his hand, stared at it in horror. "They

made me forget something? Like Garza did when you helped him?"

"You remember that, though," Sylvie said. "That I dealt with Garza in the Keys?"

"*Maudits*, you said."

"I did." This was part of what was making her crazy. The results of the memory wiping seemed so scattershot. Secondhand info relayed to someone who hadn't been a part of the original scene stayed just fine. Sylvie wondered what would have happened if Garza had written up truthful reports. Would they have altered like the video feeds? Would all the cops who read the report have their minds altered, like the TV viewers?

Sylvie thought the answer was probably yes.

"Who's doing it?" Suarez said. "And why?"

"Witches," Sylvie said. Witches were the most likely suspects. Anything more powerful—like a god—would be doing a better job. Anything less powerful than a full coven of witches, and the memory plague wouldn't be so wide-spread. The *Mundi*, as Sylvie had noted before, didn't cooperate with each other, and that ruled them out.

"*Brujas?*" Suarez seemed skeptical, which Sylvie thought was unfair of him. Azpiazu had nearly ripped Miami apart, which Suarez knew, and he'd started off as a witch.

"A whole coven of witches. More specifically than that, I can't tell you. Why? I don't know. I'm not sure who's benefiting. Whether it's 'to protect society' bullshit, or whether they're protecting the *Mundi* from discovery."

"Nothing good comes from secret workings," Suarez said. "Those who hold power should be transparent in their use of it."

"Don't have to sell me on that," Sylvie said.

"So, how will you identify this coven if you don't know its motive?"

Sylvie's phone buzzed. "Hold that thought."

"She got to Miami," Alex said. Her voice was thin and tight. Worried. "Victor found a flight attendant who remem-bered her—tried to carry on too much luggage, threw a bit of a fuss. Zoe is kind of a pain, but I guess, in this situation, it's a good thing."

"Alex," Sylvie snapped. "You're stalling. Where is she?"

"Four men in fancy suits and guns snagged her as she stepped out of the gate. Gate attendant noticed because Zoe dropped her carry-on, and they didn't bother to pick it up. Said the suits had to be official since they were armed within the terminal."

"ISI," Sylvie said.

"That's what I'm thinking."

"But they're dead. The flood destroyed their base. How in hell do they have time to hunt down Zoe?"

Suarez leaned in, shamelessly eavesdropping. Sylvie didn't care; she was recalculating. The mermaids had killed the ISI agents who were *there*. But, like Yvette, maybe others had been out of the office.

". . . want me to see if I can get video feed?"

"No," Sylvie said. She was slow, so slow. How had she forgotten? When the ISI had tear-gassed her office and kid-napped her, she had woken up in a different facility than the downtown hotel. "I'm going straight to Dominick Rior-dan. If the ISI is grabbing my sister, he's got to be alive."

· · ·

IT WAS LONG PAST FULL DARK BY THE TIME SYLVIE MANAGED TO retrace her path from the frantic night three months prior. Then, she'd been concentrating more on getting away and stopping Azpiazu, the Soul-Devourer, than on figuring out where she'd been held.

By starting at Vizcaya, still being repaired from the showdown with Azpiazu, and working her way back, she thought she was on the right track. It had been on a frontage road near the airport, but it hadn't been one of the dozens of warehouses that sprouted in that area; it had been a business-office type of building, with at least two floors.

She slowed her already crawling pace, and the driver behind her honked and cut around her. Sylvie peered into the dark, trying to focus, trying to remember. There had been a parking garage full of matching SUVs. White-painted concrete already going green. A shadow in her memory smelling like mold—everything underground in Miami smelled like mold.

Up ahead, a sign flashed in her headlights, a time-faded declaration that Miami's Best Bank would be opening soon. A bank she'd never heard of. *Opening never,* Sylvie thought. Not if it was a front for the ISI.

She jerked the wheel, garnered another series of traffic complaints, and crossed a narrow bridge over a watery ditch with pretensions to canalhood.

Sylvie bumped over the rough pavement, remembered that jarring sensation from her previous visit, and turned again sharply, picking a darker space out of an unlit lot that turned into a parking garage. One level down, lights bloomed distantly, showed a shiny row of dark SUVs and water glistening in thin trails down the walls. It made Sylvie think about mermaids.

Her nerves coiled and twisted. God, she wished Demalion had picked up a phone, wished he'd given her some way to contact him. She was used to going it alone, but right now, she wanted backup, and he was her first choice. Now and always.

Erinya could be called, but Erinya came with her own problems. If Zoe was in the ISI building, then Erinya was the last thing she needed. Zoe wouldn't thank Sylvie for causing all her witchy powers to be burned away.

Sylvie backed into a parking slot, put the truck in park, and stared into the depths of garage and the discreet elevator. She didn't see any surveillance cameras, but she didn't doubt they were there. The ISI liked to watch.

She wondered, if things went wrong—if she disappeared into their holding cells instead of pulling Zoe out of them—if Alex would call up the video feed to be witness to it. Wondered how many agents were left. Riordan to give the orders. Four to pick up Zoe.

Don't forget Demalion.

An uneasy squirm of unpleasant emotion crawled

through her at that thought, made her jaw clench and her heart sink—unhappiness? betrayal? worry? Rather than dwell on it, she climbed out of her truck and went to face the music.

It sounded sooner than she'd expected. She rounded her truck's scarred nose and found Dominick Riordan holding the elevator open for her, spotlighted in the otherwise-dimly-lit garage. A faint smile crossed his patrician face, showing a sliver of polished teeth. "Well, it's about time. I was beginning to think we were going to have to send up flares."

His voice was lovely, mellow and deep. It worked like nails on a chalkboard for Sylvie.

"I have an office, with office hours," Sylvie said. "I know you know where it is. You gassed it, robbed it, and wrecked it just three months ago. If you wanted to talk, you knew where to find me."

Riordan said, "Your office also has a guard dog of a particular ferociousness, and I'm down men already. Did you bring her with you?"

"Does it look like I brought anyone in with me? Do you see her sitting in my truck? Or launching herself at your throat?"

"No," he said. "I don't. Which is odd to me, Shadows. Here you have this powerful attack dog, and you're not using her." He smiled again, a fuller thing that made his eyes bright with pleasure. Made him look like a nice guy. "Which makes me think you *can't* use her."

"Or maybe I don't need her for the likes of you. Seems to me your lot is folding all on your own. Mermaids, Riordan? Sand wraiths? Succubi? I don't need to call on Erinya. You're fucked."

Riordan's lips flattened, but he wasn't goaded into temper. That was the problem with him, Sylvie thought. He was always so measured. So damn rational. Usually people shot off their mouths around her, goaded into it by her rudeness, by the desire to prove her wrong. Riordan just observed, calculated, then struck.

"Tone down your glee," Riordan said. "You have hostages to fate here, or did you forget who brought you to my door?"

Sylvie swallowed back her retort, caught by the plural. *Hostages.* She hadn't expected a plural. Zoe, yes. Who else?

Riordan said, "Your sister's actually been helpful, though I doubt that was her intention. She saw a certain agent in the halls and hailed him by a dead man's name. Pled with him for help that he's now in no position to give. Come along, Shadows. Let's talk."

He stepped back from the entry of the elevator, gestured her in. Sylvie saw no option but to follow his lead.

· · ·

RIORDAN WASN'T ALONE IN THE ELEVATOR. AS SHE STEPPED IN, THE agent holding the door open released the button and turned his attention to her. "Hand over your weapon," he said.

"Think you can make me?" Sylvie asked.

He took a step toward her, and she took that same step closer to Riordan, a quick two-step made awkward by the close confines of the elevator. Riordan pressed his code into the keypad, selected the top floor.

"Relax, Powell. Shadows can keep her weapon. She knows to be mindful of what she does with it."

"I do?" Sylvie said, as the elevator glided into motion, ticking upward. Too much to hope for that Zoe would be at the top. More likely, she was in one of the holding cells, and Sylvie recalled the chill damp of them, thought they must be pressed up against the parking-garage wall. The elevator was taking her farther away.

Riordan said, "You're much less impulsive than your reputation states. You control yourself well enough that your crimes have raised suspicion but nothing approximating proof. Shoot an ISI agent, and you'll be in jail."

"For as long as Erinya left me there. She doesn't like me in distress. You should have seen her with the mermaids."

"I am honestly sorry to have missed it," Riordan said.

"Wait," Sylvie said. "You know about the mermaids?"

"My son told me about them."

"He remembers them?" Sylvie thought back. The other witnesses didn't. But then, he'd fought off their song also. "That's right. He's a witch."

"Of course he's not," Riordan said. Faint distaste drew his mouth down.

Before Sylvie could delve deeper, the elevator motor traded its whisper for a sudden whine and grind of machinery. The lights snapped off, plunging them into darkness.

Sylvie dodged Powell's inevitable lunge, put her elbow into his ribs, put her gun to his throat, and pushed him back. He went.

"Shoot her, boss, don't worry about me," Powell said, voice strained.

Riordan sighed. "No one's shooting anyone. Shadows, you doing this?"

"Trapped in an elevator doesn't get me closer to Zoe."

"Boss," Powell said.

"Shut up, Powell. Listen. We have bigger problems than an unexpected stop."

Through the muffling thickness of the elevator doors and shaft, Sylvie heard rapid cracks of gunfire and shouts made distant by architecture. A battle being fought.

"Shadows, let go of my man and let's get this door opened."

"How about instead of just plain out, we go up and out," Sylvie said. "Just in case someone's aiming those guns at the elevator door. Your doors might be bulletproof, I'm not."

"My men are in trouble. I don't want to waste time clambering up a shaft. We're going through the doors," Riordan said.

Even under stress, he sounded calm, in control. Sylvie envied him. She hadn't felt in control for days. She released Powell. The big man shoved past her to help Riordan pry open the doors. Sylvie leaned against the back wall and tried to stay out of their way.

The air in the elevator, against the laws of probability,

was cooling instead of growing stuffier with three people's trapped breath and bodily exertion. She fumbled through her pockets, hunting for the tiny penlight she kept on her keychain. She pressed the button down, illuminating the small space before her. Something darkly vaporous jerked back from the light, streamed up into the elevator vent. It looked like smoke, but moved like ink in water, spreading and seeking.

"What was that?" Powell asked, jerking around in the shift of light and shadow. His eyes were wild. Riordan, Sylvie noticed, was unruffled.

"Your saboteur," Sylvie said. "I don't think it's human. I think it's come to finish the job the mermaids started."

"Powell, the doors." Riordan eyed Sylvie in the eerie greenish glow of the penlight, and said, "You ready?"

"Yeah," Sylvie said.

"Don't shoot my men. Shoot everything else," Riordan said.

Powell and he made progress; the elevator doors grumbled but slid apart. "Go," he told Sylvie.

Sylvie studied the gap. Definitely wide enough, split by two levels, leaving her with a choice—to enter the upper floor crawling, her gun hand hampered, or to drop an unknown distance into a darkness deep enough that her little penlight couldn't begin to penetrate it. Neither idea appealed, but she chose to drop. Zoe, after all, was beneath them somewhere.

She passed Riordan the useless light.

She braced herself in the width of the space, heard voluptuous movement in the darkness, like velvet rolling over stone, and tightened her grip on her gun. One last breath, and she dropped.

The floor was farther down than she'd hoped—one of those office buildings that prided itself on high ceilings—and forced a grunt out of her. Her free hand felt damp marble; she smelled fear sweat and blood and bile, and it was cold enough she thought her breath must be clouding the air before her. It made no sense. It was Miami, for

God's sake, and the power was out. The rooms should be gaining heat, not losing it.

It was the cold of morgues, of underground mausoleums, dank like an abandoned animal's lair. Empty of everything but death.

Sylvie's fingers were sticky, clammy with old blood; she brushed them against her sleeves, felt the contaminant liquefy and seep into the fabric, chilling her. She was the only breathing thing she could hear, her heart a desperate drum looking for an echo. Death rolled over her like a shroud.

She was alone, and everyone else was dead and gone—rotting—and she was alone. Her breath seized.

Riordan dropped to the ground beside her, said, "When you enter a hostile room, clear the area and get out of the way, dammit, do you know nothing?" It was like a wave breaking. An external influence breaking. Her ears popped; the sound of the world returned in a roar of gunfire and Riordan muttering about untrained lone wolves with delusions of competence.

Even her skin felt dry and warm again, the cold blood only an illusion of some kind. She should have known better.

"Powell, get down here," Riordan said.

Harsh panting was the only answer, and Sylvie turned. Riordan flashed the penlight once, briefly, and Powell jerked. His eyes had iced over, gone cataract white, faintly luminescent in the blackness. He pointed his gun at them, and said, "You're trying to kill me! It's a trap, and you want to grind me up in it!"

Sylvie darted away from the elevator doors, running blind in the darkness, away from Powell's shooting after them. She heard Riordan keeping pace, a rhythm of footsteps and breath beside her. He veered suddenly, tackled her to the floor.

She punched him. He reeled, and said, "There's a staircase, Shadows. You were heading straight for it. Say thank you."

"You deserved it anyway," Sylvie growled. "My sister's somewhere in this nightmare, isn't she?"

"She should be safe," Riordan said. "Locked up nice and tight. Do you know what we're dealing with?"

"Something that's radiating influence. I think your men are killing each other, losing it like Powell did."

"Like you did?" Riordan said.

Sylvie swallowed, said, "How better to know what's going on than to let it affect me for a moment?" Sounded good. She wished it were true. "What about you. You going to start shooting at me?"

Her eyes were finally adjusting to the darkness. She couldn't see anything much, but she got the sense of shapes, the slightly paler black where the walls were, the endless black gap where the stairs were, the moving darkness where Riordan shifted to a crouch. If she read the space right, they were on a balcony overlooking the lobby below. Stairs ahead. Offices to her left. A glass barrier between her and a long fall. Echoes of gunfire bounced off the ceiling and made it hard to tell if fights were going on above and below or just echoing upward. A sudden draft, a rush of displaced air suggested a body falling from above. The gruesome *thud* and *crunch* of that same body hitting the floors below suggested that both directions were treacherous.

Riordan swore quietly, said, "If I shoot you, Shadows, you can be sure I'll be doing it of my own will. Not someone else's."

"You're immune?"

"I've never been one for feeling fear. What are we facing, Shadows?"

"Headaches and a good possibility of bullet holes? I don't know. I didn't know in the elevator, and I don't know now. I can make some guesses. It's a monster. It's not happy."

"Can you kill it?"

Sylvie shivered. Her little dark voice whispered. *We can kill anything.* "First I have to find it." That wouldn't be hard, really. The monster would be ground zero, the only calm place in the midst of chaos, spreading its influence— those inky tendrils—wider and wider. "It'd be easier if there were lights. I thought you agency types were big on emergency power supplies."

"We are," Riordan said. "But our generators are inside the building. Vulnerable to bullets, or men under the influence."

"Okay. Two questions. How many men do you have left?"

"None of your business."

"If I have to fight my way through them, it is. I'm not bulletproof."

"You keep saying that."

"It bears repeating." It was comforting in a panic-inducing sort of way. She might be immortal, but she was still human.

"More men than you'd like," Riordan said. "We were transitioning from the hotel to this building after the earlier attacks on the other ISI branches, trying to minimize civilian risk."

"Good job, then," Sylvie said. "Too little, too late."

"This is hardly the time to assign blame," Riordan said. "Would you prefer to argue or survive?"

Sylvie hated to admit it, but he was right. "Fine. Second question. Flashlights?"

He passed her back the penlight, and she said, "That's not gonna cut it. I need to see what I'm walking into."

"Demanding," he said. "Wait here."

"Get two if you can."

He shifted around her, made her realize that their drop-and-hide spot was more sheltered than she'd thought—she reached back, felt a jut in the wall. An alcove looking over the lobby. If this were a real office building, it would probably have held a water fountain.

She had time to think. Time to kill. She laughed, soundlessly, a little closer to hysteria than she'd admit. Hunting monsters in the dark to save her sister, and God, Demalion—where was he in all this? Locked up tight with Zoe? Safe? Or roaming the halls, shooting at everything he could. If

Demalion was out there, prone to the same panic that Powell had fallen prey to, he'd be lethal. Paranoia plus psychic abilities? Ugly.

She wished she knew what she was dealing with. It wasn't a succubus. Wasn't anything attached to elements: no sand wraiths, no mermaids, no fiery salamanders, and, despite the smoky tentacles in the air, she didn't think it was any type of air elemental.

It wasn't a succubus, but it was something that worked on a similar principle. Used the body to overwhelm the brain. Whatever this was spread panic and paranoia as easily as a succubus spread lust and hunger.

Movement near her, and she turned, a "Took your time" on her lips. It wasn't Riordan. She caught the faint glimmer of eyes with an icy shine and held her breath. The tainted agent went past, limping, his breath wheezing and whispering out insanity. *Not my teeth. Can't take them. Not for you. Kill you first.*

Sylvie wiped her face. This was all a little too zombie apocalypse for her. She wondered if Zoe was terrified, pissed, or trying to work magic. She wondered if Zoe was still alive.

Riordan returned, passed her a flashlight, kept his hand over the switch, and said, "Don't turn it on yet."

"Not stupid," Sylvie murmured. "You get one for yourself?"

"I did."

"Good. While I'm hunting monsters? You're going to fix the damn generator."

7

Bureaucracy & Other Monsters

ONCE RIORDAN LEFT HER SIDE—A BRUSH OF DARKNESS, HIS FOOT-steps fading, his warmth receding—and Sylvie was certain that she was the only living thing in close proximity, she hit the switch of the heavy Maglite. The beam shot out like a laser; dark, vaporous tendrils scattered beneath it, left roiling crimson ghosts behind. Sylvie swept the light across in precise arcs, illuminating the space around her, the stairs ahead of her—pale marble streaked with blood—a bulky shadow of a dead man on the first landing, two more on the landing below that, but overall, a clear enough path for her to tread. She raised the light higher—swept out across the lobby, dispelling darkness, swept the light across, down, over, and around, trying to memorize every-thing in a second's worth of illumination.

Then she flicked the light off, traded positions for another sheltering alcove, this one in the doorway of an empty office. Once certain she had a moment, she closed her eyes and played it all back.

The lobby proved that the building had been designed to throw off any casual looky-loos who might suspect the bank was more than it seemed. The lobby was a classic bank lobby, a central atrium stretching up all four floors, the walls and floors a symphony of dark marble, pale inlaid wood, and polished brass and glass. Around the core, offices and hallways branched off, dark arteries that she diagnosed by their stubborn refusal to reflect light, and by the echoes of gunfire coming from them. Everyone in the atrium was dead.

Not everyone, her little dark voice reminded her.

Everyone, Sylvie insisted. The only thing standing down there wasn't a person.

No matter what it looked like—a woman in a dark dress standing dead center in the atrium, surrounded by bodies, uncaring of the continuing gunfire, the shouting, or the blood wicking up her skirt—three floors below, stood a monster.

Something horribly, terribly unnatural that was mimicking a human form. Just recalling her made Sylvie's heart stutter a beat.

Nightmares, her little dark voice said.

Her skin, her hair, her clothes were the void of a starless night; her face seemed featureless but for the gloss of eye shine, the sudden shocking scarlet of a tongue that had swept across her lips. That icy vapor swirled around her, waiting her commands. No, she *was* the vapor, a constant release and collection that blurred the lines of her being. Around her, agents died, and the perfect void of her face held a smile.

And somewhere down there, Zoe and Demalion.

Riordan was a bastard, but he'd reacted to this disaster as neatly as if he'd planned for it. She had her gun, a light, a motive to go down and solve his problem for him. To kill the monster between her and her sister. To save his wretched agency. Again.

All she had to do was kill the monster before the remaining agents, maddened by the monster's presence, found her and added her blood to the scarlet slicks already greasing the floors.

Sylvie clutched the flashlight—the vapor pulled back from the light, that was something—and her gun. Anticipating trouble below, she was caught by surprise by the agent who loomed out of nowhere right next to her, his eyes frosted over, gleaming in the dark, his breathing harsh and giving way into manic babble. *I'm falling. I'm falling. You pushed me. Falling.*

She slashed the flashlight beam across his face, and he didn't even flinch, blind to the real world, blind to the darkness around him. On his eyes, the frost crackled, and he leaped at her. She reversed the flashlight, caught him solidly in the head, and he dropped.

"Didn't shoot him," she muttered. "Hope you're happy, Riordan."

The stairs beckoned, and she started down them, the temperature plummeting with every step she took, raising goose bumps on her flesh.

Her shoes whispered on the edges of the stairs, the soft sandpaper guides warning her when to step, but they also woke rhythmic echoes of the babbling panic from the two affected agents. *Not my teeth. Can't take them. I'm falling. You pushed me.* Bizarre. Disquieting.

Oddly familiar.

She ran her tongue over her own teeth, tasted the scent of blood in the air, and paused. Imagined tipping over a cliff and falling.

Nightmares, her little dark voice had said.

Not nightmares. The *creator* of them. Sylvie fished through her memory banks, overstuffed due to Alex's non-stop researching. *The Mora.*

She tasted the words on her lips, realized she'd said it aloud, and felt the icy vapor pour up the stairs toward her. With one careless moment, she'd betrayed her presence to the monster.

As Demalion had said: Nothing got someone's attention like the sound of their name.

• • •

"DO YOU COME TO CHALLENGE ME?"

The Mora's voice, without even a shred of humanity in

it, evoked the sound of a creaking door in a dark house, a footstep where none should be, the last breath of a man who had just stepped off a cliff. It made Sylvie's steps falter; she tasted fear, felt sweat spring up along her hairline.

She kept her mind focused, one step at a time, following the remembered beam of light downward. The Mora waited below with the deadly patience of a high-ranking predator.

When Sylvie reached the lobby, black vapor swirled away from her like smoke in a draft and bared marble floors to her dark-adjusted eyes. A pathway, leading directly to the monster. "Why do you face me?" the Mora asked. "What makes you think you can?"

"I want answers." She forced bravado into her voice, made it harsh and rough and *vital*. Everything this creature wasn't.

"I have no answers for you," the Mora said in her cracked-ice voice. "Only fears."

Between one step and the next, the vapor rose over Sylvie and her flashlight like a cresting wave, and dropped her into a carousel of horrifying images. Sylvie's parents dead. Demalion dead. Riordan gutting Zoe on a dissection table. Erinya devouring her whole. Nightmare imagery circling her like a swarm of stinging insects.

As if they were stinging insects, Sylvie swatted them away and kept moving forward. "I've looked into a Fury's eyes. Your nightmares don't compare to that. Tell me who sent you here."

"Sent me? This is my city, my home. I traveled here in frightened men's minds, coming across the sea. I thrive here, feeding my dreams into human minds, eating their last breaths as their hearts give out.

"Everyone is weak in their nightmares," the Mora said. "Even you."

More images, closer to home. Less death, more trauma. Failing her clients, failing Lupe, watching the city crumble about her, while she stood powerless, her gun emptied.

Sylvie took those nightmares and used them to hone her

purpose. She wouldn't fail. Her sister depended on her. "But you're not feeding. You're making a statement. It's not your statement. Whose is it?"

"For all our kind," the Mora said. "To show your world that they would do well to remember us." The words whispered around Sylvie, brushed her skin like the first warning tingle of frostbite.

"No argument from me," Sylvie said. "But why now? From what I understand—"

"You understand nothing—"

"—there's not a lot of sharing and caring in the *Magicus Mundi*. A sand wraith, succubus, mermaids. You all get the same bee in your bonnet at the same time? No. Someone's guiding you." Her mouth and throat were sore, as if some part of her was shrieking under the constant bombardment of nightmare imagery. It was getting harder and harder to keep the Mora in focus. If she blinked, the real world, already hazy and dark as dreams, was replaced by the Mora's questing imagery. Trying to find Sylvie's weaknesses, the things that made her sick and mindless with terror.

"You'll never know," the Mora said, and the black wave of nightmare slammed over her, shoving her back physically, knocking her to the floor, pouring itself down her throat, through her eyes, and took her into dream hell. "You'll die alone in your dreams."

Unlike the mermaids and their killing waves, which wanted to crush the life out of her, this dark undertow took her out of herself and dropped her into the Mora's turbid, icy darkness. Took away all the images that she had been bombarded with, all the mundane horrors of losing family and friends, of her failures. Sucked into the Mora's empty heart.

Alone.

Disarmed.

Naked.

Helpless.

Pain lanced through her joints—shoulders and knees and elbows and ankles—spears of dragging agony, and she jerked her head against the weight, trying to see. Trying to assess the threat, even as she tried to scream. Dreamlike, her voice was sucked away. Fine golden cables, slicked with her blood, jutted out from her body in a familiar pattern.

God's little marionette, the Mora whispered, and flicked one of the cables. Sylvie's body jerked in helpless reaction.

You can fight but only so far as he allows you to do. You're prideful. Useless. A puppet.

No, Sylvie said. Silence throttled her, brutalized her throat.

All alone. Eternally alone.

Sylvie shuddered; the cables hissed and sang with her trembling.

You'll kill or outlive them all.

You'll be alone, and when he starts speaking to you, you'll be grateful, so grateful for a voice that you'll be obedient. A perfect killing machine, mindless, falsely rebellious . . . a lonely puppet.

Voice, Sylvie thought. There was already a voice in her head. One that never left her. One that even now swarmed up through her blood, through the dark backbrain in her mind, growling, flashing feral teeth. The cables pinning her shoulders snapped, lashed out into the darkness like striking snakes.

The Mora's whispered torment stopped.

Sylvie felt her little dark voice, that bitter, angry piece of Lilith, clawing its way through her throat, bursting through that dream silence.

"The thing is," Sylvie gasped, and her words birthed themselves physically, fell into her hands, each of them a gleaming silver bullet, "I'm not sure I'm alone in my head."

A full clip of bullets, slammed into a gun created out of the dream-darkness, aimed unerringly at the darkest spot, the black-hole heart of the Mora. Sylvie pulled the trigger and filled the monster full of gun flare and silver light. The darkness spiderwebbed and dissolved like ink under bleach. The Mora shrieked, and Sylvie rolled to her feet, slipping on the wet marble, rubbing blood away from her ears, the corners of her eyes.

The darkness in the bank lobby changed, tinted toward a more regular darkness, one being slowly thinned by the false dawn penetrating through the glass facade of the building.

The Mora was gone; only a black stain and cracked marble showed where she had stood. Sylvie crouched, touched the floor, her fingertips mapping holes where imaginary bullets had had real impacts.

Sylvie backtracked, found the flashlight and her gun, both dropped when the Mora had attacked her.

In the Mora's absence, the building seemed racked with silence, that hush after a disaster. It wouldn't last long, and in fact, as soon as Sylvie thought that, she heard screaming— not the desperate shouts she had heard earlier, men and women reeling under the Mora's manipulation—but true horror. Sylvie wondered bleakly how many agents were coming back to themselves with spent clips and dead colleagues at their feet.

Sylvie hated the ISI but could still spare a brief spurt of sympathy for that type of awakening. Then a woman's voice rose sharp and shrill over the rest, echoing through the open spaces, and Sylvie thought, *Zoe.*

Her sympathy fled.

Hallways stretched off the lobby, dark holes in the world, and Sylvie tried to orient herself. The cells were near the garage. *Which way is the garage?*

Sylvie turned on the flashlight, wincing as it took out her dark-adapted eyes, hoped she wasn't making herself a clear target, and chose a hallway.

Even with the flashlight's beam, the hallways had dark edges. She juggled the gun and the flashlight, trying to keep the light far enough away from her body that a shooter couldn't use it as a crosshairs.

Some part of her brain made a note: Buy tac light for gun. Too many of the things she hunted prowled the darkness.

Sound up ahead, almost animal. Rasping breaths, a low whine. Sounds that were entirely human. The rasp of fabric, the scrabble of hands on a hard surface. At least one agent, more likely two, still fighting, trapped in the darkness.

Or one agent and Zoe, trying to tear each other's throat out.

Sylvie hastened into the dark more quickly than was wise.

. . .

THE FLOOR BENEATH HER WAS HARD AND SLICK, GREASED WITH what she hoped was recent waxing, a spilled drink, anything but the lake of blood she imagined. If it were blood, she'd expect to smell it, strong as sun-warmed pennies, but with the Mora-induced fighting, the entire building stank of blood and desperation. This was just more of the same.

A sudden sharp gasp, a pained groan, and a man's curse—Sylvie hastened her steps. She recognized that groan, that curse, breathless with effort and pain—*Demalion*.

God, she wanted lights!

For once, something in the world went her way. An angry mechanical grinding started, a motor revving up, then the emergency generator kicked in and set amber lights flickering throughout the building. Riordan had finally come through.

After the Mora's darkness, it seemed as bright as sunlight and made her blink tears away. She found herself about to walk into a wall, thanked the lights for coming back at just the right moment, and made the hard jog to the right.

Demalion and an agent were a tangled knot half on the floor, half against the wall, both of them grimacing in pain. Demalion's face showed a grim determination, while the agent's showed confusion—coming out of the Mora's spell, the realization there was no enemy. His grip slackened and Demalion lunged forward, head-butted him, and sent him to unconsciousness. Demalion rose, swayed dizzily, and said, "Bastard's got a hard head."

As if to prove it, the man started groaning and twitching again, fighting his way back to awareness. His gun holster was empty, and Sylvie sought the gun first, just in case. She found it, unfired, full clip, beneath a narrow, decorative table. When she turned, she realized she was leaving bloody footprints on the pale marble. Guess it hadn't been a spilled drink after all.

"Where's Zoe?" Sylvie said. "I thought you were being held with her."

"Yeah. Your sister's not real big on keeping her mouth shut, is she? Riordan's guys drag her in, and before I can even start thinking of a way to get her out, she starts bitching at me, calling me by name."

"You were going to get her out?"

Demalion shot her an ugly look. "Jesus Christ, Sylvie. Of course I was. She might be a pain in the ass, and a witch wannabe, but she's your sister, and more importantly? She hadn't done anything wrong."

"Where is she?" Sylvie repeated. She didn't have time to apologize, didn't have time to explore the warmth that bloomed—he was choosing her.

Of course, his cover's been blown, the little dark voice said, purveyor of all things cynical. *Choosing you is just sensible.*

Sylvie stifled a wild giggle. Choosing her was many things. Sensible wasn't one of them. No one sane threw his lot in with her.

"This way," Demalion said. He paused. "Grab his legs, would you? We'll throw him in a cell. See how he likes it."

Sylvie shook her head. "I want my gun hand free."

"You killed the monster, right?"

"Monster's gone. The agents aren't."

"You can't shoot—"

"Demalion! Zoe. Now. Move."

Demalion yanked off his belt, flipped the agent over, bound his hands together, and said, "Fine. But when he gets out of that—"

"We'll have Zoe and be long gone."

Demalion pushed through a nondescript door, and Sylvie found herself back on the ISI cellblock. Three months after her own incarceration, and she was pleased to see that it was still just a few cells; she was less pleased when she realized all the doors were standing open.

Her heart plummeted.

Open and *empty*.

She turned that crushing disappointment and fear on Demalion, turned to shove him away from her. "Where the hell is she?" Farther down the hall, she saw a crumpled body, but it was wearing a grey suit, another ISI agent.

"She was there," Demalion said, shaking her off, peering into the end cell as if she had simply missed seeing her sister.

"You got out," Sylvie said, "and you left Zoe?"

Demalion checked each room, checking the shadows beneath the bunks, his mouth set in a grim line. Sylvie felt her heart jerk. Looking for a body.

"I saw the monster coming in my mind. I kicked up a fuss. None of the agents wanted to listen, but, finally, one did. He opened the door to find out what I was talking about, and the lights went out. The agent in the hall started shooting a second later. I told Zoe to hide. When I left, she was whispering spells. I was going to scope out our escape route, then my guard dog tackled me."

"So where is she now? There's only one door in or out of here, Demalion." She put her back to him, stared into the empty cell as if she could will secrets out of it. All she got was a sink, a bunk, and a noted absence of people.

"It's not my base," Demalion said. "I don't know who or how."

"Whatever. Let's find her." She couldn't have gotten far, would still be within the ISI's confines.

"We still need to have that talk, Shadows," Riordan said, coming around that blind corner with three of his men on his heels. They looked the worse for wear and ready to take it out on her and Demalion.

"Just tell me where she is, and you can consider it coming out ahead. I killed your monster after all."

Demalion's hand tightened on Sylvie's forearm, tension

translating through touch. She read it clearly. Don't get sucked in.

Easy for him to say. He was out of the cage. He was close to free, and Zoe was God knows where.

"Let's deal, Shadows. I get what I want from you, and I don't dissect your sister to see what witchcraft looks like on the DNA level."

Sylvie tore free of Demalion's grip, slammed into Riordan, got him against the wall, her gun in his throat, before the guards could act, slowed by their shock and long night. "I saved your son's fucking life this morning. And you repay me by snatching my sister? What the fuck is wrong with you people? No wonder the *Mundi*'s coming after you. I wish I could watch you all burn."

Riordan coughed, tilted his head away from her gun as much as he could, and said, "That's why I took her. Someone's gunning for the ISI? Your sister's my bullet shield. At least that way I don't have to worry about you as well as the monsters."

"Monsters," Sylvie said. "Look in any mirrors, recently?"

"Get her off of me," Riordan said. "She won't shoot. It's a bluff."

"You sure?" Sylvie said.

"You could kill me," he said. "But Zoe's with my son, and he has standing orders."

"Now who's bluffing?" Sylvie said.

"Can you risk it?"

Sylvie's blood beat hard in her temples.

Demalion said, "Sylvie."

She holstered her gun though her throat felt like she was swallowing battery acid. "A bullet shield's only effective short-term. You took Zoe for a reason. Stop fucking around, Riordan, and tell me. What do I have to do to get Zoe back?"

Demalion's warmth was like a brand at her back; his shoulders were tight against hers, letting her know, even without looking, that he was watching the other agents.

"Let's talk privately," he said. "You men can go. I

believe Shadows can be reasonable. Given the circumstances."

They disappeared, reluctantly, the last man baring bloodied teeth at her.

"Please," Riordan said. He gestured toward one of the holding rooms.

"You first," Sylvie said.

"Of course," Riordan said.

He was back to smug; Sylvie fought her baser instinct to shut the door on him and walk away. Wouldn't help anything.

"You're right," Riordan said, as she and Demalion filed in after him. "I do want something from you. I want you to kill a man."

Sylvie frowned, felt skepticism bubble up in her blood again. Demalion twitched hard beside her. Having his remaining illusions broken, she thought. Today, he'd learned the ISI was willing to kidnap teenagers for ransom, willing to farm out murder.

"What, Marah's too busy?"

"Too invested," Riordan said. "I'm not sure it would be a good idea."

"She has a softer side? Where is she, anyway?"

"Ms. Stone is like the ISI cat. We feed her. But she's not tame. She comes and goes. So, how much has Demalion told you?" Riordan asked. He leaned against the table, hitching his hip to sit on the edge. His loafer-shod foot dangled—*Gucci,* Sylvie thought. Zoe would know.

"About Marah?" Sylvie said.

"About the ISI."

"Too late to worry about what she knows, I think," Demalion said. "What with the monsters slaughtering us all. Get to the point, Riordan. Who do you want her to kill?" He stuck the gun he held into his shoulder holster and crossed his arms over his chest.

"The ISI was created to study—"

"That part I know," Sylvie said. "Skip to the point. This is about the attacks. You think you know who's behind it."

"I do," Riordan said. "I believe these attacks on the ISI are manufactured internally by William Graves."

"Dallas got hit first," Demalion said. "His own branch. You really suspect him?"

Riordan said, "Classic misdirection. You've been working for Yvette Collier; hasn't she taught you anything?"

"Mass homicide seems overkill for a bump up in salary and prestige," Sylvie said. "I don't buy it."

"You don't have to believe me."

"Right. All I have to do is kill your political rival, a high-ranking government agent. Nice for you. You get one enemy dead, and another on the run, 'cause I'm sure you're going to be damn free with my name as the killer."

"That would be a bonus," Riordan said, "but I'm an honorable man. You play fair, and I keep your name out of it, return your sister. Everyone's happy and the ISI is safe." He slid off the table, moved between her and Demalion, a physical show of confidence.

"I'm just supposed to trust you?"

"Demalion. You've got the inside scoop. Tell her. What's my reputation within the ISI?"

"Honest," Demalion said. "Though it's hard to see why when you're blackmailing Sylvie into killing for you. Distrustful, so you research all your agents in scrupulous detail—"

"I'd have uncovered *you*," Riordan said. "No matter whose body you stepped into. The point, Shadows, is simple. You play fair. I play fair."

"When did assassination become fair?" Demalion said. "It's not the agency way. You think Graves has turned? Report him. Arrest him. Try him. Convict him. You don't murder him."

"The result would be the same. It's treason, what he's doing, Demalion."

"I could report you and him to Collier," Demalion said. "Make your life difficult."

"That would benefit no one," Riordan said. "Certainly not you. You think Yvette's going to be pleased to find she's been hosting a revenant like you? You think Collier would believe anything you say?

"It wouldn't benefit Sylvie. She wants her sister. Not even the world. You think Graves would go quietly? No. He'd ruin everything we've been working for. Listen, Shadows, you know how I feel about the *Magicus Mundi*."

"You don't like it," Sylvie said. "You don't trust it. You think it should be controlled or exiled, kept out of human affairs."

"You remembered, how charming," Riordan said. "But why wouldn't you? You and I might be on opposite sides, Shadows, but I think, big picture, we agree."

"And Graves? What's his side?"

"Graves thinks the *Magicus Mundi* should be exterminated."

"Yeah? You think he hit his head and got confused about who he hates?"

"Don't be naïve," Riordan said. "He's a zealot. He'll use any means necessary to reach his goal. If that's working with monsters to winnow his enemies, so be it. He'll betray them in the end, just as he betrays us, now."

"It does double duty," Demalion said, sounding sick. "He points monsters at the ISI in big splashy kills and gains public attention. Public acclaim for when he decides to make his cause known. He'll be the hero who fights the monsters. And those in the know who might disagree with him would be dead."

Riordan nodded along with Demalion's words. The idea didn't sit right with Sylvie, but if Demalion thought it was conceivable, she'd have to go with it.

"Except someone's working overtime erasing public memories," Sylvie said. "Graves factor that in?"

"No one factored that in," Riordan said.

"Any ideas on who's behind it?" Sylvie asked. "Since we're on the same side and all, right? I know it's a large and powerful coven that's well organized—"

"The most likely candidate is Yvette Collier," Riordan said. He didn't look pleased to be admitting it.

"No," Demalion said.

"Why not?" Riordan said. "We all have our specialties in dealing with the *Magicus Mundi*. Graves is the monster wrangler. Yvette watches the witches. And I deal with the legal aspects."

Sylvie grimaced. "Less than five years, and you're all stepping across your lines is what you're telling me. Graves is using the monsters to dispatch his enemies. Yvette is using witchcraft to thwart Graves's power play, and you . . . you'd rather use me than risk your own life or your son's. So the law is only the law until it endangers you."

"Just go deal with Graves," Riordan said. She'd ruffled him, finally. His jaw twitched; his voice deepened, rasped. "Put a rush on it. And as a gesture of good faith on my part, take Demalion with you. Get it done, and your sister will be back home before you know it. Just get the hell out."

Sylvie bit back all the fight rising up in her. It wouldn't get her anywhere and might cost her Demalion if Riordan got his back up. "You have a last known for him?"

"Dallas," Riordan said.

Sylvie and Demalion traded a glance; the likelihood that he was still in Dallas? "Fine," she said. "I'll investigate Graves. I don't promise anything more."

8

On the Run

IT WAS DAWN OUTSIDE, THE AIR DAMP AND FRAGRANT WITH SALT, the grass shading from black to smudgy green, and the second sunrise Sylvie had seen after a sleepless night. Her truck surged up the last bit of the garage ramp and brought them into morning. At least that, she thought, explained the slight tremble in her gun hand, explained why her emotions were ping-ponging from rage to fear to desperation. Another night gone without sleep. Exhaustion was beating her down.

Sylvie stepped on the gas, and Demalion snapped, "Wait!" She slammed on the brakes, hair-triggered, and nearly gave them both whiplash.

"What?" Sylvie snapped.

She glanced over at him in the uncertain morning light, and felt a chill chase over her skin. Demalion's eyes were glassy, the pupils shrunk to nothing.

"What is it?" Sylvie said. She scanned the roadway behind and before, one hand slipping from the wheel to her gun.

"Someone's waiting for you at the canal edge," Demalion said.

"Friend or foe?"

Demalion shook his head. "Can't tell."

"There's no one there."

"Not yet."

Fucking psychics. Sylvie eased forward, and sure enough, just as the truck reached the narrow bridge, a man stepped out from the piling's shadow. She stopped the truck, got out.

He didn't look like a threat. He was smaller, slighter than he had appeared on the video feeds. His head barely reached the top of the truck's cab. All he wore was a pair of low-slung jeans. His feet were bare. Everything about him suggested he was harmless.

But he was the same man Sylvie had seen shrug off the mermaids' compulsion like it was nothing more than an irritating radio station, the same man who'd been at the site of at least three of the ISI disasters. He was more than he seemed.

Even if she'd been willing to buy into his appearance, the fact remained: He was enough of a threat that he triggered Demalion's visions.

"What do you want?" she said. "This isn't a good time."

"What happened to the Mora?" he asked. His voice, even pitched low to carry only to her ears, held the same powerful resonance as an opera singer's.

"I killed her."

"Fuck," he muttered, and Sylvie knew he was *mundi*, not a witch, by the way the obscenity sounded wrong in his mouth. A language poorly learned. Imitation of humanity. But not of it.

He looked human. About five-eight, slightly olive skin tone, curly dark hair dripping water to his narrow shoulders. His eyes were dark enough that it was hard to tell pupil from iris, and his irritation creased his forehead in all the human ways. But his hair was damp; his jeans were sodden, and if she looked closely, his nose seemed more for show than for breathing, a beak with dents for nostrils instead of actual breathing apparatus.

"What'd you want with her? To congratulate her on a job well-done?"

"I was hoping she'd lead me to whoever sent her out to kill your kind. I wanted to know if she was coerced or coaxed. Now, I can't. You killed her."

"Trust me, she wasn't in the mood to chat."

"Sylvie." Demalion jerked his head toward the ISI. "Riordan's watching. Should we have this meeting here?"

"Fuck," Sylvie echoed, but kept her attention tight on the monster masquerading as a man. "You think she'd have talked to you?"

"Everyone talks to me. Even you."

Sylvie twitched and realized unhappily that it was true. On the ISI's lawn, her enemies behind her, Riordan's goad driving her onward, exhaustion fluttering in her chest, and she had stopped to chat. "What the hell are you?" Her gun hand—when had she lowered it?—started to rise.

"Don't shoot. I need to know what the Mora said to you. But not here. Not now. Your man is right."

Sylvie darted a glance over her shoulder and twitched when she felt the invasion of her personal space; she jumped back, but the stranger had laid a hand, smooth as silk, utterly uncallused, on her sternum. She swung at him, too slow, but he was already backing away. "I'll find you," he said. "Now that I've got the feel of you, I'll find you."

He took three quick steps, leaped into the watery ditch beside the roadway, attached to one of the Miami canals. Sylvie got a quick glimpse of something smooth and torpedo-shaped speeding through the shallow water, the jut of a not-quite fin. A dolphin?

"Crap," Sylvie said. She clambered back into the truck, gunned it, and pulled out of the drive with a screech. "Like we don't have enough going on."

. . .

SYLVIE DIDN'T RELAX UNTIL SHE GOT THE TRUCK OFF THE MORE deserted frontage roads and into denser morning traffic.

She wanted to get back to her office. Needed her

things—spare clips, cash—and she needed some safe space to sleep: where Riordan couldn't rush her into killing Graves; where Marah couldn't swan in at will; where Erinya couldn't come calling with tales of bloody hearts and dead witches.

"Riordan won't hurt Zoe," Demalion said, attempting reassurance.

Sylvie nodded. She believed him, but there were a lot of levels of harm: Being held prisoner was its own kind of hurt. "Your psychic skills can't home in on her?"

"I wish I could," Demalion said. He sounded sincere.

Sylvie tightened her hands on the wheel, said, "I know you hate talking about this. But you're clairvoyant. You should be able to see where she is—"

"*Was* clairvoyant. Then I died. Came back normal. Powerless."

"You're not powerless now," she said. "You used it to survive the sand wraith, to warn the ISI about the Mora. You've been really quiet about how you managed that. Makes a girl wonder what it took to recover that ability." She tried not to let her voice tighten. She kept her own secrets; he should be allowed his.

"Why do you always think the worst of me?" he said. "What do you think I did?"

"I don't know. That's the problem."

"I told you my mother wasn't happy with me, right? That she's avoiding my calls? How much do you know about the sibyls of ancient Greece?"

Sylvie took a hand off the wheel, scrubbed at her face. Exhaustion was warring with adrenaline and winning.

"Syl?"

"Uh," she said. "Nothing."

"Mythic history ascribes their abilities to various gods speaking through them, but that's not really the way it worked."

Sylvie remembered arguing with Dunne about that while she was hunting for his lover. "The gods aren't pre-cognitive. At least, most of them aren't. They can see possibilities, but it's more like men playing chess. Experience and familiarity. But the Sphinx can see the future."

"Yeah," he said. "One of the few beings who can see it clearly."

"*She* made the sibyls."

"Her bite carries a venom that can alter human abilities."

"So you found your mom, convinced her it was you, and then what, asked her to rewrite your DNA?"

"Pretty much," he said.

"And for that, she's not talking to you? Come on, Michael, I'm too fucking tired to beat around the bush. What did you do?"

"It was risky. Her venom kills more often than it changes. I was pretty sick for a couple of weeks."

Sylvie's hand flew off the wheel again, grabbed his shoulder. "Idiot. Wright died to save you, and you . . ."

She shut her mouth, felt one step away from hyperventilating, thought back to when he'd first returned to Chicago. "Those two weeks where you were 'unreachable'? You were fucking dealing with the venom. Dying, and you didn't tell me."

"I didn't die."

Sylvie let out her breath; it rushed out on a shaky stream. She counted to ten, sucked in more air, and said, "Fine. Fine. You didn't die, and I'll crash the truck if we fight now. So, give me the short answer. You have psychic powers, but you can't find Zoe."

"I have limited abilities," he said. "They're all tied in to precognition and threat. I could tell you *when* to dodge a bullet. I can tell you that we've got a car wreck in our future."

"What?" She whipped a look at him, wondering if that was an example or a prophecy.

He shrugged, apparently not sure himself.

Sylvie's phone rang shrilly in her jacket pocket, thrown over the back of the seat. "Get that," she said. "Maybe it's Zoe."

"It's not," he said, before he even reached her jacket.

"So your talent's good for crushing hope," she muttered. "Figures."

Demalion fumbled for the phone, dragging her jacket up from behind the seats. "It's not an ISI number," he said, before hitting speaker.

An agitated man started talking before Demalion could say more than, "Yes?"

"Who's this? Wait, never mind. Tell that bitch, Shadows, that she needs to come pick up whatever it is she left in my hotel. It's freaking the fuck out, and the doors aren't going to hold it."

"I'll be there, Toro," Sylvie said, raising his voice so he could hear. "Stay away from the doors."

"You owe me another $500 for this, Shadows."

"Only if my client is still present and in one piece when I get there. It'll be . . ." Sylvie checked her dashboard clock, tried to calculate distance, traffic, endless variables that flitted through her weary mind like elusive, darting bats. "It'll be as soon as I can make it," she snapped, jerking her hand across her throat, and Demalion cut the connection.

"Sylvie," he said. "Do we have time for this?"

"No choice," she said. Toro was a lot of things, but jumpy he wasn't. If he was concerned, there was reason. She pulled the truck over into the nearest convenience-store parking lot, nearly sideswiped a fast-approaching Mercedes that she just hadn't seen, and thought, Car wreck in her future. Right.

She got out of the truck, staggered into the store, bought an energy drink that looked to be made entirely of caffeine and sugar, grabbed a pack of Tums to go with it, and returned to the truck on the passenger side. "You drive."

"Where am I going?"

"Siesta-Sleep Hotel in Homestead, and hurry." She folded herself into the passenger seat, found it warmed by his skin, and nearly dropped off then and there. Instead, she buckled the belt down, and chugged her drink and two of the antacids.

"You left your client there? Jesus, Sylvie. What'd she do, try to stiff you on your fee? That place has cockroaches the size of scorpions—"

"Drive, Demalion," she said, closed her eyes, and tried to think of yet another place to keep Lupe.

· · ·

SHE WOKE WHEN DEMALION BRAKED HARD, TIRES PROTESTING, AND she woke up angry. Fucking Lupe couldn't even control herself for one damn day. *Weak-natured,* she thought, then felt something in her head click over. That wasn't her. That was the Lilith-voice making itself felt, though more quietly than usual.

Just great, she thought. All she needed. To have it go stealth, make it even harder for her to resist its brutal pragmatism.

"Good nap?"

"Not long enough." She looked out along the streets, said, "Make a left."

"I know where we're going."

"So go there faster," she said. That drumbeat urgency in her blood was the only thing keeping her moving. It kept a clock running down, the time she was wasting. Time she could be using to deal with a world going wonky under the weight of Erinya's presence, of Dunne's expectations, of the witchy manipulations.

Demalion pulled into the hotel lot, found a space in a mostly empty lot. He wasn't wrong about the hotel's ambiance; it did run toward rat and roach more than bed and bath, but beggars couldn't be choosers. "Stay here," Sylvie said. "I need you to keep the truck running."

Sylvie headed out of the truck. She'd left Lupe in Room 213, sulking and none too pleased with her environment. Then again, as far as Lupe was concerned, everything in her life had been on a downward slide since the moment she was kidnapped by Azpiazu.

Given that and the manager's call, Sylvie was less than surprised to find her knock answered by a crash and a strange animal sound. Something large, she thought, since the floorboards creaked as Lupe paced toward the door. Exactly what shape Lupe had taken, Sylvie couldn't tell. The animal protest that traveled through the door was like nothing she'd heard before. Something like a snake rattle, like a cat's purr, but high-pitched.

Tranquilizer gun. She should have invested in a tranquilizer gun. Another thing to set Alex on. God, Alex. She should have warned her about the ISI, told her to get someplace safe. Was there anyplace safe? Sylvie's head spun.

She leaned on the door frame, tried to muster patience. "Lupe. It's Sylvie."

The door jolted as Lupe crashed into it; the thick wood bowed outward, and the rattling shriek made Sylvie wince. Up close, the sound could cut glass. Or shatter it.

"What the fuck did you leave in there?" the manager said, joining her.

"Give me the key," Sylvie said. "Go away."

Toro passed her the key, backed up a few feet. Sylvie eyed him, knew he was hoping to get something on her that would net him some more cash, and thought, Fuck it. She was sick of playing censor. If he wanted to see, let him. The ISI wouldn't like it, and that was reason enough to let it happen. She waited until she heard Lupe retreat, then keyed the door open a crack. Peered inside.

"What is it? What do you see?" he asked, leaning forward.

Trouble.

Serious trouble.

Not only had Lupe changed independent of the lunar cycle, but there was absolutely no way this change could be passed off as normal. No "zoo escapee" excuse was going to cover this.

Lupe raised her head; a long forked tongue flickered out, tasting the air. Tasting Sylvie's presence. The mane of feathers around her neck shifted and fluffed. She shrieked again, and lashed her long, tawny tail. She sprang forward, and Sylvie slammed the door just in time to avoid a clawed paw.

"I'm going to need a nonlethal weapon," she told him. "A Taser, stun gun, or a tranq gun. Something."

He looked at her blankly, and she said, "Get me one."

"Shadows, I don't know what you—"

"Toro, your hotel clients are 90 percent violent offenders of one kind or another. You're telling me you don't have an entire armory in your office?"

"I got an Uzi?"

"If I wanted to shoot her, I'd use my gun," Sylvie snapped. She knew she was being irrational, that most of her anger was self-directed—she just didn't have things under control.

"I got roofies."

Sylvie grimaced. She hated the people she interacted with sometimes. "Fine. Get me a handful and a steak."

"Five dollars each—"

"Toro, I could walk away and leave her to you. Make her your problem."

"Fine," he said, and slunk off.

Sylvie shuddered. She was so going to call Suarez and sic him on Toro. There was sketchy, and then there was *sketchy*.

Demalion joined her on the second-floor balcony, ignoring her scowl. "I left the motor running. What's taking so long?"

Lupe hiss-purred through the door, and Demalion said, "What is that?"

"My client," Sylvie said. "She's having a bad day."

Toro returned with a handful of pills going chalky and damp in his hand, and a steak a couple of days past fresh. Sylvie could smell him coming.

She wasn't the only one. The door shuddered again in the jamb, the hinges jolting. Toro crushed the pills into the steak, and Sylvie took it with one hand. It took more concentration than she expected to hang on to the slimy, heavy mass, and that was the beginning of the end.

She took her eyes off the crack in the door to focus on the meat's getting away from her. Demalion stiffened like he'd been electrocuted and swept her down to the concrete walkway, scraping her arm, numbing her elbow, and knocking the breath from her.

Lupe's claws closed on empty air, and she leaped down to the parking lot. In the sunlight, she was a beautiful monster. She had a huge catlike body, tawny and stippled with tropical bird colors, blue, green, red. A ruff of bright feathers stood out around her serpentine head like an Elizabethan collar, and the scales on that massive snake head glimmered with an oily green sheen. Like a poison-arrow frog, everything about her screamed toxic.

"Lupe!" Sylvie yelled, hanging over the edge of the balcony. She hurled the steak down in front of her. It landed with a wet, messy splat and spread out across the concrete like a rooftop jumper.

Lupe flickered a skink blue tongue at the steak, then dismissed it.

"No, no, no," Sylvie muttered, scrambled to her feet, and headed downstairs, Demalion shouting behind her. Maybe if she could get Lupe into her truck, the situation could be salvaged.

Traffic on the road outside the hotel suddenly bottle-necked as first one driver, then another, saw Lupe and slammed on the brakes, and got rear-ended for their pains. Horns filled the air, and Lupe let out her freaky howl-shriek again and headed straight for the traffic in a ground-eating lope Sylvie couldn't hope to beat. Maybe with the truck, but the road was blocked.

Her breath seesawed in her chest, panic striking hard and deep. Lupe was going to get killed. Or kill someone. Or both. And it would be her fault.

Sylvie raised her gun, belatedly thinking even a flesh wound would slow her down, be better than this, but there were too many people around, and Lupe was so fast. . . .

Sylvie closed her eyes, shut out Demalion shouting at Toro, the sounds of panic and excitement on the street, the sounds of Lupe's life being destroyed step by step. There had to be something she could do.

Whether it was exhaustion or panic or the catastrophe about to happen, she could only think of one thing that might work.

"Erinya!" she shouted. "Erinya!"

Her breath felt like it was torn from her, and she didn't even know if it would work. If Erinya was listening. And if she was, if she'd come.

Lupe gained the roadway and the stopped cars, lunged atop them, and flared her neck feathers. Her clawed feet crashed through a windshield, and the carpoolers inside hurled themselves out, one man clutching a bloody shoulder.

A second later, he was convulsing in the street; Lupe was, apparently, as toxic as she looked.

Demalion said, "Shoot her. Sylvie. You don't have a choice. She's killing people."

Sylvie lined up the shot, blinking sweat out of her eyes, her vision blurring. She scrubbed her face, scented the lingering aroma of putrid meat on her skin, and gagged. The gun shook in her hands.

Demalion took the gun from her, aimed, and Lupe dropped between the cars, showing that, animal or not, she still recognized danger. Sylvie got a glimpse of that snaky head peering at them beneath the SUV she'd just trashed and had only a moment to realize that Lupe was coming for them at speed.

Demalion held his ground, took the shot—head shot, too high. The scales furrowed back, exposed thick bone— another scar for Sylvie's client should she survive turning human again—but Lupe didn't even slow.

Sylvie swiped her gun back, holstered it, and shoved Demalion toward the truck.

"Lupe," she said. "Lupe." Like the name was a spell to return her to herself.

Lupe slowed in her advance, tilted her head. Listening, Sylvie hoped.

"C'mon, Lupe. You don't want to kill anyone, right? You don't want to hurt anyone else. Remember how bad you felt when Jenny—"

The chattering blast of Toro's Uzi cut through her words, sent her seeking ground, seeking safety. Lupe leaped, slashed at Toro with a casual paw, and sliced flesh to the bone. He screamed in pain and kept screaming.

Lupe whined, her side torn by at least one bullet. Then her feathers ruffled; her scales shifted color, shading dark, and she lunged for the next nearest person.

Sylvie.

Sylvie had one terrifying glimpse of Lupe's soft underside, wished she hadn't holstered her gun, then Lupe went crashing across the parking lot, hurled away by a larger force.

Erinya had made the scene.

• • •

A BARE SECOND AFTER ERINYA'S EMERGENCE, SYLVIE'S RELIEF faded. Erinya had come ready to kill; and more, she brought the jungle with her. Vines and lianas burst from the concrete and asphalt, crumbling the ground beneath her. Scarlet flowers fell out of the air, spreading petals that oozed a sickeningly sweet scent.

"Don't kill her. Don't hurt her. Just stop her," Sylvie breathed out. Her back hurt with a growing dull heat; she put a hand to her side, felt perforated flesh and liquid, something slippery inside and out. Toro's fucking Uzi. Friendly fucking fire. She was too tired to tell how bad it was.

Erinya didn't even glance in her direction, just sprang on Lupe, rolled her over, squalling, hissing, and snapping. Greenery erupted around them, entangling them.

Demalion's hands latched tight on Sylvie's side unexpectedly, and she struck at him, hurting and half-crazed. She laughed when he swore at her, came away with his hands stained wet with her blood. "Marah thinks I'm immortal," she told him. "Guess not." Her body throbbed. Her vision blurred.

He manhandled her into her truck, dragged out the first-aid kit, and she tried to push him off. "Got to tell Erinya. Tell her to take Lupe away. Tell her to—"

"Shut up," he said. "They're on their own."

His lips were white, pressed tight between his teeth, and she said, "You're worried about me?"

"Everybody's got a hobby," he said. He leaned forward, kissed her forehead. "Now, shut up. Let me get you bandaged before you bleed out."

A thunderous crash resounded in the back of the truck, rocked them both violently in the cab, slammed her truck's nose into the wall, and the animal shrieking cut off all at once. Demalion looked up, wild-eyed, and Sylvie let out a startled yelp as Lupe's snake head crunched through the back window. But, despite the unlidded gaze, she was out. Unconscious or dead.

Erinya slid behind the wheel, all human delight. "Sylvie! Where'd you find her? She's wonderful."

"Drive," Demalion said.

"I don't take orders from you," Erinya said.

"Sylvie's in no shape to give them. Get us out of here," Demalion snapped.

Sylvie winced against the seat; the wound was beginning to feel less hot and more hurt. "Erinya—"

Sirens were thick in the air, the approaching cops, ISI—everyone she didn't want to talk to. Everyone she needed to protect Lupe from.

"Take us to Alex," Sylvie said, trying to get a last bit of thought out. If things were going to hell this fast, she needed to make sure Alex knew about it.

"Heal her first," Demalion said.

Erinya hesitated. And Sylvie thought, *Dammit, Erinya might have healed me, except that Demalion was the one to ask for it.*

Demalion slid out of the truck, and she grabbed at him, wondering what the hell he was thinking, but the effort jolted her and sent her, finally, into unconsciousness.

When she came to, she was still in the truck, and she wanted to scream in frustration. She was tired of fighting—

Never tire of fighting, her inner voice declared—

—and she just wanted to get some fucking sleep. Even as

she complained, she realized she felt . . . better. Not good; still exhausted, shaky, wiped out, and stinking of blood, but better. Also, the world outside the truck had changed. Not the hotel parking lot but someplace cooler, dimmer. Someplace without screaming and panic.

Someplace that smelled strongly of exhaust and oil, a faint overlay of mall perfume.

A parking garage?

The passenger door next to her hung open, and crouched in it, a blurry shape in the dimness, was Erinya. "Don't be mad," she said.

Sylvie threw her head back and groaned. "Erinya, what did you do?"

"Healed you," the Fury said.

"I thought I felt better," Sylvie said. "Why would I be mad at you for . . . did you kill Lupe?"

"Lupe is the monster-girl? No. I like her. She's fun."

Sylvie swallowed hard, cleared her eyes enough to see that Erinya's face was bloodstained from cheek to chin. "Demalion—" Sickness churned in her; her breath felt suddenly fragile. Ready to shatter.

"I'm here," Demalion said from behind Erinya. He sounded all right, but when she saw him, she wasn't so sure he was. His hands were bloody to the elbows, and his gaze had some of Erinya's hangdog quality to it. *Don't be mad.*

"What happened?" Sylvie said, pushing herself upright. "Where's Alex?"

"Hiding," Erinya said. "She doesn't like me much without you around."

"Where are we?"

Erinya huffed. "Questions, questions, questions. I'm bored with that." She leaped into the bed of the truck, stroked Lupe's battered feathers to smoothness, slid her hands down along Lupe's velvety hide. Sylvie wasn't the only one the Fury had healed.

Demalion reached into the truck, tugged Sylvie out. "Easy. She fixed the wound, but I think you still lost the blood."

"What happened," Sylvie repeated.

"I ripped out Toro's heart and offered it to Erinya in exchange for healing you. I—"

"Worshipped her," Sylvie said. "Gave your allegiance to a god who hates you?"

"You were bleeding out," he said, "in my arms. I did what I needed to."

"Your afterlife," she said. "Oh God." She leaned up against him, felt useless tears start in her eyes. An afterlife with Erinya, where she'd chase and torment and hate him for eternity. "I don't know that I can get you out of that."

"I won't die anytime soon," he said. "Give you time to work on it."

Sylvie sniffed hard, raised her head. "Yeah. If we get the chance. Where the hell are we?"

"Dadeland Mall," Demalion said. "You told Erinya to find Alex. She was shopping."

"At the Apple store," Alex said. She sidled around the truck with a wary glance at Erinya, still crooning over her unconscious playmate. "Amazingly enough, having a Fury pluck you out of it makes things tricky. On the bright side, I've got a new toy. Since I was holding on to it when Erinya grabbed me? I'm trying to figure out if that makes me a shoplifter or what."

Sylvie said, "The mall, Alex? With all that's going on?"

"The ISI took your sister out of the airport. I felt a little exposed at the office and at home. I've been here since it opened, waiting for you to call."

Sylvie found herself sinking more heavily against Demalion, and he said, "We need to get you a place to rest."

"I've been saying that for the last twenty-four hours," Sylvie muttered. "But Zoe, Graves—"

"Riordan's just going to have to wait," Demalion said. "We need a bolt-hole. Your apartment's not safe enough. Hotel?"

"I know where to go," Alex said. "I've been thinking about it. Enough space for all of us and maybe even safety from memory modifications? From Riordan's haranguing you to get busy?"

"Yeah, yeah, cut to the chase," Sylvie said.

From the truck, Lupe emitted a strange groan, then began to collapse inward, shifting back to human. Erinya sat back on her haunches to watch, head cocked, curious.

"Val's place," Alex said. "She's in Ischia. Which means there's an estate with both magical and high-tech security going to waste. Plus, if Zoe somehow manages to give Riordan the slip—"

"Zoe would head for Val's if she got free," Sylvie said. "You're brilliant, Alex." She grinned, but it felt weak. "Can't take Erinya, though."

"You want her around full-time?"

"Nice to have a Lupe-wrangler."

"Val's estate will have at least one safe room," Demalion said. "If she's as high-tech as Alex says."

"Great, we're all for it. Let's get there and stop talking about it." Sylvie pushed off Demalion's solid chest, staggered a bit but stayed upright, waving him off.

"We're not taking your truck," Demalion said. "Too many of us, and it's full of blood."

"Fine," Sylvie said. "Go fetch a car, then." She leaned up against her truck while he disappeared farther into the parking garage. Grand theft auto, coming up, committed by a rogue government agent. What the hell had their lives come to?

Alex said, "Are you really going to kill Graves on Riordan's say-so?"

"Demalion filled you in, then?" Sylvie said. "I don't know. If Graves *is* the one siccing monsters on the world? Probably. I'm just not sure. Something about the whole mess doesn't sit right. But I can't think straight. I'm making bad choices. Careless choices. There's a hotel in Homestead that's proof of that." At least two dead men, car wrecks, witnesses to a monster-brawl, and she really doubted Erinya had tidied the jungle away without Sylvie to harass her into doing it.

Demalion rolled up a minute later in an enormous, gas-guzzling Escalade, big enough to hold them all and ostentatious enough to be unnoticeable in Val's fancy driveway.

Erinya transferred Lupe's unconscious shape into the back bench seat, strapped her in with careful precision, and said, "When can I see her again?"

"Later," Sylvie said. "We're trying to fix her. I don't suppose you—"

"Fix her? She's wonderful," Erinya said.

"Yeah," Sylvie said. "Never mind. Eri, can you do one more favor for me? Get rid of the truck?" If they left it here, bloodstained and battered, the cops would be looking for her, either as victim or as a criminal. She didn't have time for it.

Erinya waved a hand; Sylvie's truck dissolved. It stung, watching it go. She'd loved that damn thing, battered as it was.

If she was immortal, if Marah was right, then it'd only be one of a thousand things she'd lose in her eternal life.

She stood there, shivering in the garage, blaming blood loss, until Alex tucked her into the second seat and shut the door on her. Alex took the passenger seat, and Demalion drove them smoothly into the afternoon.

9

Regrouping

LUXURY HAD ITS PLACE, SYLVIE THOUGHT AS SHE SETTLED MORE comfortably in the leather seat. The motor hummed quietly, the ride was smooth, and the car was pleasantly dim in the midday heat. Sylvie fumbled out her cell phone, found it cracked through, and said, "Alex. Phone?"

"Calling Val?" Alex asked, passing her phone back.

"Yeah. Her estate isn't going to be much of a safe haven if it kills us as we try to get in."

Demalion grunted from the driver's seat. "We've had enough near-death moments today. I'm forbidding any more of them. My nerves can't take it."

"Aw, poor baby," Alex teased.

Demalion's glance toward her was not amused.

Sylvie ignored the start of their bickering and dialed Val. Usually, Val refused to answer Sylvie's calls, but Sylvie was betting that with Zoe AWOL, Val would answer, no matter the time. Sylvie turned her watch, thought, actually her timing wasn't that bad. Ischia was about six hours ahead. Dinnertime.

"Sylvie," Val said.

She sounded so calm and competent that Sylvie felt

strange, choking tears rise in her throat. "God, Val, I need your help."

The line hummed between them for a long moment, then Val said, "What do you need?"

Ten minutes and copious notes later, Sylvie disconnected from Val, feeling better about their strained relationship than she had in ages. Nothing like knowing that your friend—no matter how justifiably pissed off—wasn't going to leave you high and dry when your life was on the line.

Sylvie passed one part of the list to Alex, said, "We're going to need to make a stop for supplies."

Alex nodded.

Behind Sylvie, Lupe stirred and moaned, and Sylvie peered over the seat back. Lupe's eyelashes fluttered, her hand flailed weakly. Her nails, Sylvie noted, were deep blue-black, another transformation that had failed to erase itself. Sylvie just hoped that the venom hadn't made the transition back to human along with the claws. Lupe's temper was far too dangerous.

"What happened?" Lupe said.

"Too much to explain. But hey," Sylvie said dryly, "you made a friend."

"I dreamed about a monster," Lupe whispered. "Her teeth in my throat."

"Her heart in your hands," Sylvie said. "Her name is Erinya. She likes you."

"It was real?" Lupe asked. "I dreamed I killed a man." When Sylvie didn't deny it, she turned her face away, toward the dark leather seat, hiding from reality, and nothing Sylvie said after that could draw her into speech again.

Finally, Sylvie just slumped back in her seat and closed her eyes. Not sleeping. Not yet. But she could rest her eyes.

Demalion kept the SUV running while Alex grabbed items on Val's list and on hers, tearing through one magic bodega and one gun shop with an efficiency Sylvie envied.

Sylvie wanted to go in with Alex, keep an eye on her, make sure she got everything on the list, but she couldn't leave Lupe unattended. The woman seemed wrung out, unable to move, much less shift shape and rampage some more, but better not to take the chance.

Alex returned, laden down with bags, and passed Sylvie the Taser. "Here," she murmured with a sidelong glance at Lupe. "It's got a charged battery, and the cartridges are loaded."

Sylvie folded it against her side like the world's oddest security blanket and let herself drowse. Soon enough, she smelled the sea, heard the city traffic stop echoing off concrete facades, disappearing out over the waves. She opened her eyes, and they were passing the Seaquarium and the Rosenstiel School, opened her eyes again, and Demalion was pulling up to Val's driveway gate.

He stopped the SUV and she slid-tumbled out the side door; she keyed in the passcode Val had given her, and the gate rumbled into motion, pulling back. She put her hand up—wait—and went back for the bag of magical supplies. Nothing too exotic—a white feather, some salt, a few white pebbles polished to a dull gleam, a handful of red chalk. Seemed hard to believe that was all it was going to take to carve a doorway through Val's wards.

Val had said that Zoe would be the best to do the spell; that since Zoe had lived there, even briefly, the spellwork would be like turning a key. For anyone else, Val said, it was going to take brute willpower.

Sylvie felt a little low on brute willpower, but there wasn't another alternative. She knelt on the smooth black asphalt of the drive, in the shadow of the SUV, and took a deep breath. She wasn't a witch. She'd used spells once or twice. Always paid for it. Magic made her sick. Part of her Lilith bloodline. The same thing that made her resistant to magic punished her for using it. She expected it would only get worse. Lilith, at the end, hadn't been able to cast even the simplest of spells.

She marked four of the pebbles—one for each of them— with a symbol that Val swore meant *benign*. Sylvie just hoped the stone couldn't tell the truth. They were a ragtag crew who meant no harm to Val, but she wouldn't call any of them benign. Even Alex wouldn't fit that description to a witch's gaze since she was marked by Eros, the god of Love, and was burdened with an active and malevolent memory curse.

"Sylvie, do you need help?" Alex asked.

Sylvie shook her head. "Go back to the SUV. If I can't shift the spell right, it could get ugly."

Alex made a face but did as she was bid.

Sylvie plunged into spellwork with nausea growing in her chest, her heart throbbing. By the time she rose from her knees—the asphalt swallowing the chalk down, preparing to listen to her commands—the feather weighed her wrist down as if it were made of lead. She raised the feather, raised the wards with it, and nearly collapsed under the weight of something intangible but impossibly heavy. The world seemed to sway around her, as if she were peeling back the sky. The wards lifted, and she jerked a shoulder forward. Demalion, watching for her signal, moved the SUV through the ward. The feather vibrated in Sylvie's hand, and she hung on to it with nothing but a last burst of determination.

The moment the SUV was through, she let the feather drop. It burned as it fell, disappeared into ash, and the wards snapped back around them. A witch might have seen something spectacular in it. Sylvie only felt the wrongness of the world being forced away. She stumbled, fell forward, and Demalion caught her.

"Just a little bit more," he said.

Once they were through the perfectly mundane alarm on the door, Sylvie headed for the nearest bedroom on autopilot. She'd been up for sixty-plus hours, fought four pitched battles, and dealt with more chaos than even she could handle. Not to mention being shot and healed.

The floor-to-ceiling windows looked out over the ocean, and Sylvie gave the spectacular view a cursory glance, making sure no one was lurking. Then she spilled face-first onto the bed. It felt like heaven.

She was vaguely aware of Demalion tugging her one way then another, peeling off clothes and shoes, sliding her under sheets, but mostly she was aware of the yawning darkness in her brain. The dreamworld waiting for her. She had a moment to hope that the Mora's taint hadn't left a mark; the last thing she wanted was to find her sleep interrupted by nightmares.

Then she was gone.

· · ·

IT WAS TWILIGHT WHEN SHE WOKE, DEMALION A WARM PRESENCE wrapped around her, his arm heavy across her ribs. The waves outside had gone phosphorescent around the edges. Sylvie felt struck stupid and boneless with exhaustion, but the world was making itself known again: Her brain started churning out worry for Zoe, worry about what had been done with Lupe, where Alex was.

What was coming out of the waves.

She struggled out of Demalion's grip—sleeping, the man folded up like origami and took his partners with him—and stepped soft-footedly toward the windows. She expected it to be a hallucination brought on by tiredness and exertion, but the closer she got, the more real it looked. A man—slim-shouldered, dark-haired—rising out of the sea.

He was too far away to make out any expression, but his impatience seemed to reach out toward her, passing through the air and the glass, beating against her skin. *Come out and talk to me. Don't make me wait.*

A coercion charm of some kind. Sylvie felt it fluttering against her nerves, urging her toward movement. She could push it off, but truth was, she had her own eagerness adding to it. She wanted to know what the hell he was. How he was involved.

Sylvie reached for her pants, but they smelled so much of blood and char and sweat that she let them fall, too repulsed to worry about modesty. She picked up her gun and went out to meet the intruder in a tank top and her boyshorts. Hell, she had swimsuits that covered a lot less, and at least both the tank and underwear were black.

She walked down the lawn, the earth warm beneath her

feet, the grass cool as it soaked up the evening breezes. Her bare feet were cat-silent as she walked, the faint rustling masked by the sway and rattle of palm fronds. He spotted her coming, raised his head, and scowled, taking in the gun held loosely in her hand.

She stopped a healthy twenty feet from the shore—no way was she approaching him in his own environment—still within the wards. He waited, scowl darkening, his arms crossed over his chest. She shook her head, snapping his hold on her. Not happening. If he wanted to talk, he'd have to come to her.

He slogged up the sandy shore, and when he was within speaking distance, she asked, "How'd you find me?"

"I have your sense in my skin," he said. "I can track you."

"Charming," she said. She remembered that now, the feel of his hand on her skin. His other shape a dolphin . . . she tried to recall old field trips to Seaquarium, recall old marine biology classes. Dolphins had some type of electro-sensing ability, didn't they?

"On better days, you'd be surprised how charming I can be," he said. He smiled, his teeth white and sharp beneath the jut of his nose. A predator's grin. He lingered at the very edge of the ward, as if he could sense it as easily as she could. Probably easier. He wasn't human; he lived in the currents of magic.

"You got a name?" she asked. "Since you managed to cop a feel, I think I deserve a name." She supposed she should be asking him what he wanted, but she thought, just once, she'd start with the easy stuff.

He sighed, a strange half-whistled sound, widened his smile. It still looked toothily insincere. "Women. They always want a name." Something seethed beneath his skin; she thought she recognized it. Anger.

"So you answer to what? *Player?*"

He squinted up at her; apparently his English didn't go so far as modern dating references. "You don't need my name. We're not going to be friends."

"Fine by me," Sylvie said.

"I want to know what the Mora said. If she told you why she was attacking those humans."

"What's it to you?"

"Just tell me," he snapped. "I don't have time to play games with a trigger-happy human."

Sylvie crossed her arms over her chest, tapped her gun meaningfully. "Games, no. Basic courtesy? Never a bad thing."

"Courtesy." He looked back toward the glistening water, the oily snake ripples of slow waves beneath the moonlight. "This whole visit is a courtesy. I could have compelled you."

"Could have tried," Sylvie said. "Look. The Mora didn't say much. A lot of *We were here first, you should remember us*, and one small hint that maybe she was sent. She didn't give me name, rank, and serial number. Too busy trying to kill me by nightmares."

"Her words?"

Sylvie huffed out exasperation. He raked water from his hair with an impatient hand, spat salt water at her feet. The wards hissed and bubbled. The air smelled of fish.

"I challenged her. Said I knew someone had to be sending them. It's just not normal behavior for the *Magicus Mundi*."

"No," he said. "It's not." Some of the anger drained away. "You're aware of this?"

"It was the succubus that convinced me," Sylvie said. "I know them. They drain their victims over the course of several days. Weeks if they're feeling sentimental. They don't pick up automatic weapons and start mowing down government agents. They don't waste their food."

"And mermaids don't come this far inland, and sand wraiths don't like lake cities. It's anomalous. People are paying attention."

"No, they're really not," Sylvie said. "That's the other half of the problem."

"Not your people," he said, lips twisting. "*Mine*. Humans. Think you're the only ones that matter. We were here from the beginning. We've been around since before your kind had language. *We* are the people. You all are . . ."

"What?" she challenged. Both irritated and curious. His attitude was regrettable, but she couldn't help but find him intriguing. She'd never really sat down and had a conversation with a monster before—a few gods, yeah, but a monster? No. She was friends with a werewolf or two, but they considered themselves human, descendants of Lilith and regular wolves. Human, with extras.

His gaze was flat, black, and unfriendly. "Interlopers. Scavengers. Prey."

"Nice," she said.

"Are your words for us any better? Monsters? Nightmares? Creatures? *Things?*" He shook his head—another gesture that was subtly off. His neck didn't seem to have the flexibility of a human's. "It doesn't matter. That's not why I'm here. You didn't learn anything from the Mora. You just killed her. So from now on? Stay out of my business."

She felt him pressing his will on her, trying to urge her to do just that. But she was made of sterner stuff, and there was a ward between them as well. She shook it off.

"What were you going to do? Talk to her while she killed you? One thing I do know about your *people* . . . you turn on each other just as easily as you turn on us."

He turned, disinterested. A patch of darkness on his neck showed, and Sylvie leaned forward. Was that a hole?

"Hey," she said, pushing curiosity aside again. "I have a question."

"I don't care," he said.

"Don't make me shoot you in the leg," Sylvie said. "We've been getting along so well. Come on. One question."

He paused; his skin twitched and rippled like an animal pestered by an insect. Then he huffed. Water vapor burst out of his neck.

Hole, she thought. *Blowhole. Went with the dolphin shape-shifting.* She knew what he was.

"What?" he said. "Ask me your question."

"You think something's coercing or confusing the monsters who are attacking the ISI."

"That's not a question."

"There's someone modifying human memories also, more confusion and coercion. That your doing?" She couldn't believe it was Yvette, much as she'd like to. The thing was, the thing Riordan hadn't mentioned, maybe didn't know—the memory attacks had been going on for far longer than the ISI attacks. Why would an ISI witch cover up *Maudit* misbehavior, some of which wasn't even in the USA? Why would an ISI witch gunning for promotion use a power that was injuring or killing the people she was supposed to protect? It just seemed messy and disorganized. Yvette, by Demalion's accounts, was neither of those things.

She was looking for someone else. Maybe the creature in front of her. Even as she asked, she didn't believe it. His power was small; his field of influence narrow. He'd stood outside the wards and called, and the only one who woke was Sylvie. Because he'd touched her. The memory plague was affecting people citywide simultaneously. She let the accusation stand, though. To see what he would say. The more she kept him talking, the more chance she could figure out his angle.

"Why would I—"

"It seems to me that you've been sent to stop these attacks. That they're drawing heat down on your heads. You're not doing a good job at the main source. Not stopping the monsters. Are you cleaning up after them? You said you're charming. You're sure as hell working the compulsion magic. You're Encantado."

Like the fairy-tale creature he was, he shivered all over when she named him. As if she'd diminished him.

"Your name for my people. Not ours," he said. "But yes, I am Encantado."

"So, are you brainwashing my people, making them forget what your people are doing? I thought it was witchcraft, but I'm willing to adjust my theory."

He jerked his head, teeth flashing and clicking.

Sylvie took a prudent step away. Didn't look friendly. He pressed back up at the edge of the ward, leaned close. She could smell him—something salty and pungent and something faintly animal beneath the human skin. Legends said that the Encantado seduced women who wandered too close to the riverbanks. Right now, she couldn't imagine any woman touching him.

She closed her hand tighter around her gun, thought of Alex and Demalion sleeping back at the house. They seemed very far away at the moment.

The ward sizzled and sang, clicks and pops that almost sound like dolphin chatter.

"It's not our way to hide ourselves," he said. "That's yours. Sneaking and prying and stealing away in the dark. Aggressive, greedy, cowardly monkey-things. Someone's taking your memories? I don't care. Someone's taking our *lives* and using them as *weapons*."

His face closed off, his mouth snapped shut, his eyes shuttered. She expected him to leave, but instead he let out another huffing breath, and said, "Perhaps we can make a deal."

"A deal?" Sylvie said. "Sure you trust a greedy monkey?"

He parted his teeth at her again; his tongue was white in the darkness.

"My people are being used. I think by the very people they attack."

"The ISI?" Sylvie said. There was another vote for internal strife turning into a massacre.

"Yes. The better to make themselves a needed force in the world. I can't be in two places at once," he said. "I've been focusing on stopping the attacks."

"Really," Sylvie said. "Bang-up job. You're what? Always an hour too late?"

"It's my only option," he said. "Someone's leashing my people with magic. Leading them around like dogs. That person has to be close by. I'm hunting them. I don't know who I'm looking for. The ISI would know. *You* can get inside the ISI and get out again. You can get me that name. I expect it's one of their own. A secret branch within a secret branch. Your government would love to harness us."

"Like a dolphin with a bomb strapped to it."

He shot her an ugly glance. "Exactly like that. Except we don't need any weapon but ourselves."

"All right," Sylvie said. "What do I get if I pass any information on to you?"

"Stopping the attacks isn't enough?"

Sylvie shook off her ingrained urge to bargain, but before she could apologize, he said, "How about an answer to your problem. The Good Sisters."

"The what?"

"Your memory witches. The Society of the Good Sisters. They're the ones wiping out your memories. Or so the rumors say. More than that, I don't know. Is that enough for our deal?"

Sylvie eyed him in the dimness, the sleek inhuman smoothness of him, and tried to figure out his angle. He had one, that was for sure. He had no love for humans, but he might be telling the truth. She had to go after Graves anyway, and if the Encantado was being truthful, if the Good Sisters existed, the ISI would have files on them.

"Yeah," she said, but he was already moving away as smoothly as he'd come, heading for the ocean. He strode into the slow roll of the surf, smoothed into dolphin shape, and was gone.

Sylvie turned back toward the house and got light-dazzled for her pains as room after room suddenly illuminated. She headed toward the house at a careful trot, and met Alex rushing out.

"Sylvie," Alex called, her voice reaching ahead of her. She stumbled as she came, too impatient to wait for her eyes to adapt from the interior light to the darkness outside. Impatient. Or afraid. Sylvie felt her spine go cold. She guessed Alex's words even as she gasped them out.

"Someone's trying to get through the wards," Alex said, stopping before she tumbled head over heels. "How do we stop them from getting through? I know computers. Not magic."

"We can't," Sylvie said. "The wards aren't walls, Alex. They're spellwork, nothing more."

"But you did all sorts of magicky stuff to open—"

"Only because I didn't want to spend our entire time here fighting the urge to *get out, get out.* That's all the wards do. Give you the creeping terrors. Make you miserably ill. Encourage you to leave, posthaste. The magical equivalent of a pack of growling pit bulls. Otherwise, Val's house would be surrounded with the bodies of solicitors and neighborhood kids who climbed the fence. It's a pretty strong spell, though. I've never seen anyone defeat it. Did you see who it was?"

"No," Alex said. "I was watching Lupe when I suddenly got the urge to get up and check the security system—that was the wards alerting me, right? The camera shows a car at the gate, but there's no one in it. They climbed the fence?"

"It's what I would have done. Especially if I knew the house was empty of an actual witch."

Alex looked miserable, and Sylvie said, "Hey. Val's place is still safer than anywhere else I was thinking of. You did good. We have a defensible place with a good warning system. And hell, if they actually try to breach the house, we'll be swarmed with cops. Val believes in tech as well as magic."

They'd reached the house, Sylvie ushering Alex in ahead of her. Sylvie reactivated the alarm on the door she'd come through and sent Alex to the security monitors. "See if you can get eyes on our intruder. Odds are, they're probably either headed back toward the gate—chased out by the ward—or they're fighting to move forward."

"But if they got past the ward—"

"Val's wards are nasty. You go through one, and it sticks to you. They'll be fighting it until they're released from it or flee. So, at the very least, our intruder's not at their best."

The question was, who was after them now? Lupe's injured witch, coming back for revenge? The *Maudits*, belatedly realizing one of their own was dead?

"There's nothing on the monitors!" Alex called out. While Sylvie had paused to think, Alex had hit the security room just off the main hallway. Her voice was shrill, pitched to carry, and it brought Demalion and Lupe out of their rooms. Demalion looked wary, bare-chested, gun in his hand. Lupe just looked tired. And toxic. Her crossed arms were swirled with color, bleeding up from within. Sylvie grimaced. Lupe might be too far gone to go back to human.

Sylvie headed toward the front door, waving at them to stay back, jerked her head toward Demalion, toward Lupe, and saw Demalion move to cover her.

A sudden *thump thump thump* sounded at the front door, muffled by the thickness of the material—steel core beneath a wood veneer.

"Alex, get eyes on the front door?"

Sylvie was surprised the intruder had made it that far. Val's aversion spells didn't mess around. She crept to the door, peered out through the peephole. The spyhole wasn't a regular kind. Some sort of magic was laid on it. The figure leaning on the door was traced with layers of different-color lights. Some type of magical diagnostic Sylvie couldn't interpret, no doubt designed to let Val know exactly who or what she was letting in.

Sylvie didn't need the diagnostic. She recognized their inopportune caller.

"Little pig, little pig," Marah said, her voice reedy through the door. "Let me in. Or I'll huff, and I'll puff . . ."

"It's a woman. I don't know her," Alex said, poking her head into the hall.

"She's that ISI assassin I told you about. We had pictures of her, remember?"

"Sorry. Been a long few days."

Sylvie swallowed. A long few days and some evil spell-work.

"Marah Stone," Demalion said. "She's okay. Let her in."

"She's okay?" Sylvie said. "Verdict's not unanimous on that."

"Sylvie, don't be difficult," he said.

"She works for the goddamn ISI. She's part of the people who took my sister. You've seen the error of your ways. I doubt that she has."

Demalion's lips went white and tight, irritated. "Can't you just, for once, trust me? Marah and I spent fourteen hours trapped under the rubble of the ISI. She's loyal to them the same way I am. To the cause. Not the division heads."

"She kills people."

"So do you."

A low blow, and that he had said it only showed her how determined he was. Demalion put his hand on the door handle. "Turn off the alarm."

Sylvie thought of all the hell they'd been through that day, thought about Demalion's giving himself to Erinya so she could be healed, thought about the likelihood of more violence and trouble in the near future, and decided she wasn't going to fight him. Not on this.

She punched in the code, and Demalion opened the door. Marah all but fell into his arms. She didn't look so hot, her skin greased with fear sweat and effort, her body shaking. The only part of her that wasn't trembling was the Cain-marked hand, and it was rock steady as it held her gun.

She raised her head from Demalion's bare shoulder, patted his bare chest absently, then more mindfully. Looked around. Sylvie in her underwear. Lupe in expensive lounge-wear borrowed from Val's closet, Demalion's low-slung suit pants. Only Alex was still in her street clothes, and, since those were cutoff shorts, flip-flops, and a halter top, there was a lot of skin on display.

Marah forced a grin. "Slumber party? Or orgy? Can I play?"

"What do you want?" Sylvie said.

"Right now? You to lift the fright night from my bones. C'mon, Shadows. Panicky assassin with a gun? Can't be good."

"Fine," Sylvie said.

"Hey, that was easy. I thought I'd have to bribe you to—"

"Why did you come here? Riordan decide we need a babysitter?"

Demalion said, "Sylvie. Interrogate her *after* the spell is lifted?"

"Nah, it's okay. I get it," Marah said. She shivered all over, her face going grey, her eyes rolling back in her head. "Jesus, this Val is a real bitch. That was a bad one. Feels like my guts just rolled around. Feels like there are rats chewing me up from the inside; oh God, what if there are—"

"You could have hit the intercom," Sylvie said. "Asked to be let in. Demalion, bring her."

"No, wait, what?" Marah protested. "Back outside? I don't want to—"

"Shut up," Sylvie said. "We put you out; the spell drops off. Then I invite you in. Easier than trying to remove the spell while it's active."

Marah spasmed again, her hand clenching tight on Demalion's shoulder. He winced; her nails raked his skin. Sylvie took advantage of the moment to take Marah's gun from her. Or at least, that had been the plan.

For a woman fighting off a magically induced panic attack, she was damn fast. Sylvie found her outstretched hand grabbed, wrenched behind her, and her body shoved into face-first into the wall, Marah a trembling line against her back. "Don't make me shoot you, Sylvie. You owe me favors. I intend to collect. But instincts are hard to fight."

"Tell me about it," Lupe said, entering the conversation for the first time. "At least you don't turn into an animal. Sylvie, what the hell is going on? Alex only told me that we were all in danger."

"I am, Demalion is. Alex is by proximity," Sylvie said, easing herself out from Marah's grip. Marah let her go, but stepped back, wary. "You're . . ."

"Collateral damage. Again. Brought to someone's attention because of you. Fuck you," Lupe said, and stormed off toward the back of the house.

"Great, glad to know why we're all here," Marah said. "Spell. Off. Now."

Sylvie flung the door open, stalked down the moonlit driveway, wincing as her bare feet hit crushed rock, listening to Demalion telling Marah that it'd be all right, just a little bit longer. Platitudes. To reassure an assassin. Sometimes, she really wondered about him.

"So how'd you find us?" Sylvie said.

"Studied you, remember? I've got as many files on you as Demalion does, I bet. I know about Val. This was a logical place to regroup before going after Graves."

The wrought-iron gates, looming before Sylvie, still held a tiny residual warmth from the long-set sun. She keyed it open, shoved Marah out.

The woman whooped for air, dropped her hands to her knees, and just breathed. "Holy crap, I feel better."

"Great," Sylvie said, and closed the gate. *"Why did you come?"*

"You're going after Graves," Marah said. "I want in. C'mon, Syl, it's a win-win. You help me kill an asshole, and I help you get your sister, my itty-bitty baby cousin, back home safe."

"Do you know where Riordan's keeping her?" Sylvie opened the gate again, extended a hand to Marah. "Come in." Her heart thumped hard in her chest; Marah's hand in hers was cold with lingering shock, but her grip was firm.

"No. His boy's hiding and hiding good. I tried to find him. I figured you'd be sure to let me play if I brought Zoe with me. But no dice. C'mon. I want to help. I know Graves."

"Riordan said you liked the man."

"He said that?"

"No," Demalion said. "He said your instincts couldn't be relied upon when it came to Graves."

Marah grinned. "Now that just depends on whether or not the instincts go against orders. Right now, they're in sync. I want to scoop his eyeballs out with my fingernails and feed them to him. Riordan wants him dead."

"So he says," Sylvie said.

She felt like she was surrounded by power plays. It

seemed quite possible to her that Riordan would send Sylvie off with marching orders to kill Graves, secure in the knowledge that she wouldn't, not without proof that might be hard to find. That would explain why he didn't send Marah. Riordan's games were hard to figure.

Marah stepped forward gingerly, burdened by the memory of fear and sickness. Demalion scanned the surrounding area, keeping an eye out for anything that might take advantage of the open gate, ready to usher them back to the fragile safety of Val's house.

"So? What's the plan?" Marah said.

"Haven't gotten that far yet," Sylvie said.

"Jesus," Marah snapped. "It's been ten hours since Riordan gave you orders. What the hell have you been doing?"

"Mostly? Sleeping," Sylvie said.

"Look, we need to move fast. Graves has ears everywhere. Even in Riordan's crew, and he's notoriously cautious about who he talks to. I think that's why Riordan recruited his son. Just to have a single ally he could trust. I killed Powell."

Powell. It took Sylvie a moment to recall the agent. Last she'd seen him, he was holed up in the elevator taking potshots at everyone who passed. "You did."

"Graves's man. I'm pretty sure."

Demalion groaned. "You're pretty sure?"

"Well, he tried to shoot me."

Demalion and Sylvie traded glances.

Marah headed up the path to the house, said over her shoulder, "Graves is a bastard, but he's a clever one. He's got a serious yen for using and disposing of the magical freaks. And he loves spies. I used to spy on Riordan for him. Hell, he tried to have me killed the moment I stopped saying *Yes, sir* and wanted to work under Yvette, and I register pure human. He'll know we're coming, and he'll have access to all our weaknesses. It's gonna be an ugly fight. Can we get your Fury in on it? Wait, no. Never mind. I want to kill him myself, and she looks like she'd be selfish."

Sylvie and Demalion trailed after her, listening to her eager and bloody plans for Graves.

. . .

BACK IN THE HOUSE, SYLVIE EXCUSED HERSELF TO RAID VAL'S closet; she left Marah and Demalion bending their heads together, making quiet plans. She tugged Alex aside, and said, "Keep an eye on her."

"Who is she?" Alex narrowed her gaze as Marah ran a hand through her short, dark hair and stepped closer to Demalion. "Is she hitting on him? In front of you—"

Sylvie sucked in a breath. Alex knew who Marah was. She'd been told twice, once just minutes ago. Alex's memory was getting worse. But she was within Val's wards—the spells should no longer reach her. Unless she was forcing the memories by digging at the cases, which seemed entirely likely, knowing Alex.

"Just watch her. She's not a homewrecker. She's an assassin. She's dangerous."

Alex crossed her arms over her chest, nervously. "What am I supposed to do if—"

"Yell," Sylvie said. "Loudly."

She padded down the hallway, the tiles smooth beneath her feet. The room she'd crashed in with Demalion was a guest room. Alex looked to be camped out in the living room. Her laptop hummed industriously on the huge modular sofa, a woodcut image of a mermaid on the screen; a blanket was crumpled at one end of the couch, next to a bottle of aspirin and a clutter of small plates, as if Alex had gotten up for more than one snack while working. Sylvie's stomach growled. Food. Soon.

She heard Lupe swearing, detoured toward it. Found Lupe and her destination all at the same time. Lupe, apparently, was bunking down in the master bedroom.

Lupe jerked away from the mirror when Sylvie came in. "What do you want?"

"Clothes, mostly. How are you doing?"

"You're really going to ask that?" Lupe threw out her

hand toward the mirror; her talons, longer than she'd accounted for, scored four lines through the mirror glass. "Am I going to turn into that thing that attacked me?"

"Absolutely not," Sylvie said.

Lupe tilted her head in a gesture more predatory than confused. "What aren't you telling me?"

"That thing," Sylvie said, "is a god. A slightly mixed-up, violent-tempered, but ultimately lonely god. She likes you."

"Can she fix me?"

"Maybe. She's being a little bit difficult about it, though. Be patient." Sylvie opened Val's closet. Blinked at the size. There were walk-in closets; and then there were closets that were as large as bedrooms. This closet had a window, endless drawers, hung clothing, and a shoe rack that took up more room than some library bookshelves. There was even a department-store-worthy mirror stand and two chairs. Everything was cream or white or beige or grey, linen or silk or heavy, smooth cottons that felt like satin to her fingers.

Sylvie looked at the sheer quantity and thought she'd always mocked *Zoe* for being a clotheshorse.

Zoe.

Sylvie pushed the fear back. They'd deal with Graves and Riordan, and Zoe'd be home safe by the next day at the latest.

"Your friend's pretty big on island fashion, huh," Lupe said, poking her head into the closet. She sidled around the three-sided mirror and looked out the dark window. "Ocean view, too. What is she, the witch to the rich and famous?"

"Hey, don't snark," Sylvie said, though her lips twitched. "If we can't convince Erinya to think you make a better human than a shape-shifter, we're going to be dependent on Val's goodwill."

"Guess I shouldn't have broken her mirror." Lupe didn't sound like she cared. She slunk through the closet with an animal grace that reminded Sylvie of Erinya's human form. No wonder Erinya was interested. Here was someone who reminded her of her sisters, who could give her the fight but came without the bossiness.

"Did Alex show you Val's panic room?"

"You think I'm going to go monster again."

"Try not to," Sylvie said. "Demalion's already taken a shot at you, and our new guest would take killing you as a personal challenge. She's ISI. If I didn't need her info, I wouldn't have let her in." She pulled open drawer after drawer and finally found khaki jeans that she didn't think cost the earth. Sylvie dragged them on, wincing as she fastened them. Val had always been just that bit slimmer. They'd stretch.

She dragged a shirt over her black tank, sighed; Val's wardrobe didn't lend itself to black underclothing. It would do. She buttoned the shirt, realized Lupe hadn't said much in the past minute or two, and turned. Lupe was huddled up on one of the chairs, being careful of her talons on the fabric.

Sylvie replayed the conversation and grimaced. "Sorry. They're not trigger-happy or anything. You're perfectly safe. You feel the changes coming on, right? So we just get you in the panic room at that point. No harm, no foul. No shooting."

"Can't really blame 'em," Lupe said. "I'm a monster." She blinked slitted eyes at Sylvie, showed fang teeth in a wry grimace. "You know the most bizarre thing? I think I could deal with the shape-shifting. With never knowing what I might become or when it might happen.

"What I can't stand? Is not going back to human. I don't know whether it's vanity or what, but I look in the mirrors, and all I see is this. . . thing. When I've shape-shifted, I don't care."

Sylvie bit back her knee-jerk analysis: that Lupe didn't care because the animal instincts were too strong, too centered on killing things. After the attacks on her girlfriend, her nephew, the witch, and Toro, Sylvie had no doubts that any shape Lupe took would be instantly predatory. Dangerous.

"Maybe we can work with that," she said, instead. "At least, as a stopgap thing. Remove the side effects, make things more livable, let you be able to go out and about on the street. Worry about the actual curse-shifting as a separate thing." It was far from ideal. Far from solving Lupe's problem, and from the slump of Lupe's shoulders, she knew it.

"Might be the best I can get is that what you're saying?"

"Well, it gives us a more reachable goal," Sylvie said.

"If you have time for it," Lupe said. "Don't think I haven't noticed, Sylvie. Something big is going on, and you're in trouble."

"We're all in trouble, all the time. The moment the *Magicus Mundi* notices you, your life is trouble. But you're not wrong. The ISI grabbed my sister. I have to get her back."

Lupe picked at the fabric on the chair; seams popped with each idle flick of her talon, shedding fluff and creamy threads. "The ISI. The same ones who'd put me in a cage or just shoot me?"

"I think you're off their list for now," Sylvie said. "They're under attack from within."

"And they took your sister? Why? Leverage against you?" Said in the weary tones of a cynical rich kid. The Fernandezes, Sylvie recalled, had spent nearly two years in Mexico City, where kidnappings were common.

"I don't pretend to know how they think, if they even do. But I have to—"

"I get it," Lupe said. "She's your sister. She's more important than me. I'm just a—"

"Lupe, lock it down," Sylvie interrupted. The thread-picking had given way to gouging, and the skin along her shoulders was . . . sliding around like oil on water. "Or go sit in the panic room."

Lupe sucked in her breath, let it out on a growl that she seemed surprised to hear. "All right." She bolted for the panic room, Sylvie hot on her heels, and she got the door closed, just as Lupe went to her knees.

"Lock yourself in!" Sylvie said. Hoped Lupe would listen. Hoped her animal shape couldn't learn how to deal with locks. She waited until she heard the hiss and thunk of heavy bolts sliding into place, then went to find the rest of her ragtag crew, with worry a bitter taste in her mouth.

Alex dithered in the hall as she approached. "You're back? I can stop watching?"

"Yeah," Sylvie said.

"Good." Alex darted for the nearest bathroom. "Four cups of coffee!"

"Bring me some!" Sylvie yelled after her, then went in to talk to the rogue ISI.

Demalion looked up as she entered, grinned. "Nice pants."

"Shut up," she said. "They'll stretch. Tell me about Graves."

An unearthly howl resonated through the house, and Marah jerked for her gun. "What the hell is that?"

"Client," Sylvie said. "Sit down. Graves, remember?"

"Can't forget that bastard," Marah said. "He's mine to kill, you get it? Don't make this a fight."

"Saves me the trouble," Sylvie said, "and the jail time. Go for it."

Demalion shook his head but didn't even make a pro forma protest. Guess turning traitor was what it took to get the okay from Demalion on planning murder.

"He was working out of Dallas," Demalion said, "but they were the first hit."

"So we hear," Sylvie said. "Do we know that it's true? If Graves is behind the killing, what better way to start by preemptively giving his people an alibi. Do we actually know they're dead?"

Alex wandered back into the room, passed a steaming mug to Sylvie, who slurped at it, first for need, then for real appreciation. Rich friends. Excellent coffee.

"I've been looking into it. There are definitely bodies that hit the Dallas morgue," Alex said. "Gas leak was the story put out. Death by asphyxiation. Or is it suffocation in that case? Whatever. There are a lot of creature stories about things that steal breath. So *something* happened."

"Maybe it was a test sample," Marah asked. "Graves is capable of that."

Sylvie looked to Demalion. He said, "I can't confirm that. I have serious doubts that anyone psychotic enough to kill his own men in an experiment would be recruited in the first place, much less rise through the ranks."

Marah's jaw ticced. Rage flashed through her eyes. Her fist clenched; the Cain mark seemed to undulate over her flesh. Then she reached out and patted Demalion's cheek. "So sweetly naïve."

"Hey," Sylvie protested. "Watch your tone."

Marah shrugged. "Look, I know Graves. I worked for him. And yeah, he knows how to play the game. Knows how to keep himself looking clean. But he's not. He's the monster-catcher. He kills them. Experiments on them. Sylvie. You and I know killing. It gets easier each time. And *we're* not zealots."

"Fair enough," Sylvie said.

Demalion looked like he might protest, and she dropped a hand on his thigh. A quiet *not now*. She had things she wanted to discuss, but Marah was exuding a hectic, violent cheer that made Sylvie think of ticking bombs. In the back of the house, Lupe howled and whined, quieter now.

Alex said, "You need plane tickets?"

"For the morning," Sylvie said.

"Now," Marah said.

"No," Sylvie said. "You've invited yourself along. I can't say I'm sorry, but that doesn't put you in charge, Marah. We are not rushing this. The one thing we all agree on is that Graves is dangerous. If he's behind the attacks, he's a thinker, also. The kind of man who has contingency plans. We go in the morning. Well rested and researched."

"I like that idea," Alex said. "C'mon, Marah, is it? I'll find you a room."

Marah twitched like it was a physical pain to not go for Graves right away.

"Sheets are six-hundred-thread count," Sylvie said.

"Soft as silk. Hell, some of them even are silk. There's no complaining about Val's hospitality."

Marah groaned. "Not fair, using sheets against me. I suppose she's got scads of hot water also."

"Tankless system."

"I'm licked. Lead me to it. Revenge in the morning."

Demalion reached across her and pushed the papers that Marah had been holding. "She brought blueprints of the Dallas ISI."

"Do we really think Graves is still there? If he's this rogue ISI terrorist?"

"You obviously don't," Demalion said.

"I don't know," Sylvie said. She slumped down next to him, butted her shoulder up tight against his side. He draped an arm over her shoulder and pulled her closer. "I've been saying that an awful lot of late. I don't like it. I just feel like there's more going on here. Riordan's not impartial. He was slinging a lot of mud."

"If it helps, I really doubt Yvette's behind the memory spells," Demalion said. "They've been going on for some time, right?"

"Society of the Good Sisters," Sylvie murmured. "Sounds like a quilting group. That sound familiar to you?"

"Should it?"

"Dolphin boy thinks they're our memory culprits."

"When did he say that?"

She waved it off and went back to Graves. "The thing that's bugging me. The thing I can't get over. How is Graves doing it? If he is doing it? He's human. Not even magically talented from everything I hear. How's he controlling the *mundi* monsters?"

"Fear?"

Sylvie flicked his cheek. "They're the monsters, Demalion. We fear them. Not the other way around. They're committed to these actions. I talked to the Mora, saw the footage of the succubus attack. You survived the sand wraith. Did it seem frightened to you?"

"It seemed angry," he said. "I don't know what to tell you, Sylvie. I know that Yvette distrusts Graves. I know that Riordan, who's pretty damned sensible, thinks Graves is our guy. I'm willing to go on a little faith."

"Faith," Sylvie said. "Yeah. I'm not much for that. Requires too much working blind."

"Hey," Demalion said, pulling her to her feet. "Think about it this way. You're working to get Zoe back. And I can guarantee you that Graves is no innocent."

"It'll have to do," Sylvie said. She stretched, felt her back pop and crack, and thought about another few hours of sleep.

Demalion rubbed at the back of her neck, long fingers soothing as they carded through the tangles of her hair. "So. Dolphin boy was here? You let me sleep through it? Saw him alone?"

"Oh God, in the morning," Sylvie said. "I'm too tired to argue."

She tugged away from him, headed back for the bedroom. She stopped to move Alex's blanket over the young woman; Alex was facedown on the couch, a few inches from her laptop. Sylvie closed it, slid it beneath the couch for safekeeping, then just stood there.

"She's forgetting more things," she said.

"She asked me how things were going in Chicago," Demalion said.

Sylvie grimaced. "What did you say?"

"Not much. I started to, and she sort of went blank while I was watching her. Sylvie. Whoever these witches are. Good Sisters? They're getting stronger. I don't think we can count on Alex's research skills now. Researching is making her worse."

"Agreed. God, if Riordan weren't kidnapping family members, I'd send Alex home. Get her out of this mess. I just hope she remembers that Lupe is dangerous."

10

Turbulence

IT WASN'T UNTIL THEY WERE SQUEEZED ONTO A PLANE THE NEXT
morning, hip to hip and knees to chair back in front of them,
that Demalion seemed to recall her mention of the Encantado. "So tell me about your meeting with the dolphin."

Across the aisle, Marah's ears pricked up. "What dolphin?"

Sylvie sighed. Demalion had practically whispered it
into her ear. Marah was too damned attentive. "The ISI's
not the only one concerned about the attacks," she admitted. "There's a . . . party from the other side who doesn't
like the precedent being set."

"A monster," Marah said. "Told you what? That they
were *innocent*?"

"Told me what I already knew. That the ones attacking
the ISI are pawns of someone else."

"Yeah. Graves," Marah said.

Demalion, recalling Sylvie's objection from the night
before, said, "How do you think he's doing it? A human
controlling the monsters."

Sylvie found her wandering attention sharpening. Did
Marah have an answer?

"If anyone could figure out a way, it'd be him." Marah leaned back against the headrest and closed her eyes. "So what else did your informant say? Anything useful?"

"Not a lot," Sylvie said. "You know about the Good Sisters?"

"Sounds like the Daughters of the American Revolution," Marah said. "All prim do-gooders and charitable works."

"The Encantado thinks their charitable works are erasing memory—"

"Oh," Marah said. "Wait."

Demalion leaned over. "Oh?"

"SGS," Marah said. "The Society of the Good Sisters. They're a rumor. Not really real. Supposedly started in the late 1800s. Industrial Revolution witches."

"What do the rumors say?"

"That they're secret keepers," Marah said. "Men and women who use magic to hide magic. We thought they were a sort of magical police. But we never found any evidence they existed at all."

"Sounds like just the type of thing that's happening here."

Marah shook her head. "They don't exist, Sylvie. Trust me. The ISI looked hard. You know how the government loves templates. No, your guy was just telling you about the bogeyman that the monsters believe in."

Sylvie thought back. But the Encantado hadn't seemed afraid. Had seemed angry. Still, the plane was no place to get in an argument, and she had other things to worry about. Like Lupe and Alex, locked in a house together, one losing control of her shape and the other losing control of her memory.

Sylvie remembered driving out this morning, in the predawn swelter, and finding that Val's house had become Sleeping Beauty's castle overnight. Jungle blooms had twined and tangled and crawled over the low limestone walls, as pervasive as kudzu and as sweet-smelling as orchids. They'd had to hack through the greenery to free the gates from their tangled weave. Demalion and Marah had gawked, and Sylvie had felt eyes on her from the darkest heart of the thickets.

Erinya.

Right now, Sylvie wasn't sure whether Erinya's lurking presence was a good thing or a bad. She'd protect Lupe—wanted to keep her new toy safe—and she'd protected Alex before. But she was also impatient and violent and easily distracted. If she wandered off on some bloody task, would Alex remember to call on her?

Demalion's hand wrapped around hers, slid his long fingers between hers. "They'll be fine. All of them."

"Or I'll know the reason why . . . Vengeance gets old, Demalion. I'm tired of making people pay for hurting others. Be better to prevent it from happening in the first place."

Turbulence shivered the length of the plane, of air pockets shifting beneath the wings, and in the skies outside, lightning flashed, white cracks in a pale, blue sky. *Unnatural,* she thought. The plane dipped again. Demalion's hand slipped from hers; when Sylvie blinked the jagged purple afterimage from her eyes, ears popping ferociously, she wasn't on the plane any longer.

"Oh, come on!" she snapped, seeing Dunne leaning against the wall, watching her.

She was back in her office, back in Miami. Back where she started. With Zoe depending on her.

"You were supposed to stop her." Dunne's eyes were storm clouds. Lightning flashed through them, a constant angry crackle, strobing her office in washes of light.

"I don't know if you've noticed," Sylvie snapped. "But there's a lot more going on than Erinya. She's the smallest part of my problems right now. Take your godly envy and get lost."

Dunne sighed. "The problem with large events, *enormous* events—if you're in the center of it, you don't see the scope of it. You live in your city, but you haven't seen it."

Like magic—well, it was magic, wasn't it—a glassine smart board appeared between them, the city mapped across it, glowing green and red and gold. Mostly green. Key Biscayne was solid red from shore to shore, and the water around it was tinting with bloody light.

Lupe was in Key Biscayne.

"She's changing things past repair," Dunne said.

Sylvie swallowed. "So Key Biscayne goes Aztec jungle—" She couldn't finish her objection. Couldn't find anything to ameliorate what was happening. Erinya's jungle would be troublesome enough if it were just plants. Sylvie imagined Erinya's otherworldly jungle spreading outward, sending tendrils through the waters, snaring ships, eating away at the ocean floor. But her presence brought life to alligator statues, encouraged people to pray to her with blood and stolen hearts.

Dunne didn't say anything. He didn't have to.

A spark of gold washed over the red-tinged Key, traced it like lightning, then was swallowed by Erinya's power.

"What was that?" Sylvie said.

Dunne cocked his head and looked at his magical board.

"Is that real time? What's the gold? Green's real world, right? Nonmagic?" The gold light was tiny, like sparks. But it was speckled *everywhere*, from coast to coast and beyond, as pervasive as termite dust in an old house.

"Witchcraft," he said. His mouth turned down in disapproval. She shared that sentiment. "A large spell affecting multitudes."

"Witchcraft? What the hell . . . that's all from the brain-rewrite spell? Jesus. I knew they were brainwashing people, but this . . ." She sank down on the couch, stared at the board. It was easy to be angry at Graves, to declare him a rogue and an enemy, a traitor to humankind, but Sylvie thought that this was the greater sin. Erasing people's memories. Leaving a magical taint big enough to show up against gods.

"You're adding to it," he said, "by not stopping Erinya. Her power's leaking, and your witches are using it to strengthen their spells. Should I find something more personal to motivate you? If not your city, your lover? I can take him from you."

Sylvie tore her gaze from the board. "Try not to be an asshole, Dunne. I seem to recall you had a few good points. Besides, you're too late. You can't lay a hand on him. He's been god-claimed."

Dunne's gaze went human in surprise. "Let me guess. Erinya."

"Yeah," Sylvie said. "You can't attack her, or one of her followers, without making war. She doesn't have enough worshippers yet that she won't notice him going missing."

"She won't want anything good for him. If you kill her—"

"Dunne," Sylvie started, then just sagged. She was tired enough that his unsubtle manipulations felt like physical weights. "Look. Would you just get off your high horse for a minute or two? I know that your pantheon's probably making your existence maddening at the moment, all *Stop her, you created her, this is your fault.* I seem to recall that the Olympiads were big on blame. But listen to yourself. *Kill her?*

"Even if I had the time, the energy, or the inclination . . . what happens? She got this power by a god's dying. If she dies, all that power's up for grabs again. Things are bad enough down here as it is. I don't need a dozen gods and godlets descending on Miami to snarf up what she left. How would that help my city? Or, wait. Am I supposed to call you before I kill her, give you the heads-up so you can call dibs? I'm not a paid assassin, Dunne."

"You were the one who suggested you could get her to leave. No progress?" That, Sylvie thought, was as close as Dunne would come to admitting she was right.

"Some," she said. None, she thought. Worse than that. Antiprogress. Erinya's discovery of Lupe made her that less likely to leave. Earth was where her new toy lived. Unless . . . Lupe wasn't too happy about her current life.

Dunne growled, sounding rather disturbingly like the Furies he still controlled. "Shadows."

Right. Mind reading.

"Fine, there's a snag or three," she said. "But I need to be in Dallas right now. Erinya might be dangerous, might

be spilling god-power all over the place, but there's someone else who's actively killing humans and using the *mundi*
creatures to do it. Any pointers?"

"I can't intervene," he said.

"Figures," she said. "After all, dead humans are good
for swelling the soul collections. What do gods do with
them anyway?"

Dunne waved; the board vanished. "Nothing I can
explain to you. Sylvie, if it comes to it, I will remove Erinya
from the earth myself."

"You said that could start a war in the pantheons."

"Yes," he said.

She licked dry lips, tasted fear and the lingering flavor
of the cinnamon gum she'd chewed on takeoff. "Seems to
me human casualties would be higher if that happened
than if you left her be."

"She's setting precedent. There are whispers across the
heavens, especially from the forgotten gods: If she can
walk on earth, attract worshippers, why not the rest of us?"

"Give me a week," Sylvie said. "Right now, Erinya's all
wrapped up in my client, but Lupe's not interested. Let me
see if I can turn that one way or the other. Get Lupe
intrigued or Erinya tired of her new toy."

"She was created to chase," Dunne said. "She won't get
bored."

"Give me a week," Sylvie repeated. "Please." She'd deal
with Erinya, even if it took a bullet. Miami might lose out
that way, but at least the world wouldn't.

"A week," he said.

He spoke as if he was considering it, but she chose to
leap to her feet, and say, "Great. It's a deal. Now, can you
get me to Dallas? Since you interrupted my flight? I need
to take a look at William Graves's offices."

He sighed; the office grew storm damp. Her hair rose
and danced in the growing electricity. "His office or him?"

"He's alive?" Guess that answered that. The man was
playing possum. The odds of his being the guilty party just
went up.

"Yes."

"Then him, definitely him."

She collected her backup gun and spare ammo, snagged a chocolate bar from Alex's desk drawer, and took a giant, sweet mouthful. She needed the sugar rush in the come-down from the confrontation with Dunne. Finally, she took a quick moment to text Demalion that she was fine, would meet them in Dallas. Dunne sighed impatiently. The office twitched with electricity.

"Anytime, Shadows."

"I'm ready when you are," she said.

"If you don't mind," she tacked on, hastily. Better to be polite to the god who was about to fling her through space.

"Not at all," he said, as falsely polite as she. He flicked his fingers in her direction, and she was gone.

· · ·

LANDING WAS HARD; LUCKILY, THE FLOOR WAS SOFT. SYLVIE sprawled in the thick grey carpeting, and caught her breath, her bearings. Sofa to her right—chrome legs shining in the sunlight coming through the high windows—glass coffee table to her left. She spared a moment to be grateful she hadn't landed on it. She clambered to her feet, gun in hand, half-expecting to find Graves or his men drawing down on her. She hadn't landed quietly. Her ears popped, testament to the storm violence of her travel. She thought she smelled ozone, sharp and sour, in the air, and wondered if she'd traveled by lightning.

The living room was empty of people and stayed that way. She lowered her gun and moved on. A glance out the windows showed that she was sky-high, the ground multi-ple floors below, a wrinkle of grass and toybox cars. Top-floor apartment, she thought, in some Dallas condo. Judging from the size of the living room, a solid thirty feet by thirty feet, Sylvie assumed it was the penthouse. They were alone up here.

She moved through a sterile kitchen, continuing the mad-scientist theme of the living room—all grey and chrome and glass. His refrigerator doors were transparent, showed neat shelves sparsely filled. A man who wasn't home often. Or at least, not often enough to cook.

Tension tightened her jaw. She knew Graves was here. She didn't like Dunne, but she knew his word was good. He'd told her once that he could find any man on earth; she believed him.

So where is Graves?

Her boots rasped against the soft white stone in the foyer; there was dust beneath her feet like a dustpan's worth of forgotten sweepings. It was gritty to her fingers but softer than sand.

She rubbed her hands clean on Val's borrowed khakis, and checked the front door. Locks engaged; the security system was on. *Where is he?*

Sylvie headed down the white-carpeted hallway; caught her sleeve in one of the moving, metal sculptures that lined the walls. It rang like a struck tuning fork, a growing vibration of sound. She damped it with a hasty palm, listened.

A faint sound. A groan. Something that wanted to be urgent but was losing the strength to convey it. Sylvie hurried toward the sound, pushed through the bedroom door, and stopped cold on the threshold.

Dunne had played fair. Told the truth.

Graves was here.

Graves was alive.

But not for much longer.

Truthfully, Sylvie was shocked he was still breathing at all.

He was . . . His *skin* was . . .

It lifted and curled away from him in a thousand little shags, blanched and bloodless. It reminded her of nothing so much as paper birch bark. It made him nearly unrecognizable. His head lolled on the pillow; flakes of him drifted away. "Who—"

Sylvie backed up, repulsed, then shook herself.

"Graves," she said.

He tried to push himself up; close to death and still fighting. Still furious. A zealot indeed. His bare chest revealed four deep tears, edged in blood, and one shallow one; Sylvie thought of a hand pressing in, four long fingers and a shorter thumb.

"Traitor," he breathed. His lips cracked bloodlessly. His tongue rasped against teeth made enormous by white gums pulling away. "In the ISI. Good Sisters. Key. Books."

"What happened?"

"Warn—" He coughed, and his tongue blew away in the gust of his last breath. Sylvie reached out to check his pulse and his chest and neck and head disintegrated beneath her fingers. Not completely. A few curved fragments of bone remained, cradling a withered heart.

His hand fell to his side; his fingers hooked in his pocket, then crumbled likewise. His pants slowly collapsed as his body spilled out at both ends of the fabric.

Something chinked softly. Metal touching metal.

Key, Sylvie thought. His pocket. She reached in gingerly, hoping to God this wasn't some kind of magical disease, that she wasn't going to have to test her magical resistance against *mundi* plague. How would that work, would she lose a finger or two, before her resistance kicked in? She grimaced, tried not to think about it as she sorted through his remains.

A key fell into her palm. Small. She'd expected a locker key, or a safety-deposit-box key. Instead, she held a curio cabinet key. Simple. Uncomplicated. The kind of key that could be bypassed entirely with a paper clip.

Graves had thought it worth a dying word.

Sylvie toured the penthouse, found room after room full of white furniture. Nothing that the key fit. Nothing that looked like the books he'd mentioned. No reading material at all though she found several computers and an e-reader.

Graves liked technology.

Sylvie looked at the key again, looked at it more closely. Smiled.

It was a key, but not the kind she'd thought. There was a glass bead at the tip, with a glimmer of light behind it. It was an electronic key, disguised.

She went back to his bedroom, grimaced at the remains on the bed, and started tossing the room as carefully as she could; she didn't want to stir up his dust. Really didn't want to breathe him in.

Behind a wall mirror, she found a safe with a blank black face. She waved the key across it and it popped open, a tiny vacuum dispersing.

A book.

Journal, rather. White leather. The man was compulsive.

Sylvie dragged it out, wondered what was in it that he had felt the need to hide. To bypass his tech toys and commit to paper.

Easy enough to find out.

She sat, gingerly, on the edge of the bed, flipped it open to the first page.

It finally talked today.
  It asked for water.

Sylvie grimaced. Nice. A torturer's diary.

I had it put in the tank, and it shrieked as its torn skin hit the salt water. Hovarth looked squeamish. Weak-willed. I told him to leave. Better not let him come back. The monster's a seducer. I'd destroy it, but . . . I need it.
  It knows things.
  Things I need to know.
  Things I will know.

Sylvie flipped ahead, skimmed through accounts that turned her stomach. Mentions of how well electricity traveled through salt water, mentions of food deprivation and sound bombardment and isolation.

Mermaid? Sylvie wondered.

Maybe Marah was right. Maybe Graves did have a way of making monsters obey: He broke them.

It talked again.

It told me that I was so busy worrying about the world, I was missing what was happening in my own house.

It told me there were those who had infiltrated the ISI. It wouldn't tell me what. Or who.

It laughed at me.

I left it in the tank for a week without food. Without any water but what surrounded it. In the dark.

I knew it would survive. I could hear it singing to itself at night. It made the weak-minded among us cry. I had to send them away.

That's one thing the monsters have over us. Survival. Look at Shadows. She keeps surviving. Just a woman. On the outside.

I'd love to get her on my table.

Marah was supposed to bring her to me. Fickle, stupid, bitch. Thinks I don't see her courting Riordan. Trying to get away from me.

Sylvie flinched. It was one thing to tell Demalion that the ISI wanted her dead and dissected. Another to come across Graves's eagerness for it.

She slid off the bed, too repulsed to sit near his corpse any longer. Any sympathy she had for his outré death fled. She hoped it had hurt.

Something wrapped fingers like steel hawsers around her ankle and yanked her off her feet. She kicked out, thinking, *Stupid, stupid, stupid!*

The door had been locked, the apartment sealed. Dunne had dropped her inside and made a locked-room mystery of her presence. Graves had been still alive; his wounds fresh, his body whole. All signs that the monster was still here. Had only retreated to the nearest hiding space as a startled creature would. And she'd blissfully sat down to read on top of it.

The monster under the bed.

Sylvie's kicking hit something that hissed, that felt like metal jarring her bones. She twisted, got free, her gun drawn, just as the creature scuttled out into the room, as ungainly as a grounded bat, but *fast*. Sylvie backpedaled with all her might, skidded to the wall, and braced herself for further attack.

It leaped to its feet, revealed itself to be human-shaped, skeletal, with a crumple of burned parchmentlike skin stretching from joint to joint. When it moved, it sounded like paper tearing. Long, bone-bladed fingers jabbed at her, and she jerked aside. Her ankle throbbed and trickled blood.

"Cost me the best part of my meal," the thing hissed. "The last, labored breath." A withered tongue flicked.

Night Hag, her Lilith voice reported. *Feeds on suffering. Eats children and leaves dust behind in their beds. Parents think the children have been stolen, then the Night Hag feeds on their suffering for weeks.*

Graves wasn't a child, she thought. He hadn't been suffering. How had the Night Hag gotten to him?

"You followed Graves home from work," Sylvie guessed. Fitting fate for a torturer.

"His prisoner's cries drew me in, but it was gone when I found my way into his labs. His frustration was sweet. I rode home in his bodyguard's skin, ate him from the inside out, left him dust. Then slid in and sampled Graves slowly; he tasted of rage and panic and blood. You, I'll kill quickly."

"No, you won't."

The adrenaline had worn off. Sylvie just felt tired. Felt like she had all the time in the world. The Night Hag lunged at her, bony fingers diving for her chest, and Sylvie shot it three times in the chest. Bone splintered and cracked.

The creature looked surprised, as if it hadn't expected the bullets to affect it at all. Sylvie was getting used to that expression. She liked it. The Night Hag crumbled inward, its bones crunching under the weight of that leathery skin.

Sylvie kicked it away from her as it fell, left it a broken, skeletal nightmare stretched obscenely across a white carpet. Huffed and went back for the journal. She flipped it open to the last entry; if there was ever a time for skipping to the end, it was now.

Her throat was dry; she dragged herself and the journal to the kitchen, pulled a bottle of springwater from the glass-front fridge, and sat at the white-marble counter to read it.

> *The creature's escape means nothing. Only proves that one of mine has turned traitor. Hovarth, probably. I think he's Yvette's man. Traitor to me, the ISI, the country. Mankind.*
>
> *Doesn't matter. One monster free. What can it do? It told me what I needed to know. I'll stop it. I won't be beaten by the Good Sisters.*

That was it. Sylvie groaned, flipped back and forth, trying to piece together the narrative. Graves's captive, not surprisingly, ended up responding better to crumbs of kindness: food, fresh water, the faint promise of freedom. A lie—Graves gloated for a page about how desperate the creature must be to believe him. Once it started talking, it had things to say, things that must have made Graves feel like all his paranoia was worth it.

> *It told me that I had only caught it because it was fleeing a more dangerous foe and stumbled into my net. It told me about the Society of the Good Sisters, told me that they were witches who tried to control monsters, the better to increase their own powers. Then it told me that they had infiltrated my organization.*
>
> *I did the research. It was right.*
>
> *The Society is a secret, a rumor, a ghost, but I'm a determined hunter. I found proof. Shreds of history, shreds of evidence. Their motto. Keep the secret world secret. They harvest it, steal its powers to fuel their*

*spells, protect it, hide it from society. They will go to
any lengths to hide their resources, including erasing
people's minds.*

There was her answer to her memory plagues. Motive
and perpetrator laid out in Graves's cramped penmanship.
The Good Sisters. The Encantado had been right.

*They are in the ISI working against us, working to
increase their power, working to hinder us in our war
against the monsters. I've found the head of the snake.
Yvette Collier and her secretive cabal of witches and
freaks. Have evidence and photographs to prove it. It
shouldn't be a surprise. You can't trust magic-users,
not when the power they use is dependent on the Magicus Mundi's existing. Can't trust them to wipe out the
monsters when scavenging power keeps them strong. I
told DC that they shouldn't allow witches in the government. Now I'll prove it.*

Sylvie closed the journal. Graves had never had the
chance to prove it. The Night Hag had latched on, followed
him home; while he lay trapped and dying, his base had
been attacked, his men killed. If the much-scorned Hovarth really had been Yvette's man, if Yvette was the Society, *then* the attacks made sense. He released the monster
and ran to Yvette, telling her that they had been unmasked.

The Encantado had been right, but so had Riordan.
Sylvie's objections had all been based on Yvette's being
genuinely a member of the ISI. If Yvette wasn't ISI, then
suddenly she became a lot more likely as a suspect. The
only suspect.

Infiltrating the ISI had to have been a simple way to
keep an eye on their competitor, to make sure that Graves's
xenophobia didn't win the day. They put in their own man,
or woman, and undermined him. Then the ISI accelerated
their ten-year plan, was thinking of opening up the *Magicus Mundi* to public knowledge. Regulating it.

For the Good Sisters, who seemed to farm the magical world, it would mean sharing their resources. If the rest of the world knew about magic, everyone would be poking at it. The number of witches would skyrocket, as all the would-be latent talents suddenly gave it a go. Boys and girls like Zoe.

Until they killed themselves messing with power they weren't ready for, her little voice said.

Until equilibrium was reached, Sylvie responded. Every system, no matter how chaotic, eventually settled. Humans were adaptable, and they learned fast. Look at the technology—science had gone from Model Ts to the moon, from the inklings of genetics to DNA mapping, from the first snowy TV to the ubiquitous Internet. They'd kick and fuss and panic and slowly make space for the new knowledge.

Sylvie wouldn't have to fight alone any longer. When something went wrong in the *Magicus Mundi*, people would be able to defend against it. They'd know what they were dealing with.

It wouldn't be the end of things, only a new beginning. A beginning that the Good Sisters opposed to the extent that they were willing to wipe out government agencies, to wound or kill civilians to keep from happening.

Why wouldn't they? When they could erase their own tracks, what would stop them?

The Encantado couldn't get close enough.

It left her and Demalion. And Marah and Riordan. If they could be trusted. They wanted Graves dead, but Riordan, at least, had suspected Yvette of manipulating memory. He didn't seem to mind, but that was when he thought Yvette was working her spells on behalf of the ISI.

She needed to tell him. He'd want proof. The journal was a start. Graves had mentioned photos and files. Sylvie checked the computers, found each of them required a password to enter. She groaned. She didn't have time for this. Maybe Alex would be feeling better and could crack whatever security the paranoid Graves had put on his machines.

A glance at her watch showed her the flight from Miami to Dallas should be landing any moment now. She needed to get there, pick Demalion up. And Marah. The eternal, unwelcome afterthought.

Sylvie packed up the journal, the two laptops—one ISI issue, one personal use—and the external drive she'd found in the locked drawer beneath. It hadn't been a very good lock.

For the hell of it, she packed up his weapon—standard-issue Glock—and ammo. It left her with quite a pile. She stared at the keys on the kitchen counter and thought, in for a penny . . .

Besides, Graves was dead. He didn't need his car any longer.

When she left the apartment, stepping over the dust pile that had been an unfortunate ISI bodyguard, the alarm went off. She cursed and clattered down the stairwell, trying for haste without dropping any of her armful of things.

Twelve floors later, Sylvie came out into the parking garage and thought, penthouse apartment. Graves would have a prime parking spot. She waved the key fob at the closest spots, and a slate grey SUV chugged to life.

She should have time to pick up Demalion and Marah and make new plans before the car was reported stolen. Any cops who responded to the alarm's going off would be far more occupied with the two bodies left in the apartment—Graves's half-disintegrated corpse and the unearthly Night Hag.

11

The Good Sister & the God

SYLVIE HAD JUST MANAGED TO MAKE HER WAY INTO THE DALLAS/ Fort Worth terminal, remembering at the last that, no matter how much she liked her gun, she couldn't get it inside without causing a major fuss. She left it in Graves's glove box, along with his Glock; she chose to carry the laptops with her, stuffed into a single, overstretched laptop case.

Two small children raced past, screaming and fighting, their mother chasing after, shouting vainly for them to behave. Amusement and relief sparked in Sylvie's chest. Those were the children that had been fighting on the plane in the seats before her. At least, Dunne's travel express had spared her three plus hours of whining children.

Her gaze left them, scanned for Demalion; for once, she didn't have to remind herself to look for blond instead of brunette. It seemed her brain had finally accepted Demalion in the new form. Defaulted to it in her memory.

While looking for them, she grew tense. One suited man lingering in a terminal was nothing. A businessman traveling. But one suited man lingering in a terminal trying to not look at another suited man . . . it could be a potential hookup, but Sylvie knew better, even before she saw them avoid looking at two more suits. The ISI net was laid out.

Sylvie moved smoothly toward a coffee kiosk, then kept moving until she was behind a pillar. They didn't notice, all their attention trained on the exiting passengers. Sylvie dialed Demalion hastily, hoping he had been quick to turn his phone back on.

"Sylvie," he said, "Nice disappearing act you pulled. Think you can stay disappeared?"

"They're waiting for you—"

Demalion and Marah crested the curve, and Sylvie bit off the heartfelt curse she wanted to emit. She wasn't that far away from the ISI herself.

"I know they are," Demalion said. A woman that Sylvie had not marked as ISI peeled herself out of a chair and strode over. Late forties, a face like a beautiful blade—all sharpness and intent—and cropped, tight curls. Unlike the rest of the ISI, she wore a dress in a eye-catching teal.

Marah tensed all over, and the woman laid a hand on her arm. The movement looked gentle, a casual touch, but Marah sagged beneath it. The suits moved in and gripped her arms tight.

"What's the point of having psychic abilities if you don't use them!" Sylvie said.

"I did. This is the best-case scenario," he said. His gaze swept the concourse briefly, lit on hers for the barest moment of contact, then swept on. "This way leaves bread crumbs—"

The witch—she had to be a witch, a strong one, to affect Marah with a touch—took the phone from Demalion's hand.

"Sylvie," the woman said. Her voice was as sonorous and warm as a viola. "Will you join us?"

"Yvette," Sylvie said. Really, the woman could be no one else. Even if she weren't the witch in charge, she looked like Demalion's type: strength before prettiness. "I don't think so. I'm still in Miami."

"The first time we get to talk, and you tell me a lie? Not a good start, I'm afraid. I've cast a seeking spell. It won't be long before we find you."

"Finding isn't catching," Sylvie said.

She grabbed another look at Demalion; he'd shouldered aside one of the agents, a red-haired man, and was holding Marah up himself. Stupid, Sylvie thought, he wouldn't be able to move quickly if he got the chance. Then again, though Demalion had flaws, stupidity was not one of them. He didn't think they were in immediate danger; burdening himself was a signal to her that she should flee without guilt.

Something brushed over her skin, as damp and breathless like a dog's nose, all snuffling curiosity—Yvette's spell.

"I feel you now," Yvette said. "You're close, aren't you? You're watching us."

"You think?" Sylvie shifted with the crowd's tide, let the seeking spell fall off her. She mingled with a group of stewards moving quickly through the concourse, heading for the hotel shuttles. Time to go.

"You took the high road, borrowed a god's power to bring you to Dallas. Riordan has you searching for Graves. I bet you found him. How was he? Dead yet?"

"You knew the Night Hag was there?"

"Couldn't have happened to a more deserving man," Yvette said. "I know you'll agree."

"If I don't, you and your Good Sisters will erase the memory of it."

Yvette's breath caught, the tiniest of tells.

"Surprised, yet?"

"It doesn't matter. You're not getting out of here, Sylvie. My people are at all the exits. You're not armed. We are."

Sylvie let Yvette have the last word, disconnected. The witch was right—Sylvie could see other agents lurking near doors, made the mistake of meeting eyes with one of them. The man's hand dropped to his gun, then he came after her, close enough that she could see an earpiece. What one knew, they all knew.

Fuck.

She could just let them catch her, trust that among Demalion, Marah, and herself they could get free and make Yvette's life miserable. Demalion had suggested she disappear, though. More psychic premonition?

She had to trust him and his instincts. She had to get out, stay free. She starting dialing. "Alex? Is Erinya still outside?"

A pause on the line, then Lupe said, "No. She's inside."

Sylvie went cold. "Why are you answering Alex's phone? Why is Erinya inside?"

"Because Alex fell over and starting foaming at the mouth."

"Did you do it?" Sylvie remembered those poisonous nails, the touch-me-not colors that lurked beneath Lupe's skin, wondered if Alex had called Erinya for help.

"Fuck you," Lupe said. "No."

"Put Erinya on," Sylvie said. The agents were closing in; Sylvie clutched the phone tight and ran. Hardly discreet behavior in an airport, especially when she didn't have luggage—no pretense at running for a plane. She dodged two rent-a-cops, who were all too willing to get involved, and they paid the price, getting hit with a spell meant for her. They went down, blinded, paralyzed, neat packages ready to be collected.

Yvette's personal team was all witch, Sylvie thought, and they could and would use witchcraft at will since they could cover it up, afterward. Up ahead of her, illusions spread like disease, unreal police clearing the concourse. Unreal police dogs lunged before them, pulling leashes taut, scaring people back. Isolating Sylvie, who didn't react to the illusions.

Yvette had studied her enough to turn Sylvie's immunity into a disadvantage. Yvette was a thinker.

"I don't want that thing. It's plastic," Erinya's voice resonated through the phone even at a distance.

"It's Sylvie," Lupe said. "Just take the damn thing."

"Plastic!"

"Erinya!" Sylvie snapped. "Come get me! Now!"

"Not the boss of—"

"Erinya!" Lupe said. "Please! Go to her!"

A moment later, the airport carpet shredded under the stress of a blossoming jungle; the witches nearest Sylvie, nearest Erinya's sudden arrival, screamed as their spells overloaded in the god's presence and burned them out as inevitably as a flame following a trail of gasoline. Erinya crossed her arms over her chest and smirked.

Too much to hope that Yvette had fallen prey to Erinya's magic-burn. Sylvie knew better. The moment Sylvie had hung up on her, Yvette had taken Demalion and Marah and gotten the hell gone. Yvette was a thinker; Yvette had files on Sylvie, knew her strengths, her weaknesses. Yvette knew Sylvie would use every weapon she could if cornered. Even a god. Knew she'd done it recently in Miami.

Erinya snarled, made to go after the witches, who were scattering as best they could. Sylvie grabbed her shoulder, said, "Miami. We don't have time."

"We have nothing but time," Erinya said. "We're immortal. And we're hunters. We could play. You could get payback for their harassing you."

"I need to get back to Alex. I need to talk to Riordan." Reminders to herself as much as to Erinya. It would be so easy to turn the hunt around. So tempting. Sylvie hated the ISI, but at least they had some interest in people's welfare. The Good Sisters? None.

And they had taken Demalion.

Sylvie savaged her lip, remembered Zoe. Remembered Alex, ill and alone with Lupe who couldn't be trusted.

Erinya ran a red tongue over black-painted lips, looking after the fleeing Society agents. "It wouldn't take long. Really. I could drop some of them from here." She held up a hand and proved her point. Sylvie turned to see two of the agents explode into a fine mist. The glass wall along the stairwell exploded, spitting shards everywhere. People screamed. Civilian casualties. The roof cracked, parted; sky peered through, mercilessly blue.

Somewhere, something was burning.

Erinya laughed. "Like nipping the heads off birds! Could cripple some others, let you catch up to them . . ."

"This is why Dunne wants you dead. This is why you can't stay on earth."

Before Erinya could take offense and disappear, Sylvie grabbed hold of her sleeve, and changed the subject. She didn't bother with subtlety. Erinya didn't do subtle. "So you've been hanging out with Lupe?"

"I played in her dreams, sent whispers in with the swaying of my flowers, spoke to the beast in her, and she called to me."

"Don't you want to get back to her?"

Erinya shot Sylvie a flat glare, a clear reminder that Erinya might not be subtle, but she wasn't stupid. "I could leave you here. Let you fly back the regular way. I've cleared the witches out for you."

"Eri—I'm worried about Alex. Worried about my sister. Just plain worried. I'm going to go hunt Yvette, but I need to prepare first." Like it or not, she was going to have to talk to Riordan. Not only to get Zoe back but to get a better scoop on Yvette. Find out if Riordan had been lying this whole time. Find out if he was Society also.

Thinking about his stance on magic, Sylvie doubted it.

Erinya sidled foot to foot, hissed at a single remaining security guard who had the balls to creep up on them, gun drawn, concussion be damned. He was bleeding from his forehead; his eyes looked glazed. He came on anyway. Erinya said, "Go away," and he was gone. Vanished. He screamed as he went.

"Eri—"

"What!" the god snapped. She spun around, shifting shape as she did, her tail lashing at the air. "Do not presume on our friendship. You keep telling me what to do. What not to do. I do what *I* want to do. You asked for my help. You don't get to dictate how I grant it." The spikes on her neck were not only standing up but quivering with rage.

Sylvie couldn't muster up any argument. It was true. It was why she'd tried not to ask for help, even when Erinya's presence loomed like a solution to so many problems. Erinya wasn't the right solution, just an easy one.

Sylvie wondered if she'd jumped the gun. If she could have escaped Yvette and her goons on her own. A year ago, she would have had to. Then again, a year ago, she'd barely been on the ISI radar.

"All right," she said now. "You're right. Can we go home now?"

Erinya's tail lashed, then the Fury growled concession. Given that they'd destroyed and cleared most of the airport, and there was no one left to stop them, Sylvie took the time to collect her guns from the car and to make sure the laptops hadn't been damaged in her mad dash. She remembered ricocheting off a wall at one point. If Riordan was involved, Graves's protected files would name him a villain also. Alex would need the computers.

• • •

TRAVELING VIA ERINYA'S GOD-POWER WAS NOTHING LIKE THE smooth hiccup in reality that was Dunne's method of movement. Sylvie understood why the guard had screamed; her bones felt like they twisted inside her skin, yanking her forward through landscapes that seemed slick and hungry, predatory. It was all stone and jungle and broken edges; nothing ran in any sensible way. It was as if someone had taken a puzzle of a landscape and forced it together any which way, heedless of shape or image.

Sylvie clung tight to her sense of Erinya and managed to wait until there was real earth beneath her feet to throw up. Her nails dug into damp Key Biscayne soil. Cool grass tickled her palms, and the salt air started to ease the twisting nausea. When she looked up, Erinya was peering back at her with curiosity. "You survived."

"Was that in question?" Sylvie said. She remembered the child that Erinya had vanished and wondered wildly what had happened to him. If he had felt that pain. If he had died someplace utterly alien to the world he knew, scared and alone. It didn't make sense. Erinya was all about justice for children.

"He's fine," Erinya said. "I took him the safe way. I took

you through the realm I inherited from Tepeyollotl. Do you like it? I don't. Even someone like me needs a peaceful place to call home."

Sylvie put her hand up, a quiet demand for assistance in getting to her feet. Erinya grudgingly provided it. "I do understand, Eri. I do. But you have the power to change that place. Make it what you want."

"It fights me," Erinya said. "It remembers Tepeyollotl. He's there, somewhere. Slinking around, a sulking remnant. Urging it to rebellion by his very presence."

"You've never shied from a fight," Sylvie said.

"I like to fight face-to-face, not against sneaking, crawling things. It makes me twitchy," Erinya said. She shot Sylvie a sidelong glance. She managed to look sheepish. Sulky. Human.

A teenage pout from a creature that had just injured or killed any number of people in the Dallas airport. Sylvie scrubbed her face, frustrated. At a loss. The *Magicus Mundi* was, paradoxically, easier to understand when it was inexplicable. At least then she could just label it as such. Erinya, with her inhuman abilities and human predilections, kept her veering between horror and sympathy.

"Are you two going to stand out there all day?" Lupe leaned out the front door.

"We'll work something out," Sylvie said. "Just. Don't go off half-cocked anymore."

"Unless *you* ask me to?" Erinya showed her teeth, sharp and thin behind her painted lips.

"I won't ask."

That was a promise Sylvie meant to keep.

Erinya shrugged, raced for the house, rubbed her cheek up against Lupe's neck, coiled an arm around her shoulders. It was breaking Sylvie's brain, but Erinya looked small and fragile next to Lupe's lanky height. Then again, Erinya changed her height as easily as she changed her shape.

Lupe petted Erinya's hair, met Sylvie's gaze with a flush on her cheeks. "What. You wanted us to get along."

Dream-courting, Sylvie thought. Whispering flowers.

Beast calling to beast. Obviously, it was an efficient woo-
ing mechanism. There was a bite mark on the back of
Lupe's neck.

"No, it's great. Rah-rah, love, and all that," Sylvie said.
"Where's Alex?"

"Still on the couch. I wanted to call the ambulance,
but . . ." Lupe's mouth twisted, showed fangs of her own, the
strange skink blue tint to her tongue. She gestured broadly
at herself. "What was I going to say when they came to keep
them from grabbing me instead? I called Erinya. She said
Alex was ill, but not in danger. I had to believe her."

"Thanks," Sylvie said.

"She really wanted to talk to you," Lupe said. "She
found out something. Something important. She said, wake
her up, no matter what when you got back. She wouldn't
shut up about it."

"You have any idea what she was doing?"

"Hitting the computer hard. I think she was looking for
leverage against Riordan?"

"She would," Sylvie said. "Thanks again. I mean it,
Lupe." She clapped the woman on the shoulder, jerked her
hand back when Erinya growled possessively, and went to
check on Alex.

As Lupe had said, Sylvie found Alex on the couch, but
instead of chattering and poking at her laptop, drinking coffee by the mugful, Alex was curled into a tight knot beneath
a blanket; her face seemed comprised of bruising and shadows, hollows under her eyes, her cheeks, her throat.

Sylvie touched her shoulder. It felt thin. Fragile. Sylvie
hated to do it, but she shook her awake. It didn't take much.
Alex jerked to awareness, panting and startled.

"Sorry," Sylvie said.

"Sylvie—" Alex flailed for a moment, reaching for her
computer. "I found something. What did I find. I can't
remember. I found it. It was important."

"Easy," Sylvie said.

Alex sat up, shook her head, clicked the laptop open.
"So frustrating. I know I know things. A lot of things.

Important things. But the more I try to remember it, the more it's like a whirlpool in my head." There were tears in her voice, in her eyes. Her hands shook. Sylvie was going to kill Yvette for that alone. For putting her best friend through this hell. The Good Sisters had held sway for far too long. There was nothing beneficial in turning a brilliant young woman into a nervous wreck.

"Just sit a second," Sylvie said, pushing back anger. Pushing back her own urgency—the need to deal with Riordan, retrieve Zoe, rescue Demalion, deal with Yvette— pushing it all away. Reaching for a tranquility and patience she had never possessed.

All the time in the world, her Lilith voice murmured.

For the first time, that soothed.

Alex calmed. "Okay. Okay."

"Lupe said you were looking into Riordan."

Alex winced, but nodded. "Dominick Riordan. Head of the Miami ISI. In charge of studying the legal ramifications of . . . of . . . the *Magicus Mundi.*" She spat the last two words out, panting. She tightened her jaw. "Just about him. It's just about him. I can remember about him." Talking herself away from all the memories connected to Riordan that the Society had erased or rewritten. "Oh God, Syl, it's hard. It hurts. Riordan . . . He's fast-track. He's smart. He's careful. He's scrupulous. He's a good guy. I mean, for a fed. He's given everything to his job. He has no life outside it, no friends . . . *no family.*"

Her breath caught, eased. She looked up at Sylvie, clutched her hands. "Sylvie. He has no son. He just thinks he does. How do you get control of an incorruptible agent?"

"Plant a spy he'll trust," Sylvie said. John Riordan. Dominick Riordan's son. The man she'd saved from the mermaids. The man she'd thought a witch. He *was.* Guess that meant Riordan Sr. wasn't Society after all. His so-called son was. It meant something else, as well. She tried to keep the anxiety off her face, but felt her expression freeze along with her blood. Alex picked up on it, anyway. Her face crumpled back toward tears.

"God, Sylvie. Riordan's son has Zoe. I should have called you sooner. I should have—"

"You did your best," Sylvie said. "Really."

"It doesn't feel that way," Alex said. "If something happens to Zoe—"

"Hey," Sylvie said. "The Good Sisters are collecting people. Not killing them. Yvette took Demalion and Marah. She could have killed them. She went for the kidnap. She wants them alive. They'll be okay. I have time. Maybe Riordan's son will give Zoe back. To keep his cover, he'll have to be obedient to Riordan's deal." She tried, fiercely, to believe any of it.

Alex nodded along with her, but even as she did, a frown crawled across her face. "Who's Yvette? Do I know . . . Oh God, have I forgotten her, too?"

"Don't worry about it," Sylvie said.

Alex eyed her distrustfully, but finally nodded. "All right."

"Get some sleep. Real sleep. In a bed," Sylvie said. When Alex staggered off obediently, Sylvie confiscated the laptop, studied the open files on Riordan's life, the identity search Alex had set in motion on his not-son—no wonder her memory was failing so fast. The only image she had of so-called Riordan Jr was the altered film of the mermaid's attack. Just looking at it would set her off. Sylvie added the computer to her heap of Graves's stolen tech. She had hoped that Alex could hack Graves's computers, ID the rest of the Society agents in the country, figure out where they were based.

Maybe Sylvie could do it herself. Alex had programs to crack passwords. Sylvie opened the laptops, looked at the blank password fields. The programs were slow. She didn't have time.

All the information she could want on the Good Sisters and it was as inaccessible as if it had died with Graves. Sylvie closed the lids. She couldn't even ask Riordan to deal with it. The man harbored one Society spy in his ranks; there might be more. She looked at the files Alex had brought up on Riordan's false son, and grimaced.

"What the hell is wrong with her?" Lupe asked. "I thought she'd had a stroke, at first. But then she was convulsing. It didn't make medical sense. Another reason I didn't call the ambulance."

"Relax," Sylvie said. "You did the right thing."

Lupe stared at the door Alex had retreated through. "Can you fix her? She's really scared."

"If I can break Yvette's memory spell, I think so."

"You haven't broken the spell on me," Lupe said, her voice low and quiet. As if she regretted saying it even as the words crossed her lips.

"I don't know what to do with you, Lupe," Sylvie admitted.

Lupe grimaced. "So fucking unfair. You finally find all these powerful witches, and they're bad guys." Scales ran her skin, the beast within her threatening to surface. Sylvie tensed, then Erinya slipped into the room soundlessly, chased the scales away with a brush of her hand.

"We'll devour their hearts," Erinya murmured into Lupe's tangled hair. "We'll make them all pay."

Twelve hours ago, Lupe would have shied from that idea. Now, her snake eyes gleamed with a certain eagerness. Sylvie was losing her completely, even if Erinya was keeping her form more or less stable.

"Erinya, you healed me," Sylvie said. "Can you heal Alex? Chase the spell out of her mind?"

"Thought you weren't going to ask anything more of me," Erinya said. She leaned back, let Lupe take her weight.

"Can you do it?"

"You aren't claimed by any god," Erinya said. "Alex is marked. If I do it, Dunne will know. I don't want to—"

Lupe shoved her forward. Erinya whirled, hair flaring out into spikes. Lupe's arms grew multicolored scaly armor; her teeth lengthened, dripped venom.

Sylvie reached for her gun, but the two women only had eyes for each other.

"Do you know what I was before all this?" Lupe spat. "I was a physical-therapy student."

It seemed a non sequitur, and Erinya looked impatient. Lupe lashed out, scratched four lines across Erinya's throat. "Pay attention, Eri."

"I always pay attention," Erinya said. The vines creeping along the wall bloomed with dark flowers, set small stinging insects into the air. Her irritation making itself felt.

"I was going to help people," Lupe said. "I was going to teach them to regain control of their bodies—ironic, seeing where I've ended up. When I think about it? When I remember what I was, what I wanted to be, what my dreams were? I go crazy. This is my nightmare. I've lost control of everything I used to own instinctively. My body. My mind. I was supposed to be helping people. Now I'm *killing* them."

Erinya moved forward, reaching out, and Lupe lashed out with her claws again, etched another four lines over Erinya's throat. Like the first set, they healed at once, but Erinya hesitated.

"It's Alex's nightmare," Sylvie said. She got what Lupe was trying to say. "She's all about knowledge. It defines who she is, what she does, how she interacts with the world. You take it away from her—"

"And there's nothing left," Lupe finished. "You helped me. You made me not want to die. You can help her. Don't you stand there and do nothing if you can do something."

"But Dunne," Erinya wailed. "If I heal her, Dunne will know, and he'll—"

"Do it anyway," Sylvie said.

"Please," Lupe said.

Erinya reached for her again, and this time Lupe allowed Erinya's touch. Erinya shifted uncomfortably like a cat at the vet's, but sighed. "When she wakes up," Erinya said. "I need her awake to find the broken bits."

"Thank you," Sylvie said. It was one weight off her shoulder. Maybe two. Erinya was telling the truth. Healing another god's devotee was a definite infraction in the godly rules. It might be the thing that got the gods to come to a consensus. Alex's god—Eros—was mostly hands off, but he wouldn't like another god's mark on his worshipper. Still, in Sylvie's admittedly biased heart, Alex's cure was worth the risk to Erinya.

"So what are you going to do?" Lupe said.

Sylvie walked down the hall, peered in on Alex, curled in her tight, uncomfortable ball, the memory witches plaguing her even into her dreams, and hesitated.

"I've got this," Lupe said. "I can watch over her."

Sylvie shivered. It was one thing to leave Alex in charge of Lupe, with strict instructions to call Erinya and run like hell if something went wrong. Another to leave Alex at the mercy of two monsters. Lupe and Erinya had good intentions. . . .

Lupe said, "You have to deal with the witches. You have to get your sister. You have to trust that we can step in and take up the slack."

Her Lilith voice protested any giving up of control, but the thing was, Lupe was right. She had to trust these two. They were all she had.

Sylvie looked back at the house as she left and wondered how it had come to this. Sylvie had spent years fighting the *Mundi*; now the monsters were her only allies.

12

Unmasking

AN HOUR LATER, SHE WAS BACK IN HER OFFICE, WAITING FOR RIOR-
dan to meet her, Zoe in tow. Their phone call had been
short. Sylvie had dialed, said, "Graves is dead. Bring me
Zoe. At my office." She didn't want to give him any reason
to renege on his deal. She could hit him with all the
truths—that Graves had died at a monster's hand, that
Graves was a scapegoat, that Riordan's son was no such
thing—when he got there.

She was poking at the phone, realizing that the other
person she needed to call, she couldn't. The Encantado,
who had given her the Society info in the first place, who
had asked her for her help in identifying the witch in charge
of the monster wranglers, hadn't given her any way to get
in contact with him. Her mouth twisted. He hadn't expected
her to succeed.

It figured, though. He had been pretty grudging about
her involvement in the first place. It just rankled. She'd lay
bets that Riordan's fake son was the local monster wrangler. She didn't think the Encantado had it right: There
wasn't just one of them. Look how ragged dolphin boy had
run himself, just trying to catch up. One human in charge

of all that chaos? Far more believable to think that the Society had trigger witches in each ISI city.

The door opened, and Sylvie jerked her attention up, hand falling to her gun. It wasn't Riordan. Wasn't even Riordan's fake son.

Detective Adelio Suarez. Showing the cop-sense of timing, arriving when she absolutely didn't want him. He was unshaven, though, looked sloppy for the first time since she'd met him. He was grey with exhaustion, slow with stress.

"I thought if I had someone posted on your office, you'd show up sooner or later," he said.

"I'm meeting the ISI head here in a few minutes."

"Then I'm staying," he said. "They're supposed to protect us against magic, right? They're not doing their job."

"Lot of your men down?" Sylvie said.

"Enough that we've all been called in to work double shifts," Suarez said. "The phones keep ringing, people reporting they've been hit by the plague. We don't have people to send out."

"Plague?"

Surprise lightened his exhaustion, sparked interest in his eyes. "You haven't been following the news?"

"Lio, I've been slung from a moving airplane to Miami to Dallas and back again just since 6:00 A.M. And today's a better day than yesterday. Alex usually keeps me abreast of the news when I'm deep in a case."

"Why isn't she?"

"The witches fucked with her memory—"

"That's the plague I'm talking about, Shadows. You and I know it's witches. But there are news reports on every channel talking about the upswing in sudden-onset dementia. They think it's catching, and people are panicking."

Sylvie groaned. "Dammit. Dammit." She should have stayed in Dallas, should have prioritized catching Yvette, but Alex was hurt, and Zoe was missing, and Demalion had *nodded*, had all but sent her away. He had a plan of his own, but she had left him . . . She just felt stretched beyond capacity.

A dark SUV pulled up outside, disgorged Riordan. He looked harried; he pushed his way into her office, already criticizing her. ". . . just got off the phone with Collier. She said you released the Fury in the Dallas/Fort Worth airport? People *died*, Shadows."

"Yeah, but does anyone remember it," Sylvie snapped back. "She drove me to it. Where's Zoe?"

On the street, the dark SUV pulled away. Circling the block, probably, doing their part for air pollution.

"I needed surety that I would walk away from this meeting. She's with my people."

"Your people, or your son?" Sylvie asked.

In the same moment, Suarez said, "Your agency kidnapped her sister? This isn't communist Cuba. There are rules—"

"There are *no* rules," Riordan said. "They're all broken, and I'm just trying to pick up enough of the pieces to glue us all back together."

"By sending me out to kill people. By kidnapping my sister. By condoning memory magic."

Riordan's aristocratic face closed off. Suarez grumbled deep in his chest, rested a hand on his service weapon. Sylvie was belatedly glad he was there.

"We have a real problem, I agree," Sylvie said. "But I'm not sure it's centered where you think it is. You're blaming the monsters. You're blaming Graves. You're listening to the wrong people."

"Right now," he said, "I'm listening to you. You killed Graves, so obviously you judged him guilty—"

"No," Sylvie said. "I didn't. But he's dead all right. Been dying for days. Not behind the attacks.

"My problem is, he managed to identify the villain of the piece, but I don't know if you're part of the solution. Yvette Collier, the woman you just talked to . . . She's not ISI. Never has been. Her loyalty's to something older. The Society of the Good Sisters."

Sylvie paused, waiting for denial, for Riordan to declare the Good Sisters a magical urban legend as Marah had done, but, she'd forgotten bureaucracy—knowledge was doled out in increments, and only the upper-ups knew the score.

"You think she's one of the Society?" Riordan said, shaking his head.

"She's a ringer," Sylvie said. "Joined up, just so she could suss out the competition. Apparently, the ISI goals of study, contain, control, are not the Society's goals. She's been turned from a sleeping agent into a saboteur. She's taking out the competition, using witchcraft learned in the Society to leash monsters, then, she's using the memory spells to clean up after herself."

"No," Riordan denied.

"Sounds sensible to me," Suarez chimed in, and Riordan ignored him after a brief, why are you even here, glance.

"Yvette's driven and yes, magically talented, and yes, she's surrounded herself with other magically talented agents, but . . . no. I can believe she's behind the memory plagues, but she's just trying to help by making people forget something they're not ready to accept—"

Suarez slammed his hand down on the table, cut Riordan off, and sent papers cascading to the floor. "Take a look around, Agent Riordan. Does this city look like it's being helped? The hospitals are overflowing."

Sylvie said, "She doesn't give a shit about the regular people. She's not protecting them. She's protecting herself and the magical resources. Did she tell you that? Witches are scavengers, you know. They're born with the ability to manipulate power, but the power's not theirs. It's shed by the *Magicus Mundi*. By the gods, by the monsters, by the very things Graves wanted to eradicate. No wonder they went after him first.

"*Yvette Collier* is your enemy, Riordan. Not Graves. While you were blaming him for the attacks, he was at his penthouse apartment having his life suctioned out of him by milliliters. He's dead. I didn't kill him. The Night Hag did. Yvette knew about it. Let it happen. Graves was a vocal opponent of magic. She wanted him dead. Want more proof? Circumstantial to be sure, but thought-provoking. Her agents helped Graves's prisoner escape before the attack. She didn't want to kill monsters. Just men.

"And, Riordan, pay attention, this is where it gets personal. She keeps tabs on the players in the ISI, close tabs. Graves's aide turned out to be hers. She's got one close to you, too."

Riordan shook his head. "They're all ISI agents, and we vet them all. I vet my personal staff yet another time. Their loyalty is to me."

"*Almost* all of your personal staff," Sylvie said. She almost felt bad for the man. He was clinging to his convictions, but his grip was shaky. What she was about to show him wasn't so much something that would pry his fingers free as blow up the ground he clung to completely.

She pulled Alex's laptop up, set it on the desk between them. Opened it. Riordan glanced at it, looked harder. Suarez leaned in and studied it, too.

"That's my son."

"No. It's not," Sylvie said. "He's a Society witch, not even an American citizen. He was born in Victoria, British Columbia. His name is John Merrow. It's all there."

"No," Riordan said. "It's a trick. It's just a picture."

"You know witches, right?" Sylvie said. "They always end up with descriptive street names, pointing you toward their specialty. Like my necromantic friend, the Ghoul. Merrow's street name is Simon Says. He's not your son. Never has been. You just believed him when he said so. He's Yvette's spy.

"Don't feel bad. He fooled me, too. I never questioned whether he was more than he seemed, not even when he didn't fall prey to the mermaids' singing. He's been playing the long game."

Riordan said nothing but shook his head again, started to stand.

"Sit down," Sylvie said.

Suarez pushed him back. "Your agency. Your fault. You listen."

"Here's your file, hacked recently by Alex. Before she lost her mind. Before Yvette's memory plague made her curl up and wish she were dead. This is your life, Dominick Riordan. One ex-wife. No children."

He put shaking hands over his face, shuddered. Belief settling into his skin.

"That sinking feeling you have right now? That sense that you can't trust your own brain? That's what the *city's* feeling. I want my sister back now. I want Yvette's current location, and I want you to give me all the backup I need to take her down."

Riordan looked up, his face blanched white. He jerked to his feet, yanked off his watch, and crushed it underfoot. "He was listening."

"You came in wired?"

"You're dangerous," Riordan said. "Of course, I came in wired."

"Fuck," Sylvie swore. "We have to move, now."

"My men—"

"We're not waiting," Sylvie said. "Let's go—"

Too late, of course. Even as she pushed away from the desk, reached for her gun, five ISI agents were spilling in, John Merrow leading from behind, sheltered by their collective bulk.

"Bang, bang, Dad," he said, and the room erupted into gunfire. Sylvie lunged for the dubious shelter of the kitchenette, saw Suarez fling himself toward the understairs panic room.

Dominick Riordan stood his ground in the bullet fire, then raised his own weapon and shot himself in the head. His brains pulped out against Alex's desk. John Merrow grinned.

"Give it up, Shadows, come out and be shot like a good little troublemaker."

Sylvie felt the words move around her like a fisherman casting a net, compelling her to obey. It felt . . . oddly familiar.

Dammit, he'd compelled her way back when, when the

water was rising, when he insisted she hold on to him, keep him above the waterline. Bastard.

Stupid bastard. Once exposed, her resistance would kick in. She shrugged off the compulsion easily, now. "I don't think so."

Bullets stitched a ragged line across her wall, hit the fridge, shot metal-and-plastic shrapnel into the tiny kitchenette. Sylvie felt her skin burn and pop as the shrapnel tore into her clothes.

Small wounds. She'd heal. She poked her head out, aimed low, shot two of the invading ISI in their legs, took one in the thigh, splintered one man's knee. They crashed down, still firing. Determined.

Guess Riordan wasn't the only one under magical commands. Neither of the injured gunmen made any attempt to get out of her line of fire, to staunch the bleeding. They were going to die shooting, obedient to Merrow's will to the last.

Suarez stepped out into the room, reading the situation the same as she did. He squeezed off two shots, and the men's gun hands dropped. More brains on her floor. Sylvie shuddered.

Adrenaline made her mouth sour; her heart raced. Merrow grimaced behind his remaining two men. "Aim better, boys. And hurry it up. You. Cop. You're shooting at the wrong person. Shoot Sylvie."

Sylvie froze; Lio was in perfect position to shoot her. Instead, he shook his head. "No, I don't think so."

Merrow muttered, "Dammit. Name, name, name. Juanez? Anyone here know his name? Shadows, tell me his name."

"Don't pay enough attention to the little people, huh," Sylvie said.

Merrow had met Suarez once, but he hadn't paid attention to him. Thought him insignificant.

"Tell me."

Sylvie felt the force of his will batter at her, but it had its match in her Lilith core. She shook it off, breathed out.

She jerked out of her shelter, huddled between wall and

open refrigerator door, put three bullets in the next agent's stomach, felt her hair tug and pull and burn. Her ear felt wet and hot. Her cheek scalded. She rubbed her face against her shoulder, left a smear of blood behind. Creased. Not even that. Just a friction burn. From a bullet. Her stomach turned. She couldn't die here. Not and leave Yvette to her games.

Merrow backed toward the door. His lips moved, the words unintelligible beneath the continuing gunfire. Sylvie said, "Aim for Merrow! He's spell casting!"

Sylvie focused, tried to get her bullets where they needed to go—Merrow's throat, but her head was spinning. Friction burn or not, she'd been knocked for a loop. Her eyes weren't focusing quite right. Her bullets went wide. Suarez's never reached Merrow at all, impacting instead against a magical shield.

Suarez said, "He's *your* problem," and went back to picking off the remaining agent's shelter bullet by bullet, with a quick pause for reload.

Merrow's spell casting reached a high note; Sylvie felt the air in the room change, grow charged. The wall behind her burst into flame. She rolled forward, hitched up at the far-less-safe juncture of half wall and open office. The fire could be illusion. Witches loved their illusions. Given Merrow's steady retreat, Sylvie was laying bets that this fire couldn't be ignored.

The remaining agent panicked, jerked to his feet, atavistic fear of burning alive momentarily trumping Merrow's mind control, and Suarez and Sylvie shared the killing shots.

Now, for Merrow.

The wall to Sylvie's right bloomed with fire, another ignition point. Merrow angled to get the third wall, too impatient to retreat and pick them off as they tried to escape the fire. His spell casting stopped short, his muttering voice cut off midword, and he went rigid before twitching and collapsing.

The fires continued, but Sylvie barely noticed them, real as they proved themselves to be. Her attention was all for the woman who'd brought Merrow down.

Girl, rather.

Zoe yanked the buzzing stun gun away from Merrow's neck, breathing heavily. "Take that, asshole. Leave me tied up in the trunk, will you?" She held the stun gun in her Cain-marked hand, and Sylvie thought that combination would cut through any magical shielding. Zoe kicked the man while he was down, and only then turned her attention to the room.

Sylvie's relief was so enormous she couldn't muster a single word; her voice locked, her eyes watering. Zoe looked good. Alive and healthy and pissed. Her hair was a tangle; her fancy clothes were creased and stained and about two days past laundry time. But she was alive. Not brainwashed. Not broken.

"Sylvie, you're on fire," Zoe said.

Suarez lunged at her, rolled her over, smothering flames. Beneath his shirt, she felt rigid material and groaned. She really did have a bad reputation if the cops came to her office wearing their bulletproof jackets, and the government agents came wired.

Throughout it all, Zoe didn't leave her position near Merrow, ready to zap him again. When Sylvie rose, singed, a little bloody, tugged up by Suarez, Sylvie was so proud of Zoe she could burst.

She hugged her close, and Zoe leaned back into her for a long moment before she shoved Sylvie off. "Ugh. Your clothes are wrecked and you smell." Despite her words, her free hand lingered on Sylvie's sleeve, fingers tangling in the dirty fabric.

"Love you, too, sis," Sylvie said.

Two walls of the office were fully consumed now, the fires licking upward, climbing into her private office, rolling forward, reaching for the front. Sylvie thought of all her files, the computers, the upstairs office, the whole of her life's work going up in ash and flame, and said, "Lio. Grab Merrow. Let's get out of here."

13

Manipulations

THEY ERUPTED OUT ONTO THE STREET, THREE OF THEM COUGHING IN the smoke that billowed out after them, Merrow a silent deadweight at the end of Sylvie's arms. Her shoulders protested, even with Zoe taking his ankles. Suarez had refused to arrest him, saying, "I can't hold him securely. I won't put my colleagues at risk. We're in enough trouble."

"I wasn't going to give him to you anyway," Sylvie said. "He's got info I want."

For once, something was going their way. Streets that were normally busy and crowded with pedestrians were all but empty. The only witness to their exodus was a gull that shrieked and flapped toward the sea.

Sylvie said, "Where is everyone?"

"Staying home. Trying not to catch the plague," Suarez said. "Didn't you notice that traffic was lighter than usual?"

"I just thought I caught a break," Sylvie said. She shook herself. "Yeah. I should have noticed."

"You two get out of here. Talk to him. Find out how to stop the plagues."

"You're not coming?"

"I discharged my weapon. I shot and killed federal

agents. If I want to keep my job, I need to stay here and call it in."

"All right," Sylvie said. Zoe whined about Merrow being heavy and to hurry it up. "Be careful, Lio."

"Y tú. Cuidate."

Sylvie rubbed blood off her cheek, and said, "Yeah."

Merrow twitched and mumbled; Zoe dropped his feet, grabbed the stun gun and zapped him again. His eyes rolled up in his head as the newest jolt left him partially conscious but in no shape to be casting spells. Good enough.

"Zoe. Leave him some brain cells," Sylvie said.

"Whatever. Where are we taking him?"

"Val's is home base."

"You asked her first, right?"

"Of course I did. Couldn't have gotten everyone past the wards without her permission." Sylvie winced. Those wards were toast. Had been ever since Lupe ushered Erinya in. Magical wards had been replaced with a jungle that seethed and hungered. They were on the road, driving the ISI car along a pleasantly deserted highway, almost to their destination when Sylvie did a little mental head slap. She was bringing two witches to a god. While she didn't care if Erinya burned every last drop of witchcraft back out of Merrow, Zoe was another story.

"Zo, you absolutely cannot do any magic while you're at Val's," Sylvie said. Her voice cracked, the first thing said in long miles. Zoe was huddled up on one seat, her hand clenching tight on the stun gun, her gaze never leaving Merrow.

At least, Sylvie thought, she'd given her contrary sister an escape hatch from obsessively reviewing the wrongs Merrow had done her. Zoe erupted into instant protest.

"What? No! Why?"

"Because Erinya's there. The moment you fire up your magic, you burn out."

Zoe made a face. "So not fair. Gods are such bullies."

"And try to be polite. To everyone. We're all on edge."

Merrow coughed laughter in the backseat, rattled his

cuffed hands behind him. "Polite. Your little witch is a stone bitch. I wanted to rip out her tongue after twenty minutes in her company. I give your bad-tempered, impulsive god less than two minutes before Zoe's a smear on a wall."

"Don't make me send her back there with the stun gun again," Sylvie snapped.

"Won't change the truth."

"Did you ever consider that I might be nicer to someone who didn't kidnap me and keep me tied up in a basement, then a car trunk?"

"Let me go," Merrow said. Compulsion underscored his words, striking out like a lash.

Sylvie and Zoe laughed at the same moment, and Merrow subsided into a dark scowl.

"Sorry," Sylvie said. "You've lost your edge. Where'd you pick that talent up anyway? It doesn't really seem witchy. It's not a spell you cast. It's just you."

Zoe said, "He's half-blood monster. I think Merrow's not just his name. It's genealogy. A half-blood. Val says that a lot of the water monsters have a way with compulsion enchantments. Like the mermaids' song, like the kelpie who makes you want to ride even if you know better."

"Like the Encantado," Sylvie said.

"Yeah. That's the big gun," Zoe said. "The strongest of the water magics."

"Really?" Sylvie said. The creature she'd met had been pissy, tired, and losing ground on a battlefield he hadn't chosen. He hadn't struck her as particularly powerful. But she'd been behind wards when she talked to him at length. If he was that strong . . . damn, she wished she had a way to contact him. Add one more monster to her *mundi* allies.

"So Val says." Zoe looked over her shoulder at Merrow.

Merrow said, "That woman's not worthy of the title witch. All she does is hole herself away from any conflict and waste her talent on academics. She deserved to get her talent burned out."

"It's coming back," Zoe said. "Better not be rude to her, or she'll make all you Society witches cry."

"Watch out!" Merrow shouted.

Sylvie almost reflexively stomped on the brakes, bound both by basic driver instinct and by the sudden wave of compulsion. Almost.

"Don't!" Zoe snapped at the same moment.

Sylvie pressed down harder on the accelerator, taking them off of Virginia Key and onto the short expanse of Rickenbacker Causeway which connected to Key Biscayne. Merrow lunged for the side door, determined to get out, whispering spells to override the door locks, and Zoe flailed at him with the stun gun.

Merrow screamed and went limp.

The SUV bumped gently onto the key.

"I didn't even hit him with it," Zoe said.

"He got hit with something bigger. Take a look."

Key Biscayne had gone jungle. Erinya's will exploding outward, corrupting and changing everything in its path. There was little left of Crandon Park from what Sylvie saw. All the buildings drowned in an impossible vegetation and red flowers that snapped and bit. Shadows, spotted like jaguars, ghosted through the greenery, and brought to mind the dapple of sunlight over leaves. Zoe sucked in a breath and slid toward the middle of the SUV as if its steel walls could protect her.

Merrow had been spell casting when they crossed, head down, focusing all his energy into a spell, and found himself abruptly at the mercy of a magical tide he couldn't bear. Scoured out from within. No wonder he'd shouted.

Sylvie kept the SUV to the center of the road; the jungle encroached fast on either side. At least, Merrow wouldn't be a threat now. At least, they'd be able to question him without worrying about him spitting out spells instead of answers.

• • •

BY THE TIME SYLVIE STOPPED AT VAL'S ESTATE, SHE WAS DRIVING purely by GPS guidance. Nothing looked familiar. Or rather, it looked all-too-familiar—all of the world coated with Erinya's heaven reaching down to her. Chaotic jungles and lurking predators. Once you were out of the city proper, Miami's evening air always smelled sweet and salty—night-blooming flowers and the ever-present bite of the sea—but when Sylvie opened her door to get out and open the gate, the air was wet and heavy and rank with crushed vegetation and animal musk.

When she reached for the gate, the iron scrollwork writhed and hissed and drew back after flickering dark, forked tongues over her sweating skin. Sylvie tried not to wince. This was Erinya's world, her psyche. Like her, it would reward fear with predation.

"Erinya," Sylvie said. "We're coming in."

No response, but a tangle of dark flowers bent slowly toward the distant house. It seemed far more distant than was possible, a tiny glimmer on the horizon instead of a mansion three hundred feet off the road. Sylvie returned to the SUV gratefully. The night felt full of predators.

"Zo, you come up front and hang on to me." She didn't want there to be any misunderstandings. Bringing a witch into Erinya's realm . . . She wished she had another recourse.

Zoe clambered up, dug her fingers into Sylvie's arm without protest. Behind them, Merrow lolled in the middle seat he had dropped into, half-conscious, panting with either fear or effort.

"What about him?" Zoe said.

Sylvie wanted him alive, wanted to question him, but if he vanished from the car, if he got sucked out and devoured, she wouldn't cry.

She wanted answers, but more than that, she wanted Merrow to pay for kidnapping Zoe. Zoe was running on pissed, but whenever she stopped being cranky, Sylvie saw her hands shake, her shoulders tense, her lips bow down in that close-to-tears pout Zoe had had ever since she was a toddler. When this was over, Zoe was going to fall apart, and Sylvie wanted to be able to say, *Merrow can never hurt you again because I made him into shark chum.*

The driveway warped on them as the SUV hit concrete and brickwork. One heartbeat took them someplace that was bitterly cold with thin, gritty air and a sudden cliff to their left. *Erinya's realm,* Sylvie thought, and tried not to jerk the wheel in panicked reaction, and the next heartbeat saw her slamming on the brakes just before they impacted with Val's front door.

Sylvie felt Zoe's tourniquet grip on her arm, patted her fingers in relief, and turned to see if Merrow had made it. He had, though his eyes showed white all around the irises.

She couldn't blame him. There was basic god leakage, and then there was this. A remodeling that rearranged space and time. Erinya wasn't even trying to restrain herself. Couldn't be.

Erinya's presence in Miami was no doubt making the Good Sisters work overtime on the memory spell. Might be why it seemed to be the hardest-hit city.

Lupe opened the side door of the SUV, and Zoe bit back comment though her eyes widened, and her grip on Sylvie's arm tightened at the sight of Lupe. Sylvie felt her own breath catch. Lupe was stuck, seemingly midchange. Her skin was rippled with brightly patterned scales; her legs were . . . gone. She moved forward on a thick, snake tail, and the hand that held open the SUV door had talons that were leaving gouges in the metal.

"Coming out?" she said.

"Yeah," Sylvie said.

"Fuck no," Merrow said. He clung to the seat. "You kill me now, Shadows, and leave me out of this freak show of yours—"

A second later, he was torn from the SUV, dragged inside the house, and—by the time Sylvie scrambled to follow—gutted across the foyer, his blood wet and scarlet and dripping over Val's pale Italian marble. Erinya, in fury-god form, pawed at the remains. Lupe, hot-eyed, stared at the mess and tucked her coiled tail tighter to avoid the blood.

Zoe, on the doorstep, shrieked, turned to run, remembered the world-warp outside, and pressed up against Sylvie instead. Sylvie put an arm over her shoulders, and said, "Bring him back, Erinya. We need to question him. We need him to find Yvette."

"He was rude," Erinya said. "He came into my house, and he was rude to my chosen. I won't. Find another way."

"What, like sticking a pin in a map? Here be witches?"

Erinya lashed her tail, turned, and disappeared into the recesses of Val's house. Erinya's house, now; it bore little to no resemblance to Val's art deco mansion.

The marble floor, now drinking in Merrow's blood and bone, was the only thing left of Val's once-open foyer. The ceiling was close and stony, like the mouth of a cave. It led toward darker areas behind it, one swallowing Erinya's angry form. Sylvie stared after her, kicked at an encroaching vine. It snapped at her, and she shivered.

Lupe grimaced. "Sorry, Sylvie. I'll see if I can talk her 'round."

"Hey," Sylvie said, grabbing Lupe's arm. "Are you all right?"

"Fine, why?"

Sylvie gestured up and down, meaning *You're half snake*, a little reluctant to just come out and say it if Erinya was feeling that touchy.

"Oh. We're trying out monster shapes," Lupe said. "I keep changing. Eri says she can at least make it into a monster I like. At least in this shape, I keep control of my mind, if not my body. That's something, isn't it?"

Sylvie nodded. "That's a lot. How's Alex?"

"Sleeping, last I checked. I'll go tell her you're back." She moved off, surprisingly graceful as she swayed and slithered through the cavernous hallways.

"Jeez," Zoe said. She hadn't moved from the doorway, her arms wrapped tight around herself.

"You doing all right?" Sylvie said.

Zoe stared at her shoes, at the splatter pattern Merrow's blood had made. "These were brand-new. And expensive. An entire month's allowance worth. And look what she's done to Val's house! She could at least clean up after herself. Val's going to be peeved."

Zoe was fine. Displacing her anxiety every which way, but coping.

"Syl," Zoe said, catching her as Sylvie started after Erinya and Lupe. "Wait."

"We're kind of on a deadline," Sylvie said. "Yvette has Demalion. I'd like to get him back before he goes all Stockholm Syndrome and remembers he used to date her. Or hell, until she makes him forget they're on different sides."

"She'll be too busy keeping the Corrective running smoothly to do much with him."

"With the what?"

Zoe shrugged, took a step farther into the house. "You seem to forget I've spent the last two months in witch central. I get to *study* spells, not do them. Val's idea of teaching is setting the kid down with the *Encyclopedia Britannica*. So take that, and then stuff me in with a bastard like Merrow who likes to hear himself talk." She shuddered, and her gaze went opaque, distant.

"Your point," Sylvie prodded.

Zoe jerked back to the now with a sigh of relief. "So I know what spell Yvette and the Society's using—"

"The *Corrective*? Sounds like white-out."

"Same effect. It's a seriously complicated spell. First done in the late 1800s. The Society pioneered it. I couldn't believe it when Merrow started bragging about it—saying he could keep me for a pet, that you'd never remember that I was missing. Crazy complicated spell with really exotic ingredients."

"How exotic? Can we track them through the ingredients?"

Zoe shook her head. "Not the kind of ingredients you can buy. I still can't believe they resurrected it . . . it's such a tricky spell. It requires so much manpower to really be effective."

Sylvie leaned against the wall—damp, rough-cut stone instead of white wallpaper—and considered her sister. "All right. I want to hear all about this spell. First, though. You know how to break it?"

Zoe raised her palm, made a maybe–maybe not seesaw, and noticed a smear of blood on her skin. "I want a wash. You think the bathrooms are still in existence?"

"Zo!"

"I don't know! I mean, my books were all about how to make it work, not how to take it apart. Seriously, Syl. I've got blood all over me, and it's getting *gummy*. I really really really want a bath. If you don't let me go, I think I might cry. Or scream. Or have the breakdown I deserve. Tell me the bathrooms are still here. And not all . . . jungly."

"Lupe wouldn't let Erinya remove all the modern conveniences. Hopefully."

"Lupe. That's the . . ." Zoe checked herself, shot nervous glances around the foyer. "She's the person who answered the door?"

"Yup. Under a curse," Sylvie said.

"Your client?"

"Go shower, Zoe. And be quick about it. Miami's falling apart around our ears."

"It'll be a little bit more stable now that Merrow's dead," Zoe said. "He was the dispersal focus for the memory spell. People in Miami won't remember what they've forgotten, but they won't forget any more. Not until she gets another disperser here."

"He was part of the spell?"

"Why do you think he kept me in Miami? He wanted to take me to Yvette, one more witch for her spellwork, but he couldn't leave."

"Definitely need to talk," Sylvie said.

"Definitely need to *bathe*!"

Lupe came back into the foyer, wrinkled her nose at the mess. Sylvie wished she thought it was distaste distorting her features, but it looked more like a cat scenting something interesting.

Sylvie shuddered, wondering if she'd roll in it.

"Alex is awake," Lupe said.

"How is she?" Sylvie hesitated. This past week had been nothing but one horror after another. Still, nothing compared to sitting beside a frantic and crying Alex, unable to help her. She wasn't eager to revisit that sensation.

"Awake. Calm. Confused. Erinya's going to see what she can do."

"Don't do anything!" Zoe said, jerking to a halt.

"Why not?"

"Because I don't think Furies are good at delicate wetwork. She could probably yank out the spell, but then what? The memories go with it," Zoe said. "Because if you break the memory spell—which *is* what you're planning to do, right?—You want Alex's memories to come back. You have the Fury fuck around in her head, try to fix things, then the restore won't work as well. Because it won't be a spell releasing things back to normal. It'll be a spell beneath another spell. Her memories might not come back. If you wait, if you break the spell, you win them all back."

"Lupe, tell Eri to hold off. Zoe, with me."

"But . . . but . . . bath!"

"It can wait. I need spell info. *Now.*"

Zoe started to protest, and Sylvie grabbed her arm and dragged her toward what had been Val's kitchen. It was still a kitchen. Sort of. In some vague Erinya concept of a kitchen. There was a fire pit, nestled close to Val's slickly modern fridge. Vines carpeted the floor, as treacherous underfoot as slick cables, but sweet-smelling. There was a waterfall sliding down one wall, clear and cold and disappearing at both ends. A misty rainbow shimmered beneath the fluorescent lighting.

Zoe and Sylvie stared at the room, and said, "Freaky," at the same moment.

Sylvie poked at the table and chairs—rough-cut wood, carved with flowers. They seemed real and sturdy and most importantly, not inclined to kill them. She pushed Zoe into the closest seat, leaned back against the table, and said, "Talk."

Zoe pushed her hair out of her face, remembered she had Merrow bits on her, and grimaced. "Ebbinghaus's Corrective."

"Sounds like patent medicine."

"Eh. The Good Sisters were trying to keep a low profile. I mean, it sounds innocuous, right? Like their name? All their spells are like that. *The Helpful Cat. Serena's Trained Crow*—both of those are spying spells, by the way. *The Helpful Cat* can also be used to start fires, remotely."

"That what Merrow hit us with?"

Zoe shook her head. "That was just Pyrokinesis 101. Blow shit up. Coax all the heat in the air to coalesce in one spot. It's why he had to do one wall at a time. Burns really hot, but it burns out really fast. A little like balefire."

Sylvie said, "Zo. Trust me. That was nothing like balefire. I've seen balefire."

Zoe blanched. "You should be dead. How the hell did you—"

"Erinya," Sylvie said. "Long story. The Corrective."

Zoe stared at her, looking worried, looking impressed and Sylvie tapped her nails against the table. "Zoe, sooner you talk, sooner you get your bath."

"Okay, okay. Yeah. The Good Sisters, which you know, isn't all women, right?"

"Merrow being one of them tipped me off. Continue."

"So it's kind of chicken and egg. Whether the Society decided to keep the *Magicus Mundi* their secret first, or whether they gained the ability to do so first. Doesn't really matter—"

"Then stop telling me about it!"

"Whatever. You're being a total bitch, Syl. I've had a terrible day and I want a bath and I saved you from Merrow and he's dead and I should be glad but I'm just grossed out. And I want a bath!" Zoe's breathing was harsh; her hands clawed at the table.

Sylvie closed her eyes and reminded herself that she'd pushed enough for the moment. Now she had to be patient. Let Zoe regain her composure, her pride—those were what kept her running, as essential to her as rage was to Sylvie. She got up and rummaged through the refrigerator, still thankfully holding human-style food. She made roast beef sandwiches, heavy on the horseradish and mustard, and tried not to think about Demalion's sitting in her apartment kitchen, tasting foods to see if Wright's taste buds made a difference.

He'd be all right. He'd used his precognition to ensure it. He had a plan. He was just waiting for her to do her part.

"So at first it was like, conceptual? They weren't sure the spell would work? But it did. Honestly, from everything I hear from Val, what I heard from Merrow—I didn't think they could do it again. I think it was like a desperate experiment that went right. That kind of lightning striking twice? The Society has to have been throwing witches at it for ages trying to make it work again. Val said it was a one-time spell when I asked about it. She said there wasn't a coven alive that could get it running again."

"Val's wrong this time." Sylvie slid a sandwich Zoe's way, settled down at the table with her own.

Zoe peeled back the bread, wrinkled her nose at it. "I'm not sure it's healthy to eat when I've got blood—"

"Don't eat brain bits, don't get kuru," Sylvie said. "You'll be fine."

Zoe gave her that same startled expression, appalled and awed at once. "You eat a lot of meals with blood on you?"

"Some," Sylvie said. "Eat when you can. So, they got this uber-difficult spell up and running again. How does it work?" She took a bite of her sandwich, found herself taking a second and third bite even as the horseradish brought tears to her eyes. "Like some type of pyramid scheme? People passing it down as needed?"

"More like feed the bits they don't want people to remember into it. Tells the spell what to reach out and erase."

"And the dispersal agents?"

Zoe squirmed in her seat, something she'd always done when she wanted to know the answer and didn't.

"Best guess?"

"I think they carry something away? And it helps focus the Corrective better? Makes it work faster. Stronger." She sounded more certain by the end of it.

Sylvie groaned. "Does that mean we have to hunt down each of the . . . dispersal witches after we break the main spell, which I still don't know how to do."

"I don't think so," Zoe said. Her admission dragged out of her. Like Sylvie, she hated to admit when she was in over her head.

"Any ideas on breaking the spell? I mean, if it's that hard to create, maybe it's fragile? If I yank out the ingredients?"

"If you yank out the ingredients," Zoe said, "you'll be subject to spell backlash. You might just erase your entire mind."

"So that's a do-not-recommend approach," Sylvie said. She hung her head. "Of course, first things first. We have to find them."

"Well, you know one thing that should help," Zoe said.

Sylvie thought back, realized, yeah, that Zoe was right. "Wherever they are, there are a hell of a lot of witches present. Enough that they might get noticed."

"It's not much, but that kind of word does get around. I could ask Val."

"It's something. I'll take it," Sylvie said. "Go get your bath."

"Thank God," Zoe said, leaped away from the table.

Left alone, Sylvie pushed her sandwich around on her plate under the watchful, swaying blossoms dangling from the ceiling, and wondered what Demalion's plan was, *exactly. He let himself get captured. Maybe. Or maybe the capture was the only way to extend his life. Maybe all the other possibilities led to death. Maybe his only plan was survival, and he's waiting for me to rescue him. Maybe. Maybe. Maybe.*

Sylvie gritted her teeth. She might grow to hate precognition as much as magic. Life had enough variables as it was. Her hands clenched on her plate.

"Syl?" Alex wandered into the kitchen, frowned at the changes, and sat heavily in the seat Zoe had vacated.

"How're you feeling?"

"Better," Alex said, managed a half smile. "Lupe had some Valium. I think she's grinding it into my coffee. Is there even a coffeepot left here?"

Sylvie sighed. "Yeah. I fucked up there. I should have kicked Erinya back to her realm when Dunne asked. I bet he would have helped. Have you seen the outside world? I could see the changes as soon as I crossed over the water. I don't know what the worst scenario is. That she's not trying to control herself, or she is and failing."

"She saved your life. You were . . . shot," Alex said. That newly familiar furrow carved its way down between her brows. Her hands shook. A mug of coffee—smelling strongly of caramel and chocolate, steaming around the edges of the whipped cream—appeared between them, and the tremors in her fingers calmed.

Sylvie blinked. Erinya was, it seemed, committed to keeping Alex happy.

"She saved your life," Alex repeated, more confidently.

"Yeah, but she marked Demalion's soul in exchange—oh, fuck, I'm really stupid."

Alex grimaced. "No. That's me."

"Hey!" Sylvie said. She reached across the table, laid her hand over Alex's thin wrist. "I'll fix this. I promise. You'll be as good as new."

"And Lupe? You going to fix her, too?" Alex wouldn't meet her eyes, just fiddled with the coffee cup until it slopped over her fingers.

"No," Sylvie said. "She's beyond my help."

Alex looked up. Relief etched her features. "She's beyond you. But I'm not."

"Not you," Sylvie said. "You going to drink that?"

Alex shook her head. "It's a vicious cycle. I drink coffee, I get caffeinated, I get bored. I try to work. My brain collapses. I panic. Lupe gives me drugs. I get exhausted. I nap. I drink coffee to push away the drugs."

"You want a research project?" Sylvie suggested it tentatively. It might make things worse. Might give her something to hang on to.

Alex bit her lip, bit hard. The skin immediately around her teeth paled until it matched the enamel. "I don't know."

"Shouldn't interfere with any of the blocks—"

Alex winced.

"We need a new office space."

"What happened to ours? Did I forget that, too?"

"Nope. Just happened. Burned down." Her throat felt oddly tight as she remembered it. Her office hadn't been much—overexpensive to rent, and outdated within—but it had been hers.

"Fuck," Alex said. "I don't remember where the insurance papers are. Syl. We had insurance, right? I'm not . . ."

"Yeah," Sylvie said. "It's okay. Try not to think about the past, huh? Think about the future. That's safe."

"For how long?"

"Should be okay for a while," Sylvie said. "Apparently the magic works by dispersal, and that agent's been splattered—"

Alex shook her head fiercely. "Stop. Stop. Stop it!"

Sylvie shut up, watched Alex fight her own mind.

Lupe arrived, two-legged, mostly human, barefoot, and comfortable wandering around on a jungle carpet; the vines parted for her, caressed her legs as she walked. "Eri says you're upsetting Alex. Stop it."

"I got the memo," Sylvie said. She pushed away from the table, smelled blood and char and sweat on her skin as movement stirred the air around her. Zoe had the right idea. Bath. And then?

Yvette.

"Alex," Sylvie said. "Thank you."

"For what?"

"You reminded me of something very important."

"Okay," Alex said. She sounded like a little girl interacting uncertainly with an adult. It made Sylvie brittle with anger. Sylvie left Lupe caring for her with the sort of dispassionate efficiency that med students seemed to learn early on.

Erinya owned Demalion's soul. Even the best spell in the world couldn't hide him from her. Where Demalion was . . . Yvette and the Ebbinghaus Corrective.

Sylvie couldn't wait.

14

Sisterhood

SYLVIE GOT HALFWAY DOWN THE HALL—NOW, A WINDING STONE
tube that looked like it had been bored by a giant serpent—
and paused, her first exhilaration fading. Erinya was a
double-edged sword. She could find Demalion, but finding
Demalion also meant finding the Good Sisters. Sylvie
didn't want Erinya anywhere near them. Erinya hated
witches enough that nothing else mattered to her once she
was hunting. The airport was proof of that.

Tackling the world's most malevolent and largest coven
might be a lot to handle, but Sylvie thought she was capable
of it. With Zoe at her side, with Demalion scouting the
way. Even with Marah, should she be inclined to lend her
bloody talents. Erinya . . . she might take out Sylvie's allies
while going after the witches, leaving Sylvie attempting to
stop the witches and minimizing Erinya's massive wave of
death and destruction.

Sylvie U-turned, went back toward the sound of running
water, and stepped inside the changed bathroom. Zoe, sitting in a small pond beneath another waterfall, jerked, and
said, "What? You can't tell me I'm using all the hot water,

because I don't think there is any. Or, apparently, any privacy." She sank lower in the water.

"Sorry," Sylvie said. She crouched down near the pool, said, "Look. I need your help. I need you to do something for me."

"Right *now*?"

Sylvie had to grin. "No. When you've cleaned up to your satisfaction, found fresh clothing, maybe had a latte."

"There was no coffeepot—"

"Just ask Alex for one," Sylvie said. "The thing is I need Erinya distracted. You're a witch. You're about the biggest distraction I've got. Sure as hell the only one I trust."

"No," Zoe said. "She squished Merrow."

"She won't squish you," Sylvie said.

"You're sure? I mean, really sure. Mom would be so pissed if you got me squished."

"She hesitated to kill Marah on the grounds of being family, and she's not even close. You should be fine."

"Marah? The ISI agent that the witches were tracking?"

"Is that how they found Demalion—never mind, answer's obvious. Yeah. Marah. The point being, she actively tried to kill Erinya, and Erinya didn't turn her into chunks. But . . . don't try to kill Erinya. Just to be safe."

"Why am I doing this?" Zoe said. "What are you going to be doing?"

"Ostensibly, taking my own shower," Sylvie said. "I need some private space to talk to someone she doesn't like. I want her distracted so she doesn't notice his arrival."

"Who?"

"No names," Sylvie said. "At least, not until Erinya's distracted."

"This is important?"

"Yeah, Zo. It is. I don't know if you've noticed, but Eri's out of control."

"And you think provoking her will help keep her under control? Sounds sketchy. I mean, I'll do it. But this had better work."

"It's a total gamble."

Zoe grimaced. "Great. Hand me a towel."

"Where—"

"They're growing from that tree."

"Ah, so they are," Sylvie said. She wondered when she was going to stop feeling that dull shock of surprise. Probably around the same time her low-grade discomfort faded. Too much power in the air for the Lilith's blood in her veins. All this loose magic. It set her teeth on edge.

"Towel?"

Sylvie tossed her one and headed out. Val's mansion had six bathrooms last count. Sylvie wanted to find one as far from Erinya as she could get.

The guest room where she'd stayed with Demalion was at the back of the house, and Sylvie aimed for that with good results. Found it and its attached bath both empty, and more pleasingly, not completely changed over to Erinya's world yet. The bathroom still had a shower, still had recognizable dials amidst the twining vines. She turned on the water, stripped down, figuring she might as well get in a shower before she had to use a waterfall, and closed her eyes. She listened for magic, listened for any shivering sense that Erinya was approaching and, instead, got a sudden screech of outrage.

Zoe had distracted Erinya successfully, it seemed.

"Dunne," Sylvie said. "I need to talk to you. Now. Hurry up."

One minute she was alone in the shower, the next she was way too close to an increasingly damp god of Justice. She hadn't thought that through as well as she might. She fought the urge to leap for a towel of her own; he was a god, a towel meant nothing, and, besides, he wasn't inclined to look. Hell, he was all but wed to Eros, and no mortal could compare to him.

He shook his head, and the shower water stopped falling on him.

"You travel by storm and lightning, and you're annoyed by the shower?"

"You asked me here for that?"

"No," Sylvie said. "Look. I need your help."

"I asked for yours and you haven't done it and now you ask me for a favor? Another one? I sent you to Dallas. To Graves. I tweaked time so you'd reach him before he died."

"Thank you," Sylvie said. It didn't stick in her throat as much as she thought it might. That really had been a generous act. "I can't do it."

Dunne sighed. "You can."

"I can't kill her. Not now. I don't have the time, the energy to waste fighting her, and honestly, I don't have the heart. She's fucked-up and awful and dangerous and amazing and she's my friend. She's creating coffee for Alex whenever she wants it." Sylvie retreated into the spray, hid the flush of tears on her face with heated steam.

Dunne wrinkled his brow. "*I* can't do it," he said. "Not without causing an uproar in the heavens. We can fight to our heart's blood within our own pantheons and we do. But when you took her out of my pantheon, you took her out of my hands."

"You're no longer thinking like a human," Sylvie said. "You were going to be different. Justice. Not godly vengeance. Think back. Think to when you were human. When you caught a criminal, what did you do with them? Execute them? Every single one?"

"No," he said. "We jailed them."

"So jail *her.*"

"I can't attack—"

"You're not harming her. I'm not suggesting chaining her to a mountain while eagles eat her liver. You're just confining her. Come on, she's alone in her pantheon. Tepeyollotl's a shattered shell. He's not going to even notice, much less care."

"And the other gods? Those not in my pantheon or hers?"

"They probably won't notice," Sylvie said. "Right? I mean, if I killed her, they'd notice; there'd be a huge flare of power. If you killed her, the same. There'd be a fight. But they've been watching her trample Miami for months now. They haven't done anything."

"They're still debating."

"They're slow debaters, then," Sylvie said. Immortals tended to be slow about some things. She was grateful to it right now. "Which means, if you cage her, they'll debate that, too. Probably for generations. You can buy me time. You can teach her a lesson that she might listen to. You know she's not subtle. It probably hasn't occurred to her that there are other ways the gods might choose to deal with her beyond straight-up attacks."

Sylvie's nerves jangled. The gods might have time, but she didn't. Every second that Dunne was here was a second Erinya might notice. A second longer that Zoe courted disaster.

"It's a risk, I admit," she said. "Is it one you're willing to take?"

Dunne vanished in answer. Guess that was a no.

Sylvie punched the shower stall, winced as her knuckles impacted and shredded on the grout. She had washed the blood off and had just rinsed the shampoo from her hair when Alex came barreling into the room. "Syl, you gotta . . . Zoe and Erinya . . ."

Sylvie shook soap out of her hair, grabbed a towel, and ran, tripping over her feet, the vine-matted floor, the soil, and stone.

· · ·

WHEN SHE HIT THE LIVING ROOM, SHE FOUND THAT ERINYA HAD COR-nered Zoe, was snarling into Zoe's turned-away face. Lupe was coiled in the corner, returned to the snake-woman shape, caging a frightened nutria between her palms, watching with unblinking suspicion as Erinya and Zoe faced off.

"Aren't you going to use your witchy powers against me? Try to save yourself?" Erinya taunted Zoe.

Zoe had closed her eyes, but her face held none of the fear Sylvie had expected. Instead, she looked utterly blank, as serene as a painted doll.

"Erinya, back off," Sylvie said.

"I don't like witches," Erinya said. "I don't like her." A huge paw crashed into the stone beside Zoe, cracking it and shedding rock dust over Zoe's damp hair.

Zoe opened her eyes. "I don't like you either. But you can't bait me into using magic. Into letting you burn me out."

Erinya breathed out magic. Sylvie, who'd felt the entire island like an itch against her skin, suddenly felt like she'd stepped into poison ivy. Zoe closed her eyes again but kept talking.

"Val Cassavetes trained me. You know Val. Woman whose home you've turned into a Yucatán jungle. She's good at what she does. She taught me more than how to scavenge power. She taught me how to *refuse* it. Told me that sometimes the best skill a witch had was not sucking up the available power."

Erinya huffed. "So you're not only a thief, you're a picky one?"

Zoe grinned nastily. "I am a discerning shopper. I am educated and elegant, and I like the finer things. And you're all blunt-force power, unthinking and crude—"

"Zoe!" Sylvie shouted. "Shut up." Before Erinya stopped trying to burn her out and just bit her head off. Sylvie didn't understand why Erinya seemed so pissed. She'd heard worse before. Sylvie chalked it up to Zoe's special ability to needle in just the right way.

"I could bring Merrow back. Let him do all the things to you he promised he would. His little pet." Erinya's teeth were coated in blood, her voice thick as if she were savaging her own tongue.

Lupe had picked up the nutria and was staring at its furry face with an expression that veered between *it's so cute* and *I could eat it*. Finally, Lupe set the rodent down, watched it scamper for a bolt-hole near the river—when did the living room get a *river*? And did it run fresh or salt this close to the sea? Sylvie shook the irrelevant thoughts away in time to hear Lupe say, "Eri. Don't be silly. She's just a girl."

"So are you," Erinya snarled.

"No, I'm not," Lupe said. "She's in *high school*. I'm a junior in college. Was a junior. Now, I'm a monster."

"This place is a madhouse," Alex said, trying to add her own distraction. "Erinya, the TV just spat out little snake things. You want to go clear them away? It's freaking me out."

"No," Sylvie said. "Everyone chill out. Focus. Erinya. I need you to find Demalion for me. Then I need you to send me and Zoe there. The nice way." It was a bad idea, but it was the only one she had left. Dunne hadn't even let her ask him if he could find Demalion.

"Send me, too," Lupe said.

Erinya's teeth flashed, and she beat Sylvie to the reflexive "No!" The howl made the stones shake.

Zoe slipped away from Erinya's gaze and sidled over to Sylvie. "You owe me," she whispered. "Like new boots and a matching purse owe me."

"Dream on," Sylvie said. "I'm not enabling your fashion habit." Her eyes never left the argument before them.

Erinya paced and snarled and slunk and lashed her tail. Lupe sat calmly and made her case. "What else am I supposed to do," Lupe said. "Sit here in my jungle castle while you go and have all the fun? I'm a monster, Eri. Let me make the most of it. You said you wanted to see me hunt? Those people deserve me."

"And you need me," Zoe said, interrupting. "So don't get any funny ideas about dropping me midtransport."

Erinya growled, and Sylvie told Zoe, "You know, I'm rethinking taking you."

"Oh please," Zoe said. "I mean, I guess you're good. You keep going up against magical things without magic. And you're still alive. But you're walking into a coven of witches. How many spells can you fend off at once?"

"And Yvette's got monsters on tap," Lupe said. "Wasn't that the problem? The Good Sisters using monsters to get rid of their enemies?"

"You're a monster," Sylvie said. "By your own definition. If you go, I'll have to watch my back around you. What's to keep you from being turned against me—"

"Me," Erinya said. "I'll burn them all out."

"No," Sylvie said. "You are definitely not invited. It's witches. I can handle witches. I cannot handle massive civilian casualties."

Erinya said, "There are so many of you. Like ants. Should I be bothered by ants?"

"Is Lupe an ant?"

"No, she's mine!" Erinya flashed another burst of pointed magic at Zoe, and Zoe rebuffed it though she looked shaky.

"No one's arguing that. Enough!" Sylvie snapped. For a wonder, this time they all fell silent. Sylvie let out a breath. "Alex, you're not looking well. Go lie down, try not to listen to our plans. It's only going to tug at those sore spots in your brain. Try not to worry. We're going to fix it. Zoe. Would you pack a bag? Anything you can find in the house that might help break the Corrective."

"Yeah, like Erinya left anything useful in the house—"

"Zoe. Just go."

"New boots. New purse. New *coat*." Zoe stomped out of the room, and the tension faded sharply.

"I *am* coming," Lupe said.

"Yeah, you are," Sylvie said. "Mostly because I don't want to fight you. I want to fight witches. So you'd better damn well not let any of the Good Sisters leash you and turn you against us."

"She's mine," Erinya muttered again. "She won't be leashed or seduced."

"Fine," Sylvie said, and faced her main problem. Erinya. One part of her thought to hell with it. The Society deserved all the pain Erinya could bring them. That same part whispered, if she just made it clear enough, made Erinya understand why bystanders should be left alone, left safe, why their attacks should be pinpoint and confined . . . It was a seductive thought, but ultimately not believable. Erinya would raze everything to the ground.

"Where are they?" Sylvie asked. Easiest way to make the decision. Like she even had a say. She cursed Dunne and his god-view of time. All urgency for humans, and none of their own kind. By the time he considered her request, they'd be deep into the body counts.

"Demalion? He's surrounded by witches."

"That's good," Sylvie said. "Where, exactly?"

"There," Erinya said, waving a clawed hand in a westward direction. *Fury,* Sylvie thought. *Not good with the details.*

"Eri, I need more than that. I need a place name. An address. Is Demalion thinking anything?"

"Huh," Erinya said, "Thinking about you. He's annoyed. Thought you'd be there by now."

"Great," Sylvie said. "Just what I need. More guilt. Tell him I'd get there if he'd been a little more clear about where there is!"

"San Francisco," Erinya said.

"Oh, fuck," Sylvie said. Worst-case scenario. High population density, close quarters, and just for funsies, on a fault line. Forget involving Erinya. Forget instantaneous god-travel. It was overrated anyway. They could fly the normal way. And then hunt for witches in a big city. And Lupe would be no problem with TSA, and Sylvie's guns would be checked without comment. . . .

Sylvie gritted her teeth. Why couldn't Val have a private plane and a pilot on staff?

Erinya gloated. "You *need* me. You don't trust me. But you need me. You think any other god will come to your call? I've been gracious and generous, and you should be *grateful.* I'll take us all there, and we'll slaughter them to the last witch."

"I'm going to get my guns," Sylvie said. What was the point in arguing? She'd gambled. She'd lost. Dunne wasn't going to help. Erinya was. Sylvie just hoped she could live with the aftermath.

She found Zoe hiding out in the guest room, still less jungle than the other rooms, and said, "You ready?"

"Is she coming with us?"

"Afraid so. I can't make her not come."

"You resist her pretty well," Zoe said.

"Yeah? I don't think you've got the grounds to judge that," Sylvie said.

"You talk to her like she's your equal, not something that will rip your heart out and give it wings so she can chase it better. And you did it in a towel. Besides, this is your room, right? Where you slept? It's mostly human."

"That's because of me?"

"Your mark's all over it," Zoe said.

"Great. When she's taken over the world, I can offer my services as a redecorator. What did you say to her anyway? You really hacked her off?"

Zoe fluffed a pillow and grinned. "Yeah. It worked better than I thought."

Sylvie dragged out Demalion's shirt, left behind, put it on over another one of Val's tees, and another pair of slightly-too-tight khakis. "That's not an answer."

"Oh, I hit on Lupe. Walked right up to her in front of Erinya and Alex and kissed her cheek and told her that her scales were pretty and I bet they'd feel good against my skin."

Sylvie choked on an inborn breath, and wheezed. "It's amazing you're not dead!"

"You said she wouldn't hurt me. You were right."

Sylvie closed her mouth on a slew of protests, all made useless now. But she decided that she was going to have one last little talk with Erinya about not injuring Zoe, even by freak accident. She might even waste some bullets to make sure Erinya listened. Bad enough she was going into battle worrying about thousands of faceless strangers; she didn't need to spend the entire time sick with dread that Erinya would put Zoe in harm's way.

She calmed herself, loaded her weapons, and thought, she had a plan, she had allies—even dangerous ones— and she had a goal. Everything else was distraction.

15

Mission-Minded

THEY RECONVENED IN THE LIVING ROOM BY UNSPOKEN AGREEMENT.
Zoe, following in Sylvie's wake, was more subdued than
Sylvie liked, but as she glanced around, it was far better
than Lupe's false bravado and Alex's nervous concern.

Sylvie checked her guns again, her spare ammo, said,
"Eri. If I need more bullets—"

"You won't," Erinya said.

Sylvie decided to take that as a vote of confidence, not
another invitation to argument: She was remembering why
she had worked alone for so long. Too much at stake. Too
many viewpoints.

"Then let's go," she said. "Nice and easy. Try to bring
us in quietly?"

"Teach your mother to suck eggs," Erinya snapped, and
flung out her arms. Sylvie winced, anticipating pain, that
strange menacing chaos of Erinya's realm. But all she felt
was hideous itching as power crawled over her skin, seeking to make her part of it. A faint whimper suggested that
Zoe was having real difficulties keeping from sampling
that magic, and just as Sylvie thought she was going to

have to halt the whirlwind of movement to save her sister, they slammed to a painful halt.

Sylvie dropped deep into warm, salty waters, rife with seaweed. She flailed upward, got a breath of air, grabbed out, and brought Zoe, coughing and spitting, to the surface alongside her. Lupe rose up a moment later, startled but unharmed. Water beaded off her scales. "Did we overshoot?"

"We never left," Sylvie said looking up at the Rickenbacker Causeway from below. A furious, screeching howl ripped through the air, and all over the water, pelicans surged into ungainly flight, silvery fish dodged to the depths.

Erinya hadn't made the leap off the island.

"She's trapped," Zoe said, brushing her hair out of her eyes. "I don't think she can leave the island. There's something shielding it."

"That would be me," Dunne said. He settled on the waves before Sylvie, cross-legged, jeans staying dry despite the wave roll. "Your cage? Does it meet with your approval? It's temporary. I can get away with it for only a while. Call it a practical joke between old friends."

"Yeah," Sylvie said. "It does. Did you leave Alex on the inside? 'Cause Erinya's going to be furious."

"Eros sent her home."

Lupe shot Sylvie a betrayed glance, and Sylvie ignored it. "Can you send us to San Francisco?"

Dunne flashed inhuman, a great grey swirl of wind and storm, and the water around them grew jagged and as rough as sharks' teeth. Sylvie wished she hadn't thought about sharks. Or, God, *mermaids*. "You're asking for a lot of favors for a woman who's not even marked as mine."

"Sorry. My soul is my own."

Zoe shivered, said, "Look, I get that Sylvie's difficult, but we're wet and going to get tired of treading water and we really need your help. So if you want us to grovel . . ." she grimaced. "Okay, we won't. But I'll say please?"

"Oh, God," Dunne said, and it was so strange to hear that

word out of his mouth that Sylvie forgot to tread water. A slap of salty water going into her lungs reminded her. She surfaced in time to hear the rest of it. ". . . just like your sister, aren't you? Fine. Go. Kill witches. I'm through with you."

The water rose up around them like a waterspout, then it wasn't water at all. Sylvie had time to think she'd really angered him—this ride was rougher even than Erinya's, a far cry from the hiccup when he'd sent her to Dallas—before she lost any thought beyond trying to hold on to her allies. The hardest thing to believe was that she'd volunteered for this. The travel wasn't instantaneous; it felt endless. Cold and stormy, roiling with momentum and power. It scoured as it shoved them before it, left them blind. She gritted her teeth, determined to endure.

Zoe screamed suddenly, sharp and as brilliant as a stroke of lightning. A moment later, the storm around them eased a notch. As if the power was flowing into something else. As if it were burning through a witch. Sylvie shouted and cursed and flailed and made no headway against the power inexorably rolling them onward. Killing her sister.

They dropped hard, and Lupe snarled furiously, snapping out at everything around her—no humanity in her. Sylvie dodged her and scanned the area, taking it in, in frantic Zoe-absent chunks: nighttime sea falling away blackly and steeply to her left. Sand and stone beneath her, roughing up her skin beneath her khakis. The dark tangle that was Lupe in the night. And, finally, a white glimmer that turned out to be Zoe's blouse. Her sister was hunched tight in the shelter of a massive rock.

Sylvie scrambled to her feet, fell, scrambled up again.

This, her Lilith voice said, *is why you don't involve family. And why you don't rely on witches. They're both too fragile for the job.*

"Fuck off," Zoe said, turning to glare at Sylvie. "You know you've got a rude-ass voice in your head?"

"Uh—" Sylvie stopped.

Zoe wasn't dead, hurt, or even burned out. Power was

crackling off of her, rolling around and around the Cain mark on her forearm and hand. When Sylvie reached out cautiously, actual sparks launched in her direction. She withdrew her hand fast.

Zoe admired the silvery, stormy halo flowing over her arm, watched that stolen power spill back and forth as she tilted her arm. It lit up the dark night like she had wrapped moonlight around her skin.

"Guess this mark is good for something. Dunne's power should have overwhelmed me, fried me. Hell, I probably could have taken on Erinya."

"Don't get cocky. She would have chewed out your throat. Just be glad it saved your life," Sylvie said. She studied their environment with a less panicked and more analytical gaze. "I think it also got us dropped too early. Dunne's precise with power expenditure. No more, no less than is needed. Part of his no-carbon-footprint god style."

"Well, crap," Zoe said. "I'm really ready to take on those Society bitches." Her lips were curling into a hungry smile. "I've been studying and studying and studying, and now I've got a chance to—"

You're going to have to watch her, her little voice suggested. *She's corrupted from that much power.*

She's high, Sylvie countered.

"Shut up!" Zoe snapped. "I am not corrupted. I am not high. I am energized. I am in control. Perfect control."

"You're reading my mind."

"Yeah. A spell I always wanted to try."

"And you tried it *now*? Are you going to do anything useful with it or just going to pick fights with my brain?"

"Lupe's eating a seagull," Zoe said. "Worry about how useful she's going to be."

"What?" Lupe said, looming out of the dark on three legs at the sound of her name, the mangled bird dangling from her right front claws. "Where are we?"

"San Francisco," Sylvie said. If Zoe had sucked in enough of Dunne's power that he'd dropped them in the wrong city, she'd be more than . . . energized; she'd be a glowing trail of embers across the sky, mark of Cain or no.

"We've got to be close," Zoe said. She waved her glowing hand before her as if it could illuminate their path.

"There's *nothing* around us," Lupe said. Her nose wrinkled; her tongue flicked out, tasted the air.

"What, just because you can't smell it? Witches wash, you know," Zoe said.

Sylvie left them bickering and started walking. She had her gun; the bullets had made the trip safely with her. Her sister had made the trip. Lupe had made the trip, and, despite Sylvie pulling a fast one on Erinya, she seemed willing to fight at Sylvie's side. All systems were go, and Demalion was waiting for his rescue.

The ground sloped away from her feet, made each step forward an experiment in faith and discomfort. Each step jarred, and the rocky substrate shifted. But the sea cliff was at her back, and there was a hint of asphalt in the darkness. A minute's walk revealed the slash of car headlights passing by and, a minute after that, the long black ribbon of a California highway slipping downhill.

Zoe joined her, not slip-sliding on the rough terrain at all courtesy of her own glow. Lupe followed in her wake.

"Now what," Lupe said. "Do we even have an idea of where we're going? Are all your cases this slipshod? How do you get anything done?" That angry edge was vibrating in her voice again. Erinya's presence had tamed it somewhat. Sylvie couldn't wait to find a witch to point Lupe's bad temper at.

"I admit I've been slow about this," Sylvie said. "The Good Sisters have infiltrated the ISI. San Francisco's an ISI city. I am betting that we'll find the entire coven tucked up at ISI home base." She should have realized it was likely the moment Yvette took Marah and Demalion; they'd need a place to stash them—and the ISI buildings were all equipped with holding cells. Plus, she should have recognized the classic witchy arrogance. That a group of witches who had infiltrated the ISI easily and thoroughly would deepen the insult by running the spell that allowed them to expand their power out of the ISI bastion.

The irritation of knowing she'd been stupid itched beneath her skin. She could have gone directly from Dallas, attacked them on her own. She could handle a group of witches; she'd tackled gods.

"Going it alone would have been stupid," Zoe said. "You don't even know how many of them are there. That's not even counting the monsters they might be controlling."

Sylvie gritted her teeth. "Undo that mind-reading spell. Now."

"No," Zoe said. "It wasn't a whim, Syl. We're about to head into enemy territory. This way, I can keep up with you. Even if we get separated."

Sylvie couldn't argue with that. That was sound planning.

Zoe grinned, said, "You're going to find out I'm all sorts of useful." After picking up a scrap of broken wood and two small stones, Zoe stepped onto the empty roadway. She laid down the stones, laid the scrap across them, and whispered, "Catch and hold."

A wash of silvery light, the burning itch of magic, and the road was suddenly barricaded with a police-grade roadblock. Zoe sauntered back and said, "Next car that stops, we take."

Sylvie wanted to disapprove. Her parents would want her to disapprove—carjacking was not a skill set her family aspired to—but looking at her sister, at Lupe lurking slick and deadly in the shadows, she couldn't feel anything but pleased.

· · ·

IT TOOK SYLVIE AN HOUR TO TRACK DOWN THE ISI BUILDING IN San Francisco, and it was an enormously long hour. Zoe and Lupe, in combination, made hellish car companions, especially when the car that Zoe had liberated from a spell-stunned driver was small enough that Lupe and Zoe, divided by front and back seat, were still in constant physical contact, a fact that pleased neither of them.

As Zoe said, sliding into Lupe's outspread tail when Sylvie took a curve more quickly than the car was really capable of, "Erinya's going to be pissed enough that she's trapped. I don't need Lupe going back smelling like I've been rubbing up against her all night long."

Sylvie wanted to snap at them to shut the hell up, to just stop, to impress upon them how serious this whole matter was, but Zoe had to know. She was jacked in to Sylvie's brain after all. Knew the constant flashes of terror that she was suffering—not for herself, but for Alex, for Demalion. What if she wasn't fast enough, good enough? What if Demalion was already dead? The ISI seemed to have nothing on the Society of the Good Sisters when it came to magical experimentation. Demalion, having died once, was a curiosity they'd be dying to take apart.

If they had—

Sylvie pulled the car to a graceless halt streetside; the engine cooled and pinged, way overdue for an oil change. Or a new engine. Zoe had stolen a lemon.

But it had brought them here.

The San Francisco ISI building, unlike many of their other branches, was isolated, an entity in itself. That was a plus. It meant the only people she had to worry about were her own. No close bystanders. There were shops on the other side of the road, closed at this hour. A few houses, owned by people rich enough to afford sizable plots of land in California.

An iron gate barricaded the oyster-shell drive, which led to a dimly lit building backed up against the jagged coastline. The sea was a constant growl, unseen but threatening. Helpful, too. The crash it made as it hit the rocky shore would mask their approach.

Zoe said, "The gate's not spelled."

"Wouldn't be," Sylvie said, giving it a good shove. "Not if this hosts real ISI agents as well. With non-Talents coming in and out." The metal screeched, salt air eating away at the hinges.

Lupe slipped through the gap, darted toward the building, pulled up short, wincing. Oyster-shell drive, Sylvie thought. Sharp-edged, uncomfortable to walk on even in her boots. Lupe's bare footpads were going to slow her down.

This branch occupied a turn-of-the-century bed-and-breakfast, and it still looked more like a hotel than a government facility: The stone facade was ivy covered, the grounds were manicured and landscaped with flowering bushes that perfumed the night. The only thing that gave them away was the dull shine of replacement windows—bulletproof. Dark, angular blotches studded the roofline, and Sylvie thought they were security cameras. Inactive ones: no movement, no light.

The Good Sisters wanted privacy.

Worked for her.

"One entrance," Zoe said. "You think there's a back door?"

"Depends on whether the ISI has to abide by fire codes," Sylvie said. "But I was thinking more about hitting them head-on."

Unlike Demalion, who would have been muttering about stealth and discretion, Zoe and Lupe merely nodded, trusting her.

Sylvie checked the solid weight of her weapon, reassured herself that the spare ammo was still in her pockets, and moved up the drive, sticking to the shadows. They were nearly on the house when the tiny stone shed leaning up against the side of the building cracked open, sprouting a door where none had been.

Three people walked out into the predawn light, talking quietly among themselves. Lupe snarled in animal surprise, and the agents looked up and out and spotted them. The lead agent—*witch*—gestured at the gravel pathway, shouted out a harsh-edged word. The ground before him roiled, rolled up into the world's largest mole trail, then erupted. A monster shook dirt and sharp shells from its back and blocked their path.

Sylvie shot once at it, wondering what exactly it was

that this witch had had leashed and following him beneath the ground's surface, and where the hell its weak point was. First glance argued that there weren't any: It was all scale and scute and armored legs. Her bullet spanged off it with a sound like breaking pottery.

She wasn't even sure it had eyes. She lined up another shot, but Lupe beat her to it, lunging into her line of fire and engaging the monster directly.

Eager, but reckless.

The monster, something even Sylvie's Lilith voice struggled to name, moved like a centipede, hundreds of jointed, armored legs, and evil pincers at the head. A long, stinging tail curved above its back. It raised all the hairs on her neck, made her stomach squirm in ingrained squeamishness. She really wasn't wild about insects. Especially when this one might as well have been designed out of an insectophobe's nightmare.

Though it seemed blind, or, at least, eyeless, it moved confidently enough to get Lupe on the defensive and keep her there. Lupe whimpered after one stinger strike; her side ran blood. She fell back.

Sylvie jerked the trigger, put another two bullets into the creature, trying to maim its front pair of legs and failing, trying to keep an eye on the witches as well. Be stupid to be killed by them while focusing on a monster.

The monster ignored Sylvie, oiling back on itself to make another attack on Lupe.

Take out the witch that controls it; free the monster, the Lilith voice suggested, guided her gun hand 'round to the man who had summoned the monster out of the earth. His mouth was a black slash in his neat beard, urging the monster on.

Free the monster, and who's to say it'll run? It might want to finish what it started, Sylvie thought, but shooting a witch was well within her plans. The witch, sensing his danger, pressed back toward the shed and shelter.

Zoe stepped between the monster and Lupe just as it

charged again and slapped it hard right in its blind face. Zoe's entire body was within the cutting grasp of the pincers.

Sylvie unloaded bullets into the monster's tail end, trying to get it to turn, to forget her suicidal sister. But the monster was dissolving, starting from Zoe's slap mark and crumbling back into gravel and dust.

"Illusion," Zoe said. "Good one, though. Lupe. Stop believing you're hurt."

"Cassavetes's protégé," the illusion master said. His tone was dismissive. "You're an acolyte. Nothing more. *Your* creature illusion is unconvincing. No chimera looks like that."

"I'm a lot more than an acolyte, and Lupe's not an illusion," Zoe said. She raised her marked hand, started chanting. Dunne's stolen powers shone silver, highlighting the mark.

Sylvie, exasperated, desperate—they *had* to be attracting attention they didn't want yet—took advantage of the witch's arrogance. He'd stepped out of his shelter, all his focus on Zoe.

Sylvie's bullet made a hole through his throat; the witch managed to clutch at the wound, but nothing more, before he crumpled and died.

Zoe snarled, balked of an audience, and Sylvie thought *Get the door!* in her direction. The two witches remaining were doing their best to seal it. Lupe staggered to her feet and pounced on one of them, proving that she was no illusion. The witch, a woman whose hair was nearly as scarlet as her life's blood, managed to look betrayed as she died.

Zoe and the remaining witch played magical tug-of-war over the door until Sylvie unloaded one more bullet, this one into the last witch's head. The bullet shivered, pushing through a magical shield, before it penetrated. Sylvie wiped sweat off her face with her gun hand, smelled hot metal, thanked their lucky stars that these witches weren't carrying invulnerability talismans. Just the lesser, rudimentary spell shields. If they'd been wearing talismans, she'd have had to tackle them physically first, get the talismans off, get up close and personal with her kills.

Sylvie leaned forward, breathing hard. There was killing witches; and then there was killing people in front of her baby sister. It didn't make it better that Zoe seemed completely okay with it, was even now pushing past to grab hold of the closing door.

"*C'mon*, Sylvie. This damned door isn't happy. It knows I'm not one of them, and it's trying to close."

Sylvie looked across at the main building, looked past the shed door, and had a feeling that they could raid the main ISI building for days and find nothing but patsies. The Good Sisters had leeched on and hidden themselves, parasites who made the host forget they were there.

Lupe pressed up against Sylvie's side, her flanks wet with blood, but no wounds. Either she believed Zoe enough to erase the injury if not the signs of it, or Erinya had souped her up before the battle with some quick-healing genes. Good, Sylvie thought. She needed her team whole.

"Let's go," Sylvie said, and ignored Zoe's muttered, "Finally!" as she squeezed into the shed. She felt the quiver of angry magic as she passed. Zoe winced; her grip tightened on the door edge. It moaned like a living thing beneath her hands. Sylvie thought it said a lot about the Good Sisters that even a spell as simple as a hidden door felt malevolent.

"Lupe, come on!"

Lupe was longer than the shed was, and her tail took forever to tuck in; her fur smoked as she brushed the shimmering, twisting door frame. The moment Zoe released the door, it slammed shut and left them in darkness.

The shed, when explored, yielded another door and beyond it a steep downward ramp, leading beneath the B&B main building.

Sylvie blew out her breath. Luck, both good and bad. Since the Good Sisters had set up shop underground, the intervening earth had muffled their ingress. Once Sylvie's group was inside, that same earth would prevent anyone from hearing what happened to them if it all went wrong.

"Watch your backs down there," Sylvie said. "One way in probably means one way out. Lupe, stick with Zoe. And for God's sake, use your sense of smell. If you can't smell the monster, don't attack it."

"You shot, too," Lupe growled. The words were thick in her inhuman throat.

"Well," Sylvie said, "better safe than sorry. And I don't have your senses. Some of these witches leash monsters, remember. Stick close to Zoe."

She shot another thought Zoe's way, the warning that Lupe might turn on them and Zoe would need to be prepared and *could* she be prepared to take someone like Lupe down?

Zoe nodded once.

Sylvie thought maybe this mind reading wasn't such bad idea after all, and turned her back on Zoe's smirk. The ramp was stone on all sides, floor, walls, ceilings, lit every few feet by prosaic LED adhesive lights, battery powered. The stone was smooth beneath her shoes, worn down with age. The main building was at least a hundred years old, but the tunnel was older still.

Zoe pointed at a worn symbol chipped into the wall, blurred with age and erosion. A pentagram. "Sylvie. Think they were here first?"

Sylvie ran her fingers over it, and said, "I think it wouldn't surprise me at all. The Good Sisters obviously believe in the long game, or they wouldn't have bothered infiltrating the ISI."

The tunnel lightened ahead. Sylvie estimated they were about thirty feet below the surface and about fifty feet in. The underdwelling, whatever it would prove to be, was more than a simple cellar to the hotel above.

Animal instinct made her want to walk faster, to reach the light sooner, to step out of the dank stone tunnel. But something about the quality of the light ahead, the faint shift and flicker of it, made her heart beat faster.

She held up a hand, pausing them.

"They're waiting for us."

That was what the shift and flicker was—people between them and the light, trying to remain still. Failing.

"An ambush?"

"Let me draw their fire," Sylvie said. "I'm going first. I've got the gun, and I've got some immunity to magic."

"If they have weapons?"

"Then I'll wish I'd asked Dunne for a bulletproof vest," Sylvie muttered.

Zoe's lips twisted, but she swallowed her instinctive urge to argue.

Sylvie checked her gun, contemplated changing out the clip before going in, but didn't want them to get impatient and come after them while she was reloading, functionally disarmed. She gripped her gun tight—four bullets left in this clip. She could do a lot with that—and headed through the doorway at speed.

If Demalion wasn't somewhere in this building, she'd have gone in shooting blind.

Ten witches waited for them in the open room, a blur of suited figures, male and female, arrayed in two rows, six up close, four farther back; Sylvie got off one shot before the first spell surge hit her, saw one suited figure spin around with the force of it. Not a killing shot, dammit, but the woman stayed down. For now.

Magic crawled over her skin like fire ants, nailed her with a spell that sank in and wrapped her body like a clammy, all-encompassing shroud—cold, growing colder, tasting of clay and stone and death. It sucked heat from her skin, her heart, her breath.

Life-draining spell, Sylvie identified. Didn't matter. She had life to spare. She pushed through the paralysis the spell encouraged, blinked eyelashes that seemed weighted by sand, and sighted for the next shot. *Careful,* her voice warned. *Three bullets left.*

This time, her shot was effectively lethal. The witch in

the center collapsed silently, no time even for a shout. Sylvie had hit her square between the eyes.

Two bullets, she told it. Nine witches still alive.

Nine witches blocking a doorway behind them. There could be more of the Good Sisters waiting beyond it. There probably were. Yvette wasn't one of the opponents facing them. Sylvie's shots had to count.

The life-draining spell didn't slacken. Wrong witch.

Sylvie growled, heard Lupe echo it before leaping out of the tunnel; chameleon-like, her bright, poisonous colors had dulled, left her dark and sleek, hard to see in the dim, underground chambers.

Lupe looked like a monster, but she killed like a cat in a pack of birds, slashing wildly, doing as much damage as possible before picking a specific target to kill and eat. She scattered three witches with bloody gouges to their thighs and calves, torsos and hips. One man fell with a shriek, rolled beneath Lupe's weight and claws. Blood glossed the dark stone floor, sinking into crevices; his voice gurgled to a stop.

The other two slapped spells on each other, stopping their bleeding.

After that, Sylvie lost track of things for a bit, bombarded by spells that made her skin burn or freeze or feel like it was going to shatter. Illusions rushed the room—collapsing ceilings and panicking clouds of bats, the stink of burning sulfur and too little air.

But nothing crashed into her, and nothing slowed her breathing. *Illusion, just illusion,* her Lilith voice whispered over and over, breaking the hold the spells tried to lay on her.

Some spells *weren't* illusion, Sylvie thought, as she ducked a lash of impossibly scarlet flame.

The next fiery lash wasn't aimed at her, but Lupe and Zoe. Zoe held firm; showed the Good Sisters what a shielding spell should really be able to do.

With the witches' focus split over three targets, Sylvie figured out fast who held the life-draining spell on her—

the fiftyish woman with hard, green eyes. Sylvie met that challenging gaze and fired directly at her. The bullet veered in defiance of all natural law and disappeared. One bullet wasted. One bullet left.

Invulnerability talisman, Sylvie thought. This witch was one step up from the ones she'd killed outside, probably the leader of this little coven. Made sense. Ten here, plus the three outside. Witches did like their traditions.

Sylvie fought against the life-draining spell, tried to peel herself out of it, even as the struggle exhausted her, made her feel like the air she breathed was full of sand and sharp edges. She felt years being whisked away from her with each labored breath.

"Why aren't you dead?" the coven leader shouted. She looked irritated, outraged, even as she directed the other witches with clipped phrases in a language that meant nothing to Sylvie. Zoe seemed to understand just fine, and countered each attempt. She made it look easy, but Sylvie saw the trembling strain in Zoe's corded neck and braced legs.

"Because I hate to oblige you," Sylvie snapped. "Tell your goons to leave my sister alone."

"Only when she's dead."

Lupe's marauding had drawn to a halt; she slunk behind Zoe's shielding, baring bloody teeth, her eyes flaring in the firelight.

"You'll go first," Sylvie said.

The coven head sucked in a breath to object and Sylvie used her last shot to take out the witch aiming fireballs at Zoe. No invulnerability shield there. The man died spectacularly; his spell backlashing on him as the bullet penetrated, wreathing him in fire. His fellow witches twisted and fled him, and Zoe took the opportunity to let loose some offensive spells of her own.

Sylvie gaped for half a moment, watching her baby sister create a whirlwind to drop a witch directly in Lupe's waiting claws, then started reloading.

"Sylvie!" Zoe shouted. "Go. Get Demalion. We've got this."

Not a bad idea, but not quite yet. Sylvie shot two witches who tried to prove Zoe wrong; her bullets slipped through their shielding—a quick shimmer the only sign that there'd been anything to slow her bullets down. She was getting faster at finding the weak spots in their shields. Some instinct kicking in.

The coven head turned her attention back to Sylvie, began whispering another spell, no longer content to wait for Sylvie to drop dead from the life-draining spell, and Sylvie decided the woman had to go.

She lunged forward, the exertion of pushing past the spell still wrapped around her, making her heart beat hard and heavy and labored, but she had the satisfaction of watching the coven leader's eyes go shocked just before Sylvie tackled her.

Stupid witches. Even the Good Sisters, who used guns and technology, still seemed stunned when someone got physical with them. *Of course,* the Lilith voice muttered nastily, *it might have more to do with the life-draining spell coming into solid contact with an invulnerability talisman.* Warring magic was never fun, and while the coven leader squirmed and fought, Sylvie used the burn of the conflicting magics to locate the woman's talisman—a thin, golden bracelet—and rip it off.

The witch shrieked; age wrinkled her skin, and Sylvie put a stop to that with a bullet.

She felt better instantly, scrambling to her feet, panting, but energized. Zoe nodded determinedly at her. Another *go, go, go.* Sylvie dodged another spell and bulled her way through the door into the deeper recesses of the Society stronghold. The door closed behind her and cut off Lupe's snarls and the sounds of witches fighting for their lives.

She'd never wanted this life for Zoe. Right now, though, she was damn grateful that the girl seemed built for it.

16

Clearing the Way

AS SYLVIE RUSHED THROUGH THE DOORWAY, SHE FOUND HER FEET skidding out from under her. An unexpected blessing when the air above her was strafed with bullets. Sylvie let momentum roll her over, shot in the direction of the gunfire, and had luck on her side. She cut the witch off at the shins, and when the man fell forward, having dropped his gun to clutch at his legs, she finished him off. It made her gut churn, but that was the problem with witches. If they could talk, they could kill. She just didn't have the time to bind and gag every witch she disabled. Not tonight.

She got back to her feet, wincing as her hip protested— she'd landed hard, and the floor was unyielding as well as slick. She kicked the door shut behind her, latched it just in time to shut it in a pursuing witch's face. The door rocked on its hinges, but then Sylvie heard the witch shout, saw the quick, poisonous shine of Lupe's claw tips as they penetrated the wood, blood tipped.

Sylvie backed away, studied her surroundings. Where the first room had been an antechamber—bare stone floor and walls, a few punitive bench chairs—this one was more obviously used. The stone floor had been overlaid with glossy marble that shone like malachite, and dark, heavy, sound-muffling curtains lined the walls. Still, someone should have heard the shots.

Sylvie grabbed the first curtain to hand, yanked it back, and found herself in the coven's workroom. Silver and gold lines etched a pentagram into the floor, the lines dulled by years of footsteps.

But no one around. No Yvette. No Demalion. No caged monsters waiting for their cue. No memory spell. The room was cold, and the only magic left in it was residual, as subtle as a sheen of oil.

The curtain along the wall swayed. She skirted the pentagram, thought maybe the reason no one had come to fight her was simply that they'd left her a trap to walk into.

Vaporous wisps rose from the pentagram as she passed, licking at her ankles. Sylvie stepped away from them and found herself suddenly fighting the curtains themselves.

Effective, she thought. Stupidly so. Nothing to shoot, no one to fight, difficult to breathe as the fabric did its best to pour itself down her throat. When she tried to tear the fabric, it gave beneath her nails like water and re-formed around her wrists.

But the curtains were mindless, and she was too damn stubborn to lose to home furnishings. She fought steadily, sank lower and lower until she was slipping free of their grasp. The curtains went limp, motionless once again, and left her where she'd started. She needed to find Demalion.

Priorities, her little dark voice suggested. *Kill the witches; stop the spell. Then, worry about rescue.*

It wasn't the worst advice the voice had ever given her. But the thing was, the bigger the witch, the bigger the spell that broke, the worse the fallout. In this enclosed area, Sylvie had concerns that the minute Yvette went down, so would the whole structure. She wasn't going to have time to search for him, after.

You just want your lover back, her dark voice growled.

Sylvie refused to engage it. Mostly because, as usual, it was telling the truth.

More silvery wisps rose from the pentagram, and Sylvie bent down and smashed the corner of the star with her gun butt. The metal inlay dented. She pried at it, yanked a brittle segment of old brass out of the floor, and turned to the next curtain. She used the metal to pry back an edge of the curtain. Without human touch, it behaved like normal fabric and gave her a glimpse of three open doorways down a dark hall. It reminded her of monastery cells and gave her yet another glimpse of the fanaticism that drove the Society.

She peeled back the next curtain, found another four cell doors, closed this time, and, more to the point, three witches guarding the cells. They looked up as Sylvie slithered through the curtain gap. The room, like all the others she'd been through, was dimly lit, but she found two men and one women waiting. The leader of this small crew snarled her name, "Shadows."

She knew him. Dennis Kent. That slate grey hair and roman nose were memorable. She'd last seen him laid out by one of Tierney Wales's soul-biting ghosts. Had thought him a typical ISI agent. She should have let Wales's ghost eat his fill.

Before she could take a shot at him, he held up the amulet around his neck, and said, "I wouldn't. We're all wearing talismans. And the only vulnerable people around are your friends. You try to shoot us, your bullets will probably hit them instead."

"Didn't help the bitch at the front door," Sylvie said, had the satisfaction of seeing shock cross his face.

"What?" she added. "Did you think she just let me pass? Or that I patted her on the head and sent her home? We're past that. We've been past that since your lot started deciding what the rest of the world was allowed to know or remember. It's you or me."

"You," he said. The first two cell doors opened and birthed snarling wolves. Werewolves by their size. Sylvie took a steadying breath, looked past the wolves' bristling fur, into the room behind them. She didn't even need the Lilith voice's assessment.

She laughed and lowered her gun, and when the wolves charged her, whining and snarling, claws scratching the stone floor, she let them brush into her, through her, and disappear. "My baby sister casts better illusions than that, Kent." Two pissed-off, slavering werewolves and the room behind them was neat as a pin?

While he gaped, and the witches behind him held a hasty spell consultation, Sylvie ran forward. The floor here was the same malachite-shaded marble. And it let her drop and slide into him as solidly as she had ever managed while playing high-school baseball. She seized the talisman around his throat and yanked. Wouldn't hurt him, but it jerked him around, let her use him as her own shield. She kicked out at the other two witches, disrupting their spell casting, tangling her legs in theirs.

Dangerous, her voice shouted, ringing in her ears.

Dogpiled with three witches who were wearing invulnerability talismans and wanted to kill her? Yeah, thanks, she knew. If her voice didn't have useful suggestions, it could shut the hell up.

She tangled them all closer; the spells warred and sparked. The remaining locked door shuddered in its frame, and Sylvie turned her head to bite down hard on Kent's throat. Couldn't hurt him, but people had atavistic reactions hardwired. He flinched, ducked his head, trying to get her off his throat, pulled away. Perfect setup. She yanked the talisman's cord over his head, got her gun up, and shot him in the soft underside of his jaw.

She deafened herself, stunned herself with the concussion of it, but managed to cling tight to both the talisman and her gun. Another distant crack sounded; she rolled to her feet, staggering, preparing for illusion or magic or—

Marah Stone, furious, diving directly for the witch nearest her. She got her Cain-marked hand around the woman's throat and squeezed. The marks on her hand seemed to pulse with the woman's labored breaths.

Invulnerability talisman or not, the woman choked.

Marah was another of God's killers, Sylvie thought, swaying. Blood scent burned thickly in her nose, rested heavy on her hair and skin.

The remaining witch dithered between Sylvie and helping his partner, and Sylvie made the decision for him. She shoved him hard, pushed him off balance, pushed him right into Demalion's waiting arms.

Demalion skinned his hand down the man's neck, yanked up, and pulled out another talisman, the twin to the one Sylvie had removed from Kent. "Always had to ape Kent. See what it gets you, O'Neal?" Before the man could mouth a single spell, Demalion broke his neck.

Sylvie had a sudden and unwelcome flashback. The last time Demalion had broken a man's neck for her, he'd died half a second later.

This time, he merely let the body drop. "Sylvie."

"Good timing," she said. She couldn't stop her gaze from lasering up and down his body, looking for injury.

"Saw you playing Twister with Kent's crew and thought you'd appreciate a hand."

"Another point for precognitive skills," she said. "Remind me to send your mother a thank-you note. Not to sound ungrateful, because I'm thrilled, relieved, blissfully happy, all those things, but why the hell aren't you dead?"

Demalion flashed a smug grin. "Well. Marah told Yvette she'd join her if the price was right, so they locked *her* up until they had time to haggle."

Marah said, "She can't afford me, but I was curious."

"As for me . . ."

"Yvette thinks if she kills him, he'll just change bodies, again," Marah put in. She was searching the witch's clothes, stripping her of anything that might be useful. Small charms, a knife, a .22 that Marah sneered at but pocketed anyway.

"I freak Yvette out," Demalion said. "She's scared that if I get killed, I'll take over one of her men, and she won't know which one."

"Wonder how she got that impression," Marah said. Her grin wasn't nice at all.

"Paranoia working for us," Sylvie said. "Doesn't happen nearly enough."

"Is it paranoia?" Marah asked. "I bet he could do it."

Demalion said, "I'd rather not test the theory."

"Yeah, let's not," Sylvie said. "I've just gotten used to you as a blond."

A muffled concussion vibrated through the stone. Hard to tell directionality when it was beneath her feet, but Sylvie knew.

"Zoe—Oh hell, I left them fighting witches. They're outnumbered."

"In the antechamber?" Marah said. She pulled the witch's talisman off the body, held it up before her, spinning at the end of its cord. The talisman, an etched, wooden scapular, looked burned. Marah's handprint discolored the lines of spellcraft on it. Marah closed her fingers, and the wood crumbled. "Give me Kent's, Sylvie. You don't need it. Your sister might."

Sylvie passed it over without hesitation, blood-spotted and sticky as it was.

"For Lupe, then," Demalion said, handing Marah O'Neal's talisman. "Did you see Yvette, Syl?"

"Every other witch in the world, seems like. But not her."

"Two covens' worth," Demalion said. "There was one maintained here, when we were brought in. And Yvette brought her own. Well, most of her own. You killed five at Dallas."

"Killed Merrow, too," Sylvie said. "Shit. We're missing at least four. And however many monsters they can control."

"So what," Marah said. "You shoot them. They die." She tucked both talismans into her jacket pocket.

"You make it sound easy," Sylvie rasped. Her throat was dry. She wanted a glass of water. Fighting was thirsty work. "Some things are immune to bullets. Yvette's not likely to let me get close enough to yank off her talisman, and you can't tell me she's not wearing one."

Marah lunged forward, shoved Sylvie against the doorjamb, and said, "You still don't get it, do you? It's not your bullets that do the job. It's *you*, pulling the trigger. You kill things that can't be killed by regular means. And you do it with a gun. *Because you like guns.* You kill things. That's who you are. The gun is irrelevant. You're the weapon."

"Weirdest pep talk ever," Sylvie said. Her heart thudded. The little dark voice crowed, *Yes, yes, yes.*

The ground vibrated again, arguing that whether Zoe was behind the mini-earthquakes or not, she was still fighting.

Demalion stepped closer to the curtain, and Sylvie winced, hissed his name in warning. He shook his head. "Spell's one-way."

"You know this place?"

"Guards talk," he said. He peered through the curtain, let it drop. "Still empty."

A third, sharper force vibrated through the room, this time shaking the doors in their frames. She took a step back the way she'd come. Zoe . . .

"Don't be stupid," Marah said. "You don't have time. You've got to stop Yvette."

"Why can't you do it? I've let you out of your cell," Sylvie said.

Marah said. "The thing about being a government assassin—you know when to leave the work to the specialists. In this case, that's you. You take care of Yvette and her little memory-modification business. I'll take care of your sister, your monster, and watching your back."

"Awfully generous of you," Sylvie said. Her neck was going to be sore from the quick glances she was casting around. Checking to see that the witches stayed dead, checking the curtain, checking the doorway that Yvette had to have gone through. Checking to make sure Demalion was at her side, still living.

"Don't worry. I'm running a tab. When all this is done, I'm going to ask you for a favor. And you're going to give it to me." Marah licked her lips. "You have a spare gun? A .22's not much unless you're right up close. I'd like to avoid that until the numbers are better."

"Witch at the curtain edge of the pentagram dropped his."

Marah nodded, started to move. Sylvie caught her arm. "Marah. Nothing happens to Zoe."

"*You* brought her here," Marah said, slipped free, ducked through the curtains, taking both invulnerability talismans with her. Sylvie hoped they went to Lupe and Zoe. Hoped she hadn't made a mistake. Hoped Marah really did have her sister in mind.

"How much of Marah's decision to help Zoe is her just wanting to be closer to the exit?"

Demalion grimaced. "Seventy-five percent, at least. She's got big plans, Syl. She needs to stay alive to implement them. But you're a part of those plans. She wants you to owe her. Zoe alive will do that."

"Not reassuring," Sylvie said. She looked at the last door, the last step into the spider's parlor. "Yvette's waiting for us, isn't she?"

"Yeah."

"Let's not disappoint her." Sylvie checked her ammunition compulsively, the good, solid weight of the gun in her hand.

She turned, looked at Demalion's empty hands, and said, "You're not armed."

"Not yet," Demalion said. "Give me five minutes."

Precognitive. Right.

Sylvie took a breath and moved toward that final door— a thick, iron-banded door in a stone arch. It looked like the entry to a dungeon. Demalion caught her arm. "Wait."

She turned to look at him, scowling. "We don't have a lot of time—"

He kissed her. Chaste but heartfelt. "We have the worst dates ever," he murmured against her mouth. "Killing witches really isn't that much fun."

"Dinner and dancing afterward," she said.

"Promise?"

She kissed him again, let her breath linger with his, warmth in the midst of this chilly underground lair. "Yeah. No matter what body you end up in."

17

A Fight to Remember

AS SYLVIE AND DEMALION APPROACHED THE DOOR TO YVETTE'S sanctum, the world seemed to fade away. The concussive ripples that were the only sign of Zoe's ongoing struggle smoothed out; the *shuff* of Sylvie's shoes went from a rasp to a whisper to nothing at all. Even her heartbeat seemed smothered and silent.

She'd never felt anything quite like it. Magic, most definitely, but unlike most of the magic she'd fought before, which sought to alter or warp reality, this spell seemed to be using magic to damp down reality and magic alike.

Fragile spell, Sylvie thought. An air lock of sorts for the Corrective.

She touched Demalion's arm, tilted her head in question. Booby-trapped?

He shook his head, stepped neatly behind her. She reached out for the latch—more black iron, more magic dampening. The latch felt like . . . nothing in her hand. She saw her fingers curl around it, saw the white tension in her flesh as she pulled the weight of it upward, the sharp bits of old metal leaving black splinters in her skin—she felt none of it.

She shoved hard and fast and found herself face-to-face

with one of Yvette's bodyguards. She recognized this one, the red-haired man with the regrettably cut suit who'd dragged Marah out of the Dallas airport. He was armed, his gun aimed at her, and she stepped right into his space, so fast that his gun ended up pointing over her shoulder. She shot him in the chest; he flinched at the sound but didn't fall. She shot him again, watched the bullet disappear before touching his skin.

He tried to regroup, to get away from her gun, to get her at the end of his weapon. While he was trying to shove her away, Demalion stepped out of shadows and seized his weapon, his wrists. Sylvie lifted the talisman from his throat, and Demalion shot him dead.

Easy as pie.

It had taken seconds.

Murder in concert shouldn't feel so good. But there was a quick, wild flush in her throat and skin that pointed out how well matched they were, how well they worked together.

"Yvette," Demalion said, his voice a breath in her ear.

"And the Corrective."

They were in a short hallway that closed in smaller and smaller as it went—no wonder the guard had been waiting foolishly close to the door, probably trying to hear their approach over the suppression of sound. If he hadn't been claustrophobic before, a stint down here would jump-start it.

The door at the end was open, waiting for them. It was barely five feet tall, and the stone around it was old and dark. Sylvie crouched as she went through, preferring aching thighs to bending her head and losing sight of the room she moved into. Her breath preceded her and let her know that the room was enormous and cold. Cavernous. She stepped out and tried not to gape.

Cavernous was right.

The space stretched out ahead and around them, a hundred feet long, half that wide, maybe more, full of shadowy spaces and movement. More LED touchlights studded the walls but didn't do much for making light in the darkness.

Sylvie thought about earthquakes and tsunamis and shuddered.

Movement at the far end was too clearly defined to be anything but human, and Sylvie headed in that direction, each step cautious, testing, looking for magical traps, gun steady in her hands; Demalion had her back, stolen gun held at the ready. Something slick and glossy snaked over the floor; she stepped across it, careful not to let it touch her. She'd learned her lesson with the curtains. Here, in the Society's stronghold, everything was dangerous.

She heard Demalion's steps hitch as he adjusted to mimic her avoidance.

"Don't be so hesitant," Yvette said. Her voice rang out, full of echoes in this space. "If you've come this far, you've killed all my guards and witches. Now it's just me."

"What's he? Furniture?" Sylvie said, focusing her attention on a blotchy shadow near Yvette. It twitched against her senses like a hastily sketched illusion.

"*Nearly* all my guards," Yvette said with impatience. She waved her hand, plucked at the air, and the illusions stripped themselves off the guards bookending her. They didn't look thrilled at being exposed to her view. "Happy now?"

"Guards," Yvette had called them. Sylvie knew better. They were witches also. Yvette was a liar. Would say anything to get them off guard.

"It's hard to believe we've never crossed paths before," Yvette said. "I knew we'd meet sooner or later. I must admit, I'd hoped for later."

"Then you shouldn't have worked so hard to get my attention," Sylvie said. Yvette was exactly what she'd expected. Competent. Confident. Arrogant. All the hallmarks of a high-ranking witch.

Sylvie's eyes adjusted to the dim light, to that sense of motion when no one in the room was moving. It was the spell—the Corrective. The entire room was dedicated to the spell, and the glossy slick that she'd stepped over hadn't been a puddle or a rainwater rivulet seeping down from the earth above but actual flowing water. It traced an infinity loop around the room, following channels laid into the stone floor, but it was like no water Sylvie had ever seen or heard. It flowed in utter silence, a rush of black silk chasing itself, as heavy as oil, as black as space between the stars. It wound between two tall, slim stones like a cat's cradle spun between two upraised palms.

"Impressive, isn't it?" Yvette asked.

"Yup," Sylvie said. Something about the water was so unnatural, it was hard to take her eyes from it, even in a room with three witches and so much at stake. "Impressive. Deadly. You're making people stroke out with your shiny little spell. Ruining lives."

"Tiger by the tail," Yvette said. "I do admit that we've lost our . . . finesse of late, but you're partially to blame, crashing around without the slightest subtlety. You do keep stirring things up."

"You're the one who sicced monsters on your own people," Demalion said.

"Not my monsters, not my people," Yvette said. "Not my problem."

"You lie about everything," Sylvie said. "This is definitely your problem now. Or I wouldn't be here with a gun."

"If I had monsters at my beck and call, would I be trying to talk sense into you? Appealing to your better nature while your . . . friends are killing my people?"

"Maybe you're just tapped out, used up all your monster spells," Sylvie said. "Or maybe Merrow, with his persuasive ways, was your only monster talker. Don't know. Right now, I don't care. Shut down the Corrective, Yvette, or I will."

Yvette nodded, and Demalion growled. Sylvie echoed his irritation. She knew that gesture. It wasn't agreement, just Yvette conveying her understanding that this was how it was going to be: that Sylvie was unreasonable. "You don't want me to do that."

"I really do," Sylvie said.

"Sylvie—" Demalion said. Warning: Close her mouth, get the job done.

She kept her eyes, her gun on Yvette, but nodded that she was listening.

"I don't think it's that easy," Demalion said.

"She made it; she breaks it—"

"I don't think she did. It's not her spell to break."

"Oh, Michael," Yvette said. Her tone was disappointed and fond at the same time. "This is why I headhunted you for my team all those years ago. Why did you have to change sides? Always so quick to see the problem."

"So it's not her spell," Sylvie said. "But it's her coven, her people. She knows how to—"

"Do you know what powers this spell?" Yvette asked.

"The two stones," Sylvie said. They reeked of god-power to her. Strong beyond human skills, despite the witch sigils carved into their surfaces. "The water isn't just flowing around them. It's coming *from* them."

"It's been doing it long enough to wear a deep groove in the stone," Demalion said. "To make its own path."

Sylvie jerked her gaze downward. He was right. The lip and side of the grooves were as smooth as river rocks. The river had made itself at home.

"Those stone pillars are extraordinarily rare," Yvette said. "Do you know what they are? Where they come from? What had to be braved to bring them back?"

Water and memory together gave her the clue, and Sylvie robbed Yvette of the satisfaction of telling her. "They're from the River Lethe."

"Our founder," Yvette said, "planned it. Dedicated her lover to Hades, sacrificed him, then traveled down to Hades to barter with the god of the dead to bring him back. All a ruse, of course. Hades said no, and she begged at least, let him forget her. Hades acquiesced. Took them both to the River Lethe, where she stole a pebble from both banks before Hades ushered her out. The god thought he'd won, never thought of her again. She took the stones and ran. It took her twenty years of experimentation and effort to grow them. Another ten to create the Corrective."

"It's the same one," Sylvie said. She got it now. Yvette's

awe, reluctance, even the fear of the spell she was using. The age of the surroundings, the rarity of the ingredients. The difficulty of the spell . . . "The very same spell. You never reconstituted it; your people never let it lapse. It's been running for—"

"A hundred and seventeen years," Yvette said. "Long enough for the river to grow along with the stones. For the strength behind it to grow enormous. For it to reach out to any part of the world that we need changed. If you break this spell, the backlash of it will kill me and most likely everyone here."

"I'll take that chance," Sylvie said.

• • •

BEFORE SHE FINISHED SPEAKING, THE ROOM ERUPTED INTO MOVE-ment, their cease-fire broken. Demalion's free hand latched onto Sylvie's waist and yanked her aside just as bullets furrowed the space where she'd been.

Yvette, that liar, had only removed part of the illusions on her guards. No wonder they had stayed as still as they had throughout Yvette and Sylvie's chatter—too much movement would have revealed the truth. They were holding semiautomatic pistols.

All of this went through Sylvie's head even as she was returning fire, even as Demalion hustled them toward the nearest defensible place—ducking into the shadow of a Lethe stone. She fought him. She didn't want to duck and cover and play at armed groundhog, taking turns shooting at each other. She wanted to take the fight to them. To kill them all. To break the damn Corrective and restore the world to its regularly scheduled way of life. To give Alex her life back.

She lunged out; Demalion hauled her back. Bullets spattered the Lethe stones, doing no damage at all to them.

"Would you stop that?"

"You're going to get yourself killed," he spat.

"Is that foresight or fear?" Sylvie craned her head, trying to keep an eye on the guards, on Yvette. One guard—

dark-haired, dark-skinned, dressed to disappear, his gun held loosely but confidently in his hands—near the entryway, blocking their path out. Sylvie almost laughed. Yvette didn't know her at all if she thought that retreat was on her mind. The guard laid down another line of fire, wasting ammunition. Whatever magics were done here, the Lethe stones weren't the only things made stronger. All those bullets, and no shrapnel from the walls.

The second guard—so blond his hair was nearly white—was skirting the wall and the trapped river, trying to come up behind Sylvie and Demalion, trying to put them between two sets of gunfire.

That wasn't the real plan, Sylvie thought. The gunmen weren't even aiming well. They were distraction for Yvette. She was where the real danger lay. Sylvie had faced tougher opponents—Lilith, Odalys, a fledgling god—but Yvette was clever, and a lucky shot could kill Sylvie as easily as a powerful one.

The less time Yvette had to plan, the better. That in mind, Sylvie shifted forward again, dodged the desultory shooting from the dark guard, and rolled across the unyielding floor with a wince. She came up behind him and kicked out.

Utterly graceless, still effective. The man stumbled forward a few steps, and Demalion yanked him further off balance, yanked him directly to the edge of the narrow river and over.

The witch fell just right, slipped into the river. Sylvie had expected him to get wet, splash hip deep or so, and momentarily lose his bearings, maybe even lose his memories. Demalion moved forward as if he expected the same, expected a chance to wrest his gun away.

The witch hit the water and sank fast and silent. Disappeared, as if the river were the void it resembled. The surface didn't even change in its slow, oily rippling. Invulnerability talisman or not, he was gone.

Sylvie and Demalion exchanged appalled glances that said the same thing: *Don't you fall in!*

The second guard let his gun drop, raised his head sharply. "You're bleeding, Shadows."

She felt the sting along her arm where she'd scraped it as she rolled. It didn't seem newsworthy, but Yvette looked just as stunned. The guard growled low under his breath, began twitching beneath the skin, growing claws and fur and sprouting teeth.

Sorcerous shape-shifter, Sylvie diagnosed. Those fuckers were hard to put down; they could take a lot of abuse, and they healed fast. Mix that with a talisman that granted invulnerability, and he was going to be difficult.

"You killed my men," Yvette said, "and you didn't take their talismans? Are you that much of a purist that you'd rather die than wear a magical shield?"

"Nope. Someone else had better uses for them." She hoped like hell that Zoe and Lupe were wearing them by now. Hoped they were clearing their path out of here. Hoped they'd have enough sense to flee when Marah gave them the word to do so.

Yvette's face tightened, showed fine lines like cracks in porcelain. "Marah Stone. I wondered what had become of her. I hoped she'd join us."

"Sorry," Sylvie said. "She's got plans. They don't involve you."

Demalion shot steadily at the shape-shifter, a repetitive percussion that echoed and echoed against the walls. The man had thrown down his gun, preferring to kill up close and toothy, as so many of the shifting sorcerers did. He kept stalking Demalion, shaking bullets out of his silvery fur, scattering them like overlarge, metallic fleas.

Yvette shook her head. "They won't involve you, either. I thought you'd be better than this, Shadows. You came before me, weak?" Yvette held up her hand, fisted it suddenly and tossed the spell at Sylvie. She jerked away, almost made it out of range. Her left hand didn't, trailed behind her, and Sylvie yelped as the bones in her hand broke.

She dodged the next spell that Yvette threw; her hand

throbbed and throbbed. She felt it swelling and was thankful that it was her left hand. Not her gun hand.

Even more thankful that for all of Yvette's skills, she hadn't managed to get her hands on anything that belonged to Sylvie. A bonebreak spell was hard enough to dodge, but if Yvette had been able to fine-tune it, to use Sylvie's stolen hair, fingernails, or clothing to home in on her, there would have been no dodging possible.

As it was, Sylvie was running out of time.

Shoot her, her little dark voice shouted.

She hated those damn invulnerability talismans.

Yvette lined up another blast, and Sylvie leaped over the river, headed back toward the upright Lethe stone. The spell hit her ankle. The joint protested and swelled. Her bones . . . held this time, having learned the taste of the spell enough to reject it. Magical antibodies for the win, she thought wildly, though her left hand complained.

Yvette threw a third blast, stronger still, after Sylvie, reaching her just as she ducked behind the Lethe stone. The spell crashed over it, spilling around the sides to reach her. Sylvie felt the shivery malevolence of it vibrate her bones as it passed.

Shoot her!

The werewolf's outraged howl drew her attention, got her back on her feet, peering around the stone pillar; Demalion had the shape-shifter up off the ground, grimacing as the wolf savaged his hip, clawed at his chest. It had to outweigh him, but he took three laboring steps and tossed the wolf into the river. It clawed at the sides of the stony riverbank, never gained traction, and vanished.

Demalion staggered, leaned over the water, breathing hard. His blood dripped across the floor. Yvette snarled. She raised her hand, and Demalion raised his head, aware of the danger, but—Sylvie saw he couldn't move. Too exhausted, too sore, too slow . . .

Her heart turned over, sick with dread.

He smiled.

Shoot her!

Sylvie put her remaining shots into Yvette; she had never wanted anyone dead as much this woman who threatened to take Demalion from her. Again. Her anger was a rolling, snake-twisting cloud over her entire body and brain, a spreading, numb rage that reached out and smothered, crushed everything before it. The shots were sharp firecrackers in the sudden darkness, crisp and final.

Yvette's fisted hand splayed open. Fell to her side. The bonebreak spell cracked the floor near her feet. Yvette's other hand fumbled up toward her chest, toward the invulnerability talisman.

At her touch, while Sylvie's shots were still echoing, the talisman fell apart, split by Sylvie's bullets.

The gun's not the weapon, Marah had said. *You are.*

For the first time, Sylvie understood what that meant. She wasn't just resistant to magic used against her. She *suppressed* magic. She killed the unkillable by taking away their magical protection. She made them mortal. Vulnerable. Killable. She was the weapon. Her bullets were the coup de grace. Nothing more.

Maybe not even that.

Yvette crumpled, bewilderment frozen on her face. Her last expression. Her plans all come to nothing.

"Good timing," Demalion said. He didn't sound surprised at all.

She lunged at him, uncertain whether she wanted to kiss him or pummel him senseless. "Bastard," she snapped. "I thought she was going to kill you."

"I knew she wasn't."

Her hands were shaking, both the broken one and the one that held the empty gun. "You're bleeding all over the place. Do something about that, would you?"

"I'm all right, Sylvie. I'm all right." He dragged her close, and she burrowed into him, smelled blood, but his pulse was strong and solid beneath her cheek.

She shook off her fears and straightened her shoulders. "Yeah. You are."

Demalion looked at the liquid flutter of river water, that

oily memory sink, and said, "So, I know we don't trust Yvette's word, but I'm concerned about the magical back-lash. You're tough, but that's a century-old spell you're planning to disrupt—"

"No," she said. "Not disrupt. *Kill*. Put it down. Don't worry. I've got this."

She felt distanced from her own body, its shakes and scrapes and broken bones a thin layer above a solid, untouchable core. It seemed so easy to walk across the room, Demalion's gun collected on the way. To stand between the two Lethe stones, brought up out of a god's realm. She took a breath and shot them, one after another.

Two bullets against two stones that had deflected spells and semiautomatic gunfire, and when her bullets hit—they quavered and rang like breaking bells. The sigils along their sides wisped out like blown candle flames. The water churned furiously, steaming and bubbling, then drained away.

"Well, that's that—"

Sylvie hunched, felt oddly like someone had just punched her in the back of her head. Beside her, Demalion fell to his knees. Her vision bobbled, swamped out by memory.

. . .

THIRTEEN YEARS OLD, SULKING FURIOUSLY. THE FIRST FAMILY VACA-tion since the brat sister had been born. Her parents were ignoring her to show off Zoe. Sylvie slunk out of the aquar-ium, blinking at the cloudy sky until she stopped seeing the blue of carefully maintained tanks. The ocean, grey and jagged and wild, beckoned, and she wandered down to the pier, where dockworkers were scraping barnacles off a recently raised boat.

She sat on a boat cleat and watched their knives work, scrape and twist and scrape and twist. The salt air was soothing, and there were no crying toddlers. On the other side of the pier, a man sat beneath a beach umbrella, mind-ing three separate fishing rods wedged into the wood slats.

Then the gulls died.

They plummeted out of the sky, smacking into the pier in a splay of broken wings and twisted necks. Others slapped her face and hair and shoulders, and she screamed.

"Oye, muchacha!" *the man who'd been fishing from the side of the pier called.* "Ven aca! Hurry!" *She ran to him, and he tucked her beneath his sunshade umbrella. Birds splatted against it, and she leaned up close to the pole, smelling salt and blood and something cold beneath. Beneath the pier, the waters slapped cold and dark as if a storm were brewing in its depths.*

"Madre de Dios," *he said. Clapped a hand over her eyes.* "No mire, muchacha. Don' look." *She pried his hand away from her face. She wanted to see.*

A small boat drifted toward the pier, and even from the distance, Sylvie could see that something was wrong. The people were lying on the deck. Like the birds. All loose and empty. The air was cold.

The boat collided with the pier, shaking her world; one of the bodies on the deck slid down, giving her a clear view of the body's glazed eyes, as blank as the dead gulls'. Her stomach hurt. The fisherman rushed to the boat, along with others. Sylvie, gaping at the side of the yacht, saw a shining mist slide out through a closed porthole, curling around and around in the sky like one of the eels she'd seen in the aquarium, except they'd been just fish in water. This . . . The dockworkers shouted and jerked back; the fisherman swore in Spanish.

It was a monster. And it had human-shaped eyes. It coiled lazily, looked at her, and she felt her breathing stop; she crouched small and hoped it wouldn't keep looking at her. She thought, the monster got aboard that boat, and it looked at the people on it, like she looked at the fish in the aquarium, and the people died.

Its eye was glittering and red. The air was frigid; she couldn't stop shivering. All around her, the pier was quiet.

The monster slid back into the water and fish bobbed to the surface, silver bellies up, as it passed. A thin wake cut against the waves and disappeared into the deeper sea.

A minute later, sound and warmth crashed over her again, her mother shaking her, "We were worried, Sylvie, you can't just walk away—oh God no, don't look at them, you don't need to see that—" and dragging her away from the dock, from the dead people on the boat.

"There was a monster," Sylvie told her mother.

"No such thing as monsters," her mother said. "Come on, let's go back to the hotel."

Sylvie had gone, glad to be warm, glad to be safe, glad even to see her dumb little sister. She knew that her mother was wrong. It was a monster. She'd seen it.

The next day she went back to the pier, slipping away when her mother went to get them lunch and her father was trying to get Zoe to stop shrieking. It was closed off, yellow tape where the boat still bumped against the dock. Sylvie kicked at the gravel, studied the area.

A dark-haired woman ducked under the tape, walked out to the pier. She wasn't a policewoman; she was wearing a long, narrow skirt and lots of strange jewelry. Sylvie bit her lip, followed her. The woman turned when Sylvie approached. Her eyes were dark and hard and she didn't look nice at all. She looked interesting.

"What are you doing here?"

"I wanted to see where the monster was," Sylvie said. "The papers didn't say anything about it. It said they all died from drugs. I don't get it. The fisherman saw it. The dockworkers saw it. Why didn't they say so?"

"Because people are willfully blind," the woman said. She turned back to stare out at the sea. Her lips curled. "They want to pretend dangerous things don't exist."

"Like the eel-monster thing."

"Water spirit," the woman said. "A genus loci, do you know what that is?"

"No," Sylvie said. The woman shrugged, didn't explain what that meant. Silence fell, then the woman spoke again.

"They picked it up in the Bermuda Triangle. It gets bored sometimes. That makes it cruel and destructive."

"It killed people because it was bored?"

"You're young. The world is new for you," the woman said. "You have no idea how boring things can get when you're my age. You have to make your own amusements where you can."

"Is that why you're here? To be amused? People died."

"Aren't you the junior moralizer?" the woman said. "But not law-abiding. You're going to get in trouble if they see you behind the tape."

"I'm a kid," Sylvie said. "They'll just send me home to my parents. They might arrest you."

"Not likely," she said. She turned, put her back to the water. "So. Little moralizer. When you go home, and you're back with your little friends. What are you going to tell them? That you saw a monster? Or will you lie and tell them what the newspaper said?"

"Why would I tell them anything at all?" Sylvie asked. "They won't believe me if I do, and I'm not going to lie. I know what I saw."

The woman's hand was on Sylvie's cheek suddenly; Sylvie jerked, but the woman was strong, her nails curling beneath Sylvie's chin, scratching, hurting.

"You're an interesting kid," the woman said. "But I bet you forget. Go home, get away from the scene, think it's a dream. A nightmare. Five years from now, and you'll be shrugging and telling yourself you were an imaginative kid."

"No," Sylvie said. "I won't forget."

The woman's mouth turned down; displeasure at being contradicted or at the state of the world, Sylvie didn't know. "They always do. They like to be blind. They think it makes them safe. It doesn't. How can we be safe when he cares nothing for us?"

"Sylvie!" her mother shouted.

Sylvie jerked away, left the woman behind, even as the woman's grip left scratches on her cheek and chin. She rubbed at the welts and shivered. The woman was wrong. She wasn't going to forget.

. . .

SYLVIE *HAD* FORGOTTEN. IT HADN'T BEEN HER CHOICE. THE CORREC-tive had taken it. Now, it had given it back.

Sylvie raised her head, saw that the black waters of the Corrective had gone clear and clean, no longer muddied by stolen memories.

"Lilith," she said. Touched her cheek as if the scratches would still be there. "That was Lilith."

Demalion was curled up near the edge of the water; he looked as shell-shocked as she felt. "There was a vampire in my neighborhood," he told Sylvie. "It killed three of my friends when I was in elementary school. I forgot, even though I saw it. Touched it. This skeletal, verminous thing that grabbed me, and was going to bite me, and then . . . it smelled me and ran. Smelled Sphinx. He called me *sphinx-let* and threw me against the alley wall. How could I forget that?"

Sylvie looked back at the clear water, and said, "God. A hundred years. A hundred years of stolen memories. Anything big enough to make the news. Anything big enough to reveal the *Magicus Mundi*. The Good Sisters have been erasing it. Rewriting memories. We just gave them all back. All at once."

"Shit," he said. "What did we do?"

Sylvie licked her lips, felt an unaccountable giggle in her throat. Well, she'd always bitched about keeping the *Mundi* a secret. "We pulled off the blinders. Pulled back the curtain. Jesus, Demalion. I think we changed the world. Or at least, perception of it."

18

Getting Gone

SYLVIE AND DEMALION SPENT A FEW EXTRA MINUTES WALKING THE edges of the dead Corrective spell, Sylvie looking for any remaining cloudiness, Demalion watching her back. Unlike Pandora's box, this world-changer had emptied itself completely. Even as she walked the perimeter of the crossed loops, the water began to evaporate, revealing a smooth stone groove only two feet deep.

Neither of the witches' bodies, wolf or man, was there. They had been taken.

"Think there's going to be chaos?" Demalion asked.

"When isn't there? People never react well."

"I don't know," Demalion said. "Some of the memories won't have people to return to. A hundred-plus years? Some people are long dead."

"Not all of them. Not even most of them, I'd bet. Population goes up. So do the number of incidents. Yvette said they'd been getting more dependent on it."

Demalion grimaced, ceding the point. Sylvie winced. Her broken hand cramped and burned. She lifted it to her opposite shoulder, rested her wrist there, tried to slow the swelling.

"Syl. I remember the vampire. But I also *don't* remember it. I remember being at home, instead of the alley, watching TV, instead of being grabbed by a child-killing vampire. Double memories. False *and* real. You're always complaining about people choosing to be blind. Maybe things won't change. Maybe they'll just think they had vivid dreams about a real-world event."

"Until they realize other people had the same dreams. The Good Sisters specialized in big magic scenarios. Like the sand wraith in Chicago, the mermaids in Miami." Sylvie leaned up, kissed his cheek, tasting splash-back blood from the wound in his shoulder. "You're such an optimist. Unless you can take a look ahead with your handy-dandy psychic skills and tell me that the world just says, Oh, all right, monsters, I'm going to prepare for the worst. And stock up on ammo."

Despite her words, she did feel a little bit better. Demalion was partly correct. People did like to ignore the evidence before their eyes, even at the expense of their own memories. Things were going to change, had already changed, but maybe the change would be gradual enough that it wouldn't be a cultural apocalypse.

Maybe.

A lot depended on the Corrective itself. The spell had affected more than memories—had been the Corrective it was named. It had altered data files, video feed, Internet content, and paper reports, as well as human memory. Magical white-out par excellence. The question was, when people's memories were returned, what happened to the documentation?

Were there, even now, video files slowly changing back? Where a mangy coyote running down a Texas county road suddenly grew spikes and saber-tooth fangs and became more obviously the *chupacabra*? Where blubbery pieces of dead whales washed up on a shoreline slowly lengthened and twisted and became the sea serpent it had been before the Corrective hit?

Were there old newspapers with wild accounts of magical events, with conclusive photographs reshaping themselves on microfiche, in the recycling bins, in the landfills?

Zoe would know.

Now that she'd thought of Zoe again, the anxiety was sharp in her chest. She'd survived. Demalion had survived. Her sister? Sylvie gave Demalion's gun back to him. He raised a brow. "You don't want it?"

She readjusted her broken hand, using her good hand to brace the elbow on her bad arm, to keep it upraised. Still throbbed and complained. "I trust you to take out any stragglers we missed."

Demalion ushered her toward the door, looked back once at the cavernous room. "Amazing."

"What?"

"It's still standing," he said. "That's a first for you, isn't it? Leaving something other than wreckage behind—"

She kicked at him, and he laughed, a little wild. A little giddy. "Shut up," she muttered. "Or you'll be sleeping on the couch."

"Your apartment's probably under surveillance. We'll be sleeping in a hotel."

"Then you'll be sleeping on the floor," she said.

Rediscovering the bodies of Kent and his team drove the laughter from her voice. Yeah. She might have left the building standing, but she'd done bloody damage to the people defending it. She looked at Kent's waxy face, the gore that made a void of his throat and jaw, and couldn't regret it. It was war. She'd won.

The treacherous curtains were peaceful and motionless, and she forced herself to recall that Marah had passed through them unscathed. It still made her nerves flare to brush up against them. But they behaved as curtains should, and she took her good hand from its task of makeshift sling, and yanked the curtains down as they passed through. No more magical booby traps.

They hissed down like a rain of snakes, coiled limply across the floor. Sylvie eyed them warily, tried not to turn her back on them as they hustled—her wincing, him limping—across the ruined pentagram and back to the antechamber.

It was empty of life, and Sylvie's heart turned over. Bodies littered the floor, bloody or burned beyond recognition. Panic shivered through her, the cold coil of rage—she shouldn't have trusted Marah.

Demalion's eyes flicked over each body just as hers did, each of them racing to disprove her fear. He said, "Zoe's not here."

A yellow spark of light illuminated the dark tunnel they'd come through, and Zoe's voice, ragged and exhausted, said, "That's 'cause we got the hell out of Dodge in case you brought the roof down. Marah said you probably would."

"Zo—" Sylvie raced across the room, caught her sister up, one-handed, smelled char and fire, not just from the lighter Zoe hastily clicked shut.

"Did you do it?" Zoe asked. "Break the Corrective?"

Sylvie leaned back. "None of your memories changed?"

"Should they have?"

"Only if you ran into something big and magical before, I guess."

Weariness was settling onto her like a shroud. The earth above their head seemed suddenly oppressive, crushing her with its darkness and chill. Demalion caught her around the waist as she sagged. He groaned as he did so, and she forced herself to stiffen her spine, carry herself. He was wounded, too.

"Come on," Zoe said. "Let's get the hell out of here before someone comes to investigate."

"Investigate what?" Sylvie muttered.

"Your part of the fight might have been quiet—at least, we didn't hear it. But ours was not. We set off the ISI alarm above. Marah's up there shutting it down."

"And Lupe?" Sylvie said, following her sister's voice through the dark tunnel.

"She's . . . okay," Zoe said.

"You don't sound sure."

"She's not sure."

Sylvie stepped out into a thick fogbank tinted with dawnlight, pink and gold and palest violet. It was almost a physical relief after the closed-in dark and blood of the underground base. Two shapes swirled out of the mist and joined them. Marah Stone, a long, lean figure—the only one of them who was moving smoothly. Behind her . . . it had to be Lupe. Back in human shape. Completely human. Down to her fingertips.

"Lupe," Sylvie said. "You're—"

"I was killing them. They decided the best way to fight me was to make me normal again." Lupe's voice was blank where it should have been exultant. The bad guys had done what Sylvie couldn't. What Lupe had wanted for so long. Given her back her human life. Maybe it was just too much, all at once.

Sylvie had a bad feeling about it, though, remembering Lupe fierce and savage and powerful. That kind of feeling was addictive.

"Marah," Demalion said. "Transport?"

"SUV's waiting," she said. "Let's get out of here. I know a place we can clean up."

• • •

MARAH'S PLACE TURNED OUT TO BE A SKETCHY-LOOKING PRIVATE clinic surrounded by barbed-wire fences. Inside, Marah waved the doctor over without a word. The doctor took one look at the lot of them, bruised, broken, bleeding, and simply nodded. He whisked Sylvie away for X-rays of her hand before she could do more than blink in the bright fluorescents. The smell of burned coffee was strong, and she managed to convince him to give her a cup right after he shot her full of some powerful painkiller.

"I'm immobilizing your hand," he said. "Just to get you to your next destination. You're going to need surgery and pins. There are twenty-seven bones in your hand. Thirteen of them are broken."

"Feels like it," she said. Inwardly, she was thinking,

only thirteen? Another thing to thank her magical resistance for.

He sent her back into the room Marah had commandeered. Sylvie got her first real look at her team. Demalion's lacerations weren't as bad as she'd feared. He'd managed to do more than just lift that sorcerous werewolf up; he'd held him away from his body as best he could. Eight jagged claw marks scored his side and shoulder, but they were fairly shallow; a series of deep punctures at his hip marked where the wolf had bitten down. A crew-cut woman who looked like she belonged in army greens drew another line of sutures through his flesh.

Demalion met Sylvie's eyes and nodded. *I'm okay.*

Zoe drew her attention next by the simple gasp she let out. She stared at Sylvie's swaddled hand, braced from every angle possible. "Oh God, what happened?"

"Bonebreak spell." Sylvie took in her sister's appearance in full light and did some appalled gaping of her own. "Oh, Zoe . . ."

Zoe tossed her head; the brutal burn across her neck and jaw glistened in the white lights of the clinic, shiny with salve. Her hair on that side was a charred, frizzled mass. "It's okay," she said. "Nothing a chic haircut and a small illusion won't fix. It's not that bad."

Sylvie bit her lip hard, sat on the low, padded table beside her. Her knees felt soft, fluid. When she had control of her tongue, she said, "I'm sorry."

"I knew what I was getting into," Zoe said. Her eyes were hard and bright; she squeezed onto the table also, a line of warmth along Sylvie's side. "I opened up the earth below the witch who did it. Feel worse for her. She's down amidst the magma."

Marah grinned from her place by the door. "I like your sister, Sylvie."

"Yeah, I meant to say—what the hell, Zoe? Earthquakes in a fault zone? That was a fucking huge risk, don't you think? We were all *underground*!"

"It was not," Zoe argued right back. "Jeez, Sylvie, use

your brain. That stronghold had stood for over a century. It survived the 1906 earthquake. You know what that means?"

"They were lucky?"

Demalion rolled his eyes. The nurse in the room didn't even look up as they argued over magic and earthquakes. Sylvie wondered if she was even listening at all. She seemed utterly practiced in ignoring anything but the wounds she was dealing with. She finished the last stitch, leaned forward to reach for a roll of gauze, and revealed a handgun strapped at her spine.

Sylvie had the strong suspicion they were in an ISI chop shop. Safe enough, she supposed. There was no one left to lead the ISI. Graves. Riordan. Yvette. All dead. No one to take their places. No one to come after her for the time being.

"You don't get it, Sylvie. Those witches worked enough magic to make the ground completely stable. There are anti-earthquake charms all over the area. Hell, the rest of the world will fall into the sea before that place feels so much as a tremor."

"Yeah, that might explain why it's still standing after Sylvie got through with it," Demalion said. "I thought that was too good to be true."

"We were *damned* lucky. I kept expecting Yvette to sic one of her leashed monsters on us. I guess she was tapped out."

"Or thought she'd get caught in the cross fire," Demalion said. "Those monsters were pretty much the raze-it-to-the-ground type."

"I would have done my best to make sure she did," Sylvie said with a shrug.

Lupe slunk into the room; a toilet flushed behind her. She was changed, wearing white scrubs, and she looked very small as she curled up on another examining table. She sat silently, watching her hands open and close. Her nails shone short and soft and human. Pink and white, the traces of an old French manicure brought back from the past. She had two black eyes forming—probably a broken nose—red-yellow bruises rising on her arms, but other than that, she looked just like the girl Sylvie had seen months ago—the clean-cut college student.

Until Sylvie looked into her eyes. Lupe was never going to be that girl again, no matter that she'd gotten a reset on her humanity.

Demalion shifted in his seat, reached out, and distracted Zoe when the nurse applied one last sheen of salve to Zoe's burned face and neck.

Too little, too late, Sylvie thought, but Zoe seemed to find some measure of relief in the application. She closed her eyes, sighed into it, tilted her head so the nurse could get her cheek.

Sylvie swallowed guilt—her beautiful baby sister—and dread. Her parents were not going to be happy. The nurse nodded impartially at all of them and left.

Zoe touched her arm. "Hey. Sylvie. It really is okay. I know a lot of healing spells. And with this? Val can't object to me practicing them. She might even teach me some offensive spells. Mostly, she's just showed me defensive ones. I had to make it up as I went along."

Sylvie shuddered. "Thank you for not telling me that *before* we took on the Society. I would have died of worry." Demalion reached over, twined his fingers with her good ones, squeezed.

"Hey, I'm badass even on defense. Shielding and magical pitfalls and illusions and mind reading. You can do a whole hell of a lot with those."

Marah interrupted them. "You shouldn't play defense, Zoe. Not with Cain's mark on your hand. You're a killer. It's a waste of your talents."

Zoe shrugged. "Whatever."

Sylvie had never been so glad to hear that annoying word out of her sister's mouth.

Before she could tell Marah off for trying to—what? Recruit her sister?—Demalion said. "Airport next, Marah?"

"Yeah. I think it's safe enough. So, four tickets to Miami?"

"Four?" Sylvie said. "Where are you going?"

"So eternally untrusting," Marah said. "If you must know, DC. There's a job opening at the head of the ISI. It's got my name all over it." She smiled. Smug. More than that. Happy. Accomplished.

"*That's* what you want? That's your plan? To take over the ISI?"

Marah let her smile widen. "Oh yeah. It's been a long time coming."

"You're a lunatic," Sylvie said.

"Related to you," Marah said. "Seriously, why wouldn't I? Power, prestige, loads of excitement, and things to kill. I'm an ideal candidate. Magic resistance and everything. There's going to be more money than ever being shunted our way once people really sit down and come to grips with their shiny new memories of monsters and magic."

"You, too?" Demalion asked.

Zoe and Lupe traded left-out, puzzled glances.

"Three out of five," Sylvie said. "Odds don't look good for the rest of the world."

"Positive thinking, Sylvie. Positive thinking."

"See, I like that," Marah said. "You coming to DC with me, Demalion? There's definitely a place for you in my ISI if you want it."

Sylvie stiffened, but Demalion's answer was quick and certain. "No."

"Not even if I offer you a top position?"

"You're quick to assume no one will object to your taking over," Sylvie said.

Marah smiled. "I've got it locked. Don't you worry about that. I have persuasive and powerful friends. I even have you to back me as director of the ISI. That'll be something to show them. That I have Shadows on my side."

"You do?"

"Absolutely," Marah said. "After all I've done for you, do you really feel you can say no?"

Sylvie sighed. There might be worse things, she thought, than having Marah in charge of the ISI.

Not much, her little dark voice said. *An assassin in charge of a secret government organization.*

Probably not going to be secret that much longer, not if the *Magicus Mundi* wasn't secret. People were going to want to know that there was a plan—Sylvie studied Marah's smile and felt suspicion. Somehow, this was all working to Marah's benefit. Every step of it. The attacks that killed the ISI heads, the unmasking of the Society, Marah's easy capture by Yvette's people, even Sylvie's owing her debts. But she hadn't known about the Society. Until Sylvie told her. Right?

Just a clever mercenary. Seizing the moment.

Seizing it right *now*.

"So, you never answered me, Demalion? If I made you a division head? Rejoin the ISI? Excitement. Molding the world. Saving people?"

Zoe stiffened at Sylvie's side, all youthful indignation. Sylvie, older, wiser, thought he might say yes. He could do a lot of good as a division head. He had always believed in the ISI goals.

"No," Demalion said again. "I'm sticking with Sylvie this time. I think I'll get enough excitement and saving people working with her. And hey, we unmasked the *Mundi*. She's going to need another partner."

"Can we just go home?" Lupe interrupted. Tears slicked her face, looking painful as they squeezed past her swollen eyes. "I don't care who goes to DC as long as I get to go home."

"Seconded," Zoe said. Her shoulders sagged; her hands shook. Her bravery and adrenaline were wearing off. Sylvie wanted the inevitable crash to be somewhere other than an ISI clinic. She wanted them to think of her as strong, not to be messed with. Not the teenager she actually was. A tear smudged Zoe's face, trickled crookedly through the burn salve.

Sylvie herself wanted to get someplace familiar. Safe. There was a certain sensation in the air, a feeling that all the bad luck they'd dodged was just out there, waiting. Biding its time.

The world, Sylvie thought, was holding its breath. Waiting to see who flinched first. The human world or the *Magicus Mundi*.

. . .

MARAH PUT THEM IN FIRST-CLASS SEATING, WHICH LEFT SYLVIE feeling irritably grateful since there were fewer people to gape at them in the curtained-off area. She curled up next to Zoe, Demalion reaching across the aisle to brush his hand against hers every time she jerked awake. Lupe traveled in complete silence, not sleeping. Not talking. Sylvie didn't think it was just because she was caught between Demalion—who she didn't know at all—and the window. Sylvie thought about changing seats, thought about trying to piece together whatever made Lupe look like she was dying inside, but the painkillers swept her back under, and she didn't wake until they landed.

She staggered out, leaning heavily on Demalion's shoulder, bumping into him when he hesitated.

The security at the airport seemed . . . tense. Sylvie found herself wondering how many of the guards were reeling beneath returned memories that pointed out that there were far more exotic dangers than terrorists. Three out of five, she thought. Again, she found herself grateful to Marah for getting them back home with such speed. She had a feeling flights were about to get complicated.

"Let's get out of here," she murmured to Demalion. "We're not unnoticeable. And they're jumpy."

As they moved through the concourse, she heard whispers, watched heads turn toward the news stations playing every few hundred feet. Same two words on every lips. *Key Biscayne*. The news stations showed the Rickenbacker Causeway blocked off with police vehicles.

Shit.

Erinya was still throwing her weight around. Now there was no memory sink to hide it.

She quickened her pace though it made her hand ache, made Demalion hiss as the change pulled his stitches. Zoe adjusted her stride smoothly, kept her head down, her burned hair and cheek hidden in the shadow of Sylvie's body.

They lost Lupe; Sylvie turned and found her staring at the raised television screen, watching the flashing police lights, the line of text running beneath: INEXPLICABLE ECOLOGICAL CHANGES ON KEY BISCAYNE.

"Take me there," Lupe said, when Sylvie touched her shoulder. She twitched away from the touch.

"It's crawling with cops."

Lupe shot her a scornful glance. "You expect me to believe you're afraid of the cops? After what I've seen? No." She shook her head. Determination flared in her voice, brought life and fire to it. "Take me there."

Sylvie breathed out. "You're the client."

. . .

DEMALION GOT THEM ONTO THE CAUSEWAY AND PAST THE FIRST OF the police barricades by rolling down the window and fishing out his federal credentials. Sylvie had to smile, though it felt tight on her lips. All of the shit he'd gone through in the past week, and he still had his ID to hand? The man was born to be a Fed.

He turned Marah down, she reminded herself. His choice. She hadn't asked him to. She just appreciated it. Enormously. The blue water beyond the ocean causeway glittered in the sunlight. Lupe fidgeted in the backseat.

"How's it look up ahead?" Demalion asked the uniformed officer.

The man shrugged uneasily, cast a glance over his shoulder. "Hell if I know. They tell me that the whole island's gone weird. Strange plants sprouting overnight. Stranger animals. Waterfalls. We've had to chase tons of gawkers away."

"I see," Demalion said. He took back his ID, and the man leaned in, rested his arm on the open window.

"So, do you know what's going on, Agent Wright?"

"Yes," Demalion said, and, in a move worthy of all federal assholes, rolled up the window, making the man jerk back or lose fingers. He glanced over at Sylvie before he touched the gas pedal again. "We're sure about this? Erinya owns my soul. I don't want her to decide to collect on it because she's in a bad mood."

"I'm sure," Lupe said, leaning forward between the seat backs. "Drive."

The island loomed ahead, and Sylvie shook her head. "Erinya. No sense of discretion." Even from the far end of the causeway, the changes were blatant and undeniable. Vegetation curled above the island like greenish smoke. A sharp-edged hill rose high and bare out of the massed tree tangle. White-stone walls meandered along the top of it like an open mouth showing teeth. A pair of distinctive gates blocked the narrow, stony path toward the rearranged dwelling. Sylvie wasn't even sure there were ceilings.

"That's what's left of Val's house?" Zoe said. She slumped back, and said, "You get to tell her. Not me."

"Maybe she won't ask," Sylvie said.

Demalion pulled up at the second roadblock, this one designed to keep anyone on the Key from leaving. Sylvie wondered how many people were stuck with Erinya. Whether Erinya was leaving them alone, or whether they were all her stunned acolytes by now.

The officer who waved them to a halt was less impressionable than the first. He looked at the ID, and said, "What's your purpose here, Wright?"

"Same as yours, I'd imagine," Demalion said, nodding at the line of uniformed officers preparing to take the final few steps onto the Key. "Send a man in for recon."

"Didn't get enough information from the flyover? The Feds buzzed Key Biscayne all night. Made our choppers stand down."

Lupe growled, slid out of the car before Demalion could argue further with the policeman. "I'm going in."

"Wait," Sylvie said. She dragged Lupe around to the far side of the car, trying to keep their conversation away from prying ears. A vain attempt. The police pivoted to keep them in focus, hands on their weapons. Sylvie said, "Gentlemen. Don't get trigger-happy. You won't like the result."

They hesitated just enough that she felt comfortable putting her back to them. "Are you sure about this, Lupe? Erinya's trapped, and not in the best of moods. A drawback to being a god? Their tantrums can last eons."

"She won't hurt me," Lupe said. "She likes me."

"She liked you as a monster," Sylvie said.

"I'm still a monster. It's just . . . inside now."

"Lupe—"

"I killed people, Sylvie. I ripped them apart and ran my claws through their guts. I've done a lot of things in my life. None of it has ever been as satisfying as killing. Erinya understands that. Erinya likes me. And you know. I think I like her."

Sylvie let her go. If the world was going to change, if people were going to see the truth of things, she needed to let them act on what they knew. She couldn't play gatekeeper for the entire world. She had to trust people to make their own decisions.

Lupe nodded, walked past the armed men, walked right to the seething vines. Their chaos continued unabated, lashing and twining, but as she reached out, they parted, swallowed her down.

The cops swore and took steps back. Sylvie watched the greenery close up again and wondered if she'd done the right thing. It seemed to be a constant refrain in the back of her mind, as if she were vibrating to the uncertainty of the world.

She shook it off. She'd pulled the wool from the world's eyes. She couldn't regret it. Whatever came. Whatever happened.

Better to build a world with truth than one full of lies.

19

And After

TWO WEEKS LATER, SYLVIE WAS PUTTING TINY PINS IN A VERY LARGE map as Demalion called out city names, state names, country names, listing places that were waking up. In the states, Florida had been the first to admit that there were magic and monsters and everything people had dreamed of and feared.

Of course, they had Erinya's Key Biscayne makeover to help them along. The cops had gone in an hour or two after Lupe—shamed into it—and, surprisingly, Erinya had let them come back out, unscathed. Their report, which Alex had helped herself to, had said two women were living there, and they both could turn into monsters at will.

Then the army had invaded.

They'd been gone for four days, stumbling out with depleted weapons, shiny new PTSDs, and the word from on high: Erinya might be trapped there, but she demanded respect. Word got out. A *god* had taken over Key Biscayne.

The Christian fundamentalists claimed it was a devil and were holding prayer vigils for God to smite Erinya out of existence. So far, there was no response.

A temporary prison, Sylvie thought. She'd forgotten that

temporary meant a different thing to immortals. It might be centuries before the other gods came to a consensus on whether Dunne's trap constituted an act of war or not.

Another pin marked one final ISI attack in Seattle. While Sylvie and Demalion had been busy fighting Yvette, a sea monster had slipped out of the dense fogs and taken out the ISI building, two piers, and a homeless shelter. The sheer number of witnesses made Seattle the second city to acknowledge the truth, that humankind had neighbors they knew next to nothing about.

Sylvie didn't like that pin. Not only did it mark civilian casualties, it marked her failure to track down all the Good Sisters. There was at least one out there, and a dangerous one at that. One like Merrow, who could turn monsters into weapons. Alex was struggling to crack Graves's computer encryption. Maybe once Alex succeeded, Sylvie would have a better idea of how many more of the Good Sisters were running loose.

Demalion said, "Earth to Sylvie? UCLA just started a new scientific study on ESP."

"Yeah?" she said. She braced her cast-encased hand against the edge of the board and stuck a tiny pin in an already crowded spot. The universities, as a whole, were reacting in two ways: sheer, unbridled fascination or utter refusal to accept the magical world. That was all right. They weren't the ones she was worried about. Not really.

She was worried about the churches. It was one thing to believe in your gods, to get proof that your gods were real, concrete, *tangible*. To have your faith proved fact. It was a whole other type of shock to realize that *other* people's gods were just as real. Right now, the religious groups were being very, very quiet. It made her nervous. The whole world made her nervous, hence the board—Alex's idea to keep them up to date, trying to predict trouble spots.

"Apparently, someone at UCLA was going back through old studies and found out that the reports had—"

"Changed," Sylvie finished. "Proved that psychic powers were possible?"

"Guess whatever it was was definitive enough. The new scientists are a group of geneticists."

Sylvie grimaced. "Urgh. That . . . I don't like that. They go too far down that road in this environment, and we'll have genetic scans made mandatory. The government's already strung tight." There were seventeen red pins in DC. Each of them represented another blip on the radar, another constituent group who'd managed to get an audience with their senator or congressman for something that once would have branded them lunatic fringe.

"Tell me about it," Demalion said. He sounded strung tight himself. She stopped putting pins in the corkboard and looked at him. "Marah's been calling."

"Marah tracked you down?"

Sylvie had been expecting it. Partly because Marah was just that determined. Partly because Sylvie and her allies hadn't gone far.

Sylvie had left her South Beach office behind—not that there was much left of it—and found them discreet office space in Hialeah. It wasn't the beach, but it had everything she needed, including a lot of escape routes. Hialeah was a transport city.

Originally, Sylvie's intention was to pack up her business, her partner, her sister, and Demalion and get out of Florida for good. It would have been the wise thing to do. But Erinya was still her mess. She couldn't walk away from that. Right now, Erinya was playing nice, making a nest out of her small world for herself and Lupe. If that changed, it would be Sylvie walking up the causeway, with her gun in hand.

She hoped it wouldn't come to that. Lupe had come over for lunch a day ago, and she was happy, healthy, and bringing a peace offering from Erinya—a slew of carnivorous plants in pretty pots. Sylvie had passed them off to Alex with a grimace.

Erinya hadn't forgotten Sylvie's and Dunne's treachery, but . . . as Lupe said, "She's occupied. We've got worshippers finding their way to us, daily. Supplicants asking for vengeance and aid." Lupe had ducked her head when Sylvie asked how vengeance played out with Erinya trapped. Lupe hadn't needed to answer after that.

Lupe was dealing out punishment in Erinya's name.

Demalion sighed. "Marah's trying for the hard sell. Pushing guilt. I don't think she's even capable of feeling guilt." He stepped away from the desk, stretched out the kinks in his back. His shirt rose, revealing smooth flesh where there had been stitches.

Another benefit to the Sphinx toxin treatment. He healed better now. Sylvie would be lying if she said it didn't ease her mind. But healing wasn't where her thoughts went as she watched the small, subtle play of flat muscle over his hips. He caught her gaze and grinned, slow and wicked. "Call it a day? Head home?"

"Don't think about it," Alex said, from the front room, eavesdropping automatically. "I swear. I'm *this* close to getting into Graves's files."

"You've been saying that for days," Sylvie said. She almost, *almost* opened her mouth and teased Alex about losing her touch. Then she recalled Alex, unhappy and scared and losing her mind, and shifted direction. "You're just cranky 'cause Tex is out doing fieldwork."

"You sent him to Georgia."

"Look at the map!" Sylvie said. "There are pins all over Georgia! I have to know why. And there's only so much that facts can tell me. I want to know the feel of the—"

Their room-to-room argument was disrupted by the front door opening. The bell—a Zoe special—rang once, then twice: short bright *dings* that told Sylvie that it was a human coming in, and an armed one. Zoe had spelled the door chimes to alert them to a lot of different combinations since she couldn't be there to do it herself. Val had whisked Zoe back to Ischia. Sylvie's parents, appalled and newly aware of the dangers of the world, had thought Val offered the safest alternative.

Sylvie couldn't really argue. Look what Zoe had done under Sylvie's supervision.

This time, the chimes' special tones were irrelevant. Sylvie recognized the man coming in. "Detective Garza."

"You're a hard woman to find," he said. He gave Demalion a quick once-over, noting the gun at his hip, then, like everyone else who'd made their way to their new office, fell silent before the map.

"Those are all . . . what are those?"

"People interacting with or reacting to the *Magicus Mundi*," Sylvie said.

Garza let out a sigh that was more groan than breath. "I killed a man and covered it up, then I forgot about it."

"You had help," Sylvie said. "I helped you kill him; the Good Sisters made you forget."

"Can I help you?" The question burst out of Garza's mouth, raw. Needy.

Garza paced, thrust his hands into his pocket, looked embarrassed; Demalion left the room, closed the door behind him.

"That's not usually the way this goes," Sylvie said. "People ask *me* for help, not if I need—"

"Look. I can't do this," Garza said. "I go to work every day, and I don't even know what I'm doing anymore. We got memos from above. Telling us to stay away from Key Biscayne—it's not even in our jurisdiction. *Someone* sent down a list of likely monsters we might run into. Ways to identify witches, werewolves, even vampires. But no one really knows anything. It's not enough. I feel like I can't do my job right because I don't know enough."

"You used to do just fine—"

"I know better, now. I don't want to wait for more memos, Shadows. I want to be there, on the front line, be the one figuring this out. Not waiting for it to be a problem that crosses my path—"

Sylvie held up a hand, opened the door. "Demalion. Can I have your phone?"

He blinked but tossed it in her direction. She caught it awkwardly with her good hand, then set it down to poke through his call history. Garza vibrated with impatience.

Sylvie found the number she was looking for, hit redial. Garza said, "Shadows!"

Wait, she mouthed. When Marah picked up, her voice was triumphant. "Demalion, I knew you'd—"

"Sorry, just me. I've got a deal for you."

"What kind of deal?" Marah sounded suspicious.

"Simple. Stop trying to recruit Demalion."

"That's not a deal—"

"If you'll let me finish, I'll make it worth your while. This is Detective Raul Garza. He wants a job. On the front line. He wants to know all about the *Magicus Mundi*. He ID'd a *Maudit* sorcerer as a criminal before the *Magicus Mundi* gossip started." Sylvie passed him the phone.

A few minutes of impromptu job interview later, Garza handed the phone back to Sylvie, looking far more at ease than he had when he came in.

"I still want Demalion," Marah said into Sylvie's ear. "Do you know how useful foretelling can be in politics? I'm a professional assassin, and I tell you, I was not prepared for the cutthroat tactics."

"I'm hanging up, Marah," Sylvie said.

"I get what I want," Marah said, before disconnecting.

Sylvie, despite herself, despite Marah's cheerful tone, found her blood running cold. In the front of the office, Alex gave a sudden shriek of triumph as Graves's files gave up their secrets.

• • •

SYLVIE STOOD ON THE RIVER'S EDGE AND THREW THE WREATH OF pale flowers onto its sluggish surface. She waited for the bait to work while the water lapped up over the white petals, slowly dragging them downward.

It was quiet around her, almost peaceful here on the isolated river basin. Made her nervous. She shot a glance back toward the roadway, toward the bulk of the rental jeep, and a moving shape that was Demalion, pacing around the vehicle. He didn't think coming to Brazil was a good idea, thought it took them too far off their turf.

Sylvie couldn't blame him, but the trip had been necessary. A month had passed since Alex had cracked the encryption on Graves's files. A month since that triumph had turned to worry and set Sylvie on the hunt.

Everyone was hunting, it seemed like. Hunting for answers, for safety, for a way to stop or control the changes. All across the world, people were being drawn into the *Magicus Mundi*'s influence as surely as the wreath continued to sink.

Marah's ISI was on everyone's lips; last Sylvie had heard, before she set off on this river hunt, eight separate ambassadors from European countries had come to learn from the ISI. As if the ISI was an example of anything but what *not* to do . . .

Sylvie still worried most about the religious groups. The schisms were fast and ugly—people wanting peace, wanting communion with the gods, wanting wars to glorify their gods' names and smite the unbelievers. And people were listening to them. A lot harder to dismiss a man who declared the gods were speaking to him when Key Biscayne had an entirely-too-tangible god that could be visited, prayed to, worshipped. The Church of Wrath was growing exponentially.

Sylvie had already killed two gods who were nothing of the sort—only a jumped-up *Maudit* sorcerer and a necromancer who resurrected the dead. Taking advantage of the climate. Sylvie had managed to get herself on television once again, lecturing the would-be believers about the differences between gods and men, and why blind faith was no good for either. She had ended up being asked to consult on cases all over the US. She was flavor of the month; but when she could, she sent Demalion out to play nice instead of her. After years of keeping an unofficial profile, her sudden notoriety was nerve-racking.

A mosquito hummed at her ear, and she swatted it away, wincing as the cast on her hand caught her hair and tugged a few strands free. She was healing fast, but not inhumanly so. A mixed blessing. She might be the new Lilith, an immortal woman, but at least she was still human.

Demalion, not so much.

Hospitals and doctors were being subpoenaed all across the country by the ISI, trying to winkle out any *Mundi* living in their midst. The witches, Sylvie thought, had been the tipping point. The world seemed to accept the idea of monsters—after all, maps had declared HERE BE MONSTERS for centuries. Monsters were upsetting but part of the collective unconscious.

Witches, though, scared the fuck out of people. Made them realize that maybe they *couldn't* tell the monsters at a glance. Made them pull apart from each other instead of growing closer in the face of the *Magicus Mundi*. And then, someone let slip about werewolves and succubi and all the shape-shifting things that looked human but weren't, and the rare half-breeds . . .

Martial law had looked like a possibility for a few fraught weeks, then things settled back into a panicky détente, while the government passed law after hasty law about creatures and things they knew next to nothing about.

The water before her glossed suddenly, rolled as something slid just beneath the surface. The sinking wreath bobbed again, and the Encantado surged out of the water, shifting from dolphin to human as he did. White petals stuck to his sleek skin, and his dark eyes were languorous.

"You called for me—" He trailed off. The pleasant anticipation on his face faded to wary irritation. "Shadows. What do you want?"

"Come up here. Come out of the water," she said.

He touched the flowers over his shoulders, testing them. There wasn't a spell laid over them. Only tradition. He shrugged and walked up the bank to stand before her.

"What do you want?"

"Mostly, just to talk."

"Mostly," he said. "I don't like mostly."

"You played me," she said. "From the beginning."

If she'd thought he'd deny it, she would have been wrong. He smiled, showing sharp teeth. "You *listened* to me. Believed me. Even behind your magical wards, my words reached you. Because you *wanted* to listen."

Sylvie said, "You fed me a lot of things I was primed to hear. That the ISI was morally corrupt—which Graves most definitely was. That there were other forces working within the ISI, even gave me a name. The Society of the Good Sisters. You told me they were the ones running the Corrective. That was true."

"So you wanted to thank me?"

"You also told me that Yvette's people were the ones running the monster attacks. You . . . *encouraged* me to believe it. That's the problem with being me. I'm resistant to magic. But first I have to experience it before I can shake it off. You . . . enchanted me. Just a bit. Just enough.

"You told me that the Good Sisters could leash the monsters as weapons. That they were the ones setting the attacks.

"You know what? They couldn't. None of them could. Not even Merrow. I should have known right then. I saw Merrow when the mermaids tried to drown him. He wasn't controlling them. He *couldn't* control them. He could barely hold them off long enough for us to escape. You *sold* me that lie, and I believed it. The worst-case scenario. You sold it to Graves also, drove him mad with the possibilities."

His placid face twisted hard at the mention of the dead ISI agent.

"How did he catch you, anyway? Did you stay ashore too long with some woman? Or did you plan to be captured?"

The Encantado said, "You think I wanted to be caught?"

"I don't know; I only get to judge by the results. The results are a lot of dead humans," Sylvie said. "You ended up in his torture chambers. I thought his notes referred to a mermaid, but it was you. You told him things. Held out long enough to make it believable, and then you sent him, a paranoid man, after enemies inside his own organization. That's one way to disable an enemy."

He turned back toward the water; Sylvie caught his wrist with her bad hand, her fingertips scrabbling over the warm-rubber feel of his flesh.

"But that wasn't enough. You escaped. Then you *coaxed* the sand wraith, using your abilities to inspire belief, to go with you to Chicago, and you told it to destroy the ISI there. It obeyed. The Encantado. The strongest of the *Magicus Mundi* seducers. Then you moved on, and you did it again. Johnny-on-the-spot. You told me you were a *Magicus Mundi* troubleshooter. Trying to figure out who was controlling the monsters. A good cover story that explained your presence at all the scenes."

"You *believed* me," he said. "So eager to think that maybe we were just like you. That we cared about murder. It wasn't murder. It was extermination."

"When I stopped the mermaids, killed the Mora, you had to redirect me, to get me out of your playground. So you sent me after the Good Sisters, another set of your enemies."

"You went off like a firecracker. Funny," he said. "You *wanted* to believe that the humans were the bad guys, and my kind the innocent tools. Check your allegiances, Shadows."

"I know my allegiances," she said. She brought her good hand up, aimed the gun between his eyes. This close, she'd blow his skull to pulp.

He twitched. "What, you want me to tell you my motives, the whole of my plan? You've caught me—"

"No," Sylvie said. "I don't care about your plans. They stop today with you. I have one question left. And I want an answer."

"Put the gun down," he said. Compulsion rang through his voice; a clarion call to the back part of her mind.

She kept the gun steady, her voice even. She was in control here, and from the shock on his face, he was beginning to realize it.

"One question," she said. "Why did Marah Stone free you from Graves's torture chamber?"

Graves's files had shown that clearly enough. Two shocks in a row for Sylvie. That the monster Graves had been tormenting for answers hadn't been the mermaid she assumed, but the Encantado—her bias had blinded her. Graves had called the Encantado *it*, he had called the Encantado *creature*, and Sylvie, who'd already met the Encantado, thought of him as *he* and *man*.

The second shock had been the familiar form of Marah Stone releasing him, Cain-marked hand held protectively before her as he exited the tank on shaky legs. They had paused to speak to each other for nearly five minutes before Marah stepped back and watched him leave.

It hadn't been the much-maligned Hovarth. It had been Marah. A woman with some degree of magical resistance. A woman who'd done nothing but benefit from the chaos.

The video-feed quality was too bad to read the truth off their lips. Sylvie needed to know. Had the Encantado called Marah down, his seductive voice reaching out through the late-night building, mostly empty, and found her, heart and head full of desires for power, overriding the Cain mark as smoothly as he had evaded Sylvie's own protective instincts? Or had Marah *known* he was there and gone down looking for a tool she could use?

"Does it matter?"

"Yes," she said. "It does." The one meant Marah was what she seemed. An opportunist who took a mistake she'd made and twisted it until she landed on her feet. Mercenary, morally suspect, but understandable.

The other meant Marah was a long-range-planning murderous bitch who made Graves look like an amateur. Two hundred fifty-seven ISI agents had died in the attacks. Sixty civilians. And Marah didn't even have the fragile excuse of the ISI hunting her kind.

The one was politics. The other . . . was psychopathy.

"Yes," the Encantado said. "I see that it does." His dark eyes bore down on her, made her wonder if he had rudimentary mind-reading abilities.

He bared all his teeth, and said, "I don't have an answer for you."

"Find one," Sylvie said.

He shrugged, and the wreath slipped over shoulders

going narrower, less human, shifting back to dolphin. "Sorry. I only know my part. I killed your kind, and I loved it. I'm content. I taught my people how to fight back in a more effective way. It's funny," he said again. "Your world is running all over itself, trying to make rules to contain us. To make us play nice. We have no interest in your rules or your wants."

She shot him in the thigh, knocked him to the muddy ground; he made no real attempt to escape it, only laughed as she stood over him. His laugh sounded nothing like human, a chattering sweep of sound, but the curve to his mouth, the glint in his eyes gave his amusement away, even as he clutched at the bloody wound.

"Tell you this," he breathed. "Take it as warning or whatever you want. You don't make Cain's line feel slighted. Not if you want to live." He rolled up to his feet, lunged for her, teeth snapping, and she shot him in the head. Right between the eyes as if her sights had never left that spot.

He collapsed, dead, at her feet.

She toed him back into the river, let the water take him down, and headed back up the long slope to Demalion.

"Get an answer?" he asked. His mouth was tight and hard. He'd taken the security feed of Marah and the Encantado together worse than she had. But then, she had never really trusted Marah, and he had trusted Marah with his life. With his precious agency.

"She couldn't have planned it," he said, for the third or fourth time today. "She nearly got killed in Chicago along with me. If they were allies—"

"Being allies doesn't make them friends," Sylvie said. "One conversation between them, and death and disaster afterward. I don't think they told each other a lot of details in that time. He may not have known she was headed to Chicago."

Demalion grimaced, gestured her into the car. "So what do we do? No proof that she wasn't under his compulsion. You said he enchanted you—Marah's not as strong."

"I don't know," she said. For a phrase she hated, it was

beginning to feel all too familiar. "I do know that we have to move on from this. Monsters and gods and witches aside, Marah's the one to watch. And we helped put her in power."

Demalion started the car, the long drive back home. Sylvie rested her gun on her lap and watched the landscape go by. Trees and road and eventually houses and cities. It all looked so normal. But beneath the surface, everything had changed. She wasn't sure how it was going to work out.

Sylvie's phone rang, startling her. She'd assumed they were out of range, but it was Alex, working some type of technological miracle.

"Hey," she said.

"How's your Portuguese?" Alex asked.

"Nonexistent," Sylvie said. She laid the phone on the dash between her and Demalion, put it on speaker, caught it when it nearly slid off the dash as Demalion bounced them over a rough section of not-quite-road.

"Demalion?" Alex said.

"I can do Portuguese," he said. "What's going on, Alex?"

"The Brazilian government knows you're in the country; they'd like to speak to you."

"Why?" Sylvie asked warily. It had been a pain in the ass to get here, harder to arrange for weapons. It was well and good for Marah to say Sylvie didn't need guns, but Sylvie felt better with one. Didn't mean she wanted to explain why she was running around with an illegally purchased, illegally carried gun to the Brazilian police.

"They, apparently, have a magical snake infestation. They think, that since you're already in the country—"

Demalion spoke over Sylvie's sigh. "Are they paying? How magical?"

"Very well," Alex said. "Very magical. The snakes are apparently prone to sprouting legs and running up walls. It's a whole, big mess."

Sylvie looked across the seat at Demalion. He grinned at her. "What do you say?"

"This is going to be how it is, isn't it. Our life. Chasing snakes—"

"And getting paid," Demalion pointed out. "You like that."

"*You* like that. Missing your government paycheck?"

"Not in the least," he said. "Missing being hunted by the government?"

"Maybe a little," she said.

Alex groaned. "Stop flirting. Jeez. To think I wanted Demalion to come work with us."

"We'll take the snakes," Sylvie said. "Hey, spreading goodwill, right?"

"God, this is going to be a disaster—"

Sylvie disconnected, tucked the phone back in her pocket, and leaned back in the jeep's seat. This was how it was going to be. Bickering with Demalion. Being bossed around by Alex. Hunting magical snakes that would no doubt turn out to be venomous.

Demalion steered the jeep out of the jungle and back onto the sunlit roadway; Sylvie pulled down her sunglasses and smiled. She could live with this.